A LOVERS' JOURNEY

They were standing close together at the stile, leaning against the weathered wood. Everything around them was washed with the dying rays of the setting sun.

"I don't want to go to Summerhay, let alone become wife to a stranger," she suddenly blurted.

He turned to look down at her, his eyes glinting in the light. "God knows, *I* don't want you to," he admitted at last, softly caressing her arm. His fingers tightened as he spoke, his voice husky and intense. "I wish this journey could last into eternity. You should be mine." His mouth covered hers.

His kiss was sweet and, reeling with emotion, Adele longed to stop time, to hold the moment forever. When he kissed her again, she returned his ardor, drinking in the hot sweetness of his mouth.

Her arms slid around his strong back and she hugged him to her, thrilling to the feel of his body pressed against hers.

It was too dark to see his face, for the sunset was complete, the brilliant ball of fire burned out beyond the dark woods. "Rafe," she whispered, finding his name a joy to speak aloud. "Oh, Rafe, I wish that too."

THE SWORD AND THE FLAME

PATRICIA PHILLIPS

LEISURE BOOKS　　　　　NEW YORK CITY

For Rob, Parker, and Delainey—the next generation.

A LEISURE BOOK®

June 2000

Published by

Dorchester Publishing Co., Inc.
276 Fifth Avenue
New York, NY 10001

ISBN 0-8439-4726-8

THE SWORD AND THE FLAME

Chapter One

Adele ducked beneath a low-hanging branch, her passage loosening a shower of powdery snow. Suddenly her gelding snorted and tossed its head, while beside her the rangy black hound's ears pricked to attention. From beyond the wood came the unmistakable jingle and thud of many riders.

Quickly she drew rein and signaled to her servant lad to keep quiet. Adele slid from the saddle and led her mount behind a sheltering thicket.

She could guess the identity of these riders. For months they had been waiting for their overlord, Rafe De Montford, to bring their new castellan. It had become commonplace for castellans and sheriffs to be replaced with King John's handpicked lackeys, and otherwise the people of Esterwold would hardly have blinked an eye, but Gilbert Bohun's cruel reputation had preceded him. Even this year's Christmas celebrations had been small, for none of the castle's garrison wanted to appear derelict in their duties, afraid of punishment from their new master.

Adele's mouth tightened as she reviewed the unpleasant prospect of Bohun's rule. With a new castellan in charge, poor old Sir George would be put out to pasture. The king obviously considered the fief of Esterwold a lucrative source of revenue, a disproportionate amount of which would now likely end up in the royal coffers.

The dog growled low in warning, until Adele had to clamp her hand around his muzzle to quiet him. She had no wish to be caught out in the open by a band of soldiers. Normally her station would assure her courteous treatment, but given Bohun's reputation, she did not think it wise to put much faith in his protection.

Crouching low, she watched through a snowy screen of brush as the heavily armed soldiers passed. They rode two-by-two along the road skirting the woods. So many! Adele counted over three-score men and a fleet of baggage wagons. Bohun must have brought his own troops to bolster Esterwold's ranks. Yet again, this helmeted legion might belong to the almighty De Montford. Here, in the fading light of the winter afternoon, it was hard to distinguish one insignia from another.

To Adele's surprise, the soldiers turned east toward Myerly. Dared she hope they were not bound for Esterwold, after all? A moment later she recalled that Myerly's new lord was a favorite of the king; the travelers must be choosing a more welcoming hearth for the night.

Adele waited until it was safe to remount. Cautioning her dog to silence, she emerged from the trees with the servant lad trailing after her, a basket of herbs balanced on his shoulder.

Weary of waiting for the new castellan's arrival, today Adele had finally disregarded Sir George's advice and ventured into the countryside. How wonderful it was to feel the fresh wind in her face, to be able to ride across fields white with new-fallen snow. She had taken healing potions to her tenants, many of whom lay abed with the usual winter ailments. Without fanfare Adele had gone from cottage to cottage, asking the condition of each householder, for winter sometimes exacted a heavy toll on the serfs under Esterwold's protection.

Atop a rise of ground Adele reined in, struck by the unexpected beauty of the scene below. Esterwold's small fortress appeared dark and mysterious, adrift in a sea of white. For over a hundred years this stone keep had been the seat of the St. Clares.

If only her brother were home, they would have had no need of the king's castellan. But he was not. After their father died, Adele had written to Joce at Summerhay, where he was confined by the king to ensure their father's continued loyalty. Now with Amory St. Clare dead, the king had no need to hold her brother hostage. Jocelyn was the new lord of Esterwold.

Nearly two years had passed and still Adele had not heard from her brother. With her father's man Sir George's help, she had run Esterwold alone—and could still have done so without any need of Bohun's iron fist. But she had herself to blame for their current predicament: as the months had dragged by without word, she had written to the king asking him to release her brother. It had not been a wise move.

Until he received her letter, the king had been unaware of her father's death. If only she had kept quiet, Esterwold could have lived on in relative obscurity. Now, the royal reply had given her no news of Joce, but it had informed her that the king had appointed Gilbert Bohun as Esterwold's castellan. As a woman, and a minor, she would become a royal ward.

At least the king had not ordered her to marry Bohun, a blessing for which she was eternally grateful.

The sun slid lower in the sky, threatening to sink, and spreading gold and crimson banners over the snow as it set fire to the ice-crusted moat. Behind her, the rising winter wind moaned through bare branches. How beautiful her lands were, with an enchanted castle rising magically from the purple dusk. . . .

Behind her, the servant lad coughed loudly and moved

the heavy basket of herbs to his other shoulder. This swift reminder of the present shattered Adele's fanciful mood. She clicked to her horse, Moonlight, urging the gray forward. In a flurry, the little party descended the slope to the castle.

During the night the wind shifted to the west and brought an unexpected thaw. Adele awoke to the plop and drip of melting snow sliding off the stonework.

Pale winter sunlight slanted through windows cut high in the wall of the great hall. Where the beams met, myriad dust motes danced in the light. In the searching dawn light, Esterwold looked even shabbier than usual. Usually fiercely defensive of her home, this morning even Adele had to admit the fortress seemed primitive. Its huge, hammer-beamed hall was bare. The garrison had already broken their fast, and the room's wooden trestles were stacked back against the wall. In the massive hearth a tree trunk blazed, yet for all the leaping flames, much of the lofty room stayed cold and drafty. Braziers of coals were necessary to lessen the chill. From the cobwebbed rafters, roosting pigeons cooed, their droppings plopping on the rushes below. Though in the autumn a new floor covering had been put down, those trampled rushes were already soiled with litter and grease. The familiar surroundings looked painfully shabby.

She swallowed uncomfortably as she wondered what the new castellan would think of Esterwold. It was not completely devoid of luxury: on the dais, the lord's chair had carved oaken arms and a scarlet cushion, and the splendid arras on the west wall had come all the way from the Holy Land.

Yet, despite this fact, Adele was sure Bohun's assessment of her home would be scathing. Well and good. Mayhap he would decide not to stay. Her spirits brightened at the thought. It was even possible the man could wash his hands of the whole appointment, though Adele was not sure he could do that once the king had commanded him to come here.

At Sir George's insistence, today she had dressed in finery for Bohun's arrival. Over a red wool undergown she wore her festival gown of soft blue embroidered with gold wheat. The garment hugged her full breasts and emphasized her narrow waist. Wound twice about her curving hips was a black and gold belt with golden tassels. Adele had plaited red and blue satin ribbons into her thick auburn hair which she wore in neat coils by her ears.

The ribbons had been added to bring color to her pale oval face. This morning when she had looked in her polished steel mirror, her high cheekbones had seemed to stretch her skin, her green eyes looked enormous, and her usually soft, full lips had been thin with worry. Each time she contemplated living under the new castellan's rule, her brow furrowed; she was all too aware that the well-being of the entire household depended on his whim.

Nervously, Adele adjusted her veil. Both the fluttering blue-and-gold veil and its gold-and-black plaited circlet had come from Jerusalem, brought back by her father from his final crusade.

Adele picked up her needlework, then promptly put it down again. It was impossible to concentrate on stitching. She kept jabbing her finger, then had to suck the wound to keep the bright drops of blood from staining the linen.

She had argued for, and lost, the right to accompany Sir George and their future commander on a tour of the fiefdom. Adele chafed at the idea of waiting here beside the hearth to present Bohun with a meek and dishonest picture of simpering female obedience. She knew as much as anyone about the running of this land!

She sighed. Why were they so long in coming? She glanced again at the door which remained closed. Adele moved her stool into the crossed beams of light. Though it offered little warmth, this bright sunshine was welcome. Closing her eyes, she raised her face to the light

11

and prayed. *Please, Lord, let life here be not too terrible. Let Joce come home, and make Bohun leave.*

The great oak door swung open. In a burst of sound, dozens of stamping feet shed wet snow and mud on the rushes as many men came indoors.

The common soldiery quickly parted to make way for their commander. A barrel-chested man strode inside the great hall, his corpulent figure well matched by a deep, rasping voice. Beside him walked a taller noble man, who sometimes inclined his head to catch his companion's words above the din. They both wore mail coifs and hauberks, their sword belts slung low on their hips.

Shouts for mulled ale and wine, and for hot food to dispel the chill, came from all sides, sending castle servants scurrying to do their bidding. Though this morning's sun was bright, the fief's open, wind-wracked acres had turned the party's faces red with cold. Stamping their feet and rubbing their hands, the assembled soldiers gravitated toward the blazing hearth.

Suddenly the two noblemen stopped in the middle of the hall as if frozen in their tracks, their attention riveted on Adele. She was seated near the hearth. Light formed a bright halo around her auburn hair, imbuing upon her face an unearthly glow. Her perfect features seemed to have been chiseled from marble.

"By all the saints . . . a vision!" growled the fat one.

"Nay, 'tis just the Lady Adele," the other said. "And remember—she's already spoken for."

"More's the pity. Had I known about her, I'd have asked for her in the bargain." The heavy man's ruddy face burned with desire. "Mayhap it's still not too late."

"It's too late," the other concluded, stepping toward the lady, who had risen to greet them.

Adele swallowed nervously as the men approached. She dropped in a curtsy, her blue gown puddling around her on the rushes.

"Welcome to Esterwold, my lords," she said, not knowing who was who. One stood a head taller than the other; beyond that they were very much alike in their dull gray hauberks and mail coifs.

"So you're Lady Adele," said the shorter man. He stepped forward, his hand outstretched to bring her to her feet. "My stay here will be made more pleasant by your presence," he said with a leer. She could see that the attempt at chivalry was foreign to him.

Well, at least now she knew which was Bohun. "Welcome, my Lord Bohun," Adele answered politely, her voice tight. The other man merely nodded to her. Their mighty overlord was not nearly as old and grizzled as she had expected, she could see that, though little of his face was visible under his close-fitting mail hood.

Turning to him in appeal, Adele said, "Lord De Montford, we've no need of a castellan here." Her voice cracked. She licked her lips, preparing another plea when she realized he was not listening.

The men strode to the table. There Sir George offered them refreshment, hobbling about, his bad leg obviously giving him pain after the morning ride.

Determined not to be ignored, Adele followed. The men-at-arms milling about the hall glanced appreciatively at her and politely moved aside to let her step up to the dais.

She recognized De Montford as the more important of the two, and she offered him the lord's chair. He smiled, so Adele knew he understood, but to her surprise he shook his head.

"Nay, though I thank you, Lady Adele, I can't stay. I've pressing business elsewhere today. However, I will take a cup of wine."

Sir George handed him a brimming goblet. De Montford quickly drained the warm spiced wine. Then, nodding to them in parting, he signaled to his men to accompany him. Over half the mailed soldiers in the hall set down their cups and moved as one to follow their lord.

His abrupt departure left Adele feeling slighted as she watched them file outdoors. Unfortunately, Bohun was still there, making himself at home in the lord's chair. His squire came to help him out of his mailed coif; next came the padded hood. Without the armor his head appeared far smaller than she'd expected. Bohun's iron-gray hair was cropped short and the back cut high in the old Norman fashion. His heavy square jowls were mottled with cold, his thick lips turning purple as he greedily emptied his wine cup and shouted for a refill.

"Now, Lady, we have men's business," he said, smiling indulgently at her, displaying his blackened teeth. "Best go along with your women and attend to your sewing. There's no need to bother your pretty head with details."

Adele's blood boiled at his condescension. Swallowing hard, she fought not to show her anger. "I'm familiar with the working of the fief."

"Yes, yes, I'm sure you are." Bohun dismissed her, gesturing for Sir George to put down the two ledgers he held.

The grizzled old knight complied with relief. Though he was trying hard to hide it, the morning's ride had tired him and he was thankful to be able to sit and drink a cup of spiced wine.

"Now send your steward to me." When no one moved to do his bidding, Bohun's face tightened and he growled, "Come on, hop to it. I haven't all day."

"Steward," Sir George repeated, glancing at Adele, unsure how to proceed.

"Yes. Your steward, you old fool. The one charged with keeping the books, with running this place—or should I say, attempting to," he added scathingly. Puzzled by the old knight's confusion, he glanced about the room to find that no other had stepped forward. "Surely it's not *you*."

Sir George smiled slightly and shook his head. "No, my lord."

"I thought not. You're too old to even see the figures." The cruel taunt caught Sir George off guard and he blanched. "Well, man, are you addled too? Have your steward come forward to explain matters to me."

"You're looking at him," Adele said at last, her voice

14

harsh with repressed anger. Stepping close to Sir George, she laid her hand protectively on his stooped shoulder. "We have no steward, Lord Bohun. At Esterwold I'm both master and mistress, steward and cleric."

It was Bohun's turn to pale. For a moment her statement shocked him speechless. At last he growled, "You! Surely you jest."

"Since my father's death I've run the fief with help from Sir George—who has loyally served my family all his life." She added the latter as a reminder to Gilbert Bohun to curb his tongue. Though at first he had attempted civility, the man reverted to his reputed ill temper.

Gathering himself, Bohun laughed derisively.

"Oh, Lady, this explains much. Now I know why the place is so rundown. Being handled by a woman and a doddering old fool accounts for much. 'Tis a wonder your peasants aren't fled and the buildings falling round your ears."

Adele drew in her breath, trying to master her anger before she replied. "Our land's fertile and produces good yield. The peasants here are happy and well cared for, so they have no cause to run away. I admit, by some standards our castle is small and somewhat shabby . . ." She wanted to throttle him as he interrupted her rebuttal with a hoot of derisive laughter.

"Small? Shabby?" He hooted. "This place is of no more importance than a pimple on my arse, Lady. You could put the whole fief inside the bailey of one of my castles," he boasted unpleasantly. "I'm only here to please the king, to try to turn this hopeless midden productive. The king has expressed concerns about conditions here, and it's obvious they were justified."

"If he's so concerned, why doesn't he send my brother home to assume his rightful place as lord?" Adele demanded, her eyes flashing in anger. Sir George cleared his throat in warning.

Bohun glared at her, visibly angered. He motioned to a man who waited in the shadows. "Mayhap I'll ask the king that very question when next we meet," he snarled.

"Odo here will help me decipher your accounts, that's if you can sheathe your claws long enough to keep from scratching my eyes out."

Oh, how she longed to do just that. Biting her tongue to keep back angry words, Adele moved to stand at the new lord's side where she stiffly awaited his next order. Had she been given the choice, she would have had Bohun thrown out of the hall. She savored that pleasant thought, though she knew it impossible. Odo, Bohun's black robed steward, smiled at her as he came to his master's side and opened Esterwold's books.

As they went through them, with great glee, Adele realized that Gilbert Bohun could not read well. He was clever at hiding it, always repeating what Odo said, yet his eyes never followed the correct columns. She hugged the discovery to herself. She could read, write, keep accounts, speak some Latin—it would incense Bohun to know that a mere woman was more skilled than he. All his bluster and bravado was a front to hide his own shortcomings.

"What are you smirking about, woman?" the man growled, glancing at her.

"Why, nothing, my lord," Adele replied sweetly. "I'm merely waiting to explain matters to you."

For the next several hours they went over the ledgers, and any explanation needed was requested civilly by Odo. All was in order. Bohun then went through her records of the lord's court, which she had held regularly since her father's death. He growled in displeasure over the minor punishments she'd handed out. Then he complained at the meager rents she collected. "The peasants should pay three times that amount," he snarled.

Adele grew tired of standing and sat on a nearby bench. From the dais she had a perfect view of Bohun's soldiers sprawled idly at the trestles that had been set up to accommodate them. They snoozed, or gambled, bored by the inactivity as they awaited further orders.

When the manor accounts were declared satisfactory, Bohun's attention shifted to the castle's defenses. For this

Adele wisely sent for Spence, the captain of their small guard, aware that he could far better explain the garrison's capabilities than she.

It was late afternoon before Rafe De Montford rode back inside Esterwold's bailey. By now the sun was hidden by gray clouds and the wind was cold. He was glad to be in for the night.

"My lord De Montford."

The lady of the keep stepped from the wedge-shaped shadow of a buttress where she had been awaiting his return. A dark blue cloak protected her from the chill. Her bright auburn hair sprouted untidily from its plaits and her soft cheeks were flushed, but she was still stunning. Beside her stood her big black hound, its tongue lolling, alert to any possible danger to his mistress. They had been playing fetch, and she still clutched a wet ball in her hand.

Startled, Rafe's stallion threatened to shy, but with a stern word he got him in check. "My lady," he said warily, wondering why she had been waiting for him outside.

Cautioning her hound to stay back, Adele stepped closer to the horse. De Montford's soldiers were filing inside the bailey, but after glancing at her in curiosity they did not disturb them.

"Gilbert Bohun's impossible! How can I live under his rule? He's churlish, insensitive—he's already angered half the garrison. The kitchen's in an uproar. Next he'll infuriate the villagers, for he says he expects twice the work and thrice the rent. I implore you, my lord, take him back where he came from."

Adele was sure the man's mouth twitched in amusement beneath his steel helm.

"Lord Bohun does as he sees fit, my lady, for the king has given him charge here. He's used to ordering men. He's rough and blunt—and, I agree with you, at times downright churlish—but he does have Esterwold's best interests at heart."

17

Adele snorted in disagreement, searching for words to more eloquently plead her case. "Esterwold's best interests are not to make its inhabitants' lives unbearable. We were happy here. If his rules are implemented, no one will be content. We don't need him. Things have run well enough these two years past."

"Granted, the fief looks prosperous. I commend you for providing such good housing for your people, the animals are in good condition, and I've no quarrel with the way you've handled matters."

"Then why change it?"

"You forget—it's not I who changed things. Bohun was appointed by the king."

"Surely you can petition His Majesty on my behalf. You're our overlord."

"The king in turn is my liege. And he doesn't consider running a fiefdom to be woman's work."

"Then ask him to set my brother free!" she pleaded, coming closer to his snorting horse, whose eyes rolled at her approach. Nervously the stallion shifted its feet on the broken ground.

"I can do that for you, lady. Why is your brother a captive?"

"Because the king thought if he took Joce hostage, my father would prove more loyal."

"That's a common story these days. I'll do what I can."

Their conversation appeared to be at an end. Desperate for more assurance, Adele persisted. "When? How long must we suffer?"

Rafe's mouth quirked slightly at her choice of words.

"Oh, I don't think you'll have to suffer long," he said, then tugged on the reins. His horse surged forward, spattering Adele with mud.

For the next several hours she seethed over the injustice of her predicament and at her inability to change matters. She had a mind to petition King John herself, yet she doubted she would even be granted an audience. Even if she did meet him, he would likely try to lure her to his bed. It was said the king was a notorious seducer.

To Adele's surprise, their guests had chosen to spend the night at Esterwold. Bohun had already commandeered the lord's chamber for himself, forcing Adele to take a lesser room. Her alternate accommodations adjoined the solar, far too close to Bohun's quarters for comfort. Adele had to share the spare room with her two waiting women, whose presence she hoped would deter him from hopes of any nighttime forays, surely not even Gilbert Bohun would try to invade her bedchamber with the others there. Just to be on the safe side, she would have her dog sleep by the door. Val would protect her if need be.

That was not the only change. Adele had worked to provide the best meal that Esterwold could manage on such short notice. Women from the village had been called in to help prepare food for the extra mouths. Still, though the meal she had planned was ample, Adele feared it might not be as sumptuous as the two lords were accustomed to eating.

The delicious aroma of roasting meats soon filled the air, drifting from the kitchens where a whole deer and two pigs crackled and sizzled on spits. Lew, a scullion, was put in charge of turning and basting. A tasty broth of meat and vegetables simmered in a cast-iron cauldron over the fire. The sweating cook supervised the making of dozens of both meat and fish pasties, which were removed from the oven on long-handled wooden paddles as soon as they were done to make room for a fresh batch. The castle storehouse held a bountiful supply of apples, and Adele ordered these stewed with honey to be used as a filling for pies to be topped by heavy cream. Kegs of ale and cider were brought up from the cellars and tapped to serve the common soldiery; Bohun had brought his own French wine for the lord's table.

When it drew close to time to sup, Adele finally emerged from her chamber. Looking down into the noisy hall, she was surprised to see steaming tureens of soup already being passed around the lower tables, accompanied by platters of black bread and cups of ale. Slightly nettled that the meal had started without her, Adele drew herself to her full height and regally descended the staircase, every inch the lady of the castle.

She still wore her blue gown, though she had rebraided her untidy hair and scrubbed her face and hands. She'd had to wait far longer than usual to wash because a bath had been ordered sent to the lord's chamber, using all the available hot water. The request had surprised her, honestly. By his smell Adele had assumed Bohun never bathed.

It was well the castellan had brought many of his own supplies, she admitted as the great hall's noise enveloped her. The castle's provisions, though ample for their small population, would not stretch to feed so many mouths.

Her father's garrison had always been small, so Adele had never seen the hall packed to capacity. The closer she came to the bottom step, the more she was overwhelmed by the sheer number of diners. The racket of clanging vessels, loud, raucous voices, and laughter interspersed with hearty belches all combined with the serving wenches, flirtatious shrieks of laughter to assault her ears. How much more pleasant it would be to dine upstairs than to have to endure this. Aware that the choice was hers, Adele paused on the stair.

No, she would not let them make her a prisoner in her chamber. This was *her* home and it was her right to dine at the lord's table.

In the shadows at the foot of the stair, a man stood talking to another. Adele did not recognize him, though his fashionable blue tunic and short red leather boots proclaimed his noble blood. As he moved beneath the light of a torch, she saw how well the fine wool garment fit across his broad shoulders, the light color making his black hair look even darker in contrast.

Was he a visiting courtier? She had never before seen such fine fabric as that of his clothing; his red tights gleamed like silk, outlining every muscle and sinew of his well-shaped legs. If Bohun and De Montford started inviting other nobles to sup here, too, their food stores would be run through in days, she thought sourly. Was this man the lord of Myerly, beloved courtier of King John, invited here tonight to scoff at his backward neighbors?

Adele's sharp assessment freshly annoyed her. Her hands clenched in the folds of her gown and she longed to sink her fists in Bohun's fat, mottled face. How dare he take over her home at the say-so of a king to whom she was no more than a name on a parchment?

"Lady."

Adele glanced up, coming suddenly face to face with the man in blue. As he started up the stair, she stepped aside to let him pass.

"Nay, 'tis for you I'm waiting," he said, smiling at her.

His voice sounded familiar. When she looked closely at his face, it all became clear. *De Montford*. Without his helmet and mail he was transformed.

"Allow me."

Adele meekly accepted his arm, allowing him to lead her across the hall to the dais; up the shallow steps they went, straight to the lord's table. Bohun was there already. At his lord's approach, he stood and, bowing to Adele, murmured a polite greeting. She knew his false smile was only for De Montford's benefit.

"Forgive me, my lord, but at first I didn't recognize you." Adele bowed her head, lest he think her disrespectful. "I thought you were a guest."

"I *am* a guest," he said with a grin. "After a bath, with the feel of solid ground underfoot, I'm become a new man." He held out a chair for her, and Adele mumbled something incomprehensible. De Montford took the lord's chair. Bohun was to his right, and Adele sat to his left. How different he looked tonight, so much so that she could not take her eyes off him. His well-cut tunic was molded to his chest and shoulders and displayed his powerful physique. Likewise, his shimmering hose and supple, calf-high boots accentuated his muscular legs. Used to seeing him in bulky and impersonal chain mail, she thought this stylish new De Montford almost a dandy by contrast. She would never have dreamed that anyone could look so attractive. Unlike Bohun, he did not shave the back of his neck, allowing his hair to fall thick and black around his collar. In contrast to his olive complexion, his eyes were a startling blue, pale and luminous in the candlelight within their frames of thick sooty lashes. His dark skin made such light eyes all the more arresting. Though his mouth was generous, De Montford's strong, determined chin and high-bridged nose gave his face an air of unyielding authority.

It was hard to admit, but Adele conceded that Rafe De Montford was very handsome—so handsome that her heart skipped a beat each time he even smiled at her. Oh, how disloyal she was being. She inwardly chastised herself for her weakness, finding her sudden emotion distressing. De Montford was their disliked overlord, and a friend of their equally disliked monarch! How could she even stand him, let alone be drawn to him? No, it was not him, but his appearance she admired. Worse, she caught herself wishing it were he, and not the grizzled Bohun, who had been appointed castellan.

She reminded herself that a handsome man could be equally as unpleasant as an ugly one.

Adele gulped wine from her goblet, finding it heavy and slightly sweet. Steeling herself, she looked full upon this handsome, dark-haired lord. This time she made sure her heart remained steady. Good. At least she had conquered that foolishness.

Politely, De Montford helped serve her meal, offering bread and meat, ordering her cup refilled, and always courteous and distant.

Adele had hoped to further plead for their independence, but it did not happen. There was so much noise and clatter from the crowded lower tables, it was hard to make oneself heard. Besides, De Montford kept half turned from her, directing his attention to Bohun. By the man's glowering face, she assumed his liege's words were not to his liking. Was De Montford telling him to mind his manners?

Before the meal was half over, a flurry of activity at the door announced the arrival of a small band of players, courtesy of the lord of Myerly. Bohun cheered at their arrival and pitched a handful of coins to the rushes to encourage them to come forward.

Adele could see that De Montford was as surprised as she by this unexpected entertainment. Puffed up with self-satisfaction, Bohun explained that the arrangements were all his doing, designed especially to please his lord.

After gathering up the thrown coins, the players tumbled the length of the hall before leapfrogging back the way they had come. The half-dozen players finally stopped, and, bowing deep, stood before the lord's table ready to begin.

Adele was pleased by the prospect of having entertainment, for beyond what her own people sometimes provided, music and singing were rare at Esterwold. Minstrels almost never found their way to this castle, for the rewards were greater at the larger castles. She settled back to enjoy the treat.

The men's voices were tuneful as they sang to the accompaniment of pipe and lute. Adele recognized many of the country airs they performed, and she hummed and sang along with them. After a few cups of wine, however, the minstrels' songs turned bawdy—much to the delight of the soldiers who joined in the familiar chorus. Adele could not quite distinguish the slurred lyrics, though she noticed that De Montford glanced quickly in her direction, as if to assess her reaction. Encouraged by the audience's enthusiasm, several of the players donned women's garb and began to dance, gesturing lewdly to the soldiers. Several men were urged forward to dance with these damsels, to the great amusement of their fellows.

"Come, Lady Adele, this isn't entertainment for you," De Montford called a few minutes later. Curtly motioning to a servant, he told the man to escort her to her chamber. "Good night. I hope the music doesn't keep you awake."

"But there are things I must speak with you about," she protested, not regretting leaving this bawdy entertainment, but annoyed that she was being shunted away without having had her say.

"We'll discuss them in the morning."

"Do I have your promise you won't leave until you've heard me out?"

He shrugged but, as he saw a protest forming, grinned at her and nodded his head. "Aye, you have my word. Though I might not want to hear what you have to say."

Peeved by his flippant response, she glared at him. His smile turned indulgent as if she were a petulant child. "Must I remind you, I'm still lady here?" she said, her jaw tense. "Esterwold is my home, lest you've forgotten."

"Oh, I don't think there's any danger of that. You'll never let me forget," he joked, turning back to his wine.

Seething, Adele swished from the dais. Out of respect, the players temporarily halted their unseemly play. Too deep in his cups to heed who was passing, one young soldier who was romancing a fair "damsel," crushed her false breast too hard and burst the pig's bladder, his action provoking a great shout of laughter.

Margery and Kate, Adele's two women, got up from their places to follow their lady, though they kept glancing back at the festivities, curious to see what would take place next.

Adele went upstairs, dismissing her escort so the servant could return to the entertainment. She had lived here all her life and she certainly didn't need a guide to find her room.

Inside the sanctity of her darkened chamber, Adele sat on the edge of her bed. Margery closed the door to keep out the racket, but bursts of laughter could still be heard. Kate lit the candles from the fire in the hearth and set them on the chest beside the bed.

"What do you think they'll do next?" the younger maid asked her mistress, giggling.

"Probably mount the village women," Margery added sourly. "And from the randy look of the wenches, they'll welcome the diversion."

Adele shushed the two, conscious of Kate's tender years. Margery said no more. Kate, who was only twelve, had been sent by her mother to learn the ways of a noble household. Margery was a widow, ten years Adele's senior, who had served at Esterwold since her husband's death.

"Is this what our evenings with Bohun are going to be like?" Margery demanded when she came to take down Adele's hair. "If so, we'd best permanently cover our ears. You get away from that door, young Kate! There's nothing you'll learn from them downstairs except how to be a slut."

The girl pouted, but she went back to the bed to turn back the covers.

"I don't know, Margery. Probably. After all, according to De Montford, Bohun has complete charge over us all. He can do as he pleases," Adele said wearily. Her body sagged in defeat. She had hoped De Montford would be her ally, but after a few cups of wine he had become just like the others. For some reason, her disappointment at that was acute. Sheepishly, she had to admit that her hopes had been strengthened by his handsome appearance. She had wanted to make him her ally, foolishly desiring to enjoy his attentions and admiring smile.

"The young De Montford is fair, is he not, my lady?" Kate voiced Adele's thoughts as she set out her mistress's nightrail. "He's like a saint stepped from the church window," she added dreamily.

"No saint is he," Margery said with a wry look that faded to a small smile. "And I admit to almost envying the village wench he takes to bed tonight."

Adele's stomach pitched sickeningly at Margery's comment. Would he really select a village woman—or maybe one of the castle servants—to sleep with him tonight? Until now she had not considered the possibility, and it made her feel ill. Adele stared down at her lap. She was being foolish. What did it matter if he took a dozen women? She must accustom herself to the idea, that was all. Just then there was a bump and frantic scratching on the other side of the door.

"Oh, that must be Val," Adele cried. She jumped up to let in the pet, thankful for the diversion. The big dog bounded inside the room, relieved that he was not going to be shut out. After first licking his mistress in greeting, he acknowledged the other two women before stretching out at Adele's feet.

In silence, Adele made ready for bed. She suddenly felt so disconsolate she could have wept. This sadness was caused by the upheaval in her life, she told herself, not De Montford's sleeping habits. Of that she was sure. What he did at night was his own business! Yes, that was it; she had been forced to endure such astronomical changes, it was only natural that she should feel melancholy.

Trying to shake off her dark mood, she told herself that, given King John's capricious nature, Bohun could be out of favor by summer. She would dwell on that thought, not the shameful spectacle that continued unabated below, in the great hall. *Her* great hall inside *her* castle, she added indignantly. The drunken revelry was an unpleasant reminder of how little authority she had here. Once De Montford was gone, she shuddered to think what changes Bohun would impose. The villagers had always looked to her for fairness and just rule, but this time she feared she would be powerless to act.

When all the nighttime preparations were complete and the candles were snuffed, Adele lay in the dark listening to waves of sound and drunken laughter drifting from below.

Adele rose early the next day, freshly determined to present her case to De Montford. She refused to let the apparent dissolute nature in him that she'd witnessed last night sway her from her purpose.

Kate was still asleep, and Adele noticed Margery yawn as the maid helped her mistress dress for the day. Deciding upon utility over beauty, Adele drew on an everyday gown of forest green wool, over which she wore her fur-lined cloak. Her bright hair hung unadorned down her back in a ribbon-bound plait. As she slid her bare feet in her old deerskin boots, Margery clucked disapprovingly. Adele quieted her. Really, as if it were necessary to dress fine just to take Val outside!

She crossed the hall surrounded by the evidence of last night's debauchery. Several village women were still there, lying drunk and disheveled beneath the tables. To her surprise, she even found Gilbert Bohun snoring on a trestle. All around her, soldiers slept where they had fallen, amidst spilled ale cups and half-eaten food. The very sight and smell of them turned her stomach. There was no sign of De Montford.

Holding tight to Val's collar, for he growled in warning at strangers so close to his mistress, Adele escaped through the small door off the buttery. Cold air slapped her face, taking away her breath. It was still barely light and a brisk wind was blowing, yet the winter morn was a welcome change from the fusty great hall.

Adele wondered if this would be the castle's future: lewd entertainment nightly and, each morning, the sight and smell of snoring drunken men sprawled around its hall. She prayed that last night had been an exception, that Bohun had simply been trying to please his lord.

She could not help wondering why Bohun was sleeping out on a trestle instead of in his bedchamber—unless De Montford lay abed there . . . with a woman? Again a pang of emotion speared through her. She had hoped for much better behavior from their handsome liege lord; to discover he was little better than the others was a harsh blow.

Hooves thudded behind her. Adele spun about, calling Val to her side, but she had no need to fear. It was De Montford.

"You're abroad early," he said, reining in his horse. He was dressed for riding.

Surprised to find him already up and about, Adele quickly moved out of range of his temperamental mount.

"Will you hear me now, before you leave?"

"I'm not leaving yet, just going for a ride. This morning I need a dose of fresh air to clear my brain." He grinned as he added ruefully, "Strange to relate, my head seems to have become a belfry with a great clanging bell—"

"What I have to say won't take long," she cut him off.

His mood changed abruptly, the smile sliding from his face.

"Later."

"Why?" she demanded, gritting her teeth.

"Because I'm going for a ride. If you still want a discussion later, I'll listen then."

"How long must I wait?"

"As long as I choose," he snapped, his face hard. "Any more questions?"

"I want to know why you won't help me change the King's mind. Gilbert Bohun is no better than a pig. He's not fit to rule here." She longed to add he smelled like one too, but decided against it.

They exchanged hostile glares before he leaned slightly from his saddle to offer, "Then ready the sty, Lady, for he's the ruler you've got!" He gave her an unyielding look.

"You could help if you wanted," she cried, anger making her more reckless.

"There, you're wrong." His words were short, and, with them, he tugged on his reins and his horse leapt forward. He quickly rode into the outer ward without a backward glance.

Adele seethed with anger. How could she ever have thought him handsome? This man was about power, about grinding lesser people beneath his heel just to show he had command over them.

Chapter Two

Bohun woke to grief. As soon as he'd risen, Adele had vented her rage upon him, telling him in no uncertain terms what she thought about last night's entertainment and the deplorable conduct of his men.

He regarded her silently, his thoughts still muddled and his head pounding. When her mouth finally stopped moving, he chose a course of action. "You, Lady, can go to hell," he snarled, then spun on his heel and slammed out the solar door.

Down the stairs he thumped, boiling at the audacity of his charge. He had a mind to teach that flame-haired bitch a lesson she would not soon forget. And he know just how to do it. That would show her who was in charge. The idea was immensely appealing. It would be tricky to accomplish with De Montford still about, but not impossible. As he passed, Bohun kicked a couple of sleeping soldiers, growling at them that it was past time to be up and about.

He met De Montford coming inside the hall as he was

leaving. Bohun paused. "That songbird is in full voice this morning. Have a care lest she peck your eyes out. I've a mind to teach her a lesson she won't soon forget. For such a beauty, she can be a damned disagreeable crow."

De Montford laughed. "Likely long overdue for bedding, don't you think?" he suggested, glancing toward the stair. "Is she in the solar?"

"Aye, holding court with her hellhound and her damn maids. The sooner she learns who's master here, the better." He was pleased by his liege's ability to understand the situation. They would get along just fine. "Remember, my lord, later we're to ride out to assess the hunting." He stalked away.

De Montford watched Bohun walk outside, his rolling gait making him appear perpetually tipsy. The man's face had been mottled with anger, and Rafe could easily guess the punishment the beast intended for the Lady of Esterwold.

Rafe crossed the hall, shaking his head in regret. Why the king put faith in such soldiers of fortune, he didn't know, appointing them to important posts while his barons were bled dry. But then, no one had ever said John Softsword exercised good judgment.

As he walked, Rafe stripped off his hood and gauntlets and handed them to his squire. Today, the second half of his orders must be fulfilled, a task no longer to his liking.

Before, he had given little thought to Adele St. Clare; the woman was no more than a name, of no more significance than her small inconsequential fortress. He had been eager to be done with Bohun so he could go home, and by completing his orders, Rafe would head back toward Fordham. Hugh D'Avranche lived not far from his borders. Then, once Hugh's bride was delivered, Rafe would be free to do as he pleased.

But Rafe no longer felt so aloof. Fiery-haired Adele St. Clare was a beauty beyond compare. And she was alluringly high-spirited. The woman was far too desirable to be sacrificed to D'Avranche, a twin of Bohun in temperament, if not in looks. Still, he had to carry out his orders, however odious. He had been sent to deliver the woman to her future groom—and that was what he intended to do.

"Lady Adele."

She glanced up from her needlework and waved Margery and Kate to the other end of the solar.

"Lord Rafe, at last. I trust your head's cleared."

"Somewhat."

Adele motioned him to a nearby cushioned chair, but he shook his head. She forced herself to be civil, though after tangling with Bohun, she had to work hard to do so. "I assume you're ready to listen to me now."

"I am indeed. Though I suspect you're girded for battle and bloodied—I just saw Bohun on his way out."

"Yes, probably off to inspect the sty I've readied for him," she quipped acidly. To her surprise, De Montford laughed.

"Ah, Lady, you've a ready wit. Mayhap our talk will be entertaining, after all."

"It's not my intent to entertain, my lord. I'm pleading with you to help save my land, my people—my own person."

"Don't be so dramatic."

She forced herself to take a deep breath and stay calm. If she angered him, he'd likely stop listening. "It's true, especially after last night."

"I apologize for that spectacle. It was none of my doing. Barracks entertainment is out of place here. And I told Bohun as much."

"Thank you."

He acknowledged her with a nod, then motioned to the serving women to leave them alone. What they must discuss he preferred to keep between them. He pulled up a chair and straddled the seat, leaning his elbows on the back. Looking around, he became aware of her large black dog staring intently at him. Rafe clicked his tongue at the dog. After first glancing toward his lady—as if asking permission—the dog moved forward to lay his head on the baron's arm.

Adele was surprised by Val's trust; usually the hound was more selective of his friends.

"My lord, surely you realize Gilbert Bohun is unacceptable as castellan here. Besides that, he's unnecessary. Sir George is sure that if you would intervene on our behalf—"

"How old is that knight? A hundred?"

"Why do you ask? He's perfectly able to continue here."

"Is that why he's lying abed with poultices on his legs from yesterday's travel?"

Adele turned away from his challenging glare. She had been hoping to present Sir George as a virile older man still capable of helping her run the castle. Disarmed by De Montford's words, Adele looked down at her hands and anxiously twisted them in the folds of her gown.

She could hear Val groaning with pleasure as her liege scratched his ears and rubbed his chest. The dog's disloyalty annoyed her, but she could hardly yank the hound away from him. After all, Val was just a dog, unaware of their imminent unhappiness.

"He's a big, fine animal. What do you call him?"

"Val. Valiant."

"Ah, that's well suited. He wants to be my friend, Lady. How about you?"

His question caught her off guard; when she looked up she was surprised to find he was smiling. She swallowed before carefully explaining, "It's not that I don't want to be your friend, My Lord. I'm just disappointed that you show no concern for our future.

He leaned forward. "Lady, you seem to think a whispered word from me into the king's ear will change everything. That's not how the court operates. Gilbert Bohun is being rewarded with this castle. He has charge of several other castles already, and for some reason the king wants him to control this one, too. As overlord of this district, I must implement the royal will. It's that simple. I'm sorry, but I've no magic to set things right for you."

How matter-of-fact he made it all seem. When she looked closely at him, she could see he was trying to be kind. Though Adele hated her weakness, she felt the treacherous prickle of tears. Blinking rapidly, she cleared her throat. "Then you're saying there's nothing I can do to alter matters?"

He nodded. "Yes, that's about it."

As she turned away, Rafe saw the tears inching their way down her cheek. Suddenly he wanted to reach out for her, to take her in his arms and heal her pain. His unexpected reaction to her grief startling him, he kept his hands purposely looked before him. The tenderness he felt was disconcerting. Always in the past when he put his arms around a woman, it had been for only one thing.

Clearing his throat, Rafe got up and pushed away his chair.

"I'm sorry, Lady Adele, but that's the way it is." His voice was harsh as he tried to hide his own emotion.

She nodded but did not answer him, reaching instead for her dog. Laying her head against its silky head, she shut her eyes, tears spilling from under the lids.

With that picture still in his mind, Rafe strode from the room.

Damn, he had not expected to be disarmed by the sight of her tears. He could not wait to leave before he did something he regretted. And he still hadn't told her the second part of his mission. There'd be even more tears after she'd digested that piece of news. Nay, she'd be more likely to fly at him and try to rip him limb from limb. To be forced into accepting the king's choice of castellan was one thing; to have to accept his choice of husband was a far different matter. But she would accept it; she had no choice. As he had no choice.

His determination to complete this assignment was not out of affection for his sly king, but because John was king of England. Rafe had sworn to obey him, however much he disagreed.

Adele did not know how long she sat, hugging Val for comfort. The realization that nothing could be done to change matters was hard to accept. Bohun was here to stay. She scowled through her tears. Maybe if she made life as unpleasant as she could for him, he would hate Esterwold enough to leave it.

Val shifted slightly and licked away his mistress's tears. His devotion brought a wan smile to her face.

"Oh, Val, you've no idea why I'm crying, do you, my friend and protector?" Adele clasped his thick, furry neck, then dismissed the dog. "Go; do what you will."

She went to the solar's deep arched window to look out at the brown winter countryside; its bleakness matched her mood. Some time ago she had heard riders leave across the drawbridge; she also fancied she had heard returning hoofbeats, but all seemed quiet now below.

A few minutes later, Margery tapped on the solar door. "You have a guest, my lady."

Surprised, Adele turned to find a cloaked man standing in the shadowy doorway.

"Don't you recognize me, Lady Adele?" he asked.

"Why no, sir, not until you step into the light."

"Guy Cosantine, at your service. Your father and I fought side by side for many years."

Adele's face lit with pleasure. She did indeed remember that name. The man who moved into the light had changed: his familiar face was heavily lined, and his sharp pointed beard had turned white.

Limping toward her, Sir Guy gave Adele a swift embrace and a peck on the cheek. His face felt icy cold.

"Bring us some refreshment, Margery. Come, Sir Guy, get close to the fire. You must be chilled to the bone. How far did you ride? Surely not all the way from the coast?"

Adele remembered that the bulk of Sir Guy's lands were across the Channel in Poitou.

"No . . . at least not all this week," he said with a smile. He shed his heavy cloak and stretched thin hands out to the blaze. "I was sorry to hear about your father's death. How long has it been—a year?"

"Almost two."

"And since then you've managed things here by yourself?"

"Yes, with Sir George's help."

"Ah, yes, old George. We were young knights together, long before your father inherited this land. I must say, things are looking prosperous under your guidance, Adele."

"Thank you. Everything was fine until two days ago," she remarked bitterly.

"And that was when you received a surprise visit from Gilbert Bohun and his brutish retinue. Am I right?"

She was shocked by his knowledge. "Yes—but how did you know?"

"Oh, I hear things," he said, pulling up a bench. He sat down and stretched his numb legs to the blaze. "Where's Bohun now?"

"Hunting. At least, he took huntsmen and his falconer. De Montford's gone with him."

"That's why I was admitted without challenge. Your men all know me. Spence is still here, I see."

"Yes, but not for long. Bohun intends to appoint his own man. If only Jocelyn were home, we could be rid of him, king's appointee or nay. Perhaps *you* can help me, Sir Guy. I wrote to the king asking him to send Joce back—his response was to send Bohun and De Montford. Can you intervene on my behalf? De Montford just told me I must accept what I'm given."

Just then Margery brought them a tray of wine and sliced meat and bread. Sir Guy waited until the maid was out of earshot before speaking.

"He's right, Adele." When she began to protest, he held

35

up his hand. "Hear me out. He's right—for the time being. Endure Bohun a little longer; then circumstances may change."

"How?"

Sir Guy put down his wine cup and leaned forward.

"This very hour your brother's almost within bowshot of the castle," he revealed, lowering his voice conspiratorially.

With a gasp of delight, Adele seized his hand. In excitement she cried, "Joce is here! Oh, why isn't he with you?"

"Not so fast. Things are not so simple. We must be careful. Bohun will kill him if he finds out. After all, he doesn't want to lose power here. Your brother's in the woods. He has only a handful of men, and Bohun and De Montford have many."

"Oh, tell me, how is he? He was only a little boy when I saw him last," she said, her voice wobbling with emotion. She was thrilled by the prospect of having Joce home at last. "I mightn't even recognize him—he must be seventeen."

"Yes . . . something like that," Sir Guy allowed vaguely. He greedily reached for bread and cheese. He ignored her imploring glances while he ate ravenously, as if he hadn't eaten for days. At last, when he was finished, he dabbed crumbs from his mouth before saying, "First, I must have your word that you'll tell no one. We're going to need your help to get inside Esterwold."

"You have my word, but I don't understand. Why must you wait? Why can't Joce just ride in? Esterwold's his home. He's the undisputed lord here," she said.

"Do you think they'll let him live if he arrives without allies? He'll likely have a dagger in his back before morning. Jocelyn needs time to gather more men. The villagers will be loyal to him, of course, but they're hardly trained fighters to put up against Bohun's men."

"There's no need to fight. I'll simply tell Bohun and De Montford my brother's come home. They—"

"*No.* Don't tell anyone. We must plan what we're going to say and do." Sir Guy looked around nervously.

"Oh, I'm so excited! I can't wait to see him after all these years. Take me to him now. I can be dressed and out the gate in five minutes. Please, say you'll take me to him. I can convince him to come back. I don't like him hiding in the forest in the middle of winter."

Sir Guy smiled at her. "I don't think you understand Jocelyn's danger, my lady. But, yes, I'll take you to him."

"Let's go now while Bohun and De Montford are hunting. There'll be fewer questions asked if they don't know when I left the castle. Not that I'm under arrest, although that'll probably come next."

"We'll need to take food and gold. Jocelyn must feed his men and buy weapons and supplies."

Though Adele did not contradict Sir Guy, she was puzzled over his demands for secrecy. She had little gold to give besides the small bag of coins she kept behind her window seat. As for food, they could pack a bag from the kitchens, but it could not be a great amount if they did not want to arouse suspicion. Still, she could not imagine why there was such a need for secrecy. Surely even Bohun would not kill her brother in cold blood. Joce and Sir Guy seemed to think so.

Adele could hardly contain her excitement as she waited for Margery to bring the food from the kitchens. She paced back and forth in her winter cloak, the small bag of gold hidden inside her gown. Joce's arrival was surely the answer to her prayers.

Finally they were on their way. They rode out of the castle under glowering skies, heading into a brisk wind. Adele glanced about, afraid they would meet the returning hunters, but the muddy road stayed empty. Spence had been instructed to say, if asked, that Lady Adele had gone for a ride. Though at first the dog had growled menacingly at Sir Guy, Val had insisted on coming with her. He now loped along beside her horse.

They soon left the road and followed a narrow path, that twisted and turned through the silent woods. As they went deeper, the underbrush grew so dense and tangled it

37

was almost impenetrable in places. No birds sang here. There were reputed to be treacherous bogs deep in these woods, and Adele was uneasy, wondering if the paths were safe. Fortunately, Sir Guy seemed familiar with the area and he led her deftly through the wooded maze until they could hear men's voices and the clang of metal echoing through the trees.

They finally rode into Joce's camp. It was built in a clearing ringed with makeshift shelters. A campfire blazed in the center, smoke spiraling up through the trees.

Adele's knees trembled with excitement as she dismounted and waited beside her horse. These shabbily dressed men camped in the heart of the wood looked more like thieves than soldiers of her brother.

As she watched, a man hurried to the only permanent structure in the camp. Sir Guy did not dismount, preferring to stay in the saddle.

After what seemed a long wait, a stocky, blond-haired man dressed in a faded black tunic and hose came out of the hut. He stood a moment, looking at her, before his face broke into a smile of welcome. This had to be Joce, though he looked older than she'd expected. Adele's disappointment was acute: the young man before her was a stranger, and she had been cheated of watching him grow up.

They embraced warmly and she wept with joy. Her brother was returned from the dead!

"Oh, Joce, Joce, how wonderful to see you again after all this time." Adele sobbed. She clung to his broad, muscular frame.

"Joce?" he asked. "It's Jocelyn, sister."

"But I've always called you that," she said in surprise, drawing back slightly to look into his face. Reddish blond beard shadowed his square chin and outlined his upper lip. She reached up to lift a thick lock of hair off his brow. "Now you're grown and you would take on airs?"

"Nay, sister, I'd just forgotten, that's all." He grinned at her and gave her a second hug. "You can call me whatever you like. Come inside."

Together they walked into the hut. Val kept close to Adele's side, snarling in warning when Joce started to embrace her again. Her brother swore at the dog, angrily kicking out at him, and Adele was startled by his sudden temper. It was so unlike the Joce she remembered; her unease deepened.

Inside the gloomy shed they sat on tree stumps and he offered her bread and sour ale.

"It's not much, but the best we have," he said in apology.

"I brought some food, but it's not near enough for all your men."

"They won't starve," he said casually as he drained his ale cup. "If they're hungry enough, the lazy bastards can trap something in the forest." He turned back to her, studying her face. "You're very beautiful," he said. "Quite the most beautiful woman I think I've ever seen."

"Why, thank you, Joce. Brothers aren't usually so complimentary."

"Well, they should be—Adele," he said, carefully pronouncing her name. He'd acquired an unfamiliar accent which she assumed must be from spending so long at Summerhay; likely the speech was different in that part of the country.

Adele smiled at him, and Joce leaned forward and took her hand.

"Remember, you aren't to tell anyone I'm here. They'll ride into the woods to kill me if they know."

"Oh, I'm sure they wouldn't do that. You are Lord of Esterwold. All you need do is ride back to the castle with me. No one disputes your claim. Come on, come back with me."

"*No.* And you'll do as you're told, sister."

She swallowed and drew back, surprised by his ire. To change the subject, she asked, "Why didn't you answer my letters? I would not have worried so if I had heard from you."

"Never got any letters," he mumbled, his mouth stuffed with bread.

Her brother's poor manners were another surprise. It was not what she would have expected after his years at a great castle like Summerhay, unless, like Bohun, that castle's lord belonged in a sty. "Then you didn't know Father was dead?"

"Oh, aye, I heard."

Adele's heart lurched. She stared at her brother in amazement to see him so devoid of emotion. "You seem so cold," she whispered at last.

"Cold?" He laughed, and the harsh sound grated on her nerves. "Surely you didn't expect me to break down sobbing at the news."

"But he was our father."

"I barely knew him."

"Yes . . . yes. I suppose you were only a lad when you left."

"That's right, so don't you accuse me of being heartless," he countered, his tone belligerent. "Now you must return. Remember, no one's to know. You were clever not bringing anyone but him," Joce said, gesturing to Val. The hound lay on guard in the doorway. "When the time's right, I'll tell you what you can do. Fair enough?"

"Yes, fair enough," she agreed unenthusiastically.

Joce stood. Taking her hands, he brought her to her feet and drew her to him. "God, you're beautiful, sister mine. I'd have come back sooner had I known I had a sibling like you," he said huskily. He pulled her into an embrace, his mouth crushing hers.

Alarmed by his unexpected ardor, Adele struggled to be free. The adult Joce's embraces seemed far from fraternal.

"I'm glad you're safe, Joce. But I'll be happier once you're home and out of the cold. Why not come back with me today?"

"No, I told you. It's not time yet," he said, his voice harsh. "You go back now, Adele."

"How can I reach you? Without Sir Guy I'll never find my way here."

"Cosantine's staying at the priory. If you need me for

anything"—was that a suggestive grin?—"you can get word to me through him." He stood there, looking her up and down, his gaze probing her half-open cloak.

Uncomfortable beneath his scrutiny, Adele clutched the edges of her cape together. "All right, I'll remember." she agreed, aware of Val pressing against her leg. The big dog stood his ground, a low rumble reverberating through his chest when Joce started to pull her back into his arms. Adele moved away, her hand on Val's collar; she drew him closer to her side, wary of the annoyance flickering over her brother's face. Joce glared at the dog.

"Godspeed. We'll be together soon, sister." Joce smiled at her, waving good-bye as she hurried across the clearing.

Adele resisted the urge to run. She did not enjoy the curious, admiring stares of this ragtag band of followers. These men must be *routiers*, free lances—or were some even robbers? She feared so as a fierce-looking individual with a brace of knives in his belt doffed his cap to her.

"Ready?" Sir Guy asked. "We'd best hurry. The light's going. We'll be lucky to beat Bohun home. I'll take you to the edge of the wood. That's as far as I can go."

Adele mounted and called Val to her. She followed Sir Guy along the trail, sunk in gloom. This afternoon had not gone as expected. Something about Joce was all wrong. Adele had to admit that some of her unease had been caused by Val's hostility toward him. Yet why should she feel wary of her own brother? This was the grown-up Joce, not the little boy she had known. And his far from brotherly embraces bothered her.

Adele thought back to the last time she had seen him, on a rainy morning that was still clear in her mind. Poor Joce, he had turned in the saddle to wave at her as he headed toward captivity, sitting ramrod straight on his pony, his curly red hair spilling to his shoulders, his pale face wet with tears.

Today his hair was blond, the curl vanished. That slender lad with the big gray eyes had become stocky and muscular. What was stranger still, when she had looked into his eyes, she'd felt no tug of recognition. A startling thought struck—his eyes had been hazel! Shocked, she tried to recall the man she'd just met. Mayhap over the years her brother's eye color had deepened to more match her own. Also, how could she have accurately determined his eye color in that murky light?

It was also possible her memory was at fault. Adele had to admit she had been expecting to see a willowy lad with gray eyes and red hair. Instead she had met Joce the man, powerfully built, his curly red hair bleached to blond, his eyes darkened to hazel. In maturity the boy she had loved had become a stranger.

"You look distressed, my lady. Was your brother not as you expected?"

"No, Sir Guy. I knew a little boy, and this Joce is a man," was all she said, swallowing her unease. "He says, if I need to reach him, you'll be staying at the priory."

"Yes, the prior's an old friend of mine."

"Why doesn't Joce stay there with you?"

Hesitating before he spoke, Sir Guy finally said, "Well, Lady Adele, it's customary for a captain to stay with his men."

They stopped at a slope leading down to the castle. The heavy dusk made Adele uneasy, and surrounded as they were by trees, she kept glancing about for danger, glad of her dog's protection. Torches flared on the castle battlements, beckoning her home. Despite Bohun's unwelcome presence there, she felt a sudden urge to gallop down the hill to safety.

"I'll leave you here, Adele. Remember, tell no one."

"I'll remember. Good-bye, Sir Guy." She kicked in her heels and rode for home, her dog racing to keep up.

Looking back once, Adele could still see the shadow of Sir Guy's horse at the edge of the trees.

What should have been one of the most joyous days of her life had left her feeling uneasy. Beyond Joce's changed physical appearance and strange embrace, her brother's talk of fighting and the need for secrecy had done little to dispel her discomfort. And she had to admit that her biggest disappointment had been Joce himself. She knew now she had not been prepared for the way he had changed. How she had yearned for that little boy with soft hair and tender eyes, who had loved dogs and tended a garden in the sheltered angle of the castle walls. Years of captivity had robbed him of his sweeter self, leaving in its place a hardened soldier far older than his years.

The wind blew her tears across her cheeks as she rode inside the bailey, and her voice was husky as she answered the sentry's challenge.

Chapter Three

Adele longed to blurt out her discovery to Bohun. The man sat sucking winesops off his fingers while he spewed orders right and left. Yesterday, he had brought his prize falcons from Myerly where they had been temporarily kept until Esterwold's facilities were ready. There had been much scrubbing and repair to make Esterwold's disused mews fit to house his precious birds.

As she sipped from her ale cup, Adele hugged her secret to herself. Soon Joce would come home and everything would return to normal. Still, a feeling of unease marred her pleasure. This mature Joce might be difficult to handle; he might not be provident, or a wise governor. Still, Joce was rightful lord here and he would govern as he saw fit.

Bohun wiped his hands down his tunic, leaned back in his chair, and belched, but Adele hardly noticed. This morning, she felt pleasantly detached from their unwelcome castellan and the uproar swirling around him. Earlier she had met with Cedric, the village headman, to hear his complaints.

How Adele had wanted to confide her secret to him, for he had loved Joce too. But she dared not break her word to her brother and put him in harm's way. Instead she had assured Cedric that his grievances would be addressed, though she had a sinking feeling that she could do little to change anything. Bohun had lost no time in implementing his new laws requiring more work, higher rents, and fewer privileges.

"Lord Bohun," she said at last, catching his attention. "The villagers find your changes too rapid and severe. Could you not reconsider—"

"I'll reconsider nothing! As it is, they're getting away with murder, sitting on their fat arses all day instead of working. You've given them far too much leeway."

"We managed well enough before you came."

"*Managed* is the key word, lady." He grinned sourly at her, displaying blackened teeth. "Besides, this is no longer your concern. Baron De Montford has some news for you which I promise will change your entire outlook."

Adele's stomach pitched as Bohun chuckled unpleasantly. The man pushed himself away from the table and shouted for his men to accompany him, but instead of going outside, they all clumped upstairs to the lord's quarters.

She noticed De Montford crossing the hall, his stride hurried, his expression determined. He wore partial armor, his sword belt slung around his waist.

Adele wondered what unpleasant new ruling was to be given now. If only Joce had come home with her instead of hiding in the forest like an outlaw, this farce would be over. Then a chill went through her: Had De Montford found her brother? Was that why he was dressed for battle?

"Lady Adele, I would speak with you privately."

"Yes, Bohun's already prepared me."

"What?"

He sounded so shocked she stared at him in surprise. Quickly masking his feelings, he suggested, "Let's go somewhere quieter." When she started toward the solar,

45

he caught her arm and turned her about. "No, not there. Bohun's men are making too much noise up there. Come outside with me. Here's your cloak."

Surprised but unprotesting, Adele let him slip her fur-lined garment about her shoulders. Why did he have her cloak? Had he taken it from her chamber? Had one of her women brought it to him? It was strange, but since she'd come downstairs this morning, she had seen neither Kate nor Margery.

Together, they walked outside. Pale winter sunshine sprinkled the frost rimed buttresses with diamonds. The wind was light so it was not unpleasant walking in this sheltered part of the bailey.

"What did Bohun tell you?"

"That you had news that would change my outlook."

De Montford's sigh was audible. "Aye, you might say that." He steered her toward a stone bench overlooking a small garden within the sheltered angle of the walls. The once-well-tended plot had long since run to weeds. In the distance, Adele was aware of much bumping and banging; hooves clopped and there was a chorus of snorts and neighing from horses as they were prepared for travel.

"It sounds as if you're getting ready to leave," she said, sitting on the bench, her cloak folded beneath her to ward away the stone's chill.

"Yes. Today, if possible."

For some unfathomable reason, her stomach pitched at his unwelcome news. For some reason, she did not want him to go.

"It's such short notice."

"Aye, it is, and I apologize for that, Lady. You see, there's something I need to tell you and so far I haven't been able to put it into words." He paused, looking towards the bailey as if completely absorbed in watching the soldiers load the wagons.

Breathing a deep sigh of relief, Adele waited. Some-how she did not think this news was going to be about Joce, after all. She squinted against the sunlight, the better to see his face, finding his expression grim, his mouth set in a straight line.

"You're leaving me at Bohun's mercy; is that what's pricking your conscience?" she prompted.

Astonished by her question, he almost grinned. "Well, so you still think I have a conscience—that does surprise me. But no, Lady, leaving you at Bohun's mercy was never my intent."

"What, then? If you're leaving today, there is no other answer."

He moved closer on the bench so that her skirts brushed against his knee, making Adele very aware of the warmth of his body as it engulfed her in a welcome wave. He looked full upon her, and she saw either pity or remorse in his pale eyes—she did not know him well enough to know which. Her heart fluttered.

"Lady Adele, in that letter you received from the king, do you remember any mention about your wardship?"

She did remember, but had not fully understood the contents of that letter. "Yes . . . what of it?"

He sighed and shifted his feet; his booted legs coiled and uncoiled as he scuffed gravel underfoot while searching for the right words. There was no gentle way. "Lady Adele, King John has arranged a marriage for you. I'm here to escort you to your new husband's castle. We leave today."

A strangled cry escaped her lips. It was as if someone had suddenly yanked the ground out from under her. "What?"

"I'm sorry, but I have no choice. I know I've left it to the last, which I shouldn't have done. I didn't know how to tell you."

"No! I won't go! I don't want a husband—especially one chosen by the king. Who is this man?"

"Hugh D'Avranche."

"Who?"

"D'Avranche. He recently inherited his uncle's castle close to Bawtry. He's a favorite of the king . . . oh, Lady, please."

Adele had jumped to her feet and stood glaring at him, fists clenched in her cloak. "I won't go! Do you understand? You can't make me marry someone against my will. Isn't it enough to force Bohun on us? Now this! I'm not a serf bound to His Lordship like chattel. I'm a noble woman. This is *my* castle. I don't choose to marry any man."

"The king has the power to do as he sees fit with his ward. You are being offered to this man as a reward for valued service—a prize, if you will."

"I'll not be any man's trophy. No! You can tell your king that. I refuse to go."

"Your chests are already being loaded on the wagons," he revealed next, getting up to stand beside the bench.

Though he was a few feet away, she felt crowded by him; the almighty De Montford, the odious embodiment of the king's will had come to steal her happiness.

"I hate the king!"

"You've company there, Lady, but that doesn't absolve me from carrying out my duty. I apologize again for leaving it to the last. I knew you wouldn't welcome the news. At least, now you won't have to endure Bohun."

She gave him a malicious glare. "Some consolation. Doubtless this man is equally horrible."

De Montford glanced away and said nothing, his silence assuring her she had guessed the truth.

"What if I won't go?"

"Then you will be bound and taken as a prisoner . . . but you will go! Oh, Lady, don't make me do that. You know I have no choice in this. The king's orders have to be obeyed."

"You'd take me prisoner?" she gasped in surprise.

"Yes—if I must."

Adele swallowed. What had happened? In one short week all the joy had been stripped from her life. Everything was changed beyond repair.

"All your personal effects are ready—you've not that much.

You can take your dog with you and your waiting

48

women. It's not as if you're being cast adrift in the world. I'll be along to protect you until you reach your new home."

"I hate you too, De Montford, for your treachery," she spat. "For a while I thought perhaps you'd be fair, but I was wrong. Now I understand why you kept saying I wouldn't suffer Bohun long. You had this news at the first and told me not—all so that I'd think kinder of you."

He watched her walk away, his heart thudding uncomfortably. She was right. In the beginning he had lacked the courage to tell her, and as time passed, his resolve had grown ever weaker. Now, at the eleventh hour, there'd been nothing for it but the blunt truth. Without her knowledge, her women had packed her personal belongings and been forced to stay away lest she question their actions. She wasn't alone in feeling cheated. He had wanted her to soften to him—he could admit it now that it was too late. All his hopes had been dashed, but he had his orders.

Adele raced indoors, blinded by tears. What could she do now? Though she felt hopeless to stop this relentless plan from unfolding, there had to be a way. She had to think. There were too many people about to try to run away, so she ruled that out. Besides, where would she go? She knew nothing beyond Esterwold. Damn the king— and damn Rafe De Montford most of all. How could she have been lulled into admiring him, while all the time he had kept this hateful knowledge up his sleeve until she had no resort but compliance?

Kate and Margery stood together sobbing in her room. The bedding, the draperies, even the skins off the floor were gone. Adele reeled back in the doorway in shock when she saw the barren expanse, not having expected the stripping to be so thorough.

"Oh, Lady Adele, I'm sorry," blubbered Kate, her red-rimmed eyes imploring forgiveness.

Margery enfolded Adele against the comfort of her bosom, smoothing back her hair with a gentle hand. "I wanted to tell you, my lady, but Bohun wouldn't let me.

He said it would be much easier for you if it came as a surprise."

Adele took some comfort from her maid. At least they would still be together. "Where's Val?" she asked suddenly, having not seen her dog for hours.

"They took him away . . . he didn't want to go with 'em. Oh, Lady, he growled something fierce, but they—"

"Hush, Kate, that's enough," Margery said sharply, not wanting her lady to hear they had whipped her dog to force it to leave.

"It's all right, I don't blame you for anything. Don't cry, Kate," Adele said as the girl launched into another gale of weeping. "We have to stick together. We're all we have."

The statement brought sickly smiles to the maids' faces, and they took fresh courage from their lady's bravery.

"There's something I have to do, so why don't you use this time to say good-bye to everyone?"

The sniffling women readily agreed and followed Adele downstairs.

A plan was already forming in Adele's mind. She had to get word to Joce to tell him what was about to happen to her. Right time or not, surely this startling new development would force him out of hiding. Once her brother was home, she would no longer be the king's ward and would need not bow to his orders of marriage.

Adele sent for Lew, the young scullion who had family near the priory. As the boy was slow-witted, she doubted he could remember a verbal message for the time it took to get there, so she must give him a letter. Adele quickly wrote a message to her brother and addressed it to Sir Guy Cosantine. She had barely finished sanding the letter when, to her horror, Bohun appeared at her elbow.

"What's this, Lady? Begging your champion for help?"

He roared with laughter at his own wit and snatched the note from her.

Adele's heart sank. Now her last hope was gone. Then, like a heavenly reminder from above, she recalled that their castellan could barely read. "I'm writing to Kate's family about my marriage. They may not want her so far from home," she lied quickly.

"Kate," he repeated, finally turning the missive right side up. "Who's that?"

"My youngest maid. Her mother sent her to me to learn the workings of a household."

"Ah, I see," he said, turning the paper about in his hands. "Where's it going?"

"Her family might not read, so I'm sending it to Sir Guy Cosantine at the priory. He's a relative of theirs," Adele supplied quickly, afraid to gamble. He appeared to be studying the address.

As the scullion entered, Bohun rounded on him. "Where are you taking this, lad?" he snarled, thinking to trap her.

Adele breathed a sigh of relief when the stuttering, red-faced Lew finally croaked, "T'ot priory, my lord."

Mollified, Bohun nodded and thrust the letter back into Adele's hand. "Seal it, then. I'll allow it."

With that, he turned on his heel. Whistling tunelessly, he headed for the door.

Adele melted wax to seal the letter, her heart fluttering and bumping in relief. All the while, she uttered prayers of thanks that it was Bohun and not De Montford who had intercepted her letter. Most certainly Baron De Montford could read.

"Make haste, Lew. Remember, if you're stopped, tell them Lord Bohun authorized this."

Lew nodded vigorously, puffed up with pride to be on such an important mission.

Though Adele had hoped to delay their departure until tomorrow—to give Joce more time to act—it soon became evident that was not going to happen. A hasty meal was followed by De Montford marshaling his men into position for the journey. Lew would surely take most of the afternoon just to reach the priority—if only they could wait till tomorrow to leave, it would give Joce enough time to rescue her.

"Lord Rafe, wouldn't it be better to wait until morning to leave?" she suggested sweetly. "It's going to be dark soon."

"Possibly, but we leave within the hour." And with that he strode away.

Oh, how she longed to slap his arrogant face. What difference could one day make, except it was not his plan?

Adele hurried after him across the hall, alarmed to find Margery and Kate already waiting at the door dressed for traveling.

"Wouldn't it be wiser to travel after a night's rest?" She tried again.

He spun about and regarded her grimly. "Delaying the inevitable won't change matters. Look out there. What do you see?"

She followed the direction of his outflung arm. The inner bailey swarmed with men and horses as they prepared for the journey. "Mounted men and wagons, horses," she said lamely.

"And?"

Adele shrugged, growing uncomfortable under his dominating stare. "I don't know."

"The sun, lady—see how it still shines? The wind's light. There's no rain. For the most part, the roads have hardened. This afternoon will give us about four hours of good travel time. Any more questions?"

Silently she regarded him, emotion surging through her body. How she wanted to strike him in frustration, to rant and rave and give vent to her emotion, yet she did none of those things. Grimly, she compressed her lips.

When he saw she was not going to say more, he walked away.

Behind her, Adele could hear young Kate sobbing and Margery trying to comfort her. The sound of the girl's sobs was difficult to bear. Gritting her teeth with fresh determination, Adele followed De Montford across the bailey to ask him the whereabouts of her dog and horse. Bohun grasped her arm to stop her, bolder now that he was close to being in sole command.

"Well, well, Lady Adele, eager to be off, I see. How I envy your groom. He must be one of the luckiest men in the land for getting such a sweet-natured, obliging bride." He laughed sarcastically. "Poor sod doesn't know what he's in for, does he? You know, I'd always thought if you were to stay a little longer, we could have become far more friendly." He added the last with a leer, tightening his grip on her arm.

Adele glared at him and shook free as he attempted to embrace her. "Never. Not until hell freezes over," she spat, moving out of his reach.

Bohun cursed her roundly. He would have tried to keep her there, but thought better of it. It was his own fault. Had he put his plan into action sooner, she would already know her master, the willful bitch. Now it was too late; she had slipped through his fingers. His sagging face assumed its usual sour expression and he turned to yell at a nearby soldier, cuffing him for clumsily dropping a box.

Across the bailey, Adele saw De Montford explaining their route to the wagoneer who was to follow the main party with the sumpters and a mounted guard.

"What now?" he asked, finding her at his elbow. "Have you received a mystical message from the heavens forecasting rain?" he offered sarcastically.

She ignored his jokes. "I want to see my dog. I can't find him anywhere. And where's my horse—or am I to ride in a cart?"

"Your horse is being saddled and brought up, Lady."

"And Val?"

"He's crated on the wagon."

"Which one?"

He hesitated, then caught her arm, propelling her away from the others.

"The journey's long and we don't want him running off. He's in a crate in my supply wagon. I thought you'd rather have him travel with you than with the baggage. I'll take you to him, but first I have to prepare you.

Bohun's men were . . . a little rough with him."

"What?"

"Oh, he'll recover. But they whipped him."

"Oh, no! Poor Val! How bad is he hurt?"

"Don't be so distressed. I've had him doctored and he'll be right as rain. He's asleep now. I'm sorry this happened, but it was done without my knowledge and the men responsible for the whipping have been punished. He's a good dog. You should know I wouldn't condone such cruelty."

She snorted in annoyance, ignoring him as she marched ahead to the wagon he indicated. It was true; she had seen him treat the animals well. Doubtless this beating was at Bohun's command; the castellan had no more regard for beasts than he did for men. It was said he frequently whipped his own horses until they bled.

De Montford lifted the canvas on the wagon to reveal a wooden crate in which Val lay sleeping. Tears filled her eyes when she saw the dog's condition, his glossy black coat matted with blood from deep weals scoring his side. A yellow salve had been applied to the wounds.

Adele stared in horror at her dog, imagining his ordeal. She wanted to go after Bohun and tell him what she thought of his orders. She wanted to lash out and punish both him and his soldiers, but she knew all her anger was in vain; she would never be given the opportunity. Likely she should be thanking the saints it was not her who lay bleeding and bruised. All her impotent rage turned inward to become grief for the sheer helplessness of her position. Finally she could not hold back her tears; she leaned against the back of the wagon and sobbed.

"Oh, poor, poor Val," she whispered. "How you must have fought them. Why wasn't I sent for? There was never any need for this."

She felt the warmth of De Montford's hand as he squeezed her shoulder in comfort.

"I don't know, my lady. I promise to take full responsibility for his recovery. I swear, had I known . . . but there was so much to do this morning."

A great tremor seized the dog, its body shaking the crate. Adele reached through the bars to soothe him, stroking his haunch where his fur felt harsh to her touch. After a few minutes, soothed by the familiar caress, Val settled into a peaceful sleep.

Adele had fought to maintain a brave front throughout her own misfortune, even mastering her emotion after the devastating news of her arranged marriage. But to have her beloved dog so mistreated had been the last straw. Her stoicism fled. Tears ran unchecked down her cheeks, and she laid her head on her arm against the wagon and wept.

De Montford drew her against him. So grief-stricken was she, she made no protest, barely aware it was the baron who embraced her.

Strong arms bore her up when she would have sunk to the ground, feeling suddenly too weary to fight, having no strength left to endure all the earth-shattering changes in her life.

"Hush, don't cry. I promise to care for him. He's not feeling any pain now. See how quietly he sleeps," De Montford soothed, his voice tender. His hand was gentle on her hair as she unconsciously leaned against him, drawing comfort from his warm embrace.

Finally, as Adele's sobs subsided and she became aware of her surroundings, she also became aware of who offered her comfort. Shocked, she pulled away, looking up at him in bewilderment. His arms dropped from her shoulders and he stepped back, leaving her feeling cold and abandoned. Adele blinked up at him through tear-swollen eyes. Her head throbbed painfully.

"Are you fit to ride now?"

"Yes . . . I'm . . . well enough," she answered thickly.

"Good. I'll have them bring up your mount and we can get started."

He nodded brusquely before walking away. Adele was stunned by what had just taken place. Had she imagined his embrace? No, for she knew he had supported her when she would have fallen, offering her the comforting haven of his arms. He had cradled her gently against him as she'd given in to the emotion she had buried for days. Poor Val's wounds had been the catalyst to release that flood of grief, but she knew she sobbed also about the end of life as she'd known it—and for the loss of her treasured memories of Joce. Reality held a starkness for which she had been ill prepared.

The most startling discovery of all was that Rafe De Montford had taken her in his arms to offer her comfort. Even more startling, while she'd been inside the strong circle of his arms, she had felt loved and protected.

Adele turned to see her gelding being led across the bailey, already saddled for the journey. She dropped the wagon canvas back in place. De Montford had taken the reins from the stable boy and now brought Moonlight round for her to mount. When she looked questioningly into his face, his expression was impassive; his winter-pale eyes were no longer tender, nor was his mouth soft and gentle. This was the Rafe De Montford she was used to seeing, cold, gruff, in command.

"Ready, Lady Adele?" he asked stiffly.

Again she looked him full in the face, searching for some acknowledgment of what had just taken place. She saw none. "Yes, my lord, I'm ready."

He held the horse while she mounted from the block. Adele patted Moonlight's neck, soothing him. Up in the saddle, she could feel the gray's tension, the excitement surging through its body as the horse eagerly anticipated running free. How she wished she could share some of her steed's excitement over this journey. Unfortunately, her feelings were more akin to poor Val's who lay whipped and wounded in his crate.

They had not been on the road two hours before Rafe knew he'd made a mistake setting out today. The sky darkened to the north and the wind rose. His brave statement about the sun, light breeze, and drying roads had likewise been in error. Grimly he turned his face into the rising wind and rode on. He had been desperate to leave Esterwold, to begin this journey that would put Adele St. Clare safely into her bridegroom's household. He would have set out in any weather short of a snowstorm to put that plan in action, for the longer he stayed in close proximity to that lady, the harder it was to keep his distance. He greatly regretted taking her in his arms, too. The experience had been very pleasant, but it had been an absence of good sense—an affliction he had suffered much of late.

The clouds darkened, and when the wind blew a great gust, it tore loose the canvas on the wagons. The column halted. By the time the covering was resecured, the first raindrops had begun to fall from the churning sky. The travelers quickened their pace, anxious to reach a settlement to seek shelter from the storm.

The nearest village consisted of a manor house, a parish church, and a poor row of hovels. For a nominal fee, the lord of the manor gave them permission to spend the night in his tithe barn.

Adele shed her wet cloak, glad of any shelter provided by this drafty building. Rain pelted against the roof, and the cold wind gusted through the open door. There were stalls at one end of the barn which had once housed beasts; the old straw had long since crumbled to dust.

Margery and Kate were most impressed with the high-roofed barn, likening it to a church. The two women helped the soldiers spread fresh straw, and they brought blankets from the wagon to spread over the ground to make a primitive bed. Little Kate, unused as she was to traveling, was so tired that she fell asleep the moment she lay down. Margery lay beside her on the straw and a few minutes later she, too, was asleep. Adele's bed had been prepared on the other side of a wooden partition—to shield her from the gaze of the common soldiers.

She sat down and thankfully stretched her stiff limbs. Though her cloak was wet, inside her hide boots her feet were still dry. She pulled off the damp footwear and wiggled her toes, glad to be free of the constriction.

De Montford suddenly appeared at the entrance to the stall, carrying food and drink.

"Are your maids already asleep? Shall I wake them to attend you?" he asked, surprised to find her alone.

"No, let them sleep. I've no need of them. I'm hardly dressing for court," she added with a grin. Since they had begun the trip, she could not help thinking about him. And she would always remember his kindness regarding Val's beating.

"Your dog's here in the barn, if you want to see him," he offered, after placing the bundle of food on the edge of her blanket.

"Oh, yes. Let me see how he is."

"Nay, there's no need to get up," he said when she began to scramble to her feet. "Adric will bring him to you."

A few minutes later the groggy, bedraggled dog appeared at the entrance to the stall, baffled by his surroundings. When he spotted his beloved mistress, he shot forward, his injury forgotten. Adele laughed as Val licked her face with frantic delight. When she glanced up, she saw De Montford watching her, a slight smile on his mouth. His face was relaxed, and she was reminded once more of the man she'd first imagined him to be.

"He seems a little better, don't you think?" she asked, glancing from the lord to the soldier who had brought Val inside.

"I keep dosing him with my special tonic and dressing his wounds, my lady." Adric laid his hand affectionately on the dog's head. "I think he's a champion."

After the soldier had gone, De Montford crouched down to fondle the hound, quickly examining his injuries by the light of a lantern glowing on the overhead beam.

"Adric tends both my dogs and horses. His hands can work magic. I'm sure your Val will be right as rain before long."

Adele smiled in thanks, still stroking her dog. He had stretched out on the straw with a contented sigh. Even as they watched, the hound closed his eyes in sleep.

"Will you stay and eat with me?" Adele asked suddenly hardly able to believe she was actually asking the man she'd been so furious with to sup with her here in this straw-filled stall.

He hesitated, and she could tell that her suggestion had made him uncomfortable. Finally, after heaving a great sigh, he nodded, as if accepting her invitation were very taxing. She smiled to herself, aware he was probably embarrassed that she had seen his softer side; if he was like most males, it was important to be in control of both himself and his surroundings at all times.

They ate their meal in silence, each highly aware of the other's presence. He filled her wine cup before leaning back against the wooden partition, where he gnawed on a spiced capon leg. He even thanked her for the cloth she handed him to wipe his hands when he was done. This food had been prepared for their journey in Esterwold's kitchens; their future meals would be purchased on the road.

"That was good," he said at last. "I'm afraid I can't promise such tasty fare from now on."

"How long will we be on the road?" Adele asked, broaching the subject she had long avoided. The thought of arriving at her bridegroom's castle filled her with horror. "Is it far? You never told me where we are going."

His face clouded at the reminder. "A week, maybe two, depending on the weather," he said, glancing away from her searching gaze.

"So we're to be traveling companions that long?"

"Yes, it looks that way."

"Then shall we call a truce?"

"I didn't know we were at war."

"Much that I do seems to displease you, and, though it's not been declared, I still consider this a war." Defiant, and looking him straight in the eye, she said, "Well, what do you say?"

He smiled at her tenderly, and her heart began to

thump erratically. "I say 'tis the easiest battle I've ever fought. And, yes, we'll officially declare the hostilities over. I give you my word on it."

He stretched out his hand to cement the agreement. At first Adele was reluctant to touch him, for when their fingers met, a fiery spark shot along her arm. The sensation was so shocking that she gasped. It was as if all the warmth from his heart had sped along their limbs to unite them in an intimacy she had never anticipated. It was a long handshake, but finally he disengaged.

His eyes were dark in the murky half light, and when he spoke, the smile was gone from his face. "Good night, my lady," he said gruffly. Then, without further speech, he left the stall.

Adele watched him stride the length of the barn without stopping. Wistfully, she wondered what he was thinking. Had he also felt that curious fire when their hands met, or had the sparks been only in her own imagination? It was foolish to entertain romantic thoughts about Rafe De Montford. He was a man carrying out his orders to escort her to the home of her future husband. Yet fate had thrust them together, and she could not help but think he must have felt something—or why had he left so abruptly?

She sighed, feeling puzzled, aroused, and unfulfilled as she lay on her makeshift bed. All around her she could hear the assorted noises of the party preparing for sleep. After a little while, the barn became quiet and the darkness complete as all the lanterns were extinguished. Quietly, she stared at the rafters above and wished that, instead of King John's handpicked choice, her future groom was Rafe De Montford.

Chapter Four

They made such good time the following day that Adele was alarmed when she considered how far they had traveled from Esterwold. The further they went, the less chance Joce had of overtaking them.

To her disappointment, today Rafe pointedly kept his distance. He was very much in evidence riding back and forth along the column, checking the wagons, even dropping back to make sure the sumpters and their rear guard fared well, but beyond a curt "good morning," he had not given her a second glance.

Though yesterday's rainstorm was short-lived, it had been heavy enough to leave puddles on the rutted highway. Several times throughout the day the wagons stuck in the mud and they had to free them before their journey could resume. As the afternoon lengthened, the riders' pace slowed. Adele realized they were seeking a place to spend the night. Along this main road were inns and several abbeys, all offering accommodation to travelers.

Freeholme Abbey was eventually their choice for the

night. The building had a large guesthouse and ample stables. As it was still winter, there were not many travelers or pilgrims on the roads, leaving room to house their large party.

Adele was glad to have a real roof over her head. And though her whitewashed room was spare, she had it to herself. She had never thought she would consider it a blessing to have a chamber of her own, but her waiting women already taxed her patience with their complaints about stiff limbs, the cold, and everything until she was becoming heartily sick of them both. Adele sent them both to the abbey kitchens to warm themselves at the fire and to seek liniment for their aches.

The silence inside the spartan room was complete. She examined the narrow bed and found the covers to be clean. A padded bench stood beneath a window which she discovered could be shuttered for the night. She sat a moment on the bed and smiled, enjoying this rare solitude. What relief not to have to listen to a litany of complaints! Granted, their moans were not without substance—her own limbs felt stiff and she was already weary of the saddle—but there was little point in complaining, for there was at least another week of the same.

A rap on the door disturbed her peace. It was De Montford.

"Will you come down to sup, or would you rather eat here?" he asked, not coming inside the room, remaining on the threshold.

"Here, if that's not inconvenient. Will you send Val to me? In fact, while there's still light, I'd like to walk him if he's well enough."

Rafe looked surprised by her request, but he nodded. "All right, I'll see if Adric thinks it wise."

The answer soon became apparent when a few minutes later she heard excited yelps and squeaks of pleasure echoing along the stone corridor. Adric appeared at the door with Val on a leash.

"He's like a young pup, my lady—can't wait to be outside."

Adele took the dog from his handler and pulled on her cloak. She led Val down the corridor to a side door which opened onto the abbey garden with its neat cushions of fragrant herbs. Beyond the garden wall through an arch she could see open ground: the perfect place for Val to run.

Adele went through the stone archway and stopped to admire the breathtaking sunset. Sometimes such beauty made her melancholy, and today was such a time. The sinking sun burned brilliant orange across the surrounding country, gilding trees and furrowed land alike. How lovely and peaceful it was here at this mellow stone abbey. If only she could live somewhere where she could feel such peace, but lately there seemed no place on earth for that.

Adele stepped out briskly, trying to shake off her mood. For a little way Val kept up with her before he finally fell back, limping like an old dog, his painful wounds hampering his stride. Adele realized in disappointment that he was not nearly as well as she had hoped.

"Lady Adele, wait for me!"

Rafe. Her stomach pitched, or was it her heart that fluttered? Adele was not sure of the source of that surge of emotion. She had not expected him to follow her. She stopped, glancing behind to see him sprinting over the coarse grassland.

"The further north we go, the less safe it is to be out by yourself," he explained as he fell into step beside her. "How's he doing?"

"Slower than I'd hoped, but he's enjoying his freedom."

"Good. It'll take time."

They walked upon the tussocky ground. Around them stretched patches of wood interspersed with black plowed furrows belonging to the abbey. Through the trees a few early bluebells nodded and yellow primroses nestled amidst gnarled roots.

"You never told me we were headed north. Where is it we're going?" she asked at length.

"Summerhay Castle. 'Tis where Hugh D'Avranche lives."

"Summerhay!" Adele gasped in shock.

"Yes. Do you know it?"

"That's where my brother was held hostage."

"Seeing as Hugh just inherited, that must have been during his uncle's time."

Be careful, an inner voice warned. As far as De Montford knew, Adele thought Joce was still there. "Yes, it must have been, for he was only a little boy. He's never written to me." That was not really a lie, for she had never had any letters from Joce.

"I remember now, you asked me to intervene with the king on his behalf. Well, you won't need my help after all. Your brother will probably be there to welcome you. That would make things better. You'd like that, wouldn't you?"

"Yes, that would be very pleasant," she agreed, not knowing what else to say.

They walked along the path skirting the woods, crushing twigs and acorns underfoot. On this higher ground the breeze was sharper and filled with the scent of damp leaves, bracken, and woodsmoke. Great gray columns of smoke rose from the abbey's many chimneys as fires were stoked against the coming night's cold.

Around them, the sky grew a deeper crimson. De Montford paused to scan the heavens. "That red sky promises another fine day tomorrow."

"If we keep having good weather, we'll likely reach Summerhay sooner than you expected."

"Yes, I'm afraid so," was all he said.

As they walked on, Adele realized his words expressed displeasure. She was surprised. "You sound disappointed."

"Do I? Well, Summerhay is close to my lands and I'll be glad to be home. I've been away a long time and there'll be much that needs to be done, but . . ."

He said no more. They had stopped at a stile set amidst the hawthorn bordering the pasture. He did not continue, and Adele wondered at his silence. Val flopped to the ground at their feet, panting, glad of the chance to rest. Adele was highly curious about this man standing silent beside her, sensing there was much more he wanted to say.

"Does your family await you there?" she prompted, hoping he did not have a wife, and feeling silly.

"No. My father and mother have been gone a long time. My older brother lives on our lands in Anjou. I made my way on this side of the Channel instead."

"Do you like it here?"

"England suits me well enough. There used to be more peace here, though I suspect that is about to change. In France, the nobles were perpetually at war with each other. The king's there now, trying to retake his French lands. He's not pleased that I chose to stay here instead of going to fight. Many nobles decided to stay home, especially the northern lords. We're too busy fending off the Scots and the other unruly elements on our land to race across the Channel every time the king has a quarrel."

Adele listened, surprised that at, least in this instance, he had gone against the king's wishes. If only he had chosen to defy the man in other matters, she would have been far happier.

"I don't want to go to Summerhay, let alone become wife to a stranger," she suddenly blurted.

They were standing close together at the stile, leaning against the weathered wood. Everything around them was washed with the dying rays of the setting sun.

He turned to look down at her, his eyes glinting in the light. "God knows, I don't want you to," he admitted at last, softly caressing her arm. His fingers tightened as he spoke, his voice husky and intense. "I'd be content to have this journey last into eternity."

Adele could hardly believe what she had heard. She turned toward him, and he slid his arm about her shoulders to draw her close.

"Failing that, my dearest Adele, I wish you were coming back to Fordham Castle with me. For you should be mine." Then his mouth covered hers.

His kiss was sweet and, reeling with emotion, Adele longed to stop time, to hold the moment forever. When he kissed her again, she returned his ardor, drinking in the hot sweetness of his mouth.

Her arms slid around his strong back and she hugged him to her, thrilling to the feel of his body pressed against hers. She grew aware of the hard pressure of muscle and sinew cutting into her soft flesh as his arms tightened. Still highly aware of the heat of him and the throb of her own pulse, she laid her face against his hard shoulder, finding the steady beat of his heart music to her ears.

It was too dark to see his face, for the sunset was complete, the brilliant ball of fire burned out beyond the dark woods. "Rafe," she whispered, finding his name pleasant to speak. "Oh, Rafe, I wish that too."

She heard his sharp intake of breath; then the pressure of his arms increased.

For some time they stood there, wrapped in each other's arms, reluctant to part. When he kissed her again, she clung to him, her emotions swirling, her nerves jangling in a pleasant tumult she had never known before.

At last he came to his senses and stepped away from her. "Unfortunately, wishes don't come true. You're Hugh D'Avranche's bride, not mine. That cannot be undone."

His bitter words were like cold water on her rising passion.

"I'm sorry. I shouldn't have done that, my lady. I forget myself. You've every justification to chastise me."

"Nay, Rafe De Montford, I don't want to chastise you. I want to applaud you." She would not be so easily put off. "Never have I been kissed like that. And if it never happens again, I'll cherish the memory."

Her voice wavered with emotion when she spoke, but, contrary to her expectations, he did not pull her in his arms, delighted by her admission. He kept his distance, reverting once more to the old formality between them. He whistled for Val, who had wandered into the ditch to scent out rabbits.

They retraced their steps in silence. It was a very solemn and formal pair that entered the abbey's side door. Once again, Adele was left wondering if she had only imagined what had just taken place between them. He had become a different man, again. It was just like the last time, when he'd held her in his arms beside the wagon, yet when others were present, he became distant. It was as if they were polite strangers and no intimacy of any sort had ever taken place.

Rafe gave Val back to Adric. Then, bowing formally to Adele, he said he would arrange for a meal to be sent to her chamber.

She sat alone in her small room. She had not even sent for her women, needing time to master her emotions before she let them see her. Margery and Kate knew her too well not to notice her flushed face and ragged breathing. She still shook with passion; she could even taste his mouth on hers and feel the hot pressure of his body against her own. She was also hurt and puzzled by his abrupt detachment. The more she dwelled on it, the more she found it hard to believe that he had held and kissed her. The reminder that he was her liege lord, a man who'd held authority over even her father, made it even harder to believe that she had called him by his first name—or that he had admitted he wished she would be his. It was all true, she knew, yet she almost wondered if she had dreamed everything.

Now—after such a tender interlude—she was abandoned, whilst he went to sup with his men, as if she were of no more importance than an old shoe. His behavior was infuriating. *He* was infuriating.

Angrily, she punched the pillow on the window seat, wanting to pound some sense into him. Or out of him. She wanted his assurance that he cared deeply for her. Even if she must still marry D'Avranche, she would at least have memories to cherish.

Ha, she snorted in disgust, *memories to cherish indeed!* Memories would be small consolation during her captivity at Summerhay Castle. She needed far more than memories.

Leaving her food untouched, she went to the window and knelt on a bench to look outside. It was full dark, broken only by the small light of the lanterns at the abbey entrance. What Rafe had said to her amounted to an admission of love . . . didn't it? Yet if he loved her, why was he still taking her to become another's bride? Adele's heart sank when she wondered if he was merely toying with her. She had been told men did that, though it was a game she had no experience with. No one had ever courted her.

Resting her face against the window's cold stone work, Adele stared into the blackness, willing Joce to come to her rescue. Here at the abbey she would be easy to find if he were to ask around. If he came to rescue her tonight, he could take her away before that hated marriage to the king's chosen. More important than that, if Joce rescued her tonight, he would take her away from Rafe De Montford.

They departed before it was light. Joce had not come, so Adele had to grit her teeth, square her shoulders, and set forth on another unpleasant day of travel.

The wind was sharp and the yawning soldiers were gruff. Though she had not really been expecting special treatment from De Montford after yesterday, Adele had hoped for a secret smile, or a handclasp, just to assure her she held a special place in his heart. Instead, he was polite and distant, abandoning her once he had seen to preparing her for the journey.

Adele ground her teeth in aggravation. No one in the abbey courtyard would have guessed they had ever exchanged kisses or barely stopped short of declarations of love. Maybe that was the problem—Rafe De Montford had stopped short of making declarations of love because he felt none for her. As they clopped along, the cold wind found every chink in her clothing, and Adele ruminated on this possibility.

Thoroughly out of sorts, she concluded that if he was going to be indifferent toward her, then she would be equally nonchalant toward him. He might expect her to warm to him during secret moments when they were hidden from the others, but she would teach him a lesson, paying him back by staying cold and aloof. Tears stung her eyes as she admitted to herself that she would suffer also.

They rode past several small settlements without stopping, but food was finally purchased at a country market to break their fast. They ate beside the road in a sheltered hollow. The horses cropped grass alongside the soldiers who were lounging on the heath, glad of the break from the saddle.

By herself again, with De Montford nowhere in sight, Adele fumed as she ate her meal with her maids.

Later, she felt guilty when she discovered that while they had rested and supped, De Montford had ridden back to the sumpters to direct them along a more northern route, sending two-thirds of his soldiers home with the baggage to Fordham Castle.

It was a vastly reduced group, traveling with only one supply wagon, that turned to the east, accompanying their lord and his charges to Summerhay Castle.

Their journey took them past stretches of woodland and bog, over high moor springy with heather and open heath dotted with yellowing gorse. Curlews called, circling overhead, their cries mingling with the screech of gulls driven inland by an impending storm. Nestled below in a fold of hills, they saw a town, visible for some distance before the road turned downhill.

The wind had sharpened and the sky grew heavy with clouds. They would put up for the night in that town, Adele learned as one of the soldiers spoke.

It was none too soon, for the first fall of sleet stung her

cheeks a short time later. The road led into the valley to where the town nestled behind stands of birch. Hazel and sallow willow also flourished, their branches tossed in the rising wind.

Along the town's narrow cobbled streets, the houses were huddled together, leaning drunkenly against their neighbors. There were several fine dwellings belonging to the more successful merchants, but their wealth was conspicuous amidst their shabby surroundings; most of the thatched buildings were constructed of wattle and daub. Only the richest, half-timbered structures having slate roofs and painted facades seemed to bespeak any prosperity.

"We'll stay the night at the Mitre," Rafe said, suddenly riding up alongside the women. "You'll find warmth and good food there. It looks as if our fine weather's run out."

Adele listened and nodded, but she stayed tight-lipped with anger. None would have heard had he spoken a kind word. He could have asked how she fared, or if she was cold or hungry. But he had not asked because he did not care. Adele began to feel increasingly sorry for herself as sleet stung her face, blown in on the gusting north wind.

"March in these parts can be a trial," said Adric, moving alongside her to show the way. "Come, just follow me, Lady. Tomorrow is market day, more's the pity. Everywhere's full. Still a bag of gold works wonders."

They rode toward the inn. Many people crowded the yard, making it difficult to maneuver their horses, and they had to jostle for space at the big stone water trough.

Adele started to dismount, her eyes narrowed against the barrage of sleet, when she felt strong hands gripping her waist. Through the stinging white curtain, she saw it was the baron himself who had come to lift her from the saddle.

"Come, get in the warmth," he said, leading her to a nearby open door.

Adele shook sleet from her hood and pulled it off her head as she stepped inside the inn. The low-ceilinged

70

common room glowed with firelight. The innkeeper bustled forward, a leather apron about his rotund girth, a smile of welcome for the travelers. The ostler had a bag of coins already tucked safely inside his belt, and he was likely sure there would be more from this great lord's party. He intended to do his best to satisfy them.

Mulled wine, bread, and meat were set on a scarred trestle for their meal. As a lady of the nobility, Adele was ushered to the roaring hearth to dry her wet clothing. There earlier arrivals, grumbling quietly at being displaced, were thrust aside to make room for her and her maids.

Adele shuddered with pleasure as the fire's warmth thawed her numb limbs. She wondered if her legs would be permanently crooked, or if her backside would always feel numb and her fingers frozen.

Margery bustled about, taking care of her mistress, removing her cloak, pulling off her boots, and shaking them free of slush. Warming to her position, Margery even elbowed a couple of travelers out of the way when they tried to edge back to the hearth.

The inn's shutters were drawn fast against the hissing sleet. The common room was redolent with the mingled aromas of beer, roasting meat, and wet wool. A ruckus at the door announced the arrival of De Montford. The landlord bustled forward to usher his important guest to a place of honor beside his lady at the hearth.

Adele caught the innkeeper's inference that she was De Montford's lady. She also noticed that he said nothing to correct the man. His soldiers crowded round a large table toward the back of the room. At a nod from him, both Margery and Kate retreated to a corner, leaving them alone.

Adele's heart fluttered as she realized they were openly sitting together in this noisy and very public place. And he smiled at her so sweetly, her heart raced. Oh, how she longed to respond. Instead, she stared down at her trencher and continued to eat in silence. He swung his legs over the bench and sat beside her, scooping up a trencher of bread and meat for himself. He drank a cup of mulled wine.

"Well, lady," he said at last. "Has the weather frozen your tongue?"

"No. You have yourself to thank for that."

"Me! What have I done?"

She turned to him. They sat so close on the bench, her heart seemed to leap into her throat, making it difficult to speak. "Always when we're in front of others, you treat me as if we're the merest of acquaintances."

"How would you have me treat you?"

She stared at him, feeling color flush her cheeks.

"With a little more—" she stopped short of saying *affection*, though she could find no better word.

"Must I remind you, I'm escorting you to your groom?" He looked at her sharply. "Would you have me ruin your reputation by caressing you in public?"

She looked down at her hands, aware of the controlled anger in his voice. "I'd have you be much kinder to me," she said at last. "Surely I deserve that much."

He grinned as he refilled his cup. "People don't always receive what they deserve in this life. Haven't you learned that? If they did, our king wouldn't sit so easy on his throne, nor would half our noblemen have roofs over their heads. If I've slighted you, I'm sorry."

Oh, she could not get the better of him! She did not know why she had ever thought she could. "It's just that . . . well, after yesterday, I thought . . ."

His face clouded at her reminder. "Yesterday was a terrible mistake."

Adele gasped. "A mistake! Are you saying you're sorry it happened?"

"No. I'm just saying it was a mistake."

"I didn't consider it so."

He grinned at her. "Do you want me to repeat the offense?"

All her resolve to stay icily detached had melted in this

warm room, aided and abetted by his presence and several cups of wine. "We both know I've no affection for my fiancé."

"We also both know I'm honor-bound to deliver you to him. Men can languish a lifetime in a dungeon for disobeying the king. Or lose their heads." He made a motion of decapitation.

"Yet you didn't go with him to France. At least once, you've gone against his wishes," she reminded, emptying her cup.

He promptly refilled it.

"Correct. I'm no foolish courtier trotting at his heels. He's aware of that. But, in all honesty, Lady, I don't see any way out of your betrothal."

She swallowed the building lump in her throat. That was not what she'd wanted him to say. When she turned to look him full in the face, she was reminded again how handsome he was: his pale eyes were soft in the firelight, his mouth relaxed. She clearly remembered how it felt to be held in his arms, to have his warm mouth pressed against hers. She ached with longing to experience it again.

"I hoped . . . you . . . would . . . find a way."

He paused, his cup to his lips. He put the cup down.

"A way? Do you mean to take you back to Esterwold unmarried?"

"I mean, not take me to Summerhay."

He moved closer, his eyes on hers. "And where would you go instead?"

"With *you*, my lord, for I've a mind to see Fordham Castle," she boldly whispered. She was suddenly aware she was slightly tipsy as she felt the effect of the wine circulating through her blood. "That way both our wishes could come true."

He looked down at her, fighting the urge to crush her against him, to devour her soft, ripe lips. A dozen plans roared through his mind as he battled the insanity of them. He would be a fool to let her persuade him to do anything other than his duty—he would be a bigger fool to let this chance slip away.

Under the trestle he sought her hand, and Adele shuddered with pleasure as he enfolded her small hand safely inside his own. She had spoken plainly; short of asking him to take her in his arms, she could say no more.

"Surely you realize it was for your reputation's sake I have to keep my distance in public. Don't you know that is the reason I've always treated you with such . . ." He paused, searching for the right word.

"Indifference?" she supplied, feeling more than a little woozy.

"*Respect*, my lady," he answered, a grin tugging at the corners of his mouth. "But I fear respect is no longer what you want from me."

She smiled, and her voice quavered when she said teasingly, "Oh, my lord Rafe, whatever can you mean by that? You know, I heard the landlord call me your lady, and you did naught to correct him. What have you to say about that?"

Rafe glanced away, wondering how to answer. She was right. He had not corrected the innkeeper. Likely the obsequious innkeeper had readied his finest chamber for his exalted guests. He had guessed that would be done, and had said nothing to stop it, because all the while an insane idea had raged in the back of his mind, one he had discarded and retrieved a dozen times.

"Would it please you to be my lady?" he asked softly, his hand tightening on hers.

"More than anything in the world," she answered sincerely, inching closer to him on the bench until their thighs pressed together, sending a shiver of delight along her spine.

He began to speak, leaning down to her, his eyes dark with passion, when a commotion arose at the door. One of his men burst inside the room.

"My lord Rafe, come quick, it's Ivo."

Adele blinked as the world came crashing down about

her ears. In a flash her handsome Rafe was off the bench and pushing his way through the room, all his thoughts of romance forgotten.

Adele was stunned, for she was still lost in that tender mood wherein she had come close to lying back in his arms, decorum be damned. Guiltily, she straightened in her seat and surreptitiously glanced about the room. No one seemed to be paying any attention to her with the exception of Margery and Kate. Seeing she was alone, they came to sit with her.

"Should we ready you for the night, my lady?" Kate asked, her own eyelids appearing heavy in the warm room.

"Yes—after you're finished eating. Go to the room and unpack my things first. No . . . I'm not coming yet," she decided when Margery had gathered her discarded garments. "Give me my cloak and boots. I want to go outside to see what's happening."

As usual, Adele ignored Margery's protests as she pulled on her boots and cloak. At first when she stood, the room spun a few times, but she finally found her legs. All her attention was focused on navigating through the crowded room. When she finally reached the empty corridor leading outside, she was able to breathe a sigh of relief. The outer door stood open and a great commotion filled the innyard.

Many people had come to town for the weekly market, she knew. That, added to the inclement weather, had made lodgings at a premium. Many latecomers had been forced to share the stables with the animals. It was those travelers who now formed a noisy audience cheering on two men who grappled on the wet cobbles, cursing as each tried to stab the other. One of the men was Ivo, a soldier of Rafe's. Rafe was ordering the two to cease.

When nothing happened, he grabbed both men's collars, and heaved them apart. His man's assailant was only a lad whose skinny legs jerked up and down like a marionette's while he dangled from Rafe's fist.

"Stop it! Would you two fools kill each other?" he growled. "What's the quarrel, Ivo? Speak up!"

"He stole from me, my lord."

"Is that so?"

The other scowled, making a great show of rearranging his ragged clothing after he had been deposited on solid ground.

"Naw, he's a liar."

"You're a thief," shouted a woman from amongst the bystanders. "Thirkeld's well known to us, Your Lordship."

Rafe turned to the young woman who had stepped out of the crowd. Snow covered the tangled blond hair which curled about her shoulders. She sidled closer, her round blue eyes quickly assessing him.

"And you're known to us an' all, Gurda," retaliated the accused boy, "as the biggest whore this side of Ashford."

"Shut up, you," she sneered, turning her attention back to Rafe. "I seen it all. Your man here was minding his own business and 'im sneaks up and took 'is supper."

"That's it? You're fighting over a meal?" Rafe asked incredulously. His own man flushed, ashamed to look him in the eye.

"Well, that's how it started, my lord. He came after other stuff then."

"Return what you stole and I won't turn you over to the law, you worthless brat," Rafe growled, shaking Thirkeld by the scruff of his neck.

Rafe left them sorting through Thirkeld's pack, which became an object of much interest when other outraged travelers saw their own belongings there.

The sleet began again. Rafe hunched his shoulders to keep the cold barrage from slithering down his neck. He glanced toward the lighted doorway, surprised to see Adele amongst the onlookers.

Two strides brought him to her side.

"Go indoors, it's nothing. Just a quarrel over stolen goods. It's sleeting again and you'll get wet."

"And you?" she asked, hoping to rekindle the warm mood they had shared just minutes before.

"I'll be out here awhile," he said, turning her about and

urging her toward the door. "Go inside before you get chilled."

Turning, Adele saw the bosomy Gurda flouncing about, tossing her tangled curls as she moved closer to Rafe. The woman made a laughing remark Adele could not hear, but Rafe did. To her dismay, she watched him turn back to Gurda and laugh with her before he sprinted back inside the stables.

Anger and jealousy welled up in her. "Don't you dare bed that girl, Rafe De Montford," she muttered under her breath, longing to tell him but aware she had not the right. She stormed inside.

The room reserved for her was at the front of the inn overlooking the main street. A huge canopied bed, heaped with pillows and mounds of covers, virtually filled the room. The landlord himself had escorted Adele to the door. He now stood proudly pointing out the luxurious accommodations, emphasizing the room's warmth and cleanliness.

"Thank you, sirrah, it's most suitable," Adele said, trying to sound as if she used such words daily. She wondered if his outstretched hand meant he was waiting for a coin. "My lord will settle all debts," she announced airily as she swept past him.

"Is he not here?"

At this, Margery and Kate giggled in unison.

"He's overseeing his men and horses in the stables," she explained quickly, turning before anyone saw the flush on her cheeks.

His hand dropped, and with a half-hearted bow, the innkeeper retraced his steps.

"Silly sod," Kate giggled. "He thought De Montford is your husband, my lady."

"I suppose it's a natural mistake," Adele said, glancing about the room for the women's pallets. She saw none.

"And where are *we* to sleep, then?" asked Margery when she made the same discovery.

"Maybe in an adjoining room. Let's look."

77

Adele's heart fluttered when she discovered she would be in a separate room from her women. Their pallets were next door in a tiny cubicle hardly deserving to be called a room. Tonight, once again she would have complete privacy. But to what end?

Had she and Rafe truly been lovers, they could have spent this cold winter night in the huge bed under that mountain of covers. As it was, she would enjoy that splendor alone.

Though she tried not to dwell on it, Adele could not help wondering if Rafe and the blonde were together. Oh, that one had known how to get a man's attention, all right, a talent born of much experience. Though she did not envy such a woman, Adele wished she knew more about men so that she too might capture Rafe's attention entirely.

Automatically, Adele put up her arms for Margery to get her into her nightrail. She would rather have been left to lick her wounds instead of putting up a cheerful front before the servants. Rafe's disappearance was still painfully fresh in her mind. Because she was slightly tipsy, she had abandoned the strict code of behavior prescribed for unmarried gentlewomen and given in to the demands of her heart and body. She had reached out to him and, joy of joys, he had reciprocated. But then he was gone. Even though she appreciated his need to see to his men, where had he gone after that?

"Will that be all, my lady?" Margery asked. She had brushed Adele's hair and plaited it into a loose, ribbon-tied braid.

"Yes, thank you both. Good night."

Adele fought the foolish desire to weep once they were gone. A vivid picture of Rafe embracing the yellow-haired wench flashed through her mind. Oh, how she ached for someone who loved her. No, she admitted honestly, not just someone—the man she wanted was Rafe De Montford.

She had been alone most of her life, so why should that

state now make her feel sad? Always before, she had been contentdly self-sufficient, unlike the silly servant girls she'd overheard, never happy until they had a sweetheart. She had always prided herself on not needing a man to complete her life—until now.

Belatedly, Adele remembered she had neglected to check on her dog. In her newfound quest for romance, her attention had been wholly focused on flirtatious nonsense. She knew Adric would care for Val, but she disgusted herself by being so self-involved. The poor dear would think she'd abandoned him!

Of a mind to go downstairs, Adele stopped, her cloak in her hand. All those other travelers at the inn would find it strange for a lady to go out in her nightrail to care for a dog. Not only that, there were many people besides Rafe's men in the stables to gawk at her—including the yellow-haired Gurda. She knew in the back of her mind she was half afraid that she might also discover something outside to further shatter her romantic notions about her handsome escort. Was it better to take the coward's way out and leave Val's care to Adric?

Disconsolately, she sat on the edge of the high bed, swinging her feet like a little girl. Lately she always seemed emotional: angry or sad or both. But she'd also only lately known that other powerful feeling, the rush when Rafe held her in his arms—that wonderful, surging, weakening emotion which defied description.

Banging her pillows, furious with her incurably foolish mood, Adele scrambled into bed. A warming pan of hot coals had already chased the damp chill from the covers. She stretched her feet into the nether regions of the feather bed; even when she lay spread-eagled, there was plenty of room. She sighed. It was high time she abandoned silly thoughts of love and romance with Rafe and began to behave like a grown woman. She was no longer a child. She had been running her father's estate for two years, right?

Dutifully, Adele closed her eyes and said her prayers.

She had to sleep, for another day of travel lay ahead. She would have no more silly fantasies, no more disturbingly vivid memories of kisses or caresses. Rafe had played her emotions like lute strings, and she had been fool enough to let him—she had been an even bigger fool for enjoying it.

Outside in the stables, Rafe blew out his lantern. Beside him, Adele's dog snuffled in the darkness and Rafe could hear the thump of his tail.

"Go to sleep, boy. Tomorrow's another day," he said reaching through the wooden bars to pet the big black hound. It licked his hand.

"You wonderful, marvelous dog, I bless you from the bottom of my heart," Rafe whispered as he stroked Val's head. "Without you, your lady wouldn't have given me the time of day. I owe you for it and, by God, I'll make sure you're given your due." He promised that with a chuckle as he gave the dog a farewell pat.

Rafe straightened and glanced into the yard. It was still sleeting, the torrent hissing and swishing against the cobbles. Drunken laughter echoed from the common room, and a symphony of snores came from the stable's sleeping occupants. Behind him, horses shifted on their hooves and clattered and bumped against their wooden stalls.

What a night! What a week, for that matter! He stood there, debating what to do. He thought long and hard, refining and discarding several plans. Aware that he gambled with his very existence, he considered the stakes worth the risk. In truth, he now cared for nothing save the joy of making Adele his own.

There were ways to avoid the king's wrath, he thought.

Rafe laughed bitterly to himself at his ease in discounting the immediate danger of such a move, aware that the real jeopardy would come from Hugh when he failed to produce D'Avranche's bride. Would the spurned groom take his case to King John or would he take up arms himself? Perhaps D'Avranche would accept a generous payment and select another bride. If that were the case, Rafe could settle matters with John Softsword. Perhaps.

A fine could be levied against him for disobedience, the amount of which he would have to satisfy by borrowing from one of the moneylenders. Imprisonment was another possibility, though he knew the king often preferred compensation over punishment. What would be the outcome of this momentous step? He only knew he had made up his mind; Adele St. Clare would not be sacrificed to settle the king's debt.

Chapter Five

Adele jerked awake from a light sleep, sure that something had rattled the door. She listened to the muted sounds drifting from the inn's lower floors. Closer still, sleet tinkled against the shutters and the slurred songs of drunks sounded below in the street. It had likely been the singing that had awakened her. She was not sure of the time, but it could not be too late or the inn's patrons would not still be singing.

Again . . . she heard the sound at the door, a little louder this time, a little more insistent.

She slithered from the bed, shivering as icy rushes touched her bare feet. She went to the door to listen.

"Adele, open up!"

She froze. For an instant she panicked inwardly. It was Rafe, come to her chamber!

With shaking hands she pulled back the bolt.

"Why did you bolt the door?" he grumbled, slipping quickly inside the room.

"I thought it safer in a common inn," she retorted,

reaching for her cloak. She had no robe to cover her nightrail. Still shivering, she stood huddled inside her furlined cloak.

"You're right, it was wise. Sorry I grumbled," he apologized, going to the hearth. He stretched his frozen hands out near the blaze.

"Where've you been?"

"Packing up for the night. I looked in on Val and he's doing well. Your gelding's been rubbed down and fed." He paused, holding back the real news he had come to tell her. He had to speak it, for once spoken, it could not be taken back in a moment of faintheartedness.

"I've been thinking over what you said earlier," he began, getting to his feet. The ceiling was so low he had the feeling that if he straightened up he would bang his head. "I've come to a decision."

"About what?"

"I'll do all I can to prevent your marrying D'Avranche. And I promise not to leave you at Summerhay."

"Why must we even go there at all?"

"Because I hope to strike a bargain with D'Avranche. He's never seen you, nor has the king, so I could substitute some plain wench, or maybe keep your face veiled. I don't know what I'll do, I've yet to work out the details. I just wanted you to know I've made up my mind."

Adele stared at him in surprise. "To trick D'Avranche?"

"Nay, Lady. I mean to bargain for you."

"Bargain. How?"

"By claiming you for my own bride," he said in a rush. "That's if you'll have me?"

"Oh, Rafe, must you even ask?"

He smiled and held out his hands. "Come here. We've been apart far too long."

Adele could hardly believe what was happening. She took his hands, still cold from outside, and brought them to her lips.

"Do you know what I thought you were doing?" she admitted at last with a shamefaced giggle.

"No, surprise me."

"Bedding that yellow-haired woman."

For a moment he looked startled, then began to chuckle.

"How do you know I didn't?"

"Because you wouldn't be here now. Nor would you have been considering how to save me from marrying Hugh D'Avranche . . . Oh, you're teasing." She stopped in exasperation when she saw he was grinning. "How can you, Rafe De Montford, when I've suffered so greatly picturing her in your arms."

"Then, my sweetest, you tortured yourself without cause," he whispered, pulling her close. "You're the only one I want. We'll make our plans tomorrow. I just wanted to let you know what I'd decided." He stooped to kiss her brow. "And I also wanted to kiss you good night."

"I suspect you're a liar," she protested, moving back, trying to see his face in the firelight. He still held her at arm's length. "Acting so innocent in the matter, yet wasn't it you who arranged to have my women sleep elsewhere? And wasn't it you who never told the landlord I wasn't your wife?"

"Guilty as charged. I confess, in the back of my mind, I had this insane hope that you'd—"

"Welcome you to my chamber?" she completed, her legs trembling with excitement inside her thick cloak.

"You forget, it's *our* chamber," he corrected. "As you pointed out, the landlord thinks we're lord and lady." While he spoke he caressed her back, fingering her heavy auburn plait. "I've never seen you like this before." He drew the braid of hair over her shoulder and pulled loose its confining ribbon, spilling her hair in a bright silken cloud around her shoulders. "I've never even seen you with your hair loose. You take my breath away."

"It's a sight women usually save for either their husband or lover."

"Can't I be both?"

"Oh, yes, please—I'd like that very much."

Adele could hardly believe this was happening. It was as if time stood still and she were no longer in this inn room in some nameless valley town but soaring high above the clouds, drifting toward heaven. His hands were gentle as he smoothed back her hair, exclaiming over the burnished cloud glinting in the firelight. Her knees felt weak, and she wondered how much longer she could stand here athrob with emotion, how much longer her feeble legs would hold her before she fell to the rushes.

Rafe unfastened the clasp of her cloak and let the heavy garment slide from her shoulders, leaving Adele clad only in her thin linen nightrail. Never before had she been so scantily dressed before a man, and she swallowed nervously, wondering if he would find her acceptable, or whether he would compare her unfavorably to other women he had known. Once Rafe drew her against him, she stopped puzzling over such matters and allowed herself to be swept away, relying on his strength to support her.

Rafe rested his face against the top of her head, drinking in the perfume of her hair. In his arms, clad only in her nightrail through which the soft contours of her body were readily revealed, she felt small and helpless. The promise of the delectable flesh under the thin fabric made his blood pound. Fighting to contain the passion coursing through his veins and the furnace of desire burning in his loins, he listened to the more prudent side of his nature, which warned him to take care for she was wholly inexperienced.

"Adele . . . sweetheart, I love you true," he whispered, finally voicing the thought which had jangled his nerves for the past week. He could hardly believe he was speaking such words at no prompting besides that of his pounding heart.

She shivered in delight at his passionate declaration.

"Oh, Rafe, I love you too. All the time I thought I hated you, I think I wanted you even then."

He smiled in pleasure at her whispered admission.

"It's not always unpleasant to do battle," he admitted, looking down into her lovely face. "But I promise it's far more pleasant to make love."

She clung to him, her face upraised for his kiss. At the sweet touch of his mouth, fire sped through her limbs and she shivered in delight. Adele was aware of a growing ache in her legs and deep in her belly, as if something burned inside her. She clung to Rafe, instinctively knowing that his body offered balm for her yearning. The strength and the heat of him blazed beside her, and she thought she would melt from its intensity.

"Come, sweetest. The innkeeper provided such a large bed, we mustn't disappoint him."

Adele let him take her weight against his body. Her heart fluttered so wildly she was sure he must feel it. She had always known that someday she would come to this moment, yet never had she expected to share it with this man. She still found it hard to believe she was in Rafe's arms, moments away from surrender. For years she had heard his powerful name spoken in awe throughout the land. Now, his unwelcome visit to Esterwold had begun a wonderful new chapter in her life.

"I never dreamed I'd be in your arms," she marveled as he picked her up and carried her to the bed. He'd lifted her as if she were light as a child.

Rafe buried his face in her neck, his hot mouth trailing along the exposed flesh of her throat. His kisses made Adele shiver with delight.

"Nor did I ever expect this journey to prove so pleasant. In fact, had I known, I'd not have tarried so long in Northampton but come to Esterwold months ago."

The covers felt cool under her body as he laid her upon the soft feather bed. The mattress moved and dipped with his movements as he stripped off his clothing. In his haste to claim her, Rafe pitched his garments toward a bench where some came to rest and others fell to the rushes.

Adele stole a glimpse of his strong naked body. It briefly appeared immense and threatening as his giant shadow flickered over the walls and ceiling. But then he lay still beside her, and she felt more at ease. He was all hard muscular arms and legs, his torso broad, his shoulders square. A mat of dark hair furred his chest and formed a narrow line dividing his belly until it disappeared into shadow.

Tentatively Adele reached for him, shivering in delight as she felt the hot smoothness of his flesh. The hardness of his body was both surprising and arousing. She traced the corded sinews and muscles in his arms, discovering several puckered weals that she assumed to be old battle scars.

Rafe drew her against him, and she thrilled to the feel of his naked body against hers.

"You're the most beautiful woman I've ever known," he whispered. Eager to disrobe her, he struggled with the fastening of her shift, his fingers thick with passion. Finally, with an impatient oath he thrust the fabric up about her neck. Now her lovely, curving body was exposed to his gaze, perfect and gilded by the firelight. Adele heard his sharp intake of breath as he caressed her hips and thighs, trailing kisses across her belly. She lay there drinking in his response, finding his admiration more intoxicating than anything she had ever known. His adoration made Adele feel beautiful beyond words.

Rafe captured the white mounds of her breasts, pink-tipped and inviting. He shivered as he fondled her firm flesh, taking the weight of her breasts into his hands, encouraged when her nipples tightened under his attention. He caressed those buds with his thumbs, rejoicing in her shudders of ecstasy.

Adele was surprised to learn that, far from lessening her surging emotion, Rafe's caresses merely stoked the fire. There was a direct connection between her nipples and that secret place between her legs; and her reaction to his touch was so intense that she cried out with pleasure. She surged forward eagerly, thrusting her breasts into his exploring hands, craving more.

His mouth captured her nipple, and Adele gasped in surprise at the exquisite feeling. His lips drew gently and insistently on her soft flesh, driving her mad with longing. She plunged her hands into his thick dark hair, wondering if she could endure this delight a moment longer, yet desperate for him to continue.

Rafe finally sought her lips. Their mouths met and they strived against each other with such force and heat, that their lips grew tender—but the pain only intensified their frenzy. Adele's thighs strained against his, and she was suddenly aware of the insistent pressure of his manhood against her belly. Despite the burning of her blood, it was more than a little daunting.

She reached down between them and he cupped her fingers around his hot arousal. Still slightly in awe, Adele gently explored its length and girth, the intimacy of the contact making her swoon with passion.

Then Rafe stroked tentatively between her legs, and she readily opened to him. His gentle exploration found resistance, but he seemed pleased by it.

"Adele, sweetheart, I love you. I want you so," he whispered passionately against her ear, his breath searing her flesh.

His hands caressed her breasts, her back, her hips, until Adele was so consumed by passion that she sobbed deep in her throat, straining against him, and Rafe knew she was ready.

He placed a pillow behind her head, then reached down to position her hips. Adele clung to him, not knowing what to expect, yet at the same time writhing beneath his feverish flesh as she prepared to yield all.

When Rafe thrust, the pressure made her gasp in surprise. He held her fast, though, slowly and deliberately penetrating her—breaking the barrier and moving beyond. Adele cried out, but he covered her mouth with his own and absorbed the sound. He pushed himself to the hilt inside her, lost in the sweet depths of her body. For a lifetime he had been seeking this perfect union with a woman, this complete blending of body and soul; never before had he found it.

Adele's initial shocked surprise was soon forgotten as he swept her forward. She writhed under him, in awe of the powerful emotion sweeping through her. A towering wave of fulfillment began to build in her, and she moaned in ecstasy. Suddenly, she was floating free of any time and place and the world crashed in around her, drowning her in oblivion. Rafe held her close in the darkness as he joined her in paradise.

Adele slowly drifted back to earth. Her mind was numb, for she had not expected such an overwhelming experience. Rafe held and kissed her, cradling her gently in his strong arms. He tenderly kissed away the tears on her cheeks, tears she had not known she'd shed. She was both happy and sad, and overwhelmed with pleasure. Even her body felt both battered and satisfied.

"Oh, what happened?" she asked him finally, smiling as she licked tears from her lips. "That was almost like dying."

"What do you mean, what happened, you wonderful woman? You've just given me the most pleasurable experience of my life," Rafe whispered. He rolled back on the pillows, a satisfied smile on his mouth.

"Really?"

"Really."

Adele gave a contented sigh, pleased beyond measure that he too had found their lovemaking an awesome experience. She laid her face against his chest and listened to the thundering of his heart. From where she lay, she watched the flickering firelight paint the walls and ceiling with dancing light. She took it all in, desperate to capture just exactly how everything looked and felt on this magical night.

She softly stroked his chest, her hand sliding through the crinkly pelt of dark hair. When she fingered his dark nipples, by his reaction she discovered that he felt that same arousal she had known. Her hand slid over his flat belly and lower. Adele was still slightly in awe of the power of his body as she tentatively touched his manhood, surprised to discover his flesh full and only slightly yielding to her touch.

"You hurt me a little," she felt bound to point out.

"Sorry, sweetest. I hope it wasn't too bad."

"No." She laughed softly. "Considering all the horror stories I've heard servants tell, I was expecting worse."

Rafe listened and smiled without explaining how hard he had fought to be gentle. He stroked her silky shoulders and nuzzled her warm neck, his hands stealing to her chest.

"You know, you have the most beautiful breasts in Christendom, don't you, Lady?" he whispered. He leaned down to press heated kisses on those full white globes.

"No one ever told me that before," she admitted with a proud smile. "But I'm glad you think so."

He smiled at her again. "In fact, I think you're the most passionate, most beautiful woman in all Christendom," he added lazily as he turned her about to pull her back against his body. Burying his face in the nape of her neck, he nuzzled through the curtain of hair to kiss her damp skin. Adele shuddered with pleasure, and his heart fluttered. She was completely and totally his.

"Rafe, I always want to be beautiful to you," she whispered, "And I always want us to be together like this."

"We will, sweetheart, I promise," he whispered huskily, turning her around to enfold her protectively in his arms. But over her silky head he stared into the fire, his thoughts sobering. *Dear God*, he prayed silently, *let it be so*.

Tenderly Rafe held Adele and kissed her, wanting to keep her there beside him forever, wishing they never would need to leave this firelit room. But, as he knew, such wishes were as insubstantial as smoke. They had to leave, and he had to be sure he kept her at his side. Whatever he had to do to satisfy D'Avranche and his king—and at whatever cost—he would do.

Rafe's thoughts reignited his passion. He kissed and fondled Adele, no longer able to hide his arousal from her, smiling when he heard her murmured surprise as he wrapped her fingers about his expanding flesh.

"See what you do to me, sweetheart? I can't help myself," he confided, showering her with kisses as he rolled her onto her back.

"We can do it again?" she asked, wide-eyed. "You're not tired?"

He laughed in delight at her ignorance and lightly kissed the tip of her small nose. "Oh, Lady," he said, his voice turned husky with arousal. "I can do this to you all night long."

Rafe stroked his engorged flesh along Adele's thighs, tantalizing her unmercifully until she finally seized him in her hands. Eagerly she moved beneath him, sinking into a warm hollow in the feather bed. He positioned himself, aware she had steeled herself for his thrust. But this time Rafe entered her easily, kissing her tenderly. She relaxed and, welcoming him eagerly into herself, gave herself up to his capable hands.

Rafe's boast had not been idle; he made love to her all night long. Between short dozes, they made love so often that he lost count, content to drift, shipwrecked on a heated sea of passion.

The cock began to crow within the hour of their final coming together. The first fingers of daylight stole inside the shutters, and they were startled awake by the deafening tolling of All Saints' great bell. It was market day.

Chapter Six

Adele decided not to immediately wake her serving women to dress her, thinking it wise to keep last night's tryst a secret as long as possible. Soon after the great bell boomed through the inn, Rafe bid her a hurried good-bye. He dressed with lightning speed and was able to slip unnoticed down the back stairs before too many of the inn's patrons were stirring.

Though she knew it was wise for Rafe to stay publicly aloof, Adele wished their love need not be so furtive. Still, hugging her special, most wonderful secret to herself—at least she hoped last night's lovemaking was still a secret—Adele knocked on the door of the adjoining room. Not waiting for a response, she pushed it open to find her maids still asleep.

"Well, you lazy lieabeds, still asleep at this hour," she cried, tugging off Margery's bedcover.

Startled, Margery sat up and rubbed her eyes. "Oh, my lady! What time is it? I must've slept like a log. Oh, forgive me."

Like a log, or like someone drunk, Adele thought. Rafe had made sure that they'd consumed much wine last night. In more ways than one, she was glad he was her friend and not her enemy.

When they finally roused Kate from her bed, the shamefaced girl scrambled up to wait on her mistress.

Hiding her amusement, Adele waved her away. "Nay, Kate, don't fret. See, I'm already washed and dressed. I'm not completely helpless without you. Hurry and pack, then come downstairs, for we're going to leave soon. We'll break our fast in the market on the way out of town."

That morning the shabby town of Lower Marden was bursting at the seams. It was a struggle just to get their mounted party out of the inn's yard. The group moved at a snail's pace, their horses jostled in the crowd heading to market. The narrow, airless street rang with strident voices mingled with the bleating of frightened animals. Atop the racket could be heard the yelling of carters as they tried to clear a way for their goods.

At last the people were disgorged into the open marketplace. To the right stood the butcher's shambles where the powerful stench of blood and offal mingled with the odor of penned animals. Thankfully, as they moved forward, the unpleasant smell was replaced by the appetizing aromas of baking pastry, boiled honey, and spiced ale, carried on the sharp, cold breeze.

Adele welcomed this open area, for she was not used to such claustrophobic streets. Today, she rode beside Rafe at the head of their party instead of in her customary place at the rear with the servants and baggage. The milling crowd made Rafe's stallion nervous, and it needed much soothing before it could be handed over to a soldier who had been designated to watch the horses.

"Shall we have spiced ale and gingerbread this morning?" Rafe asked Adele. His smile was tender as he looked into her eyes. The shared memory of last night's lovemaking glowed in their emerald depths.

"That sounds wonderful," Adele agreed, smiling at him, trying not to betray her inner feelings, yet unable to quench the love glowing in her face. Just the memory of his touch made her body throb, and her mouth ached for the sweetness of his kiss. Recalling the magic of their stolen night was enough to set her heart racing. Startled by her swiftly ignited lust, Adele tried to focus her attention on more immediate matters. A public marketplace was hardly the place for such thoughts.

For later, they bought loaves of crusty bread and a wheel of pungent, crumbly cheese. At the pie stall, the savory meat pasties smelled so appetizing that they shared one hot from the oven, blowing on the steaming filling to keep from burning their mouths.

Between the stalls lay twisted ribbons of ice from yesterday's storm. The reminder made her smile. Had it not been for bad weather, Adele doubted they would have stopped in this town. Destiny had shaped events to make them lovers, and Adele blessed that late March squall. Though she was aware that last night's shared passion may have changed her future, nothing could erase what had happened between them.

Standing in the purple shadows of the pie stall, Rafe briefly slid his hand in hers, his grasp strong and comforting. His unexpected touch made her shiver with delight.

For a few minutes longer they strolled amidst the vendors' stalls. They walked close together, highly aware of the other's nearness, yet always careful not to touch.

Adele admired the displays of carved spoons and bowls, brightly stitched linens, and woven girdles. Then she clapped her hands in surprise, laughing at a monkey dancing across a small stage, wearing miniature cardinal's vestments.

Rafe laughed also, his amusement stemming as much from the derisive commentary on the Roman church as the monkey's capering. Rafe—and the whole country— was still angry at the pope's edict which forbade the sacraments in England. That amounted to a virtual national excommunication, all to punish their king for his disobedience to Rome. Rafe tossed the animal's handler a coin for his audacity. The man doffed his tasseled cap and bowed low in acknowledgment.

All too soon they were through the market. There, Rafe's men waited beside the road with the horses and wagon. Adele's disgruntled maids waited there also, slumped in their saddles, huddled against the cold. The women wore scowls because Rafe's soldiers had not let them browse as well. A warm fragrant gingerbread each and a cup of spiced ale helped thaw them slightly, but Adele felt slightly guilty as the party turned onto the road leading to Summerhay Castle.

As they left the valley town behind, moving gradually uphill into the wind, Rafe puzzled over what best to do about D'Avranche. He would leave Adele under guard at a nearby inn while he went to bargain with Summerhay's lord. One glance at such a fiery-haired prize and D'Avranche would stop at nothing to keep her.

And what if D'Avranche was not home? The man was often at court, so it was a distinct possibility. In that case he decided, they would go on to Fordham. That would be best, Rafe thought. It would give him and Adele a few weeks together before the truth caught up with him—that or his angry king.

The day gradually brightened as a pale sun peeked from behind silver-edge cloud. The surface of this upland road was firm and they were making good time.

Around noon they stopped to sup in the shelter of a stand of wind-wracked elms crowning a last hillock. Flanking the narrow road ahead on one side was an ancient forest. On the other, heathland stretched to the horizon, scattered with huge boulders which gave the illusion of a flock of grazing sheep.

Aware that any highway close to the woodland could be dangerous—trees often gave cover to robbers—when they resumed their journey, Rafe put the women in the middle of his men to shield them from attack.

Though the road wound along the fringe of the forest, many of the trees had been cleared away. Yet deep inside this ancient wildwood, all underplanted with thickets of holly, gorse, and bracken, its heart looked dark and mysterious.

The unnatural silence beside the forest seemed heavy and oppressive, broken only by an occasional bird call. In fact, it was so quiet that Rafe subconsciously reached to his side, reassuring himself that his sword and daggers were at hand. He was not the only one who found this silence unnerving, for several of his men did likewise as they glanced warily in either direction of the deserted stretch of land.

There was a curve ahead before the road crossed a stone bridge spanning a small brook. At the foot of the narrow bridge the way was blocked by a fallen tree.

The lead riders called out, and the column stopped. Rafe swung from his saddle to direct his men in moving the obstruction. Adele dismounted also, glad of this unexpected chance to stretch her legs. After much discussion, her maids joined her, stumbling around on stiff legs and bemoaning their lot.

The soldiers tied ropes around the fallen tree, then a horse was uncoupled from the wagon traces to move it. A shout went up to stand clear as the huge horse heaved and strained, and a triumphant cheer sounded as the tree rolled harmlessly onto the heath.

The horse was led back to the wagon and was being backed between the traces when the lookout sounded the alarm. From the cover of the trees, a swarm of men suddenly appeared. Only a handful were mounted, but all shouted as they charged forward, brandishing staves and cudgels, clearly intent on doing battle.

Inwardly cursing himself for not having suspected a trap, Rafe yelled to his men to make ready. He spun about and took a running leap into his saddle. Behind him, the two soldiers guarding the women had already drawn their swords.

In a wave, the ruffians engulfed them and with many shouts and oaths, the two parties clashed. Rafe was alarmed to find himself cut off from Adele by their attackers, and he sliced furiously at his foes as he fought to make his way back to her.

They had been engaged by close to thirty men, but, though Rafe's men were outnumbered, they managed to hold their own.

Still fighting to return to Adele's side, Rafe yelled in rage as enemy horsemen surrounded her. In a flash, she was lifted from the ground and swung screaming across a saddle bow. Suddenly, the riders were off, weaving away in a crazy, drunken fashion into the trees. Rafe spurred after them in hot pursuit, scattering the rabble that still blocked his way. Unfortunately, Adele's captors had a head start and were familiar with the twists and turns of the woodland paths. Several of Rafe's men thundered along behind him, eager to overtake Adele's abductors, but dense brush masked the retreating thieves and they finally disappeared in the heart of the forest. Hoofbeats could still be heard thudding in the distance, but Rafe was no longer sure if the sounds were made by the men they pursued or were the echoes of their own horses' hooves.

Rafe slacked off on the reins. His men fell back. It was useless to go any further, for they had no idea which route the thieves had taken. The truth was hard to face, but face it he must—he had lost them in the forest.

He galloped back to the highway to assess their position. Some of the thieves were still there, seemingly bewildered that their fellows had deserted them. Rafe seized one by the hair, hauling him from the ground where he was tied. Angrily ignoring the man's pleas for mercy, Rafe demanded to know where the woman had been taken.

When the man refused to answer, Rafe gave him several whacks with the flat of his sword. Wailing, the red-bearded bandit pleaded for him to stop.

"Then tell me where your camp is, you thieving bastard," Rafe growled, hauling the man up with his mailed fist.

"I don't know," the ruffian wailed.

Rafe leaned over the quivering fool, longing to beat him to a pulp. While the man stalled, Adele was being taken further away. Rafe's blood ran cold.

Prepared to carry out his threat to slice off the man's ear, Rafe had already drawn blood before the other capitulated.

"We have no camp. It was struck last night."

Rafe fought back his desire to kill the man outright. "What good is that news to me? Where have they taken the lady?"

"I don't know. . . . East?" the man guessed, his eyes round with fear. "We're Jack Broughton's men. And we're an army, not thieves."

"An army? Of what, muckrakers? If that's so, what's the name of the lord you fight for?"

"I don't know his name, but he's powerful. Jack has a lot of important friends." The last was said as if to impress him.

In disgust Rafe pushed the man aside. He was getting nowhere. Two of his own men were wounded. He needed to get them cleaned up and ascertain the severity of their injuries. Adric was already trying to patch up their injured horses. All in all, Rafe supposed they had given a good account of themselves—a dozen of their attackers were down; some still flailed about, but most were beyond help.

"Tie up the prisoners, search them, and throw them in the wagon. Then check the dead and see what we can find."

The search yielded little at first, a few coins and a ring, but on one of the last bodies someone found a bloodied paper. When Rafe unfolded the soiled parchment, his mood soared. It was a crude sketch of the area. That meant at least some of these men weren't locals, but had come here recently—probably in search of someone or something.

Frowning, Rafe spread out the map to identify the landmarks. The town of Lower Marden was marked with a red circle. He supposed they could have been spotted in town and marked, yet it seemed unlikely, for nothing had been taken from the supply wagon before their assistants had fled. Beyond giving battle and capturing Adele, this attack seemed purposeless.

Eyes narrowed, Rafe studied the drawing. Considering the lay of the land, an unnamed location marked by a cross had to be Summerhay Castle. Was that where the rabble were headed; perhaps to settle a grievance they had against D'Avranche? So ragged and ill equipped were they, it seemed unlikely the men could be in a nobleman's employ, though that was what the red-bearded man had implied. There were too many questions buzzing through his head for which he had no answers, at least none that made sense.

A great wailing took Rafe's attention. Adele's maids were emerging from behind the boulders where they had hidden during the attack. Damn! Why couldn't the thieves have taken them instead? Now, he was saddled with these blubbering females.

Rafe smiled reassuringly at the women and he tried to cajole them into remounting—without success. All they did was start wailing anew and wringing their hands. Finally, his patience exhausted, Rafe curtly ordered them into the saddle.

While he assessed the severity of his men's wounds, Rafe puzzled over the rabble's apparent objective. They had to have seen these women, too, for the men had lain in wait while his soldiers cleared the road. It seemed totally out of character for bandits not to take the women servants as well, if only for some passing sport. It was one more puzzle in the mix already stirring in his mind, and Rafe was more convinced than ever that this had been no ordinary highway ambush.

Rafe turned his party around, heading back to Lower Marden. He would find shelter for his injured men. While he was there, he might also learn something of value about Jack Broughton's army of thieves.

Adele's throat felt as if it would burst from screaming, but it was useless. There was no one about to rescue her. Even the couple of black-faced charcoal burners they passed in a clearing in the forest had stared at her like half-wits, making no effort to stop her abductors despite her screams for help.

Adele asked the man on whose horse she was tied who he was and where he was taking her. With a curse, he told her to shut up. When she began to ask again, he cuffed her lightly across the head. The blow did not injure her, but it greatly affronted her dignity. Smarting from the insult, Adele said no more, marking well the ruffian's pockmarked face, his tangled hair, and the perpetual odor of onions wafting from his body.

Though she tried not to let her abductors know it, Adele was very afraid. As the miles slid by uneventfully, disillusion began to set in. She had been expecting Rafe to ride forth to rescue her. She had felt safe in his presence, but now she knew that had been a false security. Adele still did not know what had happened. One minute she was watching them pulling a tree off the road; the next, everyone was fighting for their lives. She should have mounted her horse and ridden to safety, but at the time of the attack she had been stunned by their enemies' unexpected appearance. The thought never occurred to her.

It began to rain. Soon streams of water dripped off the hat of the man in front of her and ran down his face. The trickles made pale streaks in the grime. Adele huddled inside her cloak, trying unsuccessfully to stay far away from the man's body. Unfortunately, she had to brace herself against him as they bounced along, and finally he grabbed her with one arm, steadying her against his side and forcing Adele to endure his sweaty grip.

They finally entered a settlement. By now the rain had

stopped. From a row of hovels an assortment of men, women, and children emerged, as if they had been waiting.

" 'Ere, you. Don't cause no trouble and you won't be hurt," her captor hissed in her ear, his horrible breath blasting her face.

Adele did as she was asked because it seemed pointless to plead for help from these ragged people. She was untied and dragged from the horse by a second man who held her securely until her captor had dismounted. They pinioned her arms, propelling her along between them.

Feeling shaken and bruised, Adele walked on unsteady legs. As she passed them, the crowd of onlookers fell back, mouths agape, as if she were some exotic animal. Who *were* these ragged, dirty people? They reminded her of the beggars who lined church doorways exhibiting their infirmities, for wherever she looked, she saw misshapen limbs, boils, and scabrous faces.

The two men led her inside a wooden building filled with people, who ceased their chat when she was pushed inside the door. From the room's murky interior came a familiar, raspy voice.

"Welcome, sister dear."

Adele's stomach lurched in shock. "Joce," she whispered into the darkness. She blinked rapidly, trying to accustom herself to the gloom. A sea of faces swam before her, gray-shadowed in the smoky atmosphere. A cloaked man stepped forward, and when he threw back his hood, she saw her brother. Fear, joy, and relief all surged through her veins. Surely if Joce was here, she was safe—despite the menacing appearance of these people. For all that, she still felt vaguely uneasy, just like the last time she had been with him.

"Why did you let me think I was being captured by robbers?" she demanded indignantly.

"Nay, don't be angry. It was just easier that way," Joce replied, his voice pleasant. "I'm sorry if you were afraid. You've nothing to fear from my men."

"Your men?" She looked around the crowded room,

seeing familiar faces swim into focus. Yes, she did recognize some of them as they crowded around the smoky central hearth.

There was the giant from the forest, his belt bristling with daggers. The men were all grinning at her expectantly. Suddenly Adele realized they were waiting for her to thank them. In their eyes, they had rescued her from her captor; to them, Rafe De Montford represented the hated King John.

"You came all the way from Esterwold to save me?" she gasped, and the picture grew clearer.

"That's right. Isn't that what you expected?" Joce asked in a puzzled voice.

"Well, yes, but it took so long, and . . . well . . . things are different now."

"Different? How do you mean?" The smile slid from Joce's face as he caught her arm and stepped toward the door. "Come outside."

Given little chance to decline, Adele soon found herself out in the damp afternoon. Some of the women and children still stood about, but when they saw Joce, they slunk away.

"Now, explain yourself. What do you mean—different?" Joce demanded gruffly. "You're still to marry Hugh D'Avranche?"

"Well, yes . . . and no. Lord Rafe's going to bargain with him to buy him off. Oh, Joce, when I wrote to you I was so angry and afraid. Now things have changed. I'm in love with him—with Rafe."

Joce stared at her. "What?" he asked finally. "What are you saying?"

"I want to marry Rafe. He wants to strike a bargain with Hugh D'Avranche over the marriage contract. After all, the man doesn't even know me. To him I'm only a name. Oh, Joce, Rafe isn't my enemy and I don't need to be rescued from him. And once you're home, Bohun will have to leave. When you're back at Esterwold I won't be a ward of the king any longer, so he can't make me marry someone I don't know. Don't you see?" she ended lamely as Joce continued to regard her stonily, almost as if she were speaking a foreign language.

"I don't give a damn about your silly mooning about being in love. De Montford's still *my* enemy. All that matters to me is that you're still set to marry D'Avranche. That's worth money."

"Joce," Adele cried, appalled. "I want to marry Lord Rafe instead. As the Lord of Esterwold, you can arrange that."

"No." He blinked at her. "De Montford is a bastard. He's the king's man. Besides, he'd never have someone like you as his wife. He just wants to bed you, silly goose. That's all. The same as any other red-blooded man. Now, I don't want to hear any more about it."

Adele stared at him in shock. "I love him," she repeated stubbornly.

Joce curled his mouth scornfully. "Look, I know you think you love him, but I'm your brother and I know best. He was taking you to your groom and when he saw you, he fancied you for himself. That's all. My plans don't include him. He's abandoned his task, but I intend to finish it. And instead of buckets of praise from old John Softsword, my reward's going to be gold, sister. Buckets and buckets of gold."

"Please, Joce," Adele moaned, "Forget what I said in the letter. Just listen to me *now*."

"I don't know what the letter said, all right. Just forget about all this love stuff. D'Avranche will pay anything to have you. Never fear, I'll ask a ransom that fits your beauty and his fortune." Joce grinned, charmed by his phrase. "A big lord like D'Avranche won't have any use for a piddling place like Esterwold, so I'm going to ask for that back for myself."

Joce's scornful comment about their home both surprised and disturbed her.

"How can you call our home—your inheritance—piddling? And, Joce, Esterwold's already yours."

"You know, some of your appeal's probably because

you're an heiress," Joce continued, not hearing anything she said.

"Listen to me," she cried, shaking his arm to get his full attention. "Esterwold's not part of my bride price. You already own it."

For a moment Joce stared at her, stunned by her words; then his fair skin flushed. Grabbing her arm, he gave her no time to say any more as he marched her along the rutted path between the huts.

"Stop, Joce—you're hurting me," Adele cried as his viselike fingers began to bruise her arm.

He slackened his grip at once and stopped, turning her about to face him. "I'm sorry, Adele. I never wanted to hurt you," he said huskily. "Don't ever do anything to make me hurt you. Just do as I say. It's not like I'm sending you into the London stews. You'll be lady of a great estate."

"But I'll be married to a man I don't even know, and I'm already in love with Rafe. Don't you see, you're condemning me to a life of servitude with D'Avranche." She searched his face for some glimmer of sympathy. It was as if he were carved from stone. "Don't you care if I'm happy? For years I longed for your return, but you're so different now, you're like a stranger to me. We used to be close, Joce. Don't you remember when we hid in the old tunnel and pretended to be smugglers? And that boat you made that we sailed on the fish pond? It was the year the puppies were born under the cooper's shed, and we had to—"

"Shut up!" he snarled. "I don't remember and I want you to stop bringing those things up!"

"You can't have forgotten all those things."

"If you'd been beaten like I have, you'd be lucky to remember your own name," he spat bitterly. Then, forcing a smile, he added in a kinder tone, "Just be patient, Adele. Everything will be for the best. Now, I want you to stay in here tonight. It's safer. Tomorrow we'll leave." He grinned as he glanced about. "I don't see that big ugly hound guarding you today."

His tone chilled her. In vain Adele tried to twist out of his embrace. Joce held her firmly, crushing her against his hard body as he kissed her bruisingly on the mouth.

"Remember, sister, while we're here, your safety depends on me."

Chapter Seven

When she was left alone in the dark hut, Adele's forced bravery dissolved. She crouched on the floor weeping bitterly until she finally grew angry with herself for being so weak. Only fools wallowed in self-pity. She had to make an escape plan. She could expect no help from her brother.

She crept to the door. As she'd expected, it was padlocked from the outside. Adele hoped Joce had the only key, though even that thought was not especially comforting. She checked the rest of her surroundings.

It was not wholly dark within the hut, glimmers of moonlight crept between the ill-fitting wooden shutters. As her eyes adjusted to the faint light, she saw a straw-filled mattress on the floor.

Adele sat down, knees drawn up to her chest, as she tried to get her bearings. It had been a blow to discover her own brother was so heartless. The beatings he'd endured must have robbed him of far more than his childhood memories. Though Adele's love for the boy she had known was not dead, Joce the man whittled away at those cherished feelings at every turn. Had he so quickly dismissed her love for Rafe as a woman's foolishness because he had never known love himself? Or was it more because she was interfering with his plans?

She lay back on the pallet, drained, and listened for sounds. There had been much shouting and drunken merriment earlier, but it was quiet now. Then she heard muted voices outside her door. Adele froze. Were they going to break down the door and rape her? Though the door was padlocked, the wood looked so old it would not take much to kick it in.

Finally, the revelers moved away. She let out a great sigh of relief, unaware she had been holding her breath. With bands of drunken men roaming the camp, it seemed unsafe even to fall asleep and risk being caught off guard. She had to stay alert. Each time her eyes closed, Adele pinched herself awake, and when her head sank on her chest, she jerked herself upright.

Adele was startled by an unexpected knock. Soft light filtered under the door and between the shutters. Despite all her efforts, she must have fallen asleep, for it was already morning.

"Don't be afraid, Adele, it's only me."

She felt a modicum of relief to discover it was Joce at the door and not another of her abductors. With much banging and muttered cursing, he finally unlocked the rusty padlock.

The door crashed inward where it hung lopsidedly against the wall.

Joce stood in the doorway, darkly outlined against the iron-gray dawn. He was dressed for traveling. This morning he looked grubby and unshaven, his chin dark with red-gold stubble.

"Are we leaving now?" Adele asked, scrambling to her feet.

"Yes, and none too soon. Broughton's men are a pack

of thieves. We'll be well shut of them." Lowering his voice even further, Joce confided, "We're going to our own camp, closer to Summerhay."

At the mention of that hated place, Adele's stomach lurched. Joce had not changed his mind during the night. She considered pleading again with him, but decided against it. Maybe if he thought her obedient to his wishes, he would not guard her as closely, thereby giving her an opportunity to escape.

"What, no loving greeting for your own brother?"

"Good morrow, Joce," Adele said dutifully, nervously licking her lips. When he reached for her, she tried to sidestep him, but she was not quick enough and he swiftly imprisoned her in his arms.

"No kisses, and always trying to shy away from me. Are you really so cold?" he asked huskily, looking closely at her face.

Adele was glad of the gloom, for she was afraid that if it were lighter Joce would have seen her revulsion. He was holding her far too close for comfort, and Adele panicked inwardly. She was finally able to master her emotions sufficiently to force a smile. She pecked his cheek. "There, brother, there's your good-morrow with a kiss."

Horses' hooves thudded outside and Joce was momentarily distracted by the sound, giving Adele the chance to slide out of his embrace. He grunted his displeasure at her action, but said no more while he waited for her to pull on her boots.

When they stepped into the street, Adele was surprised to find that even at this early hour the shabby settlement bustled with activity. To her amazement, she saw Moonlight standing in the shadows between the buildings. She could hardly believe her eyes. The gelding whickered in pleasure when she called his name.

Joce smiled when he saw the surprise and joy in her face.

"I thought that was your gelding," he said, tugging on Moonlight's reins to bring him forward.

"Where did you find him?" Adele cried in delight as she stroked the horse's velvety nose. Moonlight affectionately nuzzled her neck, his hot breath blasting inside her cloak.

"Broughton's men took him. The bastards would have kept him, too, if I hadn't recognized him as yours. I've always had an eye for horseflesh." Joce glanced about before he added in an undertone, "Not long now before we'll be on our own."

Several fearsome men were walking toward them along the settlement's rutted street; all were armed to the teeth. The huge, red-bearded man who swaggered slightly ahead of the others was likely their leader, she thought with disgust.

When he saw the men, Joce instantly flashed an ingratiating smile and stepped forward to greet them, leaving Adele amazed by his swift change of mood. Next came back-slapping and cheerful greetings all around.

"When I get back we'll make merry, lads," Joce promised as he linked arms with the red-bearded man.

"Sure you don't need help to pull it off?" the man asked.

"Naw, Jack, you've helped enough. It's my turn now to do something for you." Joce motioned to his men to bring up their horses. "We'll soon make short work of the bastards. And if they have any of your lads, we'll bring them back with us. That wagon's loaded with gold. We'll come back here to divvy up shares."

Jack Broughton grinned, revealing blackened stubs of teeth. "We'll be waiting for that," he said, rubbing his hands together.

Another round of hearty back-slapping followed.

"Will you take your sister to the castle first?" Jack Broughton asked.

"That's my plan."

"Well, then. I'll send a couple of my lads along to show you the way."

Though Adele could tell this proposal didn't please Joce, her brother cleverly hid his feelings.

A few minutes later the small party of ten, astride their raw-boned nags, took their leave, with Jack Broughton's men riding close behind them. Adele guessed the men were being sent along to keep Joce honest. She had no idea whose wagon of gold they intended to steal.

It was only after they had been riding for some time that the truth began to dawn on her sleepy mind. Joce was talking about Rafe's supply wagon—though she was sure there were no chests of gold on board!

As they stopped to water the horses, she rode up to her brother. "Is it De Montford's wagon you have marked for robbery?"

Joce glanced about, as if making sure they were not being overheard. "There you go again, asking questions. When will you learn to trust me? It won't be your fault if you don't know what's going on."

Adele was slightly surprised that for once her question had not annoyed him. Joce further shocked her by gently taking her arm as he led her a few paces along the stream's muddy bank.

"Yes, Adele. I'm going to take De Montford's wagon." he said loudly.

"But there's no gold there."

"I never thought there was."

"But you said . . . Why steal it?"

Joce winked at her. "Shh, you'll find out soon enough, my pretty." He chucked her under the chin, his good humor intact.

At noon, they stopped at a well to wash down hunks of coarse brown bread and cheese with cold water. Curiously, Joce forbade his men to drink the ale they had brought in their flasks. Broughton's men helped themselves, however.

Adele sat on the grass, enjoying the feel of the warm sun beating on her back. They had stopped in a daisy-sprinkled meadow, and she idly plucked flowers to make a chain, splitting the stalks with her nail and threading them together. With a sigh, she stretched her limbs and, after first glancing about to make sure none of the men were nearby, she lay full-length on the grass, gazing up at the bright blue sky where fleecy clouds scudded overhead. How she longed to be able to lie there and doze, yet she knew it would not be safe to indulge that fancy. She glanced about.

Not far away, Broughton's two men were sitting apart from the rest, their backs against a boulder where they dozed in the sun, their empty ale flasks beside them. Out of the corner of her eye Adele noticed an unexpected movement from behind the boulder. She sat up for a better view, and saw the two men crouching there move forward. Sunlight flashed on steel, muffled cries rang out, and quickly the deed was done. Broughton's spies sprawled on the bloody grass, their throats cut.

Adele watched as the two assassins swaggered back to Joce, highly pleased with their achievement. They wiped the blood off their daggers on the grass.

"Good work, lads, and good riddance," Joce praised. He turned to Adele, who was watching white-faced. "Do you understand now? I never intended to take De Montford's wagon. That was a tale to keep Broughton quiet. He said I owed him something because his men helped rescue you."

Joce laughed and strode away, calling to his men to remount and be on their way.

Adele felt chilled. With morbid curiosity, she glanced toward the dead men propped against the outcropping, their hoods partially over their faces as if they slept in the midday sun. Her hands shook as she took Moonlight's reins and pulled herself into his saddle. She wanted to think she was wrong, but she could not help believing that if she stood in Joce's way, she too would be disposed of like Jack Broughton's spies.

When they finally arrived at Joce's camp, in the heart of the tangled woods, Adele was astonished to find women and children there also, making the place similar to the settlement they had just left. Perhaps Joce's people looked less like beggars, but the distinction was slim. Their dwellings were makeshift huts with roofs made from branches, and some shelters were nothing more than pieces of patched canvas strung between saplings.

At first it seemed that everyone in the camp came out to stare at her, but when Joce explained her presence amongst them, the suspicious looks changed into smiles and Adele was readily accepted as his long-lost sister.

As the days became weeks, Adele chafed at her captivity. Though she was not actually bound like a prisoner, she was never allowed outside this grassy glade. Given half the chance, she would have run away; Joce was always alert to that possibility, though, keeping her under surveillance day and night. Even the children must have been warned to stay away from the lady, for she sometimes caught them peering at her around corners before giggling and racing away.

Under the guise of providing lady's maids, Joce sent two women to serve her, though Adele was sure their true task was to watch her. Initially she hoped they might become friends, but the two rarely spoke to her, and when they did, their country dialect was so foreign to her ears that Adele could barely understand them. The women remained polite, distant, and ever vigilant. It was because their brother was Joce's second-in-command that they had been chosen for the position. Other than that, she knew little about them.

Life in this forest camp was so monotonous Adele wanted to scream with boredom. Strange though it was, she almost began to look forward to eventually going to Summerhay—if only to be able to start living again. Each day spent in this settlement was like being in limbo.

Sometimes when she felt especially vulnerable, Adele allowed herself to think about Rafe. How her heart ached with longing for him. She was sure he would rescue her. She watched daily for his men and horses to appear magically through the trees.

As the days became weeks, then months, she had to accept the painful truth—Rafe was not coming. Had the king sent him on another mission? Or did he not care enough to seek her out? Whenever that destructive thought crept into her mind, Adele pushed it out. The simple truth could be that Rafe did not know how to find her.

Besides Joce, Adele's only link to her former life was her gelding. Though she was not allowed to ride Moonlight, each day she visited his makeshift stable and spent hours grooming the gray, leaning against his warm body and taking comfort from him. While she stroked his silky hide, she poured out her heart to him, sure that the horse understood her distress. Sometimes he nuzzled her neck in comfort, his familiar presence relieving some of her loneliness.

How she wished she could also have Val for company. Hopefully by now the dog was completely healed. There were a couple of mangy hounds here who skulked about the fringes of the camp, Adele had not been able to befriend the poor creatures, for they did not seem eager for human companionship.

Summer had turned the woods lush and green, and the heavy foliage blocked out the sun. At the edge of the camp clearing grew tall rosebay willow stalks, their crimson flowers nodding in the breeze. There were birds and myriad woodland creatures in the trees; Adele could hear them scuttling about. Yet here inside the hut sat Adele and her keepers with their bland bovine faces, day after monotonous day, staring at each other, content to sit motionless for hours on end. If Adele went outside, they followed. When she strayed to gather the rosebay willow, they snatched the herbs from her, saying it was not allowed. She never learned why.

When it rained, the woods became a dripping, misty blur and Adele huddled with her handmaidens inside their leaking hut. They had a wooden bucket to catch the worst leak; the rest they dodged.

Finally the great day came. Joce, clad in his best

apparel—a russet tunic and black deerhide boots—rode out of the camp to parlay with Hugh D'Avranche, offering to return his lost bride for a generous ransom. All evening long Adele waited for his return, her stomach churning as she tried to second-guess what was taking place at Summerhay Castle.

Joce did not return that night, nor the next. Adele grew even more despondent, convinced the delay was because they were still haggling over terms. What was her asking price, she wondered bitterly as she stirred a pot of rabbit stew over the camp fire. One of her maids had made bread and it baked beside her on a flat stone at the edge of the fire.

While she stirred, Adele thrust her straggling hair out of her eyes. Since coming here, she had not seen herself, but she was sure she looked just as bedraggled as these other women with their matted hair and patched clothing. What would Hugh D'Avranche think of his bride now? Likely he would consider himself robbed when a shabby peasant girl arrived at his door instead of the beautiful noblewoman she was certain Joce had promised him.

A commotion sounded on the edge of the camp, the noise swiftly followed by hoofbeats. Adele's heart sank as Joce and his men thundered into the clearing. He skidded to a halt, showering the curious bystanders with mud.

All had not gone well at Summerhay. One glance at his angry face told Adele that much. Joce swung from the saddle, brows beetled, his mouth a hard slash in his set face. He snarled at those closest to him, and women and children quickly scrambled out of range.

Joce strode toward Adele, stopping when he saw what she was doing.

"By the Christ," he swore, lashing out at Adele's nearest maid. "What do you mean, making a kitchen wench of her? Look at her hands, you stupid bitch."

The woman cried out in pain as she tried to dodge the rain of blows.

Leaving the ladle in the stew, Adele backed away.

114

"Joce, stop. It's not her fault," she interceded, forcing a smile. "It was my idea. I'm so bored with nothing to do."

"Go on, get inside," he growled at her, grasping her shoulder and propelling her toward the hut. He turned to her maids. "You two stay outside till you're called."

Adele's stomach roiled as she went inside the gloomy hut, prepared to learn her fate. "Didn't D'Avranche want me after all?" she asked, surprising herself by her audacity.

Joce raised his hand to strike her, then thought better of it. "Go on, sit down."

Obediently, Adele sat on one of the logs they used as seats while Joce drew himself a cup of ale from the keg in the corner. Cup in hand, he went to stand in the open doorway where he glowered at the camp's inhabitants while he watched them prepare their noon meal.

"Well," Adele prompted. "Tell me the worst."

"The bastard wasn't even there!"

"What? You haven't spoken to him?" she gasped, her spirits soaring.

"I only spoke to his steward—and the whoreson tried to take me a prisoner. We had to hide in the woods or they'd've murdered us. To start with, we took the wrong road—the damned place is a lot further than I bargained for. Then the towers were bristling with guards and there's a bloody great moat."

As she listened to Joce's tale of woe, Adele grew even more puzzled. Her brother had spent most of his life at Summerhay; he should have known what to expect. Why hadn't he been better prepared?

"Are you saying things are different now?"

"What do you mean . . . *now*?"

"Well, you already knew about the moat and the guards, didn't you? You lived there for years."

"What makes you so damned clever?" he snarled as he went to refill his ale cup. "I'd just forgotten, that's all,"

Adele could see that Joce was in no mood for any more questions, so she waited silently while he emptied the cup.

"Now, you listen to me," he began, wiping his mouth on his sleeve. "No more kitchen chores. Make those two lazy sluts do all the work. I know you don't like being idle, but I've no fancy stitching or pretty playthings to amuse you. This won't last forever." While he spoke, Joce paced about the hut. "You know, I could move in here with you; then we'd have each other for company. That way I'd make sure they were both doing their work. Yes, I will. That's a champion idea."

His unexpected suggestion robbed Adele of speech. She stared at him in shock, a thousand unvoiced protests running through her mind. In his current mood, she knew they were best left unspoken. So far, Joce had kept his distance. She'd managed to sidestep his odd embraces and he'd never pursued her. She feared things were about to change.

"We're Lord and Lady of Esterwold, after all," he continued, turning to her with a half smile. "Don't you think we should start living like 'em?"

"What about Hugh D'Avranche?"

"What about him? He'll be home after the king comes back from France. What's the matter, did you think I'd given up?" he asked, seeing her changing expression. "This gives us more time to get ready. You can wash your hair and soak the dirt from your hands, maybe soften them with goose grease. We want you to look like a lady, not some kitchen slut." He paused, aware of her disappointment. "What's wrong now? Surely you're not still waiting for your handsome knight to carry you off? He's forgotten about you by now. He's probably had a dozen other wenches since you've gone. You don't need him. I'm taking care of you now. Haven't I done well so far?"

"Yes, you have," she agreed mechanically.

"All right, then. You just keep doing what you're told and nothing will change. You're safe with me. I've told my men, any bastard who dares come within sniffing distance of you gets his throat slit. And don't you think you can run away from me," Joce warned, his expression threatening. "I'll watch you night and day."

* * *

True to his word, Joce moved his few possessions into the hut. Shaken from her lethargy, Adele needed to stay alert at all times. It was as if she shared her dwelling with a wild animal that had to be constantly watched lest it catch her by surprise and devour her. Grudgingly, Joce agreed to sling a curtain on a rope to give her sleeping area some privacy. Though the threadbare curtain made a flimsy defense, Adele felt much safer behind it, hidden from his prying gaze. Though at first she had resented Meg and Joan, mainly because they prevented her escaping, she was now glad they slept beside her bed. Adele felt very uncomfortable living in such close proximity to a man who, though he was her brother, was nevertheless a stranger.

Each day, Joce and his most trusted men left the camp for hours, purportedly scouting out their surroundings. Adele suspected they were robbing travelers or stealing from nearby farms, for they never returned empty-handed.

At first the treasures he brought for their makeshift home he claimed he'd found by the roadside, conveniently discarded by some traveler. After a while, though, Joce did not even bother to explain where the objects came from. When one day he returned early carrying an inlaid chessboard with finely carved ivory pieces, Adele simply beamed in thanks. Doubtless this too had been stolen, but she knew it was wiser not to ask.

They played chess until the light faded. Adele was surprised to find him far less skillful than she remembered. To her surprise, Joce did not get angry when she beat him. On the contrary, he amazed her by praising her skill. He even took her hand and kissed it in an attempt at gallantry. The feel of his hot mouth exploring her palm sent a chill of foreboding down her spine.

Sometimes when they were playing chess companionably with the summer leaves pattering overhead, Adele was poignantly reminded of the past—those far-off days when her brother had been softhearted, quick-witted, and full of laughter; when, in fact, he had still been the brother she loved.

"You never told me how it was living at Summerhay," she ventured one night as the gathering dusk forced them to put their game aside. "Were they never kind to you, even when you first got there?"

"No," he declared, his face hardening. "For as long as I can remember, I was beaten every day as a lad. Servant boys are always treated like that, Lady Adele. Of course, you wouldn't know, living in the hall, all pretty and pampered. It's the way most poor lads live their lives."

She recoiled from the venom in his voice. "You could hardly call yourself poor, or even a servant, Joce," she interjected quickly, hoping to stem the tide of his anger. "You were a hostage, that's all. It's a common practice. Father assumed you'd be treated the way we treated the children sent to live with us."

"Well, *Father* was wrong," he growled, glaring at her.

He went to the keg and filled his cup with ale. Finally, he swallowed his anger sufficiently to ask if she wanted some.

"No, thank you. I'm just going to bed," Adele answered thickly.

Joce shrugged and went to the doorway to summon her women.

"Good night, Adele," he said, his voice softening as he came over and stroked her hair. "I'm sorry I'm not the way you'd like me to be. Maybe if I were, you'd be kinder," he said, his tone wistful.

So surprised was she by this abrupt change of mood, Adele did not know what to say. "People grow up, Joce. We can't help how life changes us." She turned away before he saw her tears.

Later, when she lay on her lumpy straw pallet listening to her maid's rhythmic snores, Adele mentally replayed the evening, and a startling realization emerged. When Joce had held out the cup of ale to her, he used his right hand. Her brother was left-handed! They must have forced him to conform to the others and use his right hand. Poor Joce. If only the family had known about his cruel treatment, maybe her father could have done something to stop it. The old Lord of Summerhay must have been a brutal man. She would probably never know what else had been done to turn her brother so hard.

Tears trickled onto her cheeks as she thought more about the past. Sometimes such vivid recollection of events was more a curse than a blessing. Tonight, she wept for her memories of a young boy, taken miles from home and all he loved, forced to endure such cruel treatment it had changed him forever.

The next morning Adele lay on her pallet, finding it unusually dark and quiet inside the hut. Her maids had already left and when she lifted the edge of the curtain, she saw that Joce had gone outside also. It was rare for her to be alone.

She lay in the gloom, uneager to get up. The monotony of her days had begun to wear on her. In this camp, no preparations were made either for bed or for the start of the day, as everyone slept in the same clothes they wore to work. Adele had known this way was the habit of the poor, yet she was still not accustomed to it. In her former life, where she had owned linen nightgowns, cotton shifts, and a hairbrush, she had never realized how fortunate she was.

A bump on the wall behind her made Adele's heartbeat quicken. Quickly scrambling from her pallet, Adele moved to the middle of the hut. Through the open doorway she could see women hauling water and stoking the campfire as they prepared the morning meal. A group of men were sitting on the far side of the fire mending harnesses and honing their weapons. Everything appeared normal. Adele then understood why she had slept so much later than usual. A thick fog blanketed the trees. Only in the clearing was there any light at all, that filtering through a hole in the brooding gray mist.

As she stood there, several more bumps shook the back wall, so forceful this time that the whole hut shuddered. Adele also noticed the sharp smell of horses. A sudden premonition of danger caused Adele's pulse to quicken and she spun about. Then, as if the world had suddenly been turned upside down, the scene before her dissolved in chaos.

From all directions, helmeted horsemen appeared out of the mist. "In the name of the king!" came a shout. Then the riders descended on the camp, slashing at those who rushed for weapons. The clearing was filled with noise.

The wall behind her cracked. With a scream, Adele bolted forward as the barrier of woven branches caved in, trampled down by a half-dozen horsemen. Before she could run to safety, she was seized from behind. Though she struggled desperately to break free, one of the horsemen scooped her from the ground and hauled her onto his saddle.

Everything happened so quickly she could barely take it all in. Now as Adele saw these invaders up close, she saw the emblazoned surcoats over their mail. For an instant, she allowed herself to hope these were Rafe's men finally come to rescue her.

Unsure, Adele looked up into the stranger's face and saw he was smiling.

"Don't be afraid, Lady Adele. You're safe with me," the man assured her in a deep voice.

How could he know her name? She had never set eyes on him before.

Around them, men were fighting for their lives. Even some of the camp women wielded staves and cudgels as they tried to batter the mounted men from their saddles. At the far side of the camp a mass exodus was under way. Those choosing not to fight had seized horses or fled on foot into the gray mist.

The soldiers were setting fire to the huts. Some structures already blazed, but for the most part they only smoldered, gushing out clouds of black smoke, too wet to burn after the recent rain. Excited horses milled about, whin-nying and snorting, their voices adding to the confusion.

"Who *are* you?" Adele asked as the stranger moved her to a more comfortable position on his saddle.

"Gerald Montsorrel, at your service, my lady," he replied courteously, then quickly maneuvered his horse about to avoid an attack from the rear.

Adele did not recognize the name. Fresh shouts and screams of fright directed her attention to the southern perimeter of the camp where those who had fled came racing back, driven like a herd of cattle before a semicir-cle of armed horsemen.

Joce was in the forefront of the men. When he saw that Adele had been taken, he drew his dagger and threw himself at her captor. Montsorrel's horse quickly side-stepped to the left, leaving Joce slashing at thin air. The humiliation of his thwarted attack only deepened his rage.

Out of the mist burst a dozen more riders who quickly cut off the fleeing rabble. These men circled about, sin-gling out Joce for capture. Though he tried to fight them off, he was soon taken prisoner. The soldiers put a rope around his neck, leading him like an animal. When Joce lost his balance and fell, he was dragged a few feet over the ground before the leading horseman was able to rein in. Adele cried out for them to stop their cruelty, afraid Joce would be dragged to death.

Joce had already staggered to his feet when the lead rider circled him and stopped. Adele found something very familiar about the man's huge chestnut stallion, the way it pawed and snorted as it repeatedly tossed its head. When the rider finally turned in his saddle, she saw that his white surcoat bore the insignia of a silver sword superimposed upon a mountain. That distinctive coat of arms told her all she wanted to know.

"Rafe! Rafe!" Adele screamed, trying to make herself heard above the din.

Urging his mount forward, Gerard Montsorrel met the

other knight in the middle of the camp, their horses' hooves scattering the charred embers of the cookfire.

Rafe quickly dismounted and handed his horse to his squire. Montsorrel helped Adele slide from her perch and she ran to meet Rafe, tripping and stumbling over the uneven ground. They met in an instant and he removed his helmet. A moment later, Rafe swept her into his arms, lifting her from the ground.

"Oh, sweetheart, you're safe! God be praised!" he breathed against her hair. His emotion was so intense his vision was cloudy.

"Rafe, oh, Rafe, I thought you'd never come," Adele sobbed joyously as she clung to him. Beneath his surcoat he wore a shirt of mail, preventing her from feeling the heat of his body or the joyous beat of his heart. It didn't matter. Her love had come for her at last.

For a moment, it was as if time stood still and all the players in the drama were frozen in place. Then, just as suddenly, the players came back to life.

Rafe lowered her feet to the ground, but he still kept his arm about her shoulders, holding her against his side. Beyond the shielding bulk of the soldiers, Joce could be heard spewing venom and hatred, cursing Rafe and vowing vengeance. The soldiers had tied together the prisoners in a shambling, shuffling line, their feet and wrists bound separately, a single rope linking them to their fellows. Only Joce was still free.

After he handed Adele into the safekeeping of his lieutenant, Rafe strode forward to face Joce. "Shut your mouth before I shut it for you," he snarled.

At the onset, these armed men had declared they came in the name of the king. Now the bound captives noisily questioned the soldiers' right to take them prisoner, Rafe's men obviously were no soldiers of the crown. Their protests bolstered Joce's resistance. Once again, his voice rang loudest.

Rafe held up his hand for silence. "This forest belongs to the king, and you are trespassing here. I have warrants for your arrest and trial—by order of Peter des Roches, the king's justiciar."

"This is free land," Joce cried. "An Englishman has the right to live where he pleases. Saxons lived here long before you Normans took over," Joce cried, his words seconded by his men.

Adele listened to him in amazement. Their own family was of Norman ancestry. Why was Joce pretending to be Saxon? Had he done so to gain the support of these common men? When she stepped forward to say her piece, Rafe silenced her with a shake of his head.

"There is no free land," he called to Joce. "Even my own land is reliant on the king's favor. And you're outlaws. You do not have that favor." Rafe turned away. No one would have faulted him had he strung them up on the nearest trees. But he would not do that. These men would be brought before the sheriff and tried. It was their right.

Even though he was now bound and gagged, Joce still raged, his face scarlet as he mumbled through the constricting cloth trying to make himself heard. The women and children were also being rounded up, though Rafe allowed those who tried, to escape to freedom off through the trees. The men he made sure to contain, however. The mist was lifting, exposing paths and trees, robbing them of their hiding places.

Rafe heard Adele calling his name, and she sounded so distressed he turned to her immediately. Just to look at her again made his heart lurch. To be sure, she looked bedraggled as a peasant lass but she appeared safe and sound. He thanked the saints once again for protecting her from harm.

Tears ran down Adele's face, and Rafe caught her by the shoulder, thinking to soothe her. "Please, sweet, don't cry."

"No, Rafe, you don't understand—that man's my brother! He's not an outlaw. You can't arrest him and put him in jail."

"Your brother? You mean the lad who was at Summerhay?"

"Yes, Jocelyn St. Clare. He didn't go straight to Est-derwold because he thought Bohun would have him killed. That's the reason he's hiding in the forest, not because he's an outlaw," she explained, her voice quavering. "I know he kidnapped me, but he thought he was saving me. Just ask him who he is."

Rafe's expression was grim. He gripped Adele's shoulders, steadying her, for now she wept in earnest. "Listen to me . . . I already know who he is."

"Then why don't you release him?"

This was not the time nor the place to tell her all he knew. In fact, Rafe wished he need never reveal that awful truth. "Adele, please trust me, I know what I'm doing. This rabble is part of a growing peasant army that plans to help overthrow the king. There are dozens of camps just like this around the country. Besides, this man isn't who you think he is."

"He's my brother!"

"No. His real name is Lorkin Yates, though God knows, he's used so many others over the years, he's probably forgotten it by now."

"No," Adele protested, grasping his arm. "You must have the wrong man. Maybe these others are all out-laws—but not Joce."

Rafe looked down at her tear stained face and trembling lips. Adele was too emotionally distraught to be sensible, and he was getting nowhere. Also, his men had now become an interested audience. Even the roped prisoners had quieted to better hear this exchange.

Gerard had dismounted and stood beside Rafe. Lord Montsorrel owned the lands abutting Summerhay Castle, and it had been him who had jogged Rafe's memory about an incident they both witnessed years ago, the incident that had led them back to Lorkin Yates. Here.

Rafe looked at Adele again. She didn't understand.

In England there were many disgruntled nobles plotting to overthrow the king. This rabble would have provided a ready source of fighting men to bolster their cause. The official ruling had been to stamp them out, every man, woman, and child. Rafe and Gerard Montsorrel were partners in this endeavor, ordered by the king's justiciar to rid the royal forest of the vermin which threatened the crown.

Though Rafe hated to ignore her pain, he turned his back on Adele, determined to finish what he had begun.

Chapter Eight

What had promised to be a blissful reunion had gone terribly wrong. Adele could not make Rafe listen. She was appalled to see Joce being led away with the others, roped and shackled like a felon. Tearful and sullen, she saddled Moonlight and rode him away from the soldiers. Why wouldn't Rafe at least hear her out? Gone was her sensitive lover, replaced by this ruthless warrior who would bow to no will but his own.

Rafe watched her go, aware she would not stray far from the main party. Adele was angry with him and stubbornly deaf to his explanations; she was letting her heart rule her head. There was far worse to come. He knew she would have to come to terms with the unpleasant truth in her own way.

They rode out of the camp, now little more than a smoldering display of the king's power. The shambling prisoners were led single-file, the dead left unburied.

After they rode out of the forest, the mounted party turned onto the rutted highway. Behind them, mist still lingered amidst the trees through here the sun shone bright and the birds were singing. When they came to a crossroads, the bulk of the party turned north, taking the shuffling prisoners with them to the local assizes for trial.

The two noblemen and a handful of their retainers accompanied Adele along the leafy lanes to Montsorrel. With nary a cloud in the blue sky, the summer sun beat down. Wild briars festooned the hedgerows, their flat pink blossoms bright against the blackthorn twigs, while the grassy ditches at the sides of the road were dotted with scarlet pimpernels and feathery yarrow. Yet this beautiful summer day was wasted on these somber riders whose dismal thoughts canceled out the blackbird's song and rendered the colorful flower carpet dull as ditch water.

Adele cried as she rode, partially in fear for her brother's safety, yet mostly because Rafe had refused to hear her out, turning deaf ears to her pleas as he carried out King John's cruel orders.

Behind her, Rafe rode silently, every sob a stab to his heart. He was sure that at the moment she thought she hated him, and had the captive actually been her brother, he could not have blamed her. But the man wasn't, and eventually she would learn the truth.

The road wound uphill, the fields on either side scarlet with poppies nodding in the breeze. At the top of the hill stood the small keep of Montsorrel, red and blue pennants waving gaily from its turrets, entirely encircled by a narrow moat. In this light, Montsorrel appeared an enchanted castle with a thousand diamonds sparkling from its new masonry. Scaffolding against the curtain wall attested to the fortress's recent construction. In fact, as they drew nearer, workmen could still be heard banging and hammering inside the walls.

As the mounted party approached, their banners waving, the drawbridge slowly descended as if by magic and without breaking their stride, the riders clattered across.

At a nod from Rafe, Gerard Montsorrel rode ahead to

escort Adele inside the bailey. It was more fitting for the
host to take charge of her comfort. Besides, as she was
still so angry with him, Rafe doubted she would have listened to anything he had to say.

"Lady Adele, welcome to my home, much of it new, as
you can see. I've been gradually replacing my grandsire's
old wooden defenses."

She smiled pleasantly and thanked him. Gerard
Montsorrel was an engaging man, and it was probably
not his fault that Joce had been taken prisoner; she was
sure Rafe was the one in charge of the arrests.

"Thank you, my lord. It will be a welcome change to
have an actual roof over my head. You probably thought I
was a scullery maid by my appearance."

"Nay, Lady, your beauty shines through all the grime
and the tangles. We'll soon have you looking yourself
again," he added gallantly as he smiled at her. Then he
glanced back at Rafe, who nodded in approval.

Adele found it novel and pleasing to be cosseted. Still,
though Montsorrel's kindness helped soothe her tearful
mood, it could not make up for her shock and pain over
Joce's arrest.

She was led up winding stairs to a pleasant south-fac-
ing chamber. There a bath was prepared for her, and for
the first time in months Adele relaxed in blissfully warm,
scented water. Though she tried to erase her mental picture of the forest roundup, she could not. Adele kept picturing her own brother with a rope around his neck like
some beast of burden, being dragged across the ground
without regard for his welfare—all at the behest of a man
she had vowed to love. Every time she thought about
Rafe's appalling lack of compassion, Adele seethed
anew.

When the bath water grew uncomfortably cool, the
maids toweled Adele dry before the blazing hearth. She
was then offered a cup of spiced wine and triangles of
white bread spread with meat paste.

The women made a bundle of her old clothes and,

holding them at arm's length, took them to be burned. When the women reappeared, they brought a clean linen shift and an embroidered gown of Lincoln green. After they had laced her into the form-fitting gown, Adele's hair was spread over her shoulders like a cloak to dry before the fire. When her hair was dry, they brushed, then plaited the burnished tresses into two long strands interwoven with silver and purple ribbons. At the last, Adele was handed a polished steel mirror in which to admire her restored appearance.

The woman gazing back at her was like some elegant stranger. How long it had been since she had approached such magnificence? With a smile of gratitude, Adele thanked the two maids and praised their splendid handiwork.

When the women had gone, she sat alone beside the fire wondering what to do. In the sudden silence, Adele became highly aware of the blood pounding through her veins, and of the duty that had been thrust upon her. It was up to her to get Joce released, to plead his cause before the magistrates; he had no other to speak for him. Now dressed in borrowed finery, she had a far better chance of being heard. As she had already appealed to Rafe without success, Adele decided to approach Gerard Montsorrel in hopes he would listen to her.

She quickly found the lord of the castle in the solar. It was a small room above the great hall with a row of windows overlooking a well-laid-out walled garden. The solar's walls were hung with fine tapestries, and the oak chairs before the hearth had blue velvet cushions. A woman's touch was evident here, from the embroidered cloth on the table to the fringed velvet cushions covering the window seats.

"Ah, Lady Adele, I was hoping you'd join me," said Gerard, rising from his chair. "That gown has never looked better."

"Your wife's?"

"Yes . . . but I'm sure she wouldn't begrudge you."

"Is she not home?"

"Nay, more's the pity—she's always bemoaning our isolation here. She would have enjoyed your company. Unfortunately, she's gone to her sister's in Bury to help with her lying-in. Perhaps you can make her acquaintance at some other time."

"Do you not have children of your own?"

His face fell and he sighed. "Not yet. We're ever hopeful."

Adele sat in the chair he indicated, wondering how best to broach the subject. Gerard Montsorrel seemed to be a reasonable man, so she took a deep breath and began, looking close into his open face with its fine dark eyes and square-cut jaw.

"As Rafe would not listen to me, my lord, I'm beseeching you to intervene. My brother's being treated like a common criminal. If we don't do something, he will likely be hanged."

Gerard's expression sobered. He leaned forward in his chair to ask earnestly, "Why are you so sure this man is your brother, my dear?"

Adele drew back. "Because he is," she retorted, aware her answer sounded childish. "I've only one brother. It's true, we haven't seen each other in years"—she paused—"what's the matter, do you doubt me, too?"

He shook his head. "Nay, Lady, 'tis not that I doubt you. It would just be better if you discussed the matter with Ra—"

"No," she cried, jumping up. "I've already tried that, to no avail."

"Please, Lady," he began, hoping to soothe her as she swished away from him, her feet crackling on the rushes. "This matter is best discussed between the two of you. There's something very unpleasant Rafe has to tell you. Don't judge him so harshly. He's trying to spare you—"

"Spare me? He's never been overly concerned with sparing anyone's feelings in the past!" She gave him a hard look. "Very well, if you won't help me, I'll go by myself."

"Go where?" Gerard asked in alarm.

She marched to the door. "To the assizes—to plead for Joce's release. Surely you and Rafe don't own the courts also."

With that she was through the door, ignoring his call for reason. Since when did reason matter to a man determined to have his own way? She had no traveling cloak, but it was still summer and she did not expect to be gone overnight.

At the stables, the groom met her request with surprise, but he obliged and saddled Moonlight, who had been rubbed down and was enjoying a bag of oats. Within minutes Adele was clopping across the wooden bridge, out into the world, with little idea of where she was headed. If she retraced her way along the road between the poppy fields, she would reach the highway, then ride back to the crossroads and turn north. That route should eventually bring her to the place where Rafe's men had taken the prisoners.

As she rode along, Adele was aware of bees buzzing lazily in the hedgerows, seeking nectar from the twining dogrose. The sun beat down on her bare head. A welcome breeze, heavy with the scents of late summer, stirred the hair which escaped in damp tendrils across her brow. Everywhere she looked, the land appeared deserted. Finally, in the distance she saw peasants reaping in the grain fields. Did these serfs belong to Montsorrel, or even to Summerhay? She did not know where one manor ended and the other began.

Ahead through the trees she could see a steeply pitched roof, and when she rounded a bend in the road, a slate-roofed parish church came into view, its spire reaching to the top of the ancient elms. Behind the church was a yew-sheltered graveyard whose mossy stones and wooden crosses protruded from a mass of wildflowers.

Adele stopped beside the lych-gate thinking to rest a

few minutes in its dense shade, when she became aware of hoofbeats. Though still out of sight, even as she listened, she could tell the horse was picking up speed until the thudding hoofbeats became a gallop. Then, suddenly, Rafe rounded the corner.

Adele gasped in surprise and automatically kicked Moonlight's flanks, urging him on, determined not to be brought to heel like some errant child. Rafe shouted after her to stop, but she ignored him, urging her horse to greater speed. At first Moonlight was delighted by the unexpected run, for he had not galloped free for a long time; his delight, however, could not make up for his lack of conditioning as, easily winded, he began to drop back.

"No, no! Come on! We have to do better than this." Adele groaned, bending low on his neck, shouting in his ear in the hope he could understand her predicament. The skirts of her borrowed gown were bound uncomfortably tight around her ankles, and she hitched the garment higher until she partially bared her legs like some peasant wench.

It was no use. Rafe was rapidly gaining on her. Abruptly Adele wheeled off the road, heading across a poppy-filled meadow where scarlet petals flew up from beneath her horse's hooves.

Suddenly it was over. The big stallion pulled ahead, turned, and blocked her way, and though Adele cleverly tried to dodge the great beast and its angry master, poor Moonlight did not have it in him for such fancy moves. He stopped. Stubbornly he refused to go further, standing there amidst the trampled poppies, sides heaving and head hanging low.

With great annoyance, Adele turned to her captor.

Rafe grabbed her reins, his mouth a grim line. "What nonsense is this, woman? Where do you think you're going? Have you even any idea where we are?"

"I'm going to plead Joce's cause. I already know better than to ask you to do it!"

Rafe swung from the saddle. When she would have

shot away from him, he grasped her reins and brought her up short, making Moonlight snort in protest.

"Get down."

She shook her head.

"Then I'll pull you down!"

Adele squealed in protest, then cried out as he dragged her from the saddle and she fell hard against his body.

"How dare you treat me like this! I've every right to go where I please."

Rafe gripped her upper arms, making her struggles futile.

"Stop it. Just listen to me. You've not the right to kill yourself. You've no money, no protection, not even any idea where you're going."

She glared at him, her eyes flashing. She would have died rather than admit he was right. As soon as he allowed it, she stepped away from him, though he kept a detaining hand on her arm.

"I'm going to set my brother free. Though I've no map, and I'm not a man, I'm capable of riding down the road to the nearest town to speak with its magistrate."

A smile tugged at Rafe's mouth before he mastered himself.

"Granted, Lady, you have that right. I'll also agree to let you carry out your proposal—after you've heard me out. If you still wish it."

"Wish it," she snorted. "Why would I not wish it?"

"You haven't heard what I have to say yet."

"I don't know that I want to hear it," she challenged, pulling free of his grasp. She stood there, panting, angrily trying to decide what to do. He could outpace her either on horseback or on foot. She could not even defend herself against him . . .

"Looks like you've no option," he said, aware that her mental wheels were turning without success. "Do you?"

"Probably not," she finally conceded.

"Good, then come over here. I see a clean boulder that looks good enough for the Lady Adele St. Clare to sit."

Her mouth tightened and she glared at him, knowing he mocked her. He was so infuriating she could hardly stand to be with him. She seethed as she marched along, trying desperately to match his stride. He held out his hand, ushering her to the boulder as if it were a throne.

Adele perched on the edge of the rock, careful to keep away from him. She saw that Rafe had already taken off his mail and wore a red worsted tunic over an undershirt of gold. He had such garish taste, dressing more like a herald than a nobleman, she told herself, reluctant to admit he looked like a god in the regal colors. They contrasted splendidly with his black hair and olive skin.

"Well," she said, angry that he was just standing there silently. "Say what it is you have to say, so I can be on my way."

"It would go down better if you weren't so angry with me," Rafe suggested as he leaned back casually against the rock and crossed his long legs.

Adele did not trust herself to comment. She noticed he was wearing the short, red kidskin boots he had worn at Esterwold. They were hardly good riding attire. In fact, she doubted it had been his intention to go riding: likely he had been torn away from his meal to track down his escaping prey. The idea pleased her; she did not want all the inconvenience to be on her side.

"Adele," he began with a sigh. "There's really no easy way to say what I have to say. When I told you the man you call Jocelyn is really Lorkin Yates, it was the truth. He's not your brother, regardless of what he's said, or what childhood memories he may have dredged up, discovered God knows how—"

She stood up, not wanting to listen. She would not be talked out of this by a man who could so easily manipulate her emotions. He knew that, and so he could not be trusted.

"Sit down and listen," he commanded, his arm shooting out to press her back against the rock. "Whatever's been said, the truth remains—he's not your brother."

Taking a deep breath, Adele braced for battle. "You may well believe that, but I believe he is. I have it on good authority."

"And on whose is that?"

"Sir Guy Cosantine. He was my father's comrade and a neighbor who's known us all his life."

Rafe frowned, wracking his brain to fit the name to the man. "Is that the Cosantine with lands in Poitou?"

"Yes. He's a loyal friend, and I don't doubt his word."

"So, this Sir Guy was the one who took you to his hiding place?"

"Yes . . . in the woods outside Esterwold."

"When I was there?"

"Yes."

"By God—and you didn't tell me, Lady."

"Why should I? At that time we were hardly friends. Or have you forgotten?"

"No, that's something I'll not soon forget," he said peevishly. "Where's this man now?"

"I don't know. At that time he was staying at a nearby abbey."

"Then it wasn't just Yates's idea to pass himself off as your brother."

"He *is* my brother," she repeated stubbornly. "Is this all you have to give—this cross-examination? I thought you had irrefutable proof, or did you just say that to quiet me?"

His face darkened, and, surprisingly fast, Adele found herself imprisoned in his embrace.

"Damn you, Adele St. Clare, you won't let me make this easy, will you? In all this time, did you never doubt him?"

Adele glanced away from him, her heart thudding uncomfortably. Oh, yes. Doubts had crossed her mind. But Joce's explanation for the changes in his character, for his failing memory, had been the daily beatings he endured. How could she subject the man who claimed to be the boy she had once loved to any more suffering? He had pain enough, and her doubt would surely be that last straw that might send him over the—

135

"Well?"

"No—not once."

"Oh, dammit, Adele," Rafe pleaded. "Don't lie to me—I can see it in your face."

"Well, maybe his appearance seemed strange. But, after all, it's years since I saw him. He looks much older than his age. But living such a tormented life could account for that. People do change; even you must admit that."

"He's not your brother, Adele. It's no shame to admit you were taken in. I know how much you loved him and how badly you wanted it to be true. But, sweetest, this man took advantage of those feelings."

"Joce was a boy when he left. Of course I wanted him back. I longed for it with all my heart." Adele hung her head, tears dimming her vision.

Rafe swallowed uncomfortably when she finally looked up at him, her green eyes brimming with tears. He wanted to take away her pain, but he could not.

"How did they deceive me? What is your proof?" she asked, subdued now. "Tell me."

"Oh, my sweet. Lord Montsorrel reminded me of an incident we witnessed years ago at Summerhay. That night's events, and what Montsorrel learned later, make me sure that the man who says he's your brother has to be an impostor."

"But what about Sir Guy? Was he taken in also?"

Rafe shook his head. "I doubt it. Likely *he* planned the deception, for I doubt Lorkin Yates has the wit to do it. Sir Guy's not the friend you imagine.

"Anyway, at that time, the Lord of Summerhay was a drunkard. His vassals wisely kept out of his way when he was in his cups. On this night, he was cruelly taunting a young dog when a red-haired lad came forward to challenge him." He paused and looked ashamed.

"Mind you, none of us were sober—we were new returned from France and full of our victory. Anyway, this lad knocked the stick out of Lord Summerhay's hand and let the pup escape. In a rage, the old man broke a tankard over the lad's head. When he fell, he struck his head. We helped him up, trying to keep the old drunk off him—the man was virtually frothing at the mouth."

Adele stared at the scrollwork around the neck of Rafe's tunic. Somehow this story had the awful ring of truth. A red-haired lad risking his life to save a dog from cruelty sounded exactly like the Joce she had known.

"Go on—what happened?"

"Montsorrel and I brought the lad back here to keep the old bastard from flaying him, but . . . he never woke up, Adele. He died in his sleep."

A sob tore from her throat and she crushed her face against his chest. "No, Rafe, no," she protested feebly, "Oh, Joce."

He held her against him, his arms wrapped comfortingly around her trembling body. "At first we didn't know who he was. Only later did Montsorrel learn he came from a noble family. Yet he was told the lad's father was dead, that he was the last of his line. That's why he never sent word to anyone. Only after Montsorrel told me the lad's name did I realize he was your Joce."

All her hopes, her dreams, those precious memories, were torn from her. If only her hope had not been revived, this news would have been easier to accept. When at last she felt able to speak, she raised her tear-stained face to Rafe.

"Thank you," she whispered. "I'm sorry I doubted you. But I wanted it to be true, so much so that I ignored my better judgment. I feel such a fool."

"No, you're not foolish. They took advantage of your soft heart. Yates was a *routier* in some knight's employ. Cosantine must have devised the plan, probably to control Esterwold through Yates. I promise you, if ever I meet Cosantine, I'll learn the reason."

"Joce—Yates was going to ransom me, but D'Avranche wasn't at Summerhay. Three months I've been his prisoner. In a way this is not all sadness. Now I know that my own flesh and blood would not barter me for gold. It was a cruel blow to accept that my own sweet Joce cared so little for my wishes he would . . ." She bowed her head and trailed off, accepting the bitter answer to so many puzzling questions.

"Were you—did he—hurt you?" Rafe asked, tormented by his imagination.

Adele smiled faintly and shook her head. "No, but I always expected him to. His actions were most unbrotherly," she admitted, placing a finger against Rafe's mouth when he would have responded in anger. "No, let it go. It's over now, thank God."

"Aye, thank God," Rafe repeated, though she did not hear relief in his voice.

"Will he be punished?"

"Aye. There's a lot he has to answer for."

They stood locked in an embrace, the breeze stirring her hair. Adele took great comfort from Rafe's strength, for she suddenly felt emotionally drained.

"Will you show me where he's buried?" she asked after a long silence.

"Now?" he asked in surprise.

"Yes. I'd like to go there."

"If you're sure."

Adele nodded and, taking Rafe's hand, walked across the meadow to catch her horse who had wandered away to drink from a brook. To her surprise, Rafe's stallion, though untied, still waited where his master had left him.

They rode back to the highway. Neither spoke: she, was afraid she would start crying again; he, unsure what else to say to comfort her. Finally they skirted a wood and arrived before a fenced area surrounded by shrubs and bright with wildflowers.

"This is where he's buried," Rafe explained, reaching up to lift her from the saddle.

Silently they walked over the bumpy ground and entered the small cemetery. To the left, several small mounds told of infant deaths, while across the back was a row of crosses, each with a single name burned into the wood.

"Servants," Rafe supplied, answering her unspoken question.

At last he stopped before a marble headstone.

Adele gasped in surprise to see the marble statuette of a small dog crouching at the foot of the headstone.

"Montsorrel thought it fitting," Rafe explained gruffly.

Still too close to tears to speak, Adele nodded as she traced the name chiseled into the marble—Jocelyn St. Clare. She found it touching that Gerard Montsorrel had shown such compassion for an unknown boy. For a long time she stood, head bowed, thinking about the child she had known, finally laying to rest her hope for his future. Though at the time she was unaware, Joce's future had stopped long ago and far from home. Now her inability to contact him was explained. The king had probably forgotten his existence long ago. Poor Joce. Here, on this hill surrounded by birdsong, he was at peace, his final resting place peaceful and full of beauty.

Rafe appeared at her side, and she was surprised to see his arms full of poppies, for she hadn't noticed that he'd left.

"Here."

He pressed the scarlet flowers in her arms. With tears trickling down her cheeks, Adele knelt to place the wild-flowers on the mossy stone slab beside the marble dog.

"Good-bye, Joce. I'll always love you," she whispered, resting her hand on his marble guardian.

"The papal edict has been lifted, Adele. If it's important to you, we can move him to the family tomb at Esterwold."

"Yes, perhaps someday I'll do that," Adele agreed. She had been unaware the church's sanctions had been removed. What had King John done to reconcile himself with the pope? The English people could now hear Masses and receive the sacraments again. Of that she was pleased. Yet the ceremonies of the church seemed unimportant in this quiet resting place.

When she was finally ready to leave, she turned to find Rafe patiently waiting for her. Her heart filled with love for him as she slid into his protective arms.

"Come, sweet, let's go back to Montsorrel. I've a little more news you might find interesting."

"What is it?"

Rafe smiled and shook his head. "Nay. That's my secret until we sit at table with a cup of wine to toast our good fortune."

And with that explanation she had to be content.

As they rode down the slope, she looked back, seeing the scarlet poppies bright against the gray stone. In a few hours, the poppies too would be dead. And somehow she took comfort that even such beautiful things as flowers would die, but in their turn and in their way, they too had brought some happiness into the world.

At Montsorrel their evening meal was served in a smaller paneled room off the great hall, which Adele was surprised to discover was half the size of Esterwold's. Her discovery reshaped her opinion of her home, which others had always referred to as shabby and unimportant. This knight's entire fairy-tale castle could fit inside Esterwold's walls, for Montsorrel Castle was no more than a turreted keep atop a hillock surrounded by a moated lower bailey. Adele realized she need make no excuse for her home's lack of luxuries. She had done well with the limited funds she had been provided.

Though Lord Montsorrel's table was loaded with crackling roast game, molded fish pastes, and assorted sweets, Adele's appetite was small. Try as she might, she could not stop thinking about Joce's tragic death. She had already thanked Gerard for his compassion in caring for her brother and providing his final resting place, to which he gruffly assured her he was happy to do it.

Though the subject was now closed, she sat toying with her spiced capon in wine sauce, picturing Joce's smiling face, her heart aching for his loss.

Minstrels played in the gallery, their music suitably melancholy to match her mood. Several times Adele wiped tears from her eyes, unable to overcome her grief.

Rafe understood her sadness and, though he had promised to tell her some cheering news tonight, he withheld his announcement. After she had slept on the news she would feel better; she would gradually come to accept Joce's death. Until then, he could wait.

Presently Adele's head began to throb and she excused herself from the table. Rafe squeezed her hand in parting, assuring her he understood. She was grateful for his acceptance. She left the men talking over wine and followed her maids upstairs to her room.

During the next couple of days, a steady stream of visitors descended on Montsorrel, filling the bailey with their horses and servants until they crowded out the disgruntled masons. The artisans had to suspend their work until a later date.

Adele had no idea why all these men were gathered here. She saw no women, and though all were not clad in mail, their manner seemed to preclude a joyful gathering. Rafe told her he had much business to discuss with these visitors. They often talked into the wee hours, their deep voices a constant hum as she drifted to sleep.

At another time Adele might have been put out that Rafe found the men's company more important than hers, yet this enforced solitude helped her accept the pain of Joce's death, Sir Guy's treachery, and the deceit of the man she had tried to love as a brother. Now she understood her reticence toward him. When she recalled Lorkin Yates's demanding kisses and caresses, it made her shudder.

Before the week was out, as suddenly as they arrived, the mystery guests departed. When Adele got up one morning, she found the bailey empty of tents. Yet though their guests had gone, the castle still buzzed with activity as if preparing for an important event. Was Montsorrel to play host to the returning king? From snatches of conversation she overheard, Adele learned that King John had been soundly defeated overseas and his French possessions were lost. On his return, his remaining barons anticipated he would demand an exorbitant scutage to refill the royal coffers. Worse, the king would doubtless blame those who had stayed at home for his French defeat.

That morning Adele took Moonlight for a ride, galloping over the lush meadows until the horse began to tire. Adele found a clear, gurgling brook edged with watercress and she took Moonlight down the shallow bank to drink. They were both resting on the daisy-splashed grass when a long shadow fell across her. Rafe.

She knew he had come back to Montsorrel late last night; she'd heard riders and looked out her window to see his standard's glittering emblem illuminated in the flickering torchlight. With luck, Rafe would now finally explain to her what all these furtive journeys and hushed conferences meant.

"Good morrow, my lady," he said politely and made a formal bow.

"We've been apart so long you've already forgotten my name," she half joked, squinting up at him through the sunlight.

He dropped down beside her on the grass and she slid into the comfort of his arms, hugging him close. "Nay, sweeting, for it's the name of my angel," he whispered, kissing her hair, her brow. "Have you missed me?"

"Yes, very much. And I also want to tell you I'm finally over my melancholy mood, so you don't need to avoid me."

"Oh, you thought that. It wasn't my intention, love. It's just that there's so much afoot and I'm right in the middle of it," he explained, frowning. He lay back on the grass with a sigh. "There's nothing I'd like better than to stay here with you."

"And can you not?"

"Nay, I'm afraid not . . . but I do have a proposition for you."

She pulled a face as she traced her fingers over the palm of his hand, examining the callused palm, the long, elegant fingers. "What kind of proposition? I doubt it's the one I'd welcome most," she added wickedly.

He grinned at her. "How would you like to come on a pilgrimage with me?"

"A pilgrimage?" she repeated, sounding so shocked that she made him laugh.

"What's this . . . you think I'm so godless I'd never go on a pilgrimage?"

"Well, not that—but I've never thought of you as the pious, saintly variety."

"Maybe you'll have to change your opinion."

"Oh, I hope not," she whispered, burying her face in the warmth of his neck as she trailed kisses across his warm flesh. He groaned, and the heat of his flesh tantalized her. They had not made love in months—or even kissed. Somehow, it had always seemed wrong. Suddenly, with his skin burning her lips, everything felt so very right.

"No one said I'd take a vow of celibacy," he assured her, hugging her close, his mouth caressing her cheek.

"That's a relief, my love." She sighed, sliding her hands over the breadth of his square shoulders. "For I've been very lonely of late."

Rafe gathered her to him, and her pulse throbbed in time to the beat of his own heart. "I know—I'm sorry I neglected you. I promise to do much better, if you come with me."

"But you're going regardless?"

"I must."

Adele drew back, looking closely in his face. "This sounds a very strange pilgrimage. Why must you go, and where is it we're going?"

His grim expression dissolved in a smile of relief. "Then you're coming?"

"Try to stop me."

Rafe hugged her to him, laughing. "Oh, sweet, I'm so happy. Unfortunately, I can't promise many female companions; it will be mostly men. And we're going to St. Edmundsbury."

"That's where Gerard's wife is staying."

"Oh, is it?" Rafe asked absentmindedly.

Eyes narrowed, Adele drew back, aware he was no longer in tune with her physically. "What is it? This is no ordinary pilgrimage, is it?"

Rafe looked sharply at her and finally shook his head. "No, and for your own good I will tell you no more. We'll enjoy our journey as simple pilgrims."

Though his explanation was far from satisfying, Adele realized it was all she was going to get.

"When do we leave?"

"This afternoon."

She gasped and pulled back. "So soon! Why didn't you tell me sooner?"

"Because I didn't know. What difference does it make? After all, my lady, you've so many gowns and jewels to be packed . . ."

Laughing at his sarcasm, Adele playfully cuffed him across the head, and Rafe caught her hands, imprisoning them in his own. "This will be a continuation of that journey I once told you I longed to take."

"Traveling together for all eternity?" she repeated, a chill going down her spine at an ominous thought. "Nay, Rafe, I'd rather we stayed in one place together."

"Oh, we shall someday, I promise."

"What was the wonderful news you had to tell me? Surely not this?"

"Nay, it's much better than this."

She waited expectantly as he drew her to her feet.

"Don't keep me in suspense. Come on, what is it?"

"Hugh D'Avranche has insulted our gracious king by leaving France without permission and . . . what does that mean?"

Adele gasped in delight. "King John will be furious?"
"Yes!"

"Oh, how wonderful! But how long will it last?"

"I hope for as long as we need. Meanwhile, I'll do my best to ingratiate myself with our monarch on his return." *If fate allows,* he added silently.

They hugged, and he looked out across the green meadows to the woods beyond where the trees were already changing color. Autumn was beginning to slip across the land.

Dear God, he thought. *If fate allows.* Now, when things were beginning to go in his favor, a new and very treasonous threat had reared its head. Worse, he did not know if he could stay out of this quarrel, balancing loyalty and good sense, or if he would make a stand from which there could be no return. For beneath those somber penitents' hoods adorning the faithful pilgrims who would converge on St. Edmundsbury would be the faces of men who were not going simply to pray.

"Come along," he said with a slight feeling of regret. He had to tamp down his lust for now. "We must prepare."

Chapter Nine

Through leafy lanes and besides meandering streams the pilgrims rode. Flocks of birds scavenging in the bare autumn wheatfields were startled into beating, cawing flight by the clop of hooves. On the hedgerows, silky white bindweed grew amidst a tangle of brambles and scarlet rose hips. Here nuts and berries grew in abundance, and the pilgrims gathered hazelnuts and late blackberries to eat as they traveled. There was a nip in the morning air.

On the whole, since they had set out the weather had been fair, making this a very pleasant journey through the peaceful Sussex countryside. The days had grown shorter and, today, morning mist lingered under the trees. The advancing season had painted the leaves russet and gold. Blazing copper beeches and bracken sprang up beside the road, colorful additions to the landscape, reminders that the year was drawing to a close.

Adele had enjoyed this pilgrimage far more than the ride from Esterwold, though that journey had provided her happiest time. She smiled as she recalled that passionate, stolen night in the crowded inn. She had anticipated a repeat of that glorious night on this journey, but as of yet, he had not touched her.

As Rafe had warned, there were few women on the pilgrimage: four others beside herself; two of those were servants. To Adele's disappointment, she found she was expected to share a room with them. Fortunately, during the day, the women stayed together. Each morning, she gladly exchanged their silly chat for Rafe's company. Only at the end of each day did they seek her out, and she would reluctantly join them in their crowded communal room. At first Adele had been annoyed by this unexpected arrangement, but she soon discovered it was customary. She had since become resigned to it.

Though she had consoled herself with the promise of stealing a few hours alone on the journey, of slipping away to make love in some romantic woodland glade, it hadn't yet happened. Each day, men rode beside Rafe as, heads down, they discussed very serious business. Their rest stops were always brief and unsuitable for any such actions. Adele had contented herself with fleeting embraces and a stolen kiss.

Though these other travelers were strangers to her, Rafe appeared to know them all. That in itself seemed odd, for Adele had expected a band of pilgrims to be mostly strangers. These men all wore somber garments, keeping their faces hidden inside their hoods, yet she suspected that most of them would feel more at home in chain mail. Curiously, these pilgrims' horses were of the finest stock and their elaborate saddles were too splendid for common men.

As they drew closer to St. Edmundsbury, the pilgrims' number swelled. Adele also sensed an undercurrent of something far removed from religious fervor. Their collective emotion reminded her of the shared excitement her father's soldiers had felt preceding a battle.

There was a large group of riders who always held

back from the rest, maintaining a discreet distance until nightfall. Were they menservants or soldiers? When she saw the gleam of steel under one of the men's cloak, she decided it had to be the latter.

Stranger still, when Adele questioned Rafe about his fellows' identities, voicing her suspicions about their armor and intent, Rafe quickly put his finger against her lips.

"Hush, sweet—there's nothing to be gained by knowing more." They stood in the innyard of the Crown and Mitre. "There, see? Likely they're here to take part in the tournament," he said, pointing to a notice board in the yard which suddenly caught his eye.

Adele sighed in exasperation, aware that Rafe had no intention of explaining matters further. She decided not to question him about the other pilgrims again, though she noticed the decidedly furtive actions of some of these latest pilgrims. The men always kept to the shadows, hoods pulled low on their brow as if they did not want to be recognized. Rafe was likely right, some of the men in armor were surely future contestants in the upcoming tournament. But, if that were the case, why did they pretend to be pilgrims?

The smell of roast meat and the clatter of dishes greeted them as they entered the inn's crowded common room that night. A few of their fellow travelers had already discarded their rough woolen garments and openly sported embroidered gloves and silken hose, further belying their guise as simple men.

Adele and Rafe still wore their plain dark cloaks, and they easily blended into the crowd of pilgrims which now contained the scrofulous and the lame. She was not surprised. She knew the infirm journeyed to the saint's shrine to seek a miraculous cure, but what was the motive of the noblemen in disguise with whom they had traveled?

Rafe led Adele to an empty place at a long table near the hearth. Adele looked in vain for the other women.

Dared she hope they lodged at another inn? The road to St. Edmund's shrine was crammed with inns and hostels all catering to pilgrims. In fact, had it not been for Rafe's foresight in sending a swift rider ahead to secure a room, they themselves might have been sleeping in the stables tonight.

Between them Rafe and Adele shared a trencher of thick stale bread heaped with sliced meat and spicy gravy. There was also a bowl of hearty pottage of lentils and wheat bread spread with honey. As she ate, Rafe filled Adele's cup with cider.

Unable to stand the suspense any longer, she finally had to ask. "Where are the other women staying tonight?"

"Surely you don't miss them already."

"No, I just wanted to know," she replied, hoping they would not suddenly appear. She chewed a piece of meat until it became flavorless. "Where am I to stay tonight?" she asked him breathlessly.

Rafe had turned to face her on the bench they shared, unable to keep a grin off his face. "Oh, I think you can guess."

Adele's heart lurched and her pulse quickened. She looked at him, seeing the blatant invitation in his eyes. Suddenly, she could not stop smiling either. They sat there looking at each other, both grinning like idiots while they relished arousing memories.

"You shock me, breaking your holy vow of celibacy. I have to admit, had I thought I'd share a room with those other women instead of you, I wouldn't have been as eager to come."

Rafe gently stroked her face, gazing intently into her green eyes. As he grazed her cheekbones with his thumbs, he said, "It was worth it, my love, if only to enjoy tonight."

"Then let's not waste another minute."

Rafe's irises were dark in the firelight, his eyelids heavy as he lazily ran his fingers along her cheek and down her chin before his hand came to rest at the neck of her gown. Aching with longing for his touch, Adele soundlessly urged him to explore further, wanting him to slide his hand inside her cloak and touch her swelling breasts. But, ever mindful of the eyes that might watch their every move in this crowded room, Rafe restrained himself.

"I've arranged a bath," he revealed. He had drained his cider cup and pushed away their little leftover food. "But they tell me there are no maids to assist us."

Adele's heart leapt as she read his thoughts. When she spoke, her voice was faint with excitement. "If you'll play servant, my lord, I'll be your lady fair," she offered, her hand stealing under his cloak to grasp his hard-muscled thigh.

"Now that's my kind of bargain."

When Rafe rose, his men, who were sitting at another table, stood also. As one, they exited the noisy common room. Rafe gave the men brief instructions about the care of his horses and tomorrow's plans; then four soldiers tramped outside to the stable. The remaining two followed Rafe and Adele upstairs to position themselves outside their master's door.

Their firelit room was nestled under the inn's thatched eaves. A feather bed heaped with covers, and a wooden chest holding lighted candles, comprised the sparse furnishings. Deep-set in an unadorned whitewashed wall were two small shuttered windows overlooking the innyard.

No sooner had they entered the room than a knock on the door announced the arrival of servants, who carried in a wooden tub and set it before the hearth. Following the men came a procession of women each bearing steaming jugs of water. The contents of the jugs only filled the bath about six inches deep, but a steadily arriving stream of hot water continued until the bath was half full. On the final trip, a little lad brought up the rear of the procession, struggling beneath an armload of towels.

Rafe glanced outside to make sure all the servants

were gone before he shut and latched the door. Then he held out his arms to Adele, and they spun about the room dancing to a tune of their own making, repeatedly circling the steaming tub in which handfuls of scented rose petals floated.

"Alone at last," he breathed into her hair as he held her against him, halting their dizzying dance. "Oh, Adele, sweetheart, how I've longed to have you in my arms, to be able to kiss and cherish you. Dear God, it seems as if we've been an eternity apart."

"I treasure that wonderful night we made love at that other inn," she whispered, upturning her face for his kiss. "Those memories kept my hope alive."

He held her close, burying his face in her hair, breathing in the longed-for scent of her body. "If I'd thought we'd never meet again, I don't think I could have gone on," he revealed, surprising even himself by the depth of his emotion. "I vowed to search the country from end to end until I found you. Thank God I did."

"All my prayers have finally been answered. Oh, Rafe, please, please, don't ever leave me again."

"I won't, I promise. We'll stay together even if I have to fight the world to keep you."

His words sent a shiver of foreboding along her spine. "No. Let us love in peace, not war."

He tilted her chin, holding up her face to his. "If God wills it," was all he said. Then, forcing a smile, he pulled her against him. "After all, we're in the right city for miracles."

"Then I'll ask holy Edmund to keep us together. What do *you* pray for on the pilgrimage?"

Caught off guard by her question, Rafe drew back. He had no plea for the saint, having spared little thought for aught beyond the completion of this mission. "There is much to request," he admitted as he released her. "Come, sweet, we must have our bath before it gets cold. You shall be first, my Princess Flame."

Thus saying, Rafe pulled out the pin which held her

plaits, separating the neat braids until her glorious auburn hair hung free about her shoulders in a shining cloud.

"We've no soap," she discovered in dismay, finding only the folded stack of towels beside the bath.

"Yes—there's some in my bags," he said as he bent to stoke the fire.

Adele unbuckled the strap of Rafe's leather saddlebag and reached inside, quickly drawing back as she felt knives inside. Three or four sheathed daggers were bound together with a leather thong. Why had Rafe brought hidden weapons with him? she wondered, chilled by her discovery.

Already, the strange behavior of their fellow pilgrims pointed to something far more sinister at work than a pilgrimage to a sacred shrine. Uneasily, Adele reached past the weapons to the oiled cloth pouch holding his razor, soap, and flannel.

Rafe watched her, aware, by her body language, that she had found his daggers. Adele did not mention it to him, though. Tomorrow, when the meeting to decide England's fate was over, he would tell her what lay ahead. Until then, he hoped she would presume the weapons were to be used in the upcoming tournament, to be held here.

In truth, the first he had known about the event was when he'd read the announcement in the innyard, but Adele didn't know that. Fulke FitzAlan was sponsoring the event, and as he was Montsorrel's brother-in-law, there was no way Rafe could beg off taking part—he was too well known as a skillful competitor.

Without comment, Rafe took the oiled cloth bag and laid its contents on the wooden chest beside the candles.

"Let me do that," he suggested when he saw Adele struggling to pull off her short boot.

Rafe knelt before her and eased off her footwear. He massaged her slender feet, then stroked the entire length of her leg until Adele was shivering in delight. Her anticipation heightened as his warm hands moved higher. The action continued on the pretext of taking off her silk hose, yet there was far too much caressing, far too much deliberate arousal, for such a simple task. Shaking with passion, Adele clasped Rafe about the neck and rested her head against his, for, in passing and seemingly quite by accident, his hot fingers had grazed the pulsating place between her legs. She ached for more. Rafe neatly rolled down her stockings, pretending to be wholly absorbed in his task.

At his command, Adele stood obediently, turning around so he could unlace her gown. The hot, unexpected pressure of his mouth against the nape of her neck excited her, and weakly Adele leaned back against him. He slowly peeled down her gown to expose her thin shift, the dark green wool slithering to rest around her curving hips.

Unable to stay unmoved by this tantalizing game, Adele swiftly turned in his embrace and pressed her aching breasts against his chest—wanting to arouse him, urging him to caress her before she went insane. Rafe cupped her breasts, and she strained toward him. When his mouth covered her hardened nipple, drawing on the pink flesh, Adele shuddered with delight. He took the weight of her full breasts in both hands, gently caressing her flesh before he gradually increased the pressure. She thrust eagerly closer.

Without conscious movement, Adele suddenly discovered she was pressed against the bed; the heaped feather mattresses offered cushioned support for her straining hips. Her desire now mirrored in Rafe's eyes. Urgently Adele tugged at his tunic, lifting it above his waist.

He pressed against her, and the pressure of his arousal increased her desire until she was shaking with passion. With a look of relief, Rafe unleashed his bursting, swollen member from his constricting clothes and thrust her skirts out of the way. With a gasp of delight, Adele strained on tiptoes, helping him maneuver his swollen flesh to the place where she burned for him. With a strangled cry of passion held too long in check, Adele sheathed him in her body. Her nerves caught fire. She dug her fingers into his crumpled tunic, clutching the cloth as she moaned in delight, abandoning herself to the all-consuming blaze of their desire.

Adele's eyes widened as he withdrew, then again drove himself to the hilt in her feverish flesh. Their aching mouths were bruised with passion and they moved as one to achieve the blinding, searing release. It was spent in a moment, leaving them weak and panting.

Dark circles had spread beneath Adele's eyes and her soft mouth was swollen with the intensity of their joining. Rafe held her close, fighting to draw an even breath.

"Oh, sweet, that wasn't what I intended," he whispered remorsefully as he stroked back her damp, tangled hair.

"Nay? It was a wonderful way to begin the night," she assured him breathlessly, nuzzling his neck and tasting the salt of his sweat. "Now we can enjoy a far more leisurely bath."

He laughed at her words. "Aye, that's true, for I was wondering how I could endure looking at your lovely body and keep my distance."

"Well, you see, we've already solved that problem for you."

"I wouldn't say it was solved," he corrected, gathering her in his arms. He carried her to the bath. "Only temporarily quenched."

She laughed and laid her flushed face in the hollow of his neck. Unable to resist, Adele traced her tongue over his smooth flesh, tantalizing him until he finally set her down beside the bath. Pressing her mouth against his in a small, chaste kiss, Adele quickly squirmed out of her garments and kicked them aside. Rafe's swift intake of breath when he finally saw her naked in the firelight made her smile.

After first testing the temperature of the water, Adele stepped into the bath, snapping her fingers. Rafe stood there mesmerized. "Come on, lad, be quick, fetch the soap," she commanded.

Rafe did as he was bid. Before he gave her the soap, though, he quickly stripped off his tunic and shirt, his boots and hose following.

Not expecting that, Adele gulped and tried to keep her attention on the bath. She soaped her hair and rinsed off the suds. Rafe obediently lathered her back, and she playfully slapped his hands when they wandered to her breasts. At his touch, her nipples peeked just above the water. Adele slithered lower to remove the temptation from him, and she rested her shapely ankles on the end of the bath. Obediently, Rafe went to lather her feet, then gently pushed her legs back into the water to rinse them. It forced her to sit up straight and again reveal her breasts.

Laughing at his guile, she chided him and pulled him closer, no longer able to ignore his growing arousal. So tempting was it and so close to her mouth, she leaned over to kiss its swelling pink tip. Then she took his pulsing flesh in her wet hand, slowly caressing its length. With a shudder, Rafe pulled away.

"Do you want to bathe, my lady, or do you want to stay dirty?" he growled, a dangerous gleam in his eye.

Her bath was finished, and Rafe held out towels for her. As soon as she stepped from the bath, she was encased in the luxury of towels warmed by the fire, yet she relished the intangible heat of his devotion far more. Tonight she felt completely cherished and blissfully happy. All the lonely abandonment of the long summer slipped away. For months she had hoped and prayed for a night like this. Her prayers had been answered.

Adele leaned against him and, wrapped in her cocoon of towels, she uttered a deep sigh of contentment. "Oh, Rafe, I'm so happy tonight. I love you."

He clasped her chin, turning her to face him. The blissful warmth of his tender kiss drew the strength from her body. She would have fallen had he not supported her with his arm.

"My Adele . . . I love you more than life itself," he

whispered. Rafe clasped her against him as if he would never let her go.

"Come now, it's your turn to play servant. Did you approve of my ministrations, my lady?"

"Yes. In fact, I might insist on my every bath being so . . ." She sought a word, distracted by his steel-hard thighs and hips pressing against hers with only a towel between them. "Cleansing," she ended breathlessly.

Rafe frowned. "Only if you always bathe with me—at home."

She smiled, wondering if he was aware he had referred to his castle as their *home*. "Yes, love, that's my dearest wish," she agreed. She looped a towel around her body and wrapped a second about her wet hair. "Come, my lord, get in the bath. Your maid's waiting.

Rafe slipped into the water.

She stood behind him to soap his hair and neck. How lovely it was to slide her hands over his smooth skin and feel the thick muscles and sinews beneath. Again she admired the hard, square breadth of his shoulders. Rafe's physique was impressive, beautiful despite the puckered scars which reminded her that he was a warrior. At least Rafe's wounds were healed; she would pray to the Blessed Mother to always keep her beloved safe. Returning to her task, she discovered that when wet, his black curly hair almost reached his shoulders. She threaded her hands in its thickness, entranced by its full soft weight.

Rafe stood and she swallowed hard, finding it increasingly difficult to concentrate. Lathering his narrow waist, his flat belly, the pronounced musculature of his chest, had all been difficult, but this was the hardest task yet. Adele slid the soap across his firm buttocks and sinewed thighs, delaying the inevitable as she tried in vain to control her thoughts.

His arousal was impossible to ignore. Dutifully she soaped the area, shivering with desire as she slid her hands along his swelling flesh. Pleased with his shudders of pleasure, she caressed its length with her fingers and admired the velvet texture of its tip. Beneath her gentle ministrations, his erection had grown until, at last, Rafe was forced to take the soap from her.

He grinned. "All right, woman, this is far too much pleasure for both of us. If I'm ever to finish my bath, I'd better take care of this part myself."

Adele stuck out her tongue at him, but when Rafe tried to grab her, she skipped out of reach. Using a pitcher the maids had left, she filled it with water and poured it over him to rinse off the soap suds. She watched as it trickled over his muscular frame, the water reflecting the hearth's golden glow, creating a gilded statue come to life. Adele swallowed at the sight, catching her lower lip between her teeth. This mutual bathing was far more delightful than she had expected.

Splashing a great deal of water onto the floor, Rafe stepped from the bath and motioned to Adele to bring him towels. He waited dripping before the hearth.

"You're a scurvy wench," he reprimanded. "I shall tell the landlord I'm most displeased with you . . . slow to obey, insolent, too much staring . . . and far too much fondling."

She threw a towel at him and he caught it, with a laugh. Between them, they soon had toweled him dry until his body glowed with a heat that owed nothing to the fire.

"Sometimes I think I must be dreaming," Adele whispered as Rafe picked her up and carried her to the bed.

"I'm no dream, Adele."

"I know, and I give thanks for it," she whispered, nibbling his ear. "Once I was in awe of you . . . of your power. People said you'd order a man hanged as readily as look at him."

"And you believed them?"

"Well, I didn't know you then."

He leaned over to lay her on the bed, but she clung to his neck, refusing to let him go until she had pulled him down beside her. They fell together in a heap of downy bedcovers, rolling over on the large bed until he lay atop her.

"And now you know me—probably better than any woman alive, I might add. What say you now?"

"I say that underneath your facade you're the most wonderful man alive."

He frowned. "What facade?"

"Your warrior-lord facade—that unblinking, unyielding knight in the mail coat who rides roughshod over his enemies, who—"

"All right, all right, I understand." He grimaced as he gently put his finger to her lips to silence her. "Sweet, if ever I showed the side of me you know to my enemies, I wouldn't stay alive five minutes. Yes, I suppose I come across as tough, hard—unyielding, if you will. But I have to. Those attributes win battles and other men's allegiance—"

"And hot kisses and caresses only win a woman's allegiance—is that what you're saying?"

"Something like that. That I have yours is all I care about."

"Oh, love, you'll always have mine."

Rafe held her close, gently kissing her face, her closed eye lids, her trembling lips. Adele did not understand the way of men. She didn't understand his need to maintain his air of invulnerability merely to stay alive. And he hoped she need never have to learn.

Pushing aside the troubling thoughts which threatened to crowd out his happiness, Rafe slid his hands over her back to her curving hips and he caressed the silken mounds of her buttocks. Tonight, at least, Adele was his.

"Now, sweetheart, let's begin the night as I intended," Rafe suggested, propping himself on his elbow so he could admire the pale perfection of her body. He desired her, for she was everything a man could want, yet there was more than that. His heart lurched and began a frenzied beat whenever he considered the depth of his emotion for Adele. This was love, just the way the poets described, a sheer insanity he had never believed existed.

"Why do you look so serious?" she asked, tracing her finger through the tangled hair on his chest.

"I swear my deepest love for you, for the rest of my days," he breathed, a catch in his voice.

"And I for you, Rafe, my love," Adele whispered, her eyes misting with tears.

"To plight my troth, I give you this," he said, reaching beneath the pillows for the ring he'd placed there earlier. In their love play they had displaced the feather pillows and he had to scrabble about before he found it.

Glinting in the mingled firelight and candleglow, the narrow gold band's engraved design decorated in enamel made Adele gasp with delight. Rafe slid the ring on her finger, and she thought she would melt with happiness. At this moment, all fears for the future were forgotten. He did not matter that their future together was uncertain, or that another man had been affianced to her. Rafe had pledged her his heart, and that was the most wonderful gift she had ever received.

Chapter Ten

The autumn night was chill as Rafe hurried through the dark streets to the abbey church of Saint Edmund. He was aware of other dark-cloaked figures emerging from the shadows, some hugging the walls of the overhanging buildings while others boldly walked through the cobbled streets.

Rafe passed a tavern whose patrons' raucous laughter and drunken songs echoed out into the narrow street. A lantern hung below the inn's creaking sign, shedding a welcome pool of light over the damp cobbles. Ahead loomed the massive bulk of the abbey church.

It was long after compline and the church looked deserted, its great bronze doors shut tight and no light showing from inside its thick walls. Yet appearances were deceiving. Within those hallowed stone walls, Rafe knew a treasonous meeting would shortly take place, as some of the most powerful barons in the realm gathered to decide England's fate.

Rafe followed the other dark figures around the build-

ing to a side door. There they were admitted by a Bene-
dictine brother, his tonsured head gleaming in the light
from a cresset mounted on the wall behind him.

Each man gave his name and rank before he entered
the church's lofty vaulted nave. Rafe glanced about for
damage; he had heard of a great fire which had taken
place here in King Stephen's day, but all appeared in
good repair.

A group of men were talking near the sanctuary, heads
down and voices low. Rafe headed toward them, recognizing several faces. These men had already shed their
costumes, and the steel of their mail hauberks glinted in
the light from the altar. Several prelates resplendent in
brocade vestments had appeared. Beside earls and bish-
ops stood men in homespun and fustian, or the plain
black cassocks of parish priests. Many had just cause to
hate the king.

"De Montford."

Eustace de Vesci, Lord of Alnwick, stepped out of the
group to greet him. Grim-faced, they clasped hands. This
lord of Northumberland was one of King John's
staunchest foes. In the north, de Vesci's influence was far-
reaching, and his open refusal to pay scutage as penalty
for not accompanying the king of France had made him a
hero amongst his overburdened neighbors.

In the shadow of a pillar stood Fitzwalter of Dunmow
and his son-in-law, De Mandeville, Earl of Essex. Beside
them was Henry Bohun, Earl of Hereford, a distant relative of Esterwold's castellan; Geoffrey De Say; representatives from the great houses of Clare and Bigod; the
Bishop of Hereford: Rafe's mental accounting seemed a
roll of England's mightiest men. Yet on second glance, he
saw mostly a preponderance of northern lords—the great
houses of the south had sent only sons and nephews.
Likely the lords of those manors had stayed safe at home,
reluctant to openly commit rebellion until they knew
which way the wind blew.

Inside the church, it was chill and dank as a tomb, the

candle flames dancing in the fierce draft that filled the building. Like many others, Rafe tucked his cold hands under his armpits as he paced about, waiting for the proceedings to begin. Such gatherings were not new, for several years ago, many of these same men had plotted to murder their hated king.

Before, Rafe had chosen not to side with them, though he had listened to their arguments. His pointed reminder that John was King Henry's son and their rightful sovereign, and that they had all sworn an oath of fealty to the crown, had not been well received. Instead, the rebels had planned to install John's nephew, Arthur of Brittany, as the new king. But Arthur had mysteriously disappeared. Most now presumed he was dead, murdered either by John's own hand or by one of his minions. It seemed wise that he had not supported them.

Given his past actions, Rafe wondered why he had been invited here tonight. Was it because he held lands in the north and wielded much power there? Still, compared to some of these malcontents, he was a minor force.

Or was it because they recognized that his allegiance had wavered? Recently, he had come to regard these conspirators less like hotheads bent on rebellion, and more like men pushed beyond endurance. Fined for the slightest offense, robbed of land and honors so that John could reward the common soldiers who fought for him, England's barons had reached their boiling point with just cause.

Out of the corner of his eye, he saw his friend Montsorrel wave to him and pick his way through the assembly to stand beside him. Surveying the crowd, Rafe was at first surprised to see Hugh D'Avranche and his brother Giles, yet, given D'Avranche's recent reputed disobedience, it seemed less odd. With a monarch as mercurial as John, friendship was a fleeting thing. Rafe debated drawing D'Avranche aside to explain his feelings for Adele, but decided this was neither the time nor place to plead his case.

Stephen Langton, Archbishop of Canterbury, stood and spoke for the clergy—trying as usual to maintain a precarious balance between factions. Rafe leaned more toward Langton's viewpoint than that of the more radical faction; there had to be a way to curb John's power without murdering him.

One by one, the barons stepped forward to air their grievances. Their charges ran the gamut from indebtedness to the king, whose trickery sought to enslave them all, to more serious charges of seduced wives and daughters. It continued until Rafe grew weary of the recounting. It was clear that the barons felt that John had overstepped his rights as king—rights which his father Henry II had agreed to by charter. Perhaps they could convince their monarch to sign a new one.

As the hours dragged by, Rafe grew more anxious to return to Adele. She had raised her brows questioningly when he said he must go out at this late hour, probably suspecting him of meeting another woman, until he'd donned his leather gambeson and thrust a brace of daggers into his belt. It was then that she'd seemed to understand that he was off to do what he had come to do, and that it had little to do with religious fervor.

Rafe peered around at his fellows. Not having studied the barons' new charter, Rafe was hesitant to accept it. From what he'd heard, it dealt with reducing royal rights over inheritance and the payment of scutage. It also curbed John's sweeping injustices and reduced the scope of the king's forestry laws. With the twelve items stated he found no fault, but to his mind, this charter did not go far enough to repair the damage inflicted by the king's trickery and deceit. But the others seemed to deem it fit.

One by one, starting with the most eminent amongst them, the mighty men knelt before the high altar and swore to go to war against King John if he would not sign their charter.

Not all men were eager to make that vow, though. Some slipped away in the shadows, unwilling to join the rebellion. Rafe and Gerard Montsorrel stood in the aisle beside a marble pillar, contemplating the wisdom of the move. Though not beloved by his king, Rafe had given his oath to support him; in breaking that vow by swearing to take up arms against King John, he would be committing treason. Was he ready for that?

He doubted the king would be overjoyed when he learned Rafe was claiming Adele for his own. That her intended groom was no longer in favor made little difference. The price of disobedience to this monarch was always high.

Rafe sighed. He had little affection for this sly little king in his high-heeled boots, who appeared without warning in the far-flung corners of his realm hoping to catch his barons at some fineable offense, but he would not commit treason by taking up arms against him. However despicable and cowardly, however unworthy of the crown, John Lackland was still England's anointed king.

As one, Rafe and Montsorrel reached that same conclusion, moving off into the gloomy nether regions of the nave, while at the high altar the swearing of those treasonous oaths continued. Rafe quietly unlatched a small wooden door and they stepped out into the dark street. He would not join the rebels, but neither would he betray them.

Gerard clasped his hand in parting before heading in the opposite direction, bound for the town house of his brother-in-law, Fulke FitzAlan. Tomorrow he and Rafe would take part in the tournament, and perhaps rethink their decision to remain neutral in this growing storm. Tonight they would snatch what sleep they could.

Returning to the inn, Rafe let himself inside his room, shivering in pleasure as a wave of heat from the fire enveloped him. The November night had turned cold, with a nip of frost in the air.

Seeing the mound of Adele's body under the covers made his heart lurch with joy, yet Rafe was no longer sure he had made tonight's judgment based solely upon what was right considering his vow of allegiance to the king. Suddenly, he feared that some part of him had hoped that his continued allegiance to John would be rewarded with Adele's hand in marriage.

This confounded honesty and soul-searching was a curse, Rafe grumbled silently as he slid into the feather bed. In her sleep Adele moved instinctively toward him, soft and smooth, her bright hair billowing out around her. Rafe cradled her gently in his arms, discovering his peace and contentment slowly returning as she snuggled against him. He would not wake her. Holding her close was enough tonight. There were many grave issues on his mind, their collective weight dampening his passion.

Tomorrow FitzAlan's tournament would allow his fellow nobles to let off steam in mock battles before girding themselves for the real thing. He had to sleep, for it was a fool's task to take part in even a sporting fight when tired—yet, for all his efforts, thoughts surged through his mind as he weighed the pros and cons of upholding his oath to the king. To disobey the man's wishes was one thing—to plot his downfall was a far more serious matter. It kept Rafe awake until the early hours of the morning.

Adele admired Saint Edmund's church with its carved rood screen and marble pillars decorated with stone lace. The gold altarpieces glittered in the light from a dozen tall white candles. The intricate vaulted ceiling arched so high that she could finally understand why the serfs thought church roofs reached into heaven.

Morning Mass was over, and the congregation quickly dispersed. Adele knelt beside Barbara, Gerard Montsorrel's wife, in a side chapel. Purportedly, the healing water from Saint Edmund's shrine had the power to make women fertile. Lady Montsorrel, who desperately craved a child, had drunk several cups from the shrine and now prayed hard and long as she beseeched holy Edmund to perform the miracle he had granted others.

Out of the corner of her eye Adele saw Rafe and Gerard exit through the stone arched door into the sunlight outside, heads down as they discussed some important issue. She had hoped the men would wait for them, but they had already tired of the inactivity and were eager to prepare for the tournament.

Barbara continued to pray as Adele shifted her aching knees on the padded velvet kneeler. Rafe's expedition last night had rekindled Adele's curiosity about the reasons for this pilgrimage, but because he had told her it could be dangerous for her to know more, she had held her tongue. She disliked the furrows deepening on his brow, though, and the growing solemnity of his expression. Rafe was not solemn with her, the man she knew laughed often. Even their lovemaking—they indulged now whenever the opportunity presented itself was sprinkled with laugher. Rafe had become her friend as well as her lover. And the growing darkness of his mood threatened that.

"Ave Maria . . ."

Adele sighed softly as Barbara began another Hail Mary. Inside the church the nose-prickling scent of incense was so strong she wanted to sneeze. Adele glanced about and saw that each small chapel had its own bank of flickering candles lit by the faithful who beseeched their special saint for favors. If she lit a candle and prayed for the return of Rafe's lightheartedness, would it be granted? Her request sounded so frivolous compared to the more serious needs of others that Adele felt ashamed even to have contemplated it.

Finally, Barbara was ready to leave. The women rose, groaning, stiff after kneeling so long. Barbara smiled wanly at Adele, her pale face tear-stained after her anguished petition. Even after weeping, Adele thought her friend looked lovely as a princess. Barbara's dark hair was plaited inside a jeweled crespine, a gold filet resting on her pale brow.

The women adjusted their cloaks before heading outside. The dark worsted garments lined with marten fur were all they had to keep out the drafts and bone-numbing chill of November air.

Adele squeezed Barbara's hand in comfort, finding her soft white fingers delicate as a child's. This woman had become a true friend. Barbara had insisted on giving Adele more gowns after she had learned all her clothing had gone to Fordham on the baggage wagon. The woman's unexpected generosity had both surprised and delighted Adele. At last she could take her rightful place amongst the other well-born ladies without feeling like a shabby kitchen wench.

Barbara's maid and a manservant had accompanied them to Mass and they now waited patiently beside the door. Outside, the sick and the lame thronged. Some were carried on pallets, others hobbled along the street on crutches. A chorus of hacking coughs filled the air, the sounds mingling with the wails of sick children and the monotonous chanting of the pious. Adele was thankful to be leaving the depressing scene behind.

Nodding to the two servants to follow them, Adele hurried the softhearted Barbara past the row of scrofulous beggars who had taken up their regular places on either side of the church's brass door. Adele continued to walk along the cobbled street, deaf to their constant whines for alms. It was not that her heart was hard, but she had been outraged to find these same cripples tippling ale at the Crown and Mitre, their deformities forgotten. Rafe had made Adele aware of several other ruses used by these malingerers—like rubbing beggar's weed on their limbs to cause ulcers, or borrowing deformed or sickly infants to play on the sympathies of the visiting pilgrims.

Once Adele and Barbara left Saint Edmund's precincts, the crowd thinned out, allowing them to move quickly through the streets to the FitzAlan house. There, Barbara's sister Margaret was waiting for them.

Adele and Rafe had also been invited to stay in the FitzAlans' home instead of sleeping at the Crown and Mitre Inn. Though Gerard and Rafe were good friends and she liked Barbara, Adele was not fond of the haughty Margaret or her pompous husband. Nor did she enjoy watching what she perceived to be Margaret's insensitive treatment of her younger sister. Undoubtedly, seeing Margaret's new baby had brought Barbara joy, but Adele could not help feeling that the newborn was too painful a reminder of Lady Montsorrel's own empty womb.

The FitzAlan house was impressive, and so large it filled half the south side of the street. The house's bulging upper stories overhanging the narrow street were painted blue and red and decorated with gold, as were the carved figures of the archangels, gold wings outstretched, that stood guard on either side of the entrance. In the front solar was a splendid glazed window with many panes, its greenish glass filtering daylight in a murky haze. This large, magnificent window advertised the extent of the FitzAlans' wealth as little else could do, and had become such a local wonder, that people stood in the street below to admire it.

As the women entered the darkened house they were met by Margaret's child's wails, the sound so shrill it pierced Adele's ears and she could not shut it out. Barbara flinched as the cries continued, and Adele tried to direct her friend's attention away from the baby.

"Are we to walk to the tournament?" she asked loudly, wishing the wet nurse would come to quiet the infant's hungry cries.

Barbara smiled wanly, aware of Adele's concern and loving her the more for it. "Nay, we're going in style. Gerard's having your horse brought over from the inn. I'd almost forgotten the tournament is today."

"How could you forget?" Adele squeaked. "I've never even been to one. I hope Rafe, or Gerard, doesn't get hurt. Is it dangerous?"

Barbara smiled indulgently at her friend's naiveté.

"If it wasn't dangerous, our men wouldn't take part," she answered sagely. "We've never had a tournament this late in the year before. But the weather's still good, and Fulke says it would almost be a crime to pass up the opportunity with so many qualified lords and their men in town."

Adele's face clouded at Barbara's words, which reminded her afresh of the unusual gathering.

"Do you know what's really afoot?"

Barbara glanced away. "No, but I can guess. Why would so many important men choose to go on a pilgrimage at the same time? More to the point—why are they now wearing mail and openly showing their colors? They could not have known about this tournament, for Fulke made the arrangements only last week. The tilting field will be bright as a summer garden with all their banners. I've even wondered if Fulke was holding the tournament just to hide such a large number of armed men."

That was something to consider. Adele's heart gave an uncomfortable thud. "Do you think they're preparing for war?"

"Not yet, not in winter—but come spring, who knows?"

Not in winter. Adele repeated that comforting phrase throughout the day. She'd never suspected that wars were deliberately arranged to take advantage of the better weather. To her mind, if a cause was important enough to die for, it could not be postponed until the sun was shining. Neither had she known that a tournament was not generally held on such short notice. Barbara claimed that tournaments were advertised well in advance to allow competitors to travel from great distances to take part. For the FitzAlan competition, however, there had been no need to attract distant contenders: the town was already full of armed men and their horses, all eager for excitement.

Barbara was right—when they arrived at the noisy lists outside the town, they found the scrubby grassland ablaze with color. The contestants' gaudy pavillions had been pitched along one side of the field, making it appear, from this distance, that immense blue, scarlet, gold, and white flowers had sprung up overnight. Dozens of shouting food vendors and assorted entertainers mingled with the growing crowd of spectators.

The women climbed the planking to their seats, which offered a splendid view of the events. The makeshift wooden stands were rickety, and Adele hoped they would not collapse under the weight of the crowd that stamped and clapped, their movements causing a dangerous sway. Adele perched beside Barbara on the edge of her seat, excited by the colorful panorama unfolding before her. When the sun rose higher, flooding the south side of the field with warmth, the two women had to cast aside their cloaks. Adele wore a red and gold patterned gown under her gold, sable-edged tunic. Her hair had been braided with gold ribbons and hung down her back beneath a fluttering iridescent gold veil secured on her brow by a golden circlet. Barbara's sumptuous new gown was of leaf-green velvet shot through with silver, worn under a long silver tunic edged with white fur. They received many admiring glances.

Of course, the common wenches who crowded the railings also received much attention, but it was not of the type she coveted. Passing men, be they lord, squire, or groom, reached out to kiss and caress the giggling wenches, their casual love play eliciting loud shrieks of laughter.

Before they moved onto the field, Rafe and Gerard came and made sure their ladies were comfortably seated. Barbara's maids had brought a hamper filled with food and drink. Adele was slightly disappointed by this discovery, for she had intended to sample the fried meat pies whose appetizing aroma swept across the stands, or the barley sugar comfits, or marchpane figures. When she mentioned this desire to Barbara, Adele was surprised by her friend's shocked reaction; both Barbara and her sister seemed appalled that she would even consider mingling with the common folk thronging the tilt field.

Margaret had arrived late, always eager to make a head-turning appearance. She had left her new infant and the other children safely at home with their nursemaids. A retinue of servants had followed in Margaret's wake, carrying Mistress FitzAlan's own cushioned chair, her pillows, and fur coverlets in case it turned cold. Like a magnet, Margaret drew many of the town's notable ladies to her side, all eager to be included in Lady FitzAlan's inner circle. The fashionable woman held court in her mulberry velvet gown, an elaborate pearl-edged head-dress and a lavender veil covering her hair. As the group gathering round them grew larger, Adele found herself crowded out by these chirruping women, until she finally had to cling to the side rail to keep from being pushed off the bench entirely.

At last, loud cheers announced the arrival of the hastily assembled marshals of this event. A herald in a blue and white tabard and broad-brimmed hat dripping with white plumes hurried to keep pace with the officials.

Adele craned her head to watch a troupe of brightly garbed tumblers and mummers who were entertaining the crowd. When the start of the joust was imminent, the entertainers scattered to await a lull between events before coming back on the field.

As Adele had never attended a tournament before, she did not miss the usual lavish opening parade in which each competitor tried to outdo the other with expensively caparisoned horses, liveried retainers, and their own magnificent attire. Here this magnificent spectacle had been replaced by a lackluster jog about the arena.

All competing knights and their retainers rode around the perimeter of the field. When Adele recognized Rafe's glittering crest carried high above the horses' heads, she waved to him and cheered. Though Rafe was accompanied by only a handful of his men, they made a good showing and appeared to be popular with the crowd.

Gerard Monstsorrel followed, riding at the head of the FitzAlan men in their murrey and silver livery.

Because this tourney was being sponsored by Fulke FitzAlan, though not a competitor himself, he had the right to ride at the head of the parade. Unfortunately, he had arrived late, for he had been escorting his wife, and to assume that position the tournament's sponsor now had to gallop forward to get ahead of the other knights. His somewhat undignified entrance caused a few irreverent titters from the crowd. FitzAlan's white horse was grandly caparisoned in murrey and silver, its magnificent saddle cloth glinting in the sun. He was a tall man who sat ramrod-straight in the saddle, moving only slightly to the side as he offered a few condescending waves to the crowd. Adele heard some definite boos mingled with the cheers as the spectators greeted today's benefactor. He seemed absurdly puffed up with his own importance. His family was undoubtedly wealthy, but Adele suspected that some of these competitors were of far greater importance than the posturing FitzAlan. He apparently had the same failings as his wife.

Musicians struck up a lively tune playing loud and very badly, Adele observed, wincing over the sour notes issuing from their instruments. Even the herald, who had swaggered forth with his bannered trumpet, blew an off-key fanfare. His voice was carried away on the wind as he announced the rules of the competitions.

The bouts began almost at once. First there was jousting over an open course, followed by a number of hand-to-hand contests. Adele paled as she understood Rafe's very real danger. These men who were battling on the field seemed unduly reckless, as if they sought to defuse some unknown tension with a show of force. These men played at war like young boys, but now their toys were deadly.

Finally there was a break between contests and the gaudily costumed entertainers ran back onto the field. At this time many spectators left their seats to buy food from the vendors. It was time for the FitzAlan hamper to be opened. Venison and fish pasties were passed around, accompanied by watered wine and crystallized fruit.

The tournament soon resumed. The contest to open the second half of the event involved six-knight teams whose sole purpose seemed to be to batter their opponents out of their saddles. Adele fretted so much over Rafe's welfare, she could not enjoy her food. She clung to her seat as she watched him sway under a rain of blows. His horse cleverly moved this way and that, helping his master to retaliate, then quickly shift out of range, and miraculously Rafe stayed in the saddle, though he had collected many new dents on his shield.

When they had discussed the tournament this morning, Rafe had convinced her this was all in sport. He also said he was not trying to win any prizes, but competed merely as a favor to FitzAlan. During the entire event, Adele expected him to be wounded at any minute, or knocked from the saddle and trampled to death by the horses' hooves. How could he withstand such fierce assaults? Though he had said it was all done in sport, the ferocity of his opponents made it indistinguishable from the real thing. Adele's venison pasty lay like lead in her stomach, and she kept chewing a crystallized apricot, unable to swallow. This tournament was far removed from those chivalrous spectacles described in song and verse. These armed men were playing at war! She supposed she should be grateful that Rafe had not taken part in the brutal hand-to-hand combats to earn more points toward a prize.

Shielding her eyes from the sun, Adele looked across the field, wondering why the competitors were now forming into two large groups at opposite ends of the field. When she asked, Barbara explained they were preparing for the Grand Melee. Adele's heart pounded in shock, for even she knew that a Grand Melee was a mock pitched battle.

"Don't they wound each other?"

"Sometimes, but it's all very exciting. The real purpose is to capture prisoners for ransom. You'll enjoy it."

Adele took a deep breath as she tried to steady her pounding heart, thinking that this upcoming event sounded far from enjoyable. In fact, the entire tournament had been vastly disappointing. True, brightly caparisoned knights had galloped courageously through the lists and engaged each other with mace and sword, but in the process both men and horses had been wounded. She was appalled by the bloodshed. Far from the colorful chivalric spectacle people had recounted to her, Adele found this tournament more like a rowdy bloodbath than a day's entertainment.

When the marshals were satisfied that the opposing sides were equally matched, the plumed herald in his blue and white tabard sounded an elaborate fanfare, his reddened cheeks puffed out like apples as the cracked notes showered forth. Adele finally put her fingers in her ears until he was finished. The announcements that followed, recounting the names and all the grand titles of today's competitors in the melee, for the most part blew away on the wind. The combatants had either red or white bands fastened around their arms to show their team colors. Rafe and Gerard were positioned side by side, their excited mounts pawing the ground and eagerly tossing their heads.

All was ready. A hush descended on the crowd, until only the flapping flags and pennants could be heard as the wind gusted across the field. A deafening blast on a horn was the signal to charge. The two small armies galloped full pelt toward each other in a shouting throng, uttering war cries and yelping like savages.

The two sides met with a resounding crash as mace, sword, and lance came into play. Steel helms and shields rang like bells, marked for immediate targets. When men toppled from their horses, they continued to fight on foot with sword and dagger. This mock war was a brilliant display of battlefield skill—yet Adele hated every minute of it. Each time a man went down, some trampled under the horses' hooves, she cried out in alarm. Bloody contestants lost their swords and resorted to daggers. Helmets came off and were kicked aside, leaving their wearers vulnerable. And all through the noisy shambles, the excited crowd screamed in delight, cheering on various special champions. Adele discovered that bets had been placed on favorite knights. When she learned that Rafe was one of these, she did not know if that was good or bad. All she knew was that he had a reputation for staying in the thick of battle, and that alone was cause for alarm.

There was much confusion on the field as knots of fighting men moved back and forth, and Adele was hard-pressed to pick out Rafe from the others. Only when the sun glinted on his shield did she catch a fleeting glimpse of him swooping down on an opponent. Time and again he survived attacks until finally he was hit from behind, the force of the blow making his horse stumble. He was thrown from the saddle.

Adele screamed in alarm as the ranks closed around him, oblivious of the fallen man. She was convinced he would be trampled to death. But she need not have worried. Soon he was back on his feet, slashing an arc with his sword as he battled with two men and got the better of them both. Then, suddenly, he was down again—and this time he did not get up.

Adele jumped to her feet. Without hesitation she pushed past the spectators, making her way down the stands. Barbara and Margaret both shouted to her, telling her not to be alarmed, but Adele would not listen. Despite their assurances, she had to see for herself.

She entered the noisy crowd milling around the base of the stands. Vendors banged into her with the corners of the wooden trays slung around their necks filled with hot, savory pies. Wherever she went they bellowed in her ears, or grabbed her sleeves, trying to stop her in the hope she would buy their wares.

At a makeshift stall against the fence, ale was being sold, and the area thronged with thirsty men. There she asked the stall's proprietor how to get to the pavilions. Several of the men pointed the way, and she ducked beneath the railings and walked along the edge of the field. Past armorers and pimply-faced squires she hurried, ignoring their catcalls and bawdy invitations. Several men were carried past on litters, their retainers clearing the way. Adele followed them to the row of pavilions. Sunshine filtered through the colored canvas awnings, creating an unnatural murky blue, red, and yellow light. Pennants were flying gaily from the roofs of the tents. Those belonging to more wealthy competitors had silk awnings with dagged edges trimmed in gold.

Here between the pavilions it was even more congested. The poorer combatants lay on the ground in the open, taking advantage of the awnings' shade while their men sponged their faces and poured reviving ale down their throats. The wounded bled onto the ground while their friends struggled to stanch the flow with wads of cloth torn from their clothing. Adele saw other women here, though she could see they were not of noble birth. She assumed they were the knights' wives and sweethearts. She knew Rafe would not be outside. Though he did not have his own pavilion, he would use the large murrey and silver FitzAlan tent at the end of the row.

People rudely elbowed Adele out of the way, cursing at her to move as they struggled past. She stood as close to the canvas walls as possible to let the stretcher-bearers pass. Some of their patients looked pale as death, though their jovial companions seemed unconcerned. Great warhorses were being led back and forth between the pavilions, stamping and snorting, their massive hooves threatening to trample her. When the horse grooms saw Adele, her style of dress immediately marking her as nobility, they tipped their caps, somewhat startled to find her here. Their reaction implied that highborn ladies usually did not enter this area.

"Who is it you seek, Lady?"

Adele turned to see a gawky lad in a red tunic who politely touched his forelock in deference to her station.

"Lord Rafe," she said breathlessly, struggling to catch her breath. "De Montford. Likely he's with the FitzAlan men."

The lad's expression changed. "Come, then, it's this way. I'll show you a shortcut. 'Tis the big pavilion at the end. Is your lord wounded? Have they carried him off the field?"

"I don't know. I just saw him go down, and he didn't get up."

The lad nodded sympathetically as he led her between the canvas walls, pointing out the guy ropes so she would not trip. Here armorers worked, clanging on metal and hammering out dents in shields and armor, making it difficult to hear. Adele still followed the youth as he weaved deftly between anvils and scrap metal, past stomping warhorses and dazed combatants. She was sure they should have reached the FitzAlan pavilion by now. In fact, they seemed to be going in the wrong direction, yet there was such turmoil taking place around her it was hard to tell. A row of wagons were parked close to the fence and men milled about, going back and forth between their wagons and the pavilions. They appeared to be mostly grooms and servants, with a sprinkling of ruffians who likely inevitably followed the tournament circuit.

"Are you sure this is the way?" Adele finally shouted to the lad, grasping his sleeve to attract his attention as he stepped between two burly men in padded gambesons. To her alarm, they moved to close the gap, and when she tried to sidestep them, they deliberately blocked her way.

"Get out of my way," she ordered, fixing them with a hard stare.

"What are you doing here, pretty?" asked one of the men, grinning as he reached for her hair. He greedily eyed the gold circling her brow.

"Help me! Someone help me!" Adele screamed in alarm as the men grabbed her arms.

Adele's cries quickly turned to screams. She kicked and punched, desperately struggling to be free. Though there were dozens of people within earshot, no one came to her rescue. She felt a heavy hand on her shoulder; then her head snapped back as a dirty palm was clamped over her mouth.

"Come on then, love, I'll help you," a man's voice hissed against her ear.

Adele's blood ran cold. That voice was sickeningly familiar—her rescuer was Lorkin Yates!

Chapter Eleven

It was cold inside the wagon, and it had begun to rain; Adele could hear the drops beating a tattoo overhead. When she opened her eyes they were sore and gritty, and when she raised her head, a giant bell clanged inside.

Groaning, she clutched her temples and fell back, lying very still. It took her several minutes to pluck up enough courage to try again. The wagon began to lurch forward, rolling her back and forth like a ship at sea. Now she had to overcome an overwhelming wave of nausea that flooded over her, lasting until the rolling motion stopped. Presently she felt well enough to sit up. She pushed her fingers through a hole in the wagon's threadbare canvas, enlarging it enough to see out.

It was still light. They jogged past rolling pastureland dotted with woods before they entered a sunken road where all she could see was a decaying tangle of vegetation. The sodden yellow growth brushing the sides of the wagon was strung with necklaces of crimson rose hips, so close she could have picked them.

As she sat there, Adele's memory slowly throbbed back to life and along with it the shock she had felt at hearing Lorkin Yates's voice. Her stomach pitched. His voice had been the last thing she had heard before everything went black. She shivered with fear.

Somehow, Yates had found her again just when she thought he had gone from her life forever. Her hands were bound, but not her feet, and she moved her legs back and forth. Her left ankle throbbed, and she recalled stepping in a rut during her struggle. She inched the canvas aside at the rear of the moving wagon, thinking to jump out and roll to safety: They were going slow enough not to cause injury, and a little rain wouldn't hurt her.

To her disappointment, as she peered through the canvas, Adele saw a donkey's head and its rider's threadbare trouser-legs. Moving to the front of the wagon, she had the same bad luck, only here there were four riders, the discovery dashing her hopes of escape. When they stopped, she would find a way.

The very thought of Lorkin's embraces, his eager wet kisses, made her shudder.

When the rattling wagon finally swayed to a halt, it woke Adele from a doze. Tense, she crouched inside the wagon's dark interior waiting for someone to come, praying it would not be Yates.

"All clear," she heard a man shout outside. Then lantern light flashed into the wagon, shining through its canvas cover.

"Hello, Adele, sweet."

All hope of escape vanished. Though she discounted it, she realized she had been clinging to the hope that she was not Lorkin Yates's captive. Now all doubt was removed, and the blow was devastating.

He stood framed in the canvas opening, holding the lantern higher to study her face. He seemed well pleased by what he saw. "At last," he breathed. "Just the way I remembered. I was afraid we'd never be together again," he said as he reached for her.

Still smiling, Joce's impostor helped her from the wagon and led her to the smoking campfire. The wood was wet after the rain, and the fire's heat was feeble, but Adele stretched icy feet and hands toward the struggling flames. She glanced about at the dense black trees, her scraggly companions, and her heart sank. Here Lorkin had her in another clearing in the woods, in another poor camp, ready to resume living a lie. Did Yates know she knew the truth?

"I thought you were still in jail," she said finally, pulling away from his restraining hand.

"There aren't many jails that can hold me, especially when I have a goal. I had to escape, if only to rescue you, sister," he explained as he reached out to stroke her cheek.

"And what do you intend to do with me now?"

His face clouded in displeasure at her abrupt question. "What, not even a greeting for your own brother? No thanks for being rescued?"

"I didn't want to be rescued," she muttered as she accepted a cup of warm ale from him. While she drank, Adele debated telling him she knew he was not Joce. On second thought, it might be a mistake. She was in the camp at his mercy again. It might be to her advantage to remain his sister, for, without their supposed blood tie, she was sure he would rape her. Also, if he knew he had been found out, there might be no further need to keep her alive. She didn't know Sir Guy's plan, and from what Rafe had said about Yates, he could be very dangerous. Rafe had said—

Rafe! A shock wave rocked her body. She had never found out what had happened to him at the tournament.

When those ruffians seized her she had been on her way to learn his fate. It was as if her mind had temporarily gone blank. Now all her pain and worry flooded back. She had to know if Rafe was hurt.

"Take me back," she demanded, setting down her cup.

"Where?"

"To St. Edmundsbury. I'm a guest at the FitzAlan home. They'll be searching for me. If you take me back now, maybe you can still escape."

"I've already escaped. See? I'm free as a bird."

"You're still an outlaw——that's not what I call free."

His eyes narrowed and he stared at her a long time in the light from the fire. At last he said, "You've changed, sister. It's not for the better. I don't know what you've been told about me, but I'm no outlaw. It's only natural for a family to live together. We'll go back to Esterwold and forget this happened."

It was all she could do to keep from blurting out what she knew. Instead she asked him, "What are you going to do about Hugh D'Avranche?"

"That bastard!" He spat in the fire. "All he's owed is a knife in the back. When I offered to bring you to him, he treated me like a beggar."

Adele sat up straighter, alarmed by his words. "When you offered me to him? What do you mean?"

"At St. Edmundsbury—he was there for the tournament—I told him I knew who held you captive and for a price I'd bring you to him. He called me a rogue and threatened to set his men on me."

"You didn't tell him I was with Rafe?"

"Aye, I did, and I offered to take you from De Montford, too. He'd have none of it."

So now Hugh D'Avranche knew that Rafe had not followed the king's orders. The idea was chilling. Perhaps D'Avranche had been fighting in that melee. It could have been he who finally unseated Rafe. She did not know the D'Avranche coat of arms.

"You fool! You might have cost him his life," she shouted as she jumped to her feet.

Lorkin Yates snarled in anger and grabbed her arm, thrusting her back down. "Don't ever call me that again," he threatened, "or I'll slit your throat!"

His threat was sufficient to silence her. The rage in his voice was a warning of what might be in store for her if she crossed him. Now, more than ever, Adele knew she had to focus her attention on escaping. If he were still able, she was sure that Rafe would search for her, yet how would he learn where to find her? He also assumed that Lorkin Yates was safely behind bars. And if Rafe was wounded, or worse . . . She thrust that terrible thought from her mind.

Where was she? During one afternoon they surely could not have traveled far from St. Edmundsbury in this old wagon. Soon all the roads in the vicinity would be swarming with knights and their retainers heading home. Perhaps she would see one of the nobles who had accompanied them on their pilgrimage; she could appeal to him for help. Until then, she must be ever ready for a chance to escape. This time, she did not have dear Moonlight for company, so if she ran away, it would have to be on foot.

Adele gnawed on the roast rabbit she was handed. These other men sitting close to the fire, had not spoken, possibly too afraid of his temper to interrupt their leader. Had they helped him escape, or were they fellow prisoners?

"It's too wet out here, so you sleep in the wagon with me," Lorkin Yates announced, finishing his meal and tossing aside the bones.

"No! I'll sleep out here in my cloak before I'll do that."

Adele's angry outburst startled him. Though at first a hard glint entered his eye, it softened. "All right, you can use the wagon tonight and we'll talk about it tomorrow," he said generously. As he spoke, he ran his hand along her arm in a lingering caress.

Adele tried to suppress a shudder at his possessive touch, longing to order him away from her. She wanted to tell him what she knew, to have done with this play-acting. In the nick of time she reminded herself that her life could depend on his remaining her brother. Tonight, at least, she had won a battle.

Disdaining his help, Adele climbed back inside the wagon. Lorkin pitched her a soiled blanket, which she threw aside. Later, as the night grew cold and the mist came down, she cast delicacy aside, glad of the extra covering.

For a long time Adele lay awake, listening to the camp sounds. To her surprise, she could hear women's and children's voices, revealing this place as another of those makeshift camps hidden in the forest. Had all his ragged companions escaped with him, or did these people follow a different peasant king and Yates had joined up with them?

Guards were posted outside her wagon, deflating any plan of slipping away during the night. Yates himself slept beneath the wagon: she'd heard his voice, and could now hear his snores. Buried under a heap of straw in the corner of the vehicle, Adele found a turnip, her discovery suggesting that her abductors had stolen the wagon at the tournament. As she lay in the darkness, she twisted Rafe's ring about her finger, praying earnestly for his safety. She prayed he would soon come to rescue her.

But she couldn't wait on that possibility. Her mind raced. There had to be a way to end this hateful captivity.

Rafe winced as his squire bound the bandage tighter on his left forearm. When he'd been unhorsed, an opponent's blade had sliced through the padded sleeve of his gambeson and slipped under his mail shirt to pierce his arm. Thankfully, the wound was not serious enough to keep him out of action. After escaping the fray briefly, he had remounted and charged back in.

Rafe and his companions had been the victors in the mock battle, unseating and capturing many of the enemy to hold for ransom. He had galloped triumphant from the field beside Gerard, eager to tell Adele about their good fortune, but when Rafe glanced toward the stands he did not see her. Barbara and Margaret were still there, though, surrounded by their chattering friends. Likely Adele had tired of their tittle-tattle and gone below to stretch her legs.

Along the path between the pavilions the triumphant knights had ridden, heartily cheered by their supporters, especially those who had placed winning bets on their team.

Inside the grand FitzAlan pavilion the fading afternoon sunlight filtered through its purple fabric, splotching its occupants' faces an unnatural hue. God, he was hot! Even in November, fighting this vigorously always raised a sweat.

Rafe's waiting squire hurried forward to help him off with his mail. His helmet was battered; he had been afraid of that. He would have to turn it in to his favorite armorer, along with his swords and daggers, which after today needed a good sharpening. Next Symme unfastened the closure on Rafe's mail coif, sliding it off his head, the padded hood following. Sodden black ringlets were plastered against his neck and forehead.

"Get me a drink, there's a good lad."

Almost at once a cool, refreshing cup was pressed into his hands and Rafe drank deep, his throat parched. Though they had fought on grass, the galloping hooves had stirred up a great cloud of dust. Thankfully, Rafe took the wet towel the lad offered and wiped the film of mud from his face.

"My lord, you're bleeding," Symme exclaimed in distress.

"Naw, it's just a scratch on my shoulder. Someone's blade slid off my helmet and struck me there. I don't think it's much," Rafe dismissed, wincing nevertheless when he moved his right arm. The blood had still not congealed and it trickled in a sticky line down his arm to pool in the palm of his hand.

Symme picked up his master's right gauntlet, which bore several dark stains that Rafe had assumed came from his opponents. Obediently, he lay on the bunk and his squire peeled off the rest of his mail, followed by the padded gambeson which was slit in several places, to

185

expose tufts of wool. Just past his collarbone lay a two-inch gash. Though he said nothing to Symme, Rafe understood now how lucky he had been.

Around his chest and under his armpit, Symme wound a clean bandage, wrapping the wounded shoulder as best he could while his master moved obediently to allow him to finish, though inwardly Rafe chafed to be up and about.

He heard Montsorrel groan as his squire compressed the wound in his thigh, trying to stop the bleeding. Rafe hoped it was only the unnatural light inside this pavilion that had turned Montsorrel's face an unearthly blue-white.

"How bad is it?" Rafe asked, sitting up and waving Symme away.

"Not bad," Montsorrel answered with a sheepish grin. "But had it been another few inches . . ." He rolled his eyes expressively. "Did you know we won a hefty purse today, my friend?"

Rafe laughed. "Aye. If we had been in it for the money, we'd have won nothing."

A commotion at the pavilion's entrance drew his attention and he glanced up to see Fulke FitzAlan stepping through the tent opening, smiling widely.

"Congratulations, my lords," he boomed, hastening to shake their hands, then drawing back somewhat delicately when he noticed the caked blood and dirt.

"A necessary evil," Rafe explained, observing the other's reluctance. "I promise that by tonight's banquet I'll be clean and presentable."

"Oh, no, no, it's just that I'm not used to . . ." Fulke stopped lamely in his explanation and stepped across to his brother-in-law's pallet, alarmed by the patch of blood which had gathered on the ground.

Behind his back, Rafe made a face and Montsorrel smiled.

"Well, brother, did we make you proud? We didn't let down the FitzAlan name."

"Proud—I'm overjoyed!" Fulke exclaimed, all smiles.

"I'd no idea you and Rafe were so good, so competent . . . perhaps you can enter more—"

"No." Rafe quickly stopped that fantasy. "Sorry to disappoint you, but there's far too much to be done at Fordham to follow the tourneys."

FitzAlan nodded, his face falling.

Suddenly Rafe understood his host's renewed interest. If Fulke could persuade them to travel the tournament circuit wearing the FitzAlan colors, they would bring fame and glory to a man too squeamish to fight. And the man could also win some lucrative bets while he was at it. *No, Fulke, my friend, not in this lifetime. No more fighting for pleasure.*

Rafe swung his legs off the bunk and motioned to Symme to take away the linens and bloody bowls. Now that the obligatory visit with his host was over, he could turn his attention to Adele, and a task far more to his liking.

"When you're both presentable, my lords, the ladies are ready to congratulate you," FitzAlan reminded, smoothing on his soft kid gloves as he prepared to leave.

"Adele hasn't been to a tourney before," Rafe commented, accepting a clean tunic from Symme. "How did she like it? Or did she find it too noisy and bloody?"

"Too much of the latter, I suspect. She's already left," FitzAlan said.

"What!" Rafe was on his feet.

"Margaret said she left some time ago, possibly feeling faint at the sight of blood."

"You're saying she left alone?"

Flustered by the other man's fury, FitzAlan shrugged. "Well, I don't know. I . . . I assumed she took a maid with her."

"But you don't know . . . and you didn't bother to find out?" Rafe challenged, anger making his voice harsh. "Good God, man, she's in a strange town with all this rabble wandering about, and you let her go home alone?"

FitzAlan colored, his full face rumpled in concern. "Put that way, I can see your concern. But, at the time, I thought nothing of it. Likely she stopped at one of the stalls. I'll go question the wenches."

"No, I'll question them," Rafe decided, already striding out of the pavilion. "Let's hope they have some good answers."

None of the maids had seen Adele leave. Though he came close to threatening them with bodily harm if they didn't stop wailing and answer his questions, Rafe held his temper. All his efforts were fruitless. No one knew where Adele had gone.

Rafe sent his men around the lists to question stall holders and sword swallowers alike in the hope that someone had seen her. Several men said they had seen a noble lady near the pavilions and Rafe suspected that many others could have come forward had they so chosen. Whether he did not offer enough silver, or if professing such knowledge was dangerous, he did not know.

As dusk drew near, it began to rain, the tents' gay bunting and bedraggled pennants whipping in the wind. Rafe stood bareheaded surveying the shambles of the festivities as tradesmen scurried to protect their goods and others took cover from the rain. All the triumph he had felt over today's victory was gone. Even the heavy decision he must make concerning his divided loyalty no longer mattered. Those vows hammered out before Saint Edmund's high altar belonged to another time. His only objective now was to find Adele.

Raising his face to the heavens, Rafe prayed as large raindrops spattered his upturned face. Not exactly a stranger to religion, still Rafe had never relied on the church before. But now that he was at his wit's end, having nowhere left to turn, he went to his knees on the churned-up ground and bowed his head. What mattered most in his life had been taken away. He prayed in earnest, the half-forgotten words coming readily to mind as he beseeched his Maker to aid him in his quest.

Nothing happened immediately. Disheartened, Rafe oversaw the packing of their gear. The horses were saddled for the journey, and his dispirited men were finally mounted after giving up all hope of learning more. They began their slow trek home, across the field, which oozed and squelched beneath the horse's hooves. There was a swift-running stream already bisecting the low-lying ground. Many carts were stuck in the mud, and men were struggling to free their vehicles, shouting and straining in the pouring rain.

What happened next made stronger his belief in the power of prayer. Rafe's soldiers had stopped to help dislodge a nearby vehicle, by habit asking the armorer and his apprentice if they had seen a noble lady near the pavilions.

"Aye, I marked her well, 'cause it's not a usual sight, nor is it common to see one so fair."

Rafe gripped his reins, abruptly drawing up. "You saw her?" he asked, overhearing the exchange. "Was she alone?"

The grizzled armorer doffed his cap. "I can tell you little more, my lord. I heard her ask directions at the ale stall. A young lad showed her. Seems like *everyone*'s asking questions today. Most is good-natured and they usually gives me a coin for my pains . . ." The man paused meaningfully.

Rafe uttered an exasperated sigh and, taking the not-so-subtle hint, motioned to Symme to give the fellow some silver. "Then what? Where did she go?"

The man scratched his head. "Last I seen, she was arm in arm with this fellow. They was a long way off, but her dress was so special like, I knows it was her. And him I'd talked to earlier."

Why would Adele be arm in arm with a man? Rafe wondered. His hopes dashed, he lost interest in inquiring further. Likely the old armorer had confused Adele with another woman. Rafe had already turned aside when the man suggested, "Reckon you'd learn more from my lord D'Avranche. This same fellow talked to him, too. Must have made him angry, for the way he bellowed—"

"D'Avranche? Hugh D'Avranche of Summerhay?"

"That's 'im. Thought you'd know 'im."

Across the field, Rafe could make out the bedraggled D'Avranche standard flapping atop a red pavilion. Like some of the other traveling knights, D'Avranche must have chosen to wait out the downpour inside his pavilion.

Rafe changed direction, riding toward D'Avranche's mud-spattered shelter. He sent a man ahead to request a meeting. It was not how he would have chosen to finally face D'Avranche—in fact, if he were honest, he knew he had been delaying the inevitable. But today fate had conspired to bring them together, and he searched for the seed of hope D'Avranche held in his hand.

While he waited, Rafe sheltered beneath the overhang of a neighboring pavilion. Inside, he could hear its roisterous inhabitants making merry, their voices incoherent with laughter and ale.

Finally his messenger returned. Hugh D'Avranche had agreed to see him.

How very generous of him, Rafe thought sourly, his jaw set as he contemplated the unpleasant meeting ahead. Urging his mount forward, he plowed through the mud between the pavilions. Outside the bespattered red tent he dismounted and handed his horse to Symme.

Rafe ducked to enter the gloomy pavilion. To his surprise, he found D'Avranche attended by only two men-at-arms. Rain pelted loudly on the canvas roof which had already sprung several leaks, and he adeptly dodged the resultant falling water.

"So, we meet at last, my lord De Montford," Hugh D'Avranche rumbled. His voice hoarse from shouting during today's contests.

A bloodied surcoat and a shirt of distinctive mail lay beside him on the floor. Immediately, Rafe recognized the regalia from the melee, but at the time he had not known this knight's identity, for D'Avranche had chosen to fight without any identifying crest. This knight had charged him with such fury, it was only with the utmost skill that Rafe had been able to avoid his crushing blows.

Now the identity of that anonymous knight and the reason behind his onslaught became clear. Hugh D'Avranche knew far more than Rafe had realized.

"First, let me congratulate you, my lord. You were a worthy opponent in today's fight," Rafe said smoothly as he accepted a cup of wine from one of the soldiers.

"I'll say the same of you," D'Avranche growled finally, leaning forward.

His surly attitude and scowl were not encouraging. Under those heavy dark brows, hostile flinty eyes regarded Rafe. Neither man spoke. Rafe drained his cup and set it down. D'Avranche did the same, following his action with a resounding belch. Immediately, Rafe was reminded of Bohun; in fact, D'Avranche had mustard stains in the selfsame place on his tunic, creating a bond of slovenly kinship between the two.

"I'll also say, you've got balls to come here after what I learned today," D'Avranche said, finally breaking the silence.

"And what was that, my lord?"

"You've got my woman!"

"Your woman? By that, do you mean the bride chosen for you by our illustrious king?" Rafe asked sarcastically.

They exchanged glares before D'Avranche, unable to contain his anger, exploded. "You've committed treason and robbed me of a bride!" Thrusting his red face forward, the veins distended in his neck, he snarled, "Worse than that, you've made me a laughingstock!"

"How's that, my lord? If you only found out today and I've been with Adele since spring, it can hardly be common knowledge."

"The king wants her to be mine, dammit!"

"After your recent dealings with the king, that may no longer be true," Rafe observed coolly. He could play this game as well as the next man.

D'Avranche drew in a breath, unprepared for Rafe's knowledge. "Well, you're hardly blameless," he finally retorted. "Lackland doesn't stand for disobedience."

Rafe shrugged. "We'll see. In view of your fall from grace, however, I did petition the king for her hand."

"You what! Damn your audacity, De Montford," D'Avranche spat, furious. "That's treachery if ever—"

"Come on, let's save both our time and tempers. You don't give a tinker's damn for Adele St. Clare. She was a gift securing your good behavior. Since you've sworn to make war on the king if he doesn't agree to your wishes, that makes you an even bigger traitor."

D'Avranche was on his feet, his hand flying to his dagger. Out of the corner of his eye Rafe caught a quick movement from the watching men-at-arms, followed by the clink of steel, warning him he was on shaky ground.

"How dare you reveal that secret?"

"Since the vow was taken before so many, I didn't know it was a secret."

"And I suppose you—you slimy bastard—will pay lip service until you see which way the wind blows."

"As that was ever your policy, I'm surprised you're belaboring me for the same wisdom. Besides, we're both aware you only sided with the rebels because you've already sucked the royal teat dry."

Realizing he was somewhat disadvantaged by Rafe's superior height, D'Avranche dropped back in his seat. They glared at each other, sizing up their opposition.

"If it's agreeable to you, I'm prepared to settle with a generous sum in recompense for the affront to your name. Or, if you want another woman in her stead, I can arrange that also."

"But you're not prepared to give up the St. Clare woman without a fight?"

"No." Rafe's face hardened. "And fighting is another option—if you choose it."

To his surprise, a smile flickered across D'Avranche's stubbly face. "Hell, no, De Montford. I want to live a while longer. Today you were only fighting for sport. I'll be damned if I'll go against you for something that matters."

Rafe's jaw relaxed, and he fought to conceal his relief.

This battle was all but won. Impulsively, he stretched out his right hand, palm up.

D'Avranche hesitated, then accepted the hand extended in peace. "I respect a warrior. We can discuss compensation at Summerhay over a cup of good wine," he offered at last. "Now, your man said you had a question for me. What is it?"

Grimly revealing the painful truth, Rafe said, "Adele vanished from the lists today. I suspect she was abducted near the pavilions. Don't ask me why she was there . . . I don't know. We're guests of the FitzAlans and I'd assumed she was safe with them. An armorer told me you spoke to the man she was last seen with. I need to know who he was, and where to find him."

D'Avranche poured himself another cup of wine and offered one to Rafe while he considered the question. "God's blood, man, that's like looking for a needle in a haystack. I've spoken to dozens of men today."

Leaning forward, his expression intent, Rafe said, "I was told this man angered you, so I was hoping you'd remember him."

"Angered me?" D'Avranche repeated. "There was an insolent *routier* who offered to bring me Lady St. Clare—for a price. That's how I learned about your part in this," he recalled with a frown.

Rafe's stomach pitched. He straightened up and took a few steps toward the pavilion flap. He had an awful feeling . . . "Stocky, medium height, blond hair and beard? Makes you want to guard your purse—"

"That's the man. His price was so ridiculous, I wouldn't pay that for the Blessed Mother herself."

Rafe's mouth set in a grim line. Why hadn't he thought about Lorkin Yates before? But he knew the answer. He had considered the bastard safely under lock and key. Somehow the criminal had escaped the hangman's noose. He'd been wrong.

Chapter Twelve

Mist obscured the landscape.

Adele shivered inside her cloak, thankful she still had the garment. Her lovely borrowed gown had not fared as well; the skirt was shredded by brambles, and it's elegant fur trimming had been sacrificed days ago in exchange for food. Such delicate garments were ill suited to hiding in gorse thickets and pushing through brambles, things she had been forced to do each time her abductors were threatened with discovery. Almost as if he read her mind, Lorkin Yates kept her gagged in case she might call out to passing soldiers to rescue her. Lately there seemed to be so many armed men moving about the countryside, Adele knew they could not all have been taking part in the tournament.

She longed to ask one of these soldiers if they knew of Rafe's fate, and she'd even tried to persuade Yates to trust her far enough to ask that one question, but he had refused.

Now hidden in a nearby thicket, Adele studied each

passing group's crest, searching in vain for the mountain peak with its glittering sword which would identify Rafe's soldiers. She did not even know if he was alive. Whenever dismal thoughts of his death entered her mind, she stubbornly thrust them away, twisting the simple ring on her finger for reassurance. Yates had taken her gown's fur trimming, her gauzy veil, and her gold circlet, but she had kept the ring as a reminder of Rafe's wonderful pledge.

Each day men casually came and went from this small camp, frequently bringing news of troops gathering and of money offered for experienced fighting men. Unfortunately, during these visits her guards never wavered in their duty, though Adele always stayed alert to the possibility.

The cold December morn struck a chill through her bones; the heavy mist felt icy on her face. Here, close to the trees, the mist was very dense. Adele's hopes soared as she considered making a break for freedom, when the unlovely tones of her guard came out of the gloom.

"Here you, get back here," growled her keeper, a surly youth with arms like tree trunks.

Adele made a face, but she obeyed. The last time she had crossed him, the youthful giant had slung her over his shoulder. Exposing her legs to all and sundry, the painful humiliation was enough to keep her from repeating the offense. Back to the dismal hut she had gone to await Lorkin Yates's return. He had left in the early hours to go scavenging. He kept telling her they would leave for Esterwold any day, but whether it was wishful thinking on his part or said merely to placate her, she did not know.

At last, Adele heard the dull thud of hooves coming out of the mist. Yates was back. She shook her head in disbelief when she realized she was almost glad he had returned, if only for the human contact. Except for the surly commands of her guard, everyone else had strict orders not to speak to her. Adele supposed the command made little difference, for she could barely understand their speech, or they hers.

"We leave tomorrow," Yates said when he finally entered their makeshift dwelling.

"Where are we going?" Adele asked, her mouth full of stale bread, what he had scavenged for their meal.

"Esterwold. Like I told you."

"It's a long way from here. Are you sure you know the way?" It appeared to be the wrong question to ask.

With a snarl he jumped up and grabbed her arm, yanking her toward him. "Look, you, I've had enough of your fool questions and all your likes and dislikes. Just do what you're told. We're headed to Esterwold. Others are joining us and we'll winter there. By spring this whole country will be on the move."

Adele digested his words. Yates obviously thought he could overwhelm Bohun's soldiers. Well, at least if they were on the road, she would have more chances to escape. This time she was keeping count of the passing days by notching a birch twig with a sharp rock each night before she lay down to sleep. It had been only a week, but it seemed like months.

"One more thing, woman. I'll expect a lot more respect from you when we're at the Castle. After all, I'm the lord there—you're just my sister," he announced, puffing himself up importantly as he swaggered to the ale jug.

Adele saw red. Anger boiled inside her, and she clenched her fists until they hurt. Almost before the words were out, she knew she was making a foolish mistake, but she could hold her tongue no longer.

"Don't ever speak like that to me again, Lorkin Yates! You're not my brother! Joce's been dead for years. You're nothing but a common *routier*, no better or worse than my humblest servant. So I'll thank you to remember that and give *me* the respect I'm owed."

Her revelation stunned him. The next moment seemed to drag on for hours, and in the ensuing silence she could hear her heart thundering in shock at what she had just done.

He stood before the ale jug like a statue, the cup

halfway to his lips. Finally, gathering his wits, he asked gruffly, "What did you call me?"

"Lorkin Yates. That *is* your name, isn't it?"

He began to protest, before abruptly abandoning all pretense. "Who told you that?" was all he asked.

"My lord De Montford."

"Damn him to hell! I should have known. How long have you known?"

"Only since you were arrested. Surely you've not forgotten you're still an outlaw with a price on your head. They'll definitely hang you for this," she observed.

"Thank you for that reminder, my lady," he said. "You're going to regret it—now the picture's changed forever."

She already regretted it. Adele twisted her skirt in her hands, wishing she could take back her hasty words. Especially when she saw the leer on her captor's face.

"There's nothing to be lost now, is there, my lady?" He put down his ale cup. "You're mine for the taking. I've never had a noblewoman before."

"Touch me and I'll kill you!"

There was such venom in her voice he took a step back. She was his captive, yet years of conditioning still kept him slightly in awe of noble blood.

"You'll soon change your tune," he snarled. "Remember, bitch, in front of the others I'm still your brother. That's your only chance to survive."

After delivering this chilling reminder, Lorkin Yates walked outside.

Adele tried to quiet her pounding heart as she considered how much damage her hasty words had done. In that respect, she knew his last advice was sound. If it were known in the camp that their purported relationship was false, whenever he was away, she would be fair game. The hideous thought made her shudder. Perhaps if these ragged men learned that Lorkin Yates was not a long-lost lord, just a common *routier*, they would not even obey him. The result of her blurted words could mean disaster for them both.

"Come on, you, get moving."

Adele was being shaken awake. After shedding a few self-pitying tears, she had fallen asleep in the gloomy dawn. How she hated to return to the present, for in her slumber all had been as before. Rafe had been coming toward her across a firelit room, his handsome face filled with love, his arms outstretched to hold her. She had quickened her step, had almost reached his embrace, almost felt that long-awaited kiss—when Lorkin Yates's rough voice shattered her dream.

Turning a look of pure hatred on him, Adele struggled to her feet. She picked up her cloak, which also served as her blanket. "What is it now? Another troop of soldiers riding by?" she asked him scornfully, shaking off his hand when he tried to touch her face.

"How clever you are," he sneered, thrusting her before him into the chill gloom. "Just get on the horse and hurry up. We have to join up with the main force."

Their current mounts were two swaybacked drays that could barely carry themselves, let alone a rider. These bags of bones were all Lorkin Yates had been able to steal this week.

Adele struggled into the saddle, pulling her skirts out of the way. She hauled herself up by the saddle's high curved front, fastening her hand in the horse's tangled mane for further leverage. This grand saddle had once been gilded and painted; red roses could still be seen on the leather. Yates had stolen it especially for her near the start of their journey, presenting his gift with such shy affection that, despite herself, Adele had been moved by his boyish confusion. It was startling to discover her heart thawing, even a little, toward him. But it had been brief. Now that his deception was out in the open, Lorkin Yates's true character shone clearly in his face.

"Whose men are they this time?" Adele asked as she kicked her mount's flank to urge him into motion.

"Mine."

Horrid thought though it was, Adele discovered he

spoke the truth. After they cleared the woods and rode onto a windswept heath, they were met by a strange, rag-tag band of men, some on horseback or riding donkeys, the rest on foot. The men were armed and menacing, carrying staves, cudgels, and what weapons they had pilfered from the dying on some long-ago battlefield.

"This, you arrogant Norman bitch, is the people's army," Yates revealed in an undertone.

He insisted she stay beside him as he rode forth to inspect his troops. To Adele it was like some preposterous dream as they reviewed the straggling ranks sitting ramrod straight on their comical steeds, as haughty as if they rode fine-blooded horses. Adele was tempted to pinch herself to make sure she was not still asleep, convinced this foolish charade could not be real. Like a king with his consort, Lorkin Yates graciously inclined his head, motioning for her to do the same. He shook hands with some of the men and listened to their brief recountings of battles both real and imagined. All the while, Adele sat up on her elaborate saddle, wanting to burst into laughter for the sheer absurdity of it all.

Then, when the mock review was over, Lorkin Yates turned to her with a malicious smile on his face, indicating she was to follow him out of earshot of the others.

"What now?" she asked warily.

"I've saved the best news for last," he said, reaching out to stroke her bright hair. "Once and for all, you'll see who's the better man—a good Saxon yeoman or some inbred Norman fool."

"What are you talking about?" she demanded irritably, moving out of his reach.

"We're going for a ride, my lady Adele. Over yon hillock are troops, hidden in the mist. We're going down to surprise them."

"What does that matter to me?" she asked wearily, anxious to be done with this foolishness. Much of the mist had already lifted, yet in the hollows of these hills, billowing clouds had drifted in dense pockets between the grassy crests. An entire army could be hiding there and no one would know. In a way, she hoped it *was* an army. Then, maybe once and for all, Lorkin Yates would meet his match.

She turned to him with a smile. "Well, beggar king, let's be done with whatever game you're playing. It's cold out here. December's not the month for a pleasant ride, especially with an empty belly."

His mouth hardened as he took to heart her jibe about his inability to provide a meal for them. "Damn you, woman, I'll soon show you who's the beggar king. I'm going down there to kill your lover!"

Adele cried out in shock, the sound echoing between the misty crevices. Behind them, against a backdrop of mist-shrouded trees, the rabble stood waiting for their leader's command.

Yates smiled cruelly at her before he turned and raised his hand to signal the attack.

Adele bolted. Desperate to give Rafe warning, she tried to kick her mount to greater speed as the surging mass of charging men enveloped her. At Lorkin Yates's insistence, they ran without their usual shouting. Had she thought it would make a difference, Adele would have screamed a warning at the top of her lungs to alert their unsuspecting quarry, but she was sure her voice would be lost in the wind.

Even while he rode toward his intended victims, Lorkin Yates considered and discarded several changes of plan. Though it was disappointing, he finally decided it would be more clever to hold the mighty De Montford and his followers for ransom instead of slaughtering them at once. His hand clenched as he anticipated the pleasure of plunging his dagger to the hilt in De Montford's heart. With the man out of the way, Adele might not be so cold and distant toward him. Once the money had been paid, he could kill him anyway. De Montford's sort already considered the common Yates a loutish, dishonorable brute only fit to die in battle; they would not be surprised when he broke his oath and delivered only their lord's head.

As he rode, he refined his plan, fueled by a vaguely remembered biblical story in which a woman demanded a man's head as reward. This time the lovely Adele needed to do nothing to earn her prize; he would gladly give her De Montford's head on a platter.

So appealing was this latest idea that Yates threw back his head in a burst of laughter and kicked his mount to greater speed. Surprised by their leader's unexpected action, the other men also cast caution to the wind and uttered their own battle cries, the sound swelling like some great wind funneling between the mist-wreathed hillocks.

As she rode, tears streamed down Adele's cheeks. How she longed for Moonlight beneath her. Her gelding would have soon outpaced Lorkin Yates's dish-faced nag, allowing her to break ahead to warn Rafe of his danger.

Then a sudden thought struck her, a thought so cheering that Adele drew in a shuddering breath of relief. The men hidden in the mist might not be Rafe's soldiers, after all; she had only Yates's unreliable word to go on. This comforting thought stanched her tears, and Adele straightened in the saddle, her mind already working on an escape plan. She could ride into the mist, then take another path, skirt the fighting, and slip away. Her spirits soared as she pushed her ancient nag to its utmost as she headed for the narrow, mist-locked valley.

A hideous sound coming out of the December morn made the men's hair prickle on the backs of their necks.

"By the Rood! What makes such an unholy racket?" Montsorrel asked, his face paling.

"Sounds like heathens," someone behind him offered helpfully.

Rafe had ridden to the head of the valley and now was galloping back. "Prepare for an attack," he shouted, rousing the last sleeper beside their glowing campfire. "I don't know who they are, but there's a lot of them."

Like Roland holding the pass at Roncesvalles, they chose to make their stand at the narrowest point of the road, standing two abreast.

Rafe narrowed his eyes, trying to pierce the billowing white mist which, even as he watched, seemed to be lifting. Miraculously, the wind had risen, or was it merely the draft from this approaching horde? Swirling away, spiraling toward the grassy uplands, the white blanketing fog slowly floated free, exposing them where they waited; twenty armed men with their lords, prepared to face an army of hundreds.

It had been against Rafe's better judgment that they had chosen to spend the night beside this meandering stream, pausing in their relentless pursuit of Lorkin Yates.

Whose army came to do battle with them, Rafe did not know. He grasped his sword hilt, knees firm against the horse's comforting bulk, and he waited.

Like a great wind the sound grew, identifiable now as human cries and shouts; there were horses too, their hooves ringing over the rocky ground. The moving mass ran into the open. Behind him a man swore, likening the enemies' appearance to the infidel horde he had encountered in the Holy Land. But these were no well-honed Saracen troops. Rafe blinked to clear his vision, unable to believe what he was seeing. He looked again, eyes slitted against a rising dust cloud as a ragtag band of men emerged from the trees. These warriors were like grotesque skeletons brandishing staves and cudgels, mouths wide open, yelling at the top of their lungs as they ran downhill. Bearded and ragged, they looked for all the world like an army of beggars.

When the rabble's leading rank saw the formation of armed men guarding the road, they skittered to a halt so abruptly that the men running behind them fell over their fellows, unable to stop. No one had been expecting mailed knights, for they had thought they were swooping down on a camp of sleeping men, to slaughter and take prisoner with ease.

Rafe cautioned his men to patience. No spears were thrown, though some of the enemy were well within range. From this disorganized mass of bodies, a single man emerged, riding a loping bag of bones. He held another horse's bridle, pulling it after him. A woman rode the second horse, for Rafe could see her flying hair and skirts. Before he had time to ponder this strange sight, the riders came closer, and his heart turned a somersault. No two women had hair like that, billowing about her shoulders, glowing coppery in the light . . .

"Mother of God! Adele!"

"Are you sure?" Montsorrel breathed beside him, as surprised as Rafe by the morning's events.

"Positive. Do nothing. Pass the word back."

Surprised by their latest order, the soldiers waited obediently like steel statues while their opponents milled about, their surprise attack halted before it began. Here a horse snorted and moved its feet, there a tail swished; beyond that, there was no movement from the men blocking the road.

Growing restless, the troops began to argue amongst themselves, trying to place blame for the slowing of their glorious charge.

After angrily quieting them, the rabble's leader rode ahead. All previous plans discarded, he had hit upon the perfect solution, something he had always dreamed of doing, something which would show Adele who was the better man.

"I'm here to challenge Lord De Montford to combat," the man shouted. "Come forward to meet me—unless you're too afraid."

"Don't be a fool!" Montsorrel hissed at Rafe as he sensed movement at his elbow. "He's trying to draw you into the open. Isn't that the bastard we're looking for?"

"That's him."

"We can take him easily. By the look of the rest of them, they'll turn tail at the first sight of blood."

"No. First we have to get Adele to safety. We've no guarantee he won't slit her throat."

"We could confuse them by moving forward."

"No. That's too dangerous. It's me he wants. I'll see what he's made of."

Rafe detached himself from the rest and slowly rode ahead, stopping in the middle of the narrow road. "Here I am. What do you want with me, Lorkin Yates?"

"Oh, so you recognize me, my lord. I'm flattered. My reputation's grown," Yates shouted back sarcastically as he too moved forward until they were close enough to speak. "I've something you want. And, if you're man enough, we can settle the issue once and for all."

"Not until Lady St. Clare is out of harm's way."

"Be damned to that! She stays where she is," Yates cried, yanking Adele's bridle for emphasis.

"You'd fight with the woman as a shield?"

Lorkin Yates was so angry his face turned beet red. An uneasy quiet descended over the squabbling men.

"Damn you, woman! I curse the day we met," Yates hissed. He dragged Adele's heaving beast about. "You've been nothing but trouble."

After a few minutes of waiting, Rafe shouted, "If you don't want to fight singly, there's nothing more to talk about. Attack us."

In amazement Adele watched as Rafe rode back to his men, leaving her at the mercy of this uncouth rabble. When she had heard his voice and known it was really Rafe, her pulse had quickened and her heart had begun to pound with joy and relief. Any minute she'd expected him to break rank and gallop forth to rescue her; Adele had virtually held her breath, waiting, her legs shaking in excitement as she saw him riding toward her. Then his cool, matter-of-fact statement came like a douse of water to extinguish her joy. Even his proposal that she be moved to a safe place before the hostilities began was no more consideration than he would have shown toward any woman in danger.

Rafe had never even looked at her, nor had he asked after her welfare, nor had he cursed Lorkin Yates for taking her captive. Adele was stunned by his apparent disregarding. All the hope went out of her and, like a deflated pig's bladder, she slumped in her saddle, hiding her grief behind a tangle of hair. How could Rafe be so coldly detached after all she had endured? Surely he was not going to abandon her? The conclusion was so earth-shattering, Adele's chest constricted and she found it hard to breathe. Rafe had delivered a cruel blow after all the faith she had placed in him.

The standoff dragged on, each side awaiting the other's first move. Adele had seen the Montsorrel pennant fluttering beside Rafe's at the head of the troop. Gerard was here also. Why didn't they come together to rescue her? Had she been on Moonlight, Adele could have easily galloped that short distance herself. Lorkin Yates's rabble clearly outnumbered them, yet they had no stomach for fighting trained knights. Yates might call them his army, but they had not eaten this morning, nor had they been paid. Before long, most of these men would seek some other employment, for loyalty was not a virtue of hungry men.

Adele tossed back her hair with new determination, welcoming the cool breeze against her hot, wet cheeks. What was the matter with these men? Behind her, the undisciplined rabble were still arguing and squabbling; before her, Rafe's and Montsorrel's armed men stood like statues. Did any of them consider her welfare in their stubborn show of pride? Lorkin Yates had dismounted, almost coming to blows with the young giant who had acted as her bodyguard.

Adele considered a daring move, excitement rippling through her body. She drew in her breath, instantly making the decision. She would not wait to be rescued: she

205

would take matters into her own hands. This poor, broken-down animal she straddled had rested; his scarred sides no longer heaved. This one final, desperate push would likely be the end of him. Adele patted the scabby, notched ears, whispering to the old horse as she stroked his rough coat. Her only chance of freedom lay with this pathetic nag.

Kicking his flanks and simultaneously yanking his bit, she brought the horse back to life. The startled nag bolted. The wind whipped Adele's face, her hair streaming behind her as she made a desperate break for freedom. In the uproar behind her, Adele could hear Yates bellowing for her to stop. Some of his men sprinted after her and tried to catch her bridle, but she ignored them all, squeezing the utmost out of the poor old horse.

Looking surprised, Rafe spurred forward, covering the ground between them with lightning speed. Almost before Yates had scrambled back in the saddle, it was over. Adele rode madly toward her lover. Rafe reached out to her. Beneath his mailed coif his handsome face was not icily impassive as she had expected, but full of love and concern. Adele's heart soared with joy as she saw that emotion, so obvious it might have been written across his face.

"Thank God! Oh, Adele, sweetheart."

Rafe swept her off the shuddering old horse and placed her before him astride his big chestnut stallion. Adele reveled in the strength of his arms as he enfolded her in that safe haven and she leaned back against his chest. How she longed to hug and kiss him, but this was not the time or place for such display.

"Rafe, you're the answer to my prayers," she said, the wind fanning her face now wet with tears of joy.

"And you, sweetheart, are the subject of all of mine," he replied, his mouth against her ear so that she felt the warm caress of his breath. Rafe had never considered she would make so daring a move, and he was impressed by her horsemanship. A lesser rider could not have gotten such speed out of the old beast she'd ridden.

Adele could hardly believe Rafe held her safe in his arms. When they reached his men, everyone cheered her daring escape. Rafe put Adele astride a new horse and placed her in the center of his men for protection. He turned the old nag loose, and it stood shuddering beside the road.

Rafe embraced her but his mail felt cold and alien against Adele's flesh. Then the heat of his mouth made up for the discomfort as he kissed her—hard and passionately. Adele gloried in the feel of his body against hers, in his tender touch and the taste of his mouth. Too soon it was over. Rafe's eyes softened as he gazed at her with the utmost love, making Adele ashamed she had ever doubted him.

Rafe smiled at Adele, and he gave a handclasp so swift that she was not even sure the touch had actually taken place before it was over and he was riding back to the head of his men.

"All right, you coward, you've got what you wanted. Come out and face me! Or are you going to hide behind your soldiers, too afraid to fight a real man?" Yates's voice bridged the distance between them, full of fury.

The chilling knowledge that the day was far from won seeped back into Adele's thoughts as she listened to Lorkin Yates bellowing at the top of his lungs.

Rafe sat in the saddle at the front of his men considering what to do.

One hurdle was overcome—Adele was safe. That was what he had needed most. But there was still Lorkin Yates to deal with. The man was now spewing venom, taunting, ridiculing, until Rafe longed to strangle him into silence.

Chivalry demanded he take the miscreant into custody, for he knew he was an outlaw. Capturing Yates would be an easy task: his men were well trained and battle-tested. He suspected that Yates's rabble would soon turn tail when the fighting turned serious. But, law aside, the score he had to settle with this man was strictly personal. Most of all, he wanted to make Yates pay for all the pain he had caused Adele.

His mind made up, Rafe rode out into the open to face his enemy across the heath. Astride his blooded chestnut stallion, Rafe's splendid appearance further belittled the ragged man astride his worn-out dray.

"Here I am, Yates. What do you want with me?"

"A fight, you arrogant bastard. Not a joust on a horse, but here on the ground, hand to hand, like a man."

Adele knew that Rafe would accept the challenge before he even spoke. But he had been wounded in the tournament; she remembered seeing it happen and had felt his bandage when they'd embraced. She now feared for that. The wound might have been minor, but it might now cost him his life.

Lorkin Yates was virtually bristling with hatred, the emotion boosting his courage, and he was also fresh. Worsen he followed no code of ethics when it came to combat. At one time, she would not have hesitated to pit Rafe against Yates, confident in his ability; today she was afraid Lorkin Yates held all the advantages.

But to publicly protest their combat would have shamed the man she loved, so Adele kept quiet, sitting white-lipped and straight, watching between her horse's ears as the combatants selected a flat area which provided a natural arena. Most of the rabble army had already sprawled on the ground, like a holiday crowd awaiting entertainment. Men were even placing bets on the outcome; though Adele could not hear what was said, their movements gave them away. In a mean-spirited way, she was pleased that most had placed their wagers on the more skillful knight.

Lorkin Yates dismounted, his flushed face a mask of hatred as he stood waiting with sword and dagger. His bravado was bolstered by a smattering of applause from his fellows. He wore a boiled leather jack and studded leather wristguards, and steel greaves were tied around his sturdy legs. He even had a borrowed helmet on his head.

Rafe dismounted also, handing his horse to Symme. He drew his sword from its scabbard and retained his favorite knife. Symme tossed him his shield, and Rafe waited until Lorkin Yates was similarly accoutered.

"You're not so big now, nobleman," Yates sneered as he swaggered back and forth, flexing his muscles.

"What are the terms?" Rafe asked.

"A fight to the death."

"And the prize to the victor? For surely I should know what I'm risking my life for."

Yates swore as he dashed sweat from his brow.

"Haven't you guessed? Yon flame-haired bitch goes to the winner."

"We fight," Rafe said, teeth gritted in anger against the other man's insulting words. He must take care—anger was not a true friend, a lesson his opponent had not yet learned.

Carefully, coolly, Rafe sized up the other man. He knew he had the advantages of height and reach, but they would work against him if Yates breached his defense and moved in close with his dagger. His opponent was also younger, and his broad shoulders and deep chest revealed some strength. Though not a trained knight, Yates had been a *routier* in the employ of several masters. More important still, he was not fighting with unhealed wounds.

Gerald Monstorrel and a designated man from Yates's army acted as seconds. Adele could hardly bear to watch. It was only a heartbeat ago that Rafe had rescued her, now she must watch him fight for his life. To have reminded him he was wounded, or that he took a needless risk in satisfying this challenge, would have been useless.

All eyes were on the two men, one tall and broad-shouldered with an emblazoned surcoat covering his hauberk, the other bearded, stocky, and fierce, clad in a foot soldier's boiled leather armor. Each man flexed his sword arm and made a few practice sweeps before declaring himself ready.

Silence descended as Montsorrel began to count.

With a hideous clang, the combatants' swords engaged. Agilely bending, leaping, the two men moved back and forth across the scrubby ground. The flat terrain favored neither man, and all rocks had been removed to prevent stumbles. Cries of warning or of triumph echoed continually from both camps as each man delivered or dodged powerful blows. Crimson stains were visibly spreading along both men's arms. Yates's blood was fresh; Rafe's came from his reopened wound.

Back and forth they went, trading blows, the metallic ring of blades and the dull thump of deflected strikes a rhythmic accompaniment to this dance of death. Rafe soon discovered that the strength and stamina of his wounded arm was greatly diminished. There had not been time enough for his shoulder to heal, or his sliced forearm to knit: growing wetness oozing inside his sleeves told him they had both burst open. He was also bruised and stiff after competing in the recent tourney, and not nearly as agile as he would have liked.

A foolish mistake and Rafe sent Yates's sword hurtling through the air. But there was little time for rejoicing as Yates came at him again with renewed vigor. To his surprise, Rafe saw that his enemy now held a dagger in each hand. The bastard must have hidden a second weapon about his person. It did not matter. This was not a tourney with a group of marshals to whom he could appeal. This was a fight to the death.

In a moment of weakness, Rafe stumbled, going to his knees. Instantly, Yates was on top of him, twisting his wounded arm, pounding his wounded shoulder, until red flashes danced before Rafe's eyes and sweat drenched his body beneath his hauberk. They both grappled for Rafe's sword until his foe finally kicked it out of reach. He tasted blood in his mouth as his head was repeatedly smashed on the ground. And he felt a sudden burning pain as Yates's dagger found a home in his shoulder.

Rafe saw his enemy's lips draw back in a feral grin of triumph. Yates was convinced he was already the victor. The overconfidence made him careless, and Rafe suddenly heaved him aside, sending him crashing in the dirt. Before Yates could right himself, Rafe was atop him, crushing the breath from his body. He grasped Yates's wrist and bent it back, struggling for the dagger, its blade already wet with his blood. Rafe bent the wrist back, keeping Yates's flailing legs imprisoned with his own. Slowly his foe yielded until he finally dropped the knife, yelling in pain as he stopped just short of having his wrist snapped.

Now they were even with one dagger each.

Rafe allowed his opponent to get up, and Yates immediately went into a crouch, his face blackened by sweat mingled with dirt. He came out of the crouch so fast that Rafe was taken by surprise and he went crashing to the ground under the force of the assault, a hollow ringing sound filling his helmet. His ears were buzzing as they rolled over and over, each man struggling to gain the upper hand. Finally, Rafe was able to force Yates's deadly blade aside as he fought him with both hands, holding his own dagger in his teeth. Screaming in pain, Yates's fingers gradually loosened their grip and his dagger fell blade down in the dirt.

With a lightning-quick move, Rafe held his dagger against Yates's unprotected throat. A gasp went up from the crowd—the fight was as good as over! Rafe knelt there, pinning his foe under his body, hesitating to complete the act. The sharp blade grazed the other man's skin. It would have been so easy to pull his dagger across Yates's windpipe, ending his evil forever.

"Adele's mine," Rafe growled, spitting blood from his split lip. "Agreed?"

Eyes rolling in fear, Yates nodded.

"I've no need to kill you. I'll leave that to the hang-man," Rafe said, slowly drawing back, his dagger poised in his hand.

"Let it be known, Lord Rafe De Montford is the win-ner of this contest. And by his choice, he allows Lorkin Yates to live."

A great cheer went up as Gerard Montsorrel made the solemn announcement that Rafe had generously given his enemy the gift of life. Rafe reached out his hand to help the other man from the ground; then he turned aside to receive his men's cheering congratulations.

Adele's tears were of joy and relief, her face aglow. It was over at last. Rafe was alive. She would fear Lorkin Yates no longer.

Symme took Rafe's helmet. Rafe unfastened his coif and padded hood and dropped the head covering back, glad of the wet cloth his man proffered to wipe the sweat and grime off his face. This done, Rafe knelt down to adjust one of his leg greaves which had come loose in the fight.

Bleeding and filthy, the glowering Yates stood watch-ing, unsure what to do. De Montford could have killed him but had chosen to spare his life. He did not want pity from that arrogant bastard. This had been a fight to the death, and one of them must die!

"No—damn it, no!" he yelled, suddenly hurtling for-ward.

Steel glinted in his hand, and a collective gasp came from the onlookers. Adele screamed in warning. Before Rafe could move, Lorkin Yates had buried his dagger to the hilt in his enemy's back. Rafe fell forward under the force of the blow. Yet when his men would have killed Yates, Rafe called for them to back off. He stood and spun about. He grasped Yates's arm, bending it back mer-cilessly until the bone snapped.

"You bastard! Doing this after I let you live," he spat. The scene began to spin before him. A deep, burning pain gripped his shoulders, virtually robbing him of the ability to think. With his faltering arm, Rafe plunged his dagger deep into Yates's chest penetrating a vulnerable place in his leather jack. In a last frenzied burst of strength, Yates grasped Rafe's throat, speaking through the blood that bubbled out of his mouth. "You've killed me, but Cosantine remains."

The two fell to the ground.

Monstorrel crouched beside his friend, paying attention to Yates only enough to pull him away. Symme and a half-dozen others frantically worked to strip off Rafe's mail shirt and hauberk, removing Yates's dagger with a great gush of blood, then working frantically to stop the spurting tide with Rafe's wadded surcoat.

Adele heard Yates's mumbled words as she stood on the fringe of the group, rudely pushed aside, shut out of this fight to stanch Rafe's blood.

"What did you mean about Sir Guy?" she asked, bending over the outlaws to hear. Someone thrust a ragged blanket in her arms and she covered him with it. He was already shaking with the chill of death.

His blood-caked lips twisted in a grimace, Lorkin Yates struggled to form the words. "I'm sorry," he whispered, aware of her kindness. "I loved you, Adele . . . though I've done a poor job of showing you. But you could never love a commoner. Cosantine's betrayed you to the king for land . . ."

He wanted to say more but seemed unable to draw breath. Several of his henchmen came to take Yates away. Adele stepped back and let him go, still puzzling over Sir Guy's role in this.

The men attending Rafe moved back to give him air, and Adele was able to slip between them to kneel at his side. She barely noticed when they carried Lorkin Yates's body away, but she was too concerned with saving Rafe's life to care.

Chapter Thirteen

As far as the eye could see, the grizzled countryside was blanketed with mist. As the travelers neared Fordham Castle, the terrain grew steadily steeper. Here bare winter trees leaned with the prevailing wind. Hidden by mist, distant sheep bleated, and beside the road the thick, shaggy coats of grazing cattle and horses attested to the region's bleak winter.

Adele scanned a range of low grassy hills rolling north. Over the first hillocks lay Fordham. Within the hour they would be home and this nightmare journey over. How strange to be thinking of an unfamiliar castle as home. This land was Rafe's, and she hoped it would be hers also someday. It had taken less time than she expected to reach Fordham, thanks to Gerard Montsorrel. The kind nobleman had escorted her to the castle along the swiftest route. Adele was grateful for his help in caring for Rafe, for she had little experience in nursing wounded men.

Riders appeared out of the dissipating mist ahead, cresting the round-topped hill and galloping down the slope. Adele heard the alarm being given, and her heart thumped in fear, aware they were a pitiful few to fight off bandits.

She need not have feared, for she heard one of the approaching riders cry, "It's our lord."

This was an advance party from Fordham, riding out to meet their wounded lord, having been informed of his impending arrival by a peddler traveling to York.

Relief washed over Adele, for in truth she had little faith in the fellow she had hired at an inn to carry her message to Rafe's castle. Thank God he had kept his word. Now everything would be in readiness for Rafe's care.

As they rode ahead, the mist lifted. Adele had a clear view of the forbidding stone walls of Rafe's turreted stronghold, perched on the craggy summit of the closest hill. Even as she looked at its gray walls, a wan winter sun struggled from behind the bank of clouds, its faint rays softening the harsh scene. Adele chose to believe it was an omen of hope.

By the time they entered the inner bailey and Rafe was carried inside the castle, the feeble December sun was already setting, a trail of wispy silver in its wake, the final pale rays fading over the nearby hills.

Arthur, the castle steward, came out to welcome his lord home, though Adele could tell her presence puzzled him. She wondered if he would be more accepting of her if she told him she was Rafe's intended bride. Her tangled hair and soiled clothes made her look like a common camp follower. When she first introduced herself as Lady Adele St. Clare, she saw a slight disbelieving smirk on his thin mouth, and his bold assessment of her person bordered on insolence. Anger bubbled inside her, but she swallowed it down, aware it was not her place to correct Rafe's servants. Yet.

The lord's chamber was at the top of a flight of stairs, and Rafe groaned as he was jostled at every step, though his men tried to be careful as they negotiated the steep treads. Finally they laid Rafe on a massive feather bed hung with gold-embroidered blue velvet curtains.

To her great relief, Adele noticed Adric standing in the shadows.

"Oh, Adric, I'm so glad you're here. Do you nurse men as well as animals?" she asked hopefully. To her great disappointment, Adric shook his head.

"Nay, Lady, I've no truck with men's ills," he said, his voice husky with grief as he looked as his lord's pale face. "And he's lost much blood, from the look of it."

Gerard Montsorrell had already given orders to the castle kitchens to prepare beef broth and milk custards, foods that Rafe might easily digest.

"I feel like a traitor leaving you alone," he apologized, taking Adele's hand in parting. "But now's not a time to be away from one's lands. He's in good hands now. His own people will soon nurse him back to health."

"Thank you for your help," Adele said, her lip quivering at the prospect of losing this familiar companion on whom she had relied. "You do truly believe he'll get well?"

Gerard grinned. "Of course, Lady Adele. Rafe'll be on his feet before Christmas. Make sure he takes nourishment, though, even if you have to feed him like a baby. Besides, having you here will be an extra incentive to get well," he added with a smile.

His face clouded when he added quietly, "If the times were not so troubled, I'd gladly spend a few days here at Fordham nursing my leg. Fortunately, I'm not too far away. I must get home to sound out tenants and neighbors, possibly prepare to defend our lands . . . no one knows what the future holds. Did Rafe tell you we may go to war unless the king comes to his senses."

"Yes. Civil war," she mused.

"Aye, but there'll be little civil about it. And choosing the right side will make or break many men."

Adele pondered Gerard's sobering statement as she sat beside Rafe, watching over him as he tossed in restless sleep. His tapestry-draped chamber was very grand, with every effort made to make it comfortable, from its padded chairs and blue cushioned settle, to the heavy bed hangings and animal pelts atop the rushes. In the corner hearth a great fire blazed, bright orange flames leaping and dancing up the sooty chimney, adding their own light to bolster the half-dozen candles burning in holders on the carved oaken chest beside the bed.

No one had given her a place to sleep, so Adele curled up on the settle beside the hearth. Now that they were at Fordham, maybe she could change her clothes, for these garments were nothing but rags, all torn and soiled, the brocade shredded where fur trimming had been ripped away. Despite her ragged dress, she still had Rafe's ring. She turned it around on her finger, smiling to recall happier times. Lorkin Yates had bullied and threatened her to give him the ring, but she had always refused.

During this past year, so much had happened to her, both good and bad. It was amazing to think it all had begun on that fateful snowy day when she watched the soldiers from the wood. . . .

A rap on the door roused her from her thoughts. A maid carried in a tray of food and set it on the bedside chest. There was meat and thick bread for her, a steaming bowl of rich broth for the invalid. The scullery maid had been told to stay to feed her master, but Adele said she would feed Rafe. She sent the maid for fresh linens to dress his wounds.

Though she tried, Adele could not get Rafe to open his mouth, so she went back to her own supper. As she chewed the tough, flavorless meat and spread the coarse bread with butter, the poor quality of the food only reinforced her suspicions that the steward thought her some common servant girl. Even the maid had stared insolently at the rents in her gown and had deliberately taken her time in following Adele's orders. After Rafe was fed and his wounds dressed, Adele would bathe and find clean clothing more befitting her station. Perhaps then these servants would give her the respect she was due.

In the meantime, the daunting task of dressing Rafe's wounds lay ahead. Adele knew that Symme, Rafe's squire, would have done it for her, but she also knew the lad was weary and needed rest. She would learn to care for Rafe herself.

Adele moved the candles closer to the bed to give more light. She lifted aside his wool tunic, slashed in places to accommodate the thick bandages. Slowly, taking care not to hurt him, she unwound the linen strips. As she feared, the bumping wagon traveling rough country roads and the jarring from carrying him up the stairs had made his wounds remain fresh. The bandage around his chest had a bright new stain. With a shudder of revulsion, Adele steeled herself as she uncovered the spongy, four-inch gash by his shoulder and the lesser cuts on his forearm. They were hot and oozing from an infection.

The maid returned with basins, cloths, and rolls of linen, and she grudgingly helped Adele wash Rafe's wounds and apply the last of the healing salve she had brought. After they had redressed these wounds, they struggled to turn Rafe over to attend to the wound on his back, but he was heavy and uncooperative. Reluctantly, Adele went to the door to call Symme. As if he had been awaiting her summons, he sprinted upstairs.

"We need your help to turn him," she explained, trying to appear calm, though her anticipation of seeing the horrid wound made her stomach pitch. Adele had not yet seen it.

"Mayhap you should send for one of the men to help—it's not a pretty sight, my lady," Symme suggested, aware of her inner struggle, his sharp features appearing drawn in the candlelight.

"No. I must learn to do it."

Symme shrugged and walked with her to the bed. Sweat beaded the young man's brow as they struggled to turn Rafe over, but they finally did. The bandages around his body were thick, but Adele uncovered him. Watty, the old soldier who cared for the injured on the road, had packed Rafe's wound with clean linen to stop the bleeding, followed by a poultice of moldy bread to fight infection.

With a gasp of horror, Adele turned away from the suppurating gash, still oozing red from its dark depth. She took a deep breath and, with fresh determination, returned to her task. Together they picked out the last of the bread still clinging to Rafe's flesh, then bathed the area and spooned the last of Watty's special salve into the opening.

As they worked, Rafe groaned, sometimes crying out in pain, the sounds making Adele stop what she was doing. When Rafe began to thrash about, Symme forced drops of poppy seed tea between his teeth. It was not enough to make Rafe unconscious, but Symme hoped it was enough to take the edge off his pain.

Before they were done, Adele had began to sweat profusely. Nausea washed over her, forcing her to sit with her head in her hands until the feeling passed. Finally, they were done.

"Thank you, Symme," Adele said when the man had finished the bandaging and stood hesitantly in the doorway.

"I can watch him tonight, my lady, if you want to sleep," he offered, before adding, "His fever's worse than ever."

Adele had also felt that raging heat when she touched his body.

"Have them send up cold water and cloths. Maybe you can show me the infirmary. There'll surely be some salve or poppy brew there."

Symme shook his head. "No. There's little of use in there."

Adele sighed, wondering where else to turn. "Is there an abbey nearby? An abbey would have medicine."

"There's no abbey for fifty miles." Symme glanced away before he finally suggested gruffly, "There's Mistress Gallett. . . . We could send for her. She's got healing salves aplenty."

With a great sigh of relief, Adele said, "Well, what are we waiting for? Get her. I'm not very skilled at treating wounds. I know we need sallow willow for the fever and something to draw out infection, but she'll know what to bring."

Symme did not move.

"Well, what's wrong now?" Adele asked, her impatience growing.

"Mistress Gallett's a witch, my lady."

Adele gasped in surprise. "You mean a wise woman," she corrected helpfully.

"No, my Lady. A witch. Lord Rafe forbade her entrance here."

"Why?"

"She tried to bewitch him," Symme mumbled, glancing away. "See yon cottage down there? Her daughter lives there."

Adele looked where the lad pointed, seeing a faint light flickering in the December night.

"Then bring her daughter also. Please, Symme, we must have healing herbs or your lord might die."

Symme blanched as he nervously twisted his hands. "You're ordering me to bring Sadie Gallett here as well?" he asked, as if she were making a mistake.

"Why not? Is she a witch also?"

Symme shrugged. "Some say so. It's just that she's known as the most beautiful woman hereabouts." He flushed and looked down at the floor. "That's why I was asking."

It was a point well taken. Aware that it could be unwise to bring such a beautiful woman here to treat her lover, Adele also knew that without medicine Rafe could die.

"All right. Send that maid in to watch him. We'll look in the infirmary before summoning the Galletts, to see if there's something I can do alone."

Adele instructed the servant girl to feed her lord broth after Symme propped him against a mound of feather pillows.

The castle corridors were dark and cold. The men-at-arms who guarded the keep watched Adele suspiciously as she walked past, curious to know why she was there. Symme took her swiftly to the castle infirmary. It seemed to be in the coldest, darkest part of the castle.

It was damp and bone-chillingly cold inside the unheated room; moisture from the moat seeped through the masonry slabs and trickled down the walls. Adele huddled inside her cloak, glad she'd had the forethought to wear it. By the light of a candle stub, she peered at the rows of cobwebby pots, delighted to find one labeled Primrose Salve. Everything here was dusty and neglected; Adele had to blow dust off the jars to be able to read their labels, the faint letters written in a spidery hand. She also found a linen pouch of unsteeped poppy heads hanging from the rafters and a tub of goose grease to use as a base for ointments. Adele unearthed several more murky linen pouches which held dried herb Robert, yarrow, and stitchwort, identifiable by their smell.

"After Mistress Gallett was sent away, things were let go," Symme apologized, quickly pushing a bundle of dried rabbits' paws and some dead toads out of sight. He was not quick enough to conceal a vessel of preserved mice floating in some yellow liquid.

Adele saw these unsavory ingredients and couldn't imagine their uses—perhaps ingredients for spells. She had no idea what other ghastly discoveries they might make under the dust and cobwebs. From what she had already seen, the evidence was stacked against Mistress Gallett. Still . . .

"Will Lord Rafe be angry if I send for Mistress Gallett?" Adele asked Symme.

He shrugged. "Well, likely he will—but if she keeps him alive . . . The priest said we'd go to hell if she stayed in the castle, what with all her spells and such."

"Where's the priest now?"

"Dead—a year come Candlemas."

They exchanged grins.

221

"Go bring Mistress Gallett."

"And Mistress Sadie too?"

For a moment Adele hesitated, aware they inviting the beautiful Sadie here could be a mistake, yet Rafe's worsening condition made her desperate and she ignored her uneasy feeling. "Yes, if she knows aught of healing, bring her as well."

Symme left, wrapped in a dark cloak and promising to slip quietly through the postern gate so as not to attract attention. Adele retraced her steps to the lord's chamber, making several wrong turns in the castle's dark corridors before she found the right passage, her steps echoing eerily. She was glad when she finally reached Rafe's lighted chamber.

The maid was most pleased to see her, for she had not been able to feed her master and was afraid she would be punished. Adele took over the task, asking the girl to bring wash water and clean clothes. The wench agreed, but her disrespectful manner made Adele want to slap her pert face.

Adele wiped Rafe's chin dry where the broth had trickled; his teeth were still clenched and he would not open them. She leaned over him, kissing his brow, stroking back his dark hair while she whispered and cajoled him, cosseting him as if he were a small child. At first Rafe did not respond; then he gradually relaxed, and by the smile playing about his mouth she knew he'd understood.

Adele was able to get several spoonfuls of rich broth in his mouth, then massaged his throat to make him swallow. Two spoonfuls. Four. Then suddenly his teeth clenched again and he would take no more.

Adele sighed, despairing of Rafe ever regaining his strength if he did not eat more than this. She took away the heaped pillows so that he could lie down, though she wondered how he could sleep with the pain in his back. His head was hot, but she still covered him with a blanket, aware that in a few minutes he would be shivering with cold.

Going back to the hearth, Adele selected herbs from the basket she'd found in the infirmary. The goose grease was so hard from being in the cold room that she could not work it, so she set the tub by the fire to soften. Adele lay back against a cushion to wait, and a few minutes later she was asleep.

A soft, damp nuzzling in her hand awakened her. Adele blinked in surprise as she saw a familiar black head resting on her lap, large brown eyes gazing soulfully into hers.

"Val!" she gasped, convinced she must be dreaming.

"Go on, lad, it's all right—she's awake now," she heard Adric urge from the shadows.

Whimpering in pleasure, Val placed his large front feet on Adele's lap and gently licked her face, his delight in seeing her attested by his wildly swishing tail, though he kept his greeting restrained as if he knew they were in an invalid's room.

"Oh, darling, you're good as new," Adele whispered after examining his sleek body. Then she put her arms around Val's muscular shoulders and hugged him. "We have dear Adric to thank for that," she said, smiling at the man, who glanced away in embarrassment. "Thank you, Adric, for nursing him back to health. Val means a lot to me."

"I know that, my lady. Yon lad was a right pleasure to care for. And your Moonlight, and all."

Eyes rounded in delight, Adele gasped. "You have Moonlight here, too! Oh, Adric, I can't believe it." Tears of happiness welled in her eyes at the joy of discovering that both her beloved pets animals were safe. "Can I see him tomorrow?"

"Oh, aye. See him tonight if you want, but if I was you, I'd wait. It's frosty out and terrible cold for visiting."

Adele smiled as with a deep sigh of pleasure Val settled at her feet. "Come here to the fire, Adric, and warm yourself," she suggested.

"Well, Lady, there's summat else I have to tell thee. You see . . . I've took your Margery to wife . . . if that suits you."

"Suits me! I'm delighted for you both," she gasped in surprise. "So Margery's here as well . . . and Kate too?"

"Nay, His Lordship thought it better to send the little lass back to her mother. Your Margery's proud to act as your waiting woman still, if you'll have her. She's a grand woman, my lady, I couldn't ask for better."

After Adric had gone, Adele sat stroking Val before the hearth, digesting this amazing news. It was more than she'd expected to have her beloved animals waiting for her. To have Margery married to Adric, of all people, who she was convinced had saved Val's life, was delightful. If only she could find someone to work the same miracle for Rafe.

She glanced over at the bed, and her good humor slipped away. How ill he was, tossing, turning, his fever unabated. None of those other delights would have meaning if she lost Rafe.

Sometime later the door creaked open, and Val gave a low warning growl. A shawled woman came quietly into the room, a wicker basket on her arm. Through the open door Adele could see Rafe's guards crossing themselves as the woman passed. Another cloaked woman walked behind her, her face shrouded inside a dark hood.

Adele stood to welcome them.

"Please come in, Mistress Gallett. I need your healing knowledge to cure Lord Rafe's wounds," she stated simply.

The old woman squinted up at Adele through a cloud of wiry gray hair, her lined face decidedly hostile. "And who be you?" she demanded, shuffling toward the hearth to warm herself. "Not another of them strumpets who's always hanging about?"

"I'm Lady Adele St. Clare. And I'm definitely not a strumpet," Adele replied indignantly, drawing herself to her full height and tossing her hair back from her face.

"Oh, all high and mighty, are we?" the old woman cackled. "Well, girlie, tonight you could pass for one."

Mortified by the truth of that statement, Adele felt her cheeks growing hot. The other woman still waited hesitantly in the doorway, until the old one motioned her forward.

"Come on, girl, you'll give him his death of cold with that door open."

Adele stared in amazement at the beautiful apparition who seemed to float inside the room. This must be Sadie Gallett. Now she understood why Symme was hesitant to send for her. Throwing back her hood, the younger woman shook out her cloud of curly black hair. She had smooth skin, bronze as a gypsy's and large, liquid brown eyes beneath perfectly arched brows, her high-bridged nose had flaring nostrils, and her pink mouth was soft and full. Sadie Gallett had a strange, exotic air about her, quite unlike anyone Adele had ever seen before. A sinking feeling returned to her stomach. It most certainly would have been wiser not to invite Sadie Gallett to the castle. She doubted that any man alive would have the willpower to refuse this woman anything.

"How bad is his Lordship wounded?" Sadie asked Adele as she came to the fire to warm her hands. Her voice was unexpectedly soft and musical. Tall and reed-slender, she wore a muted purple gown under a black tunic which flashed and glittered as she moved, reflecting the light from the fire.

Though she tried, Adele could find no fault with either Sadie Gallett's face or form.

"He has a deep knife wound on his upper back and some lesser cuts. He's fevered and chilled by turns, and whatever I give him does nothing. He can barely eat."

"Worms eat away the dead flesh," Mistress Gallett offered as she shuffled to the bed. She laid her head against Rafe's chest. "Didn't hurt his lungs none," she observed with satisfaction. "You're fortunate there."

"Mother has to get a feeling for an ailment," Sadie explained as Adele watched in concern while the old woman lifted Rafe's eyelids, pried open his mouth, and

225

felt the pulse in his neck. "I haven't seen you before. Are you his wife?" Sadie continued, reaching her elegant, long-fingered hands toward the warmth of the fire.

Adele swallowed, hearing mockery in Sadie's voice. The other woman had critically studied her shabby dress, staring at the tears in her stained skirt and the frayed edges where the once rich trimming had been torn away.

"No, though I hope to be one day."

Sadie smiled slyly. "A lot of women fancy Lord Rafe. To be his bride was my wish, too . . . once," she revealed, looking pleased by Adele's gulp of surprise at her words.

Oh, why had she not guessed there had been something between Rafe and Sadie Gallett? This woman's startling beauty, the fact that she lived within sight of Rafe's castle, and Symme's obvious reluctance to bring her here—these things should have been warning enough. Like a fool, she had not considered the possibility until it was too late. Now she knew why she had felt that inner warning. Her unexpected discovery was such a shock that Adele sat abruptly on the settee as a wave of nausea washed over her. The sly smile on Sadie Gallett's mouth revealed satisfaction over the effect of her disclosure.

Mistress Gallett came back to the hearth and crouched down to rummage through her basket. Sadie deftly picked out a packet and handed it to her. "You do want him to live?" the old woman asked suddenly, peering up at Adele.

"Of course! That's why I sent for you."

The old woman grinned her toothless grin. "That's not always the reason folks send for me. I've potions to suit either wish."

"I want you to cure him, to make him strong, just the way he was, instead of lying there like an invalid."

"Oh, yes, most definitely make him the way he was," Sadie interrupted with a throaty chuckle.

"Be quiet, girl, no one's asking you," the old woman snapped. "You had your chance."

Sadie's mouth turned down and, duly chastised, she held her tongue.

"In that case, here's what you have to do. Stop the cooling cloths, that's useless. Have 'em build up the fire. Close the shutters. Heap all the covers you can find on him ... wolf robes, blankets, anything to make 'im sweat. Then give 'im this, steeped in wine or ale." She pressed a handful of ground herbs into Adele's hand. "When the poison's sweated out of him, he'll take a turn for the better."

Eyes filling with tears of gratitude, Adele clasped the old woman's gnarled hand. Mistress Gallett swiftly turned Adele's palm uppermost, squinting as she studied what was revealed there. Finally, when she looked up, her beady eyes were brightly inquisitive. "You've suffered much of late, Lady, and all to bring you to this place—for this purpose. There he is. His life's in your hands."

Adele was unsurprised by the old woman's words. "I'll do whatever you tell me, Mistress Gallett. And I thank you from the bottom of my heart."

The crone grinned broadly, revealing a lone, blackened tooth. "Take care. You'll have to fight to take your rightful place here. Given half the chance, some of these people would boot you out with a broom to your backside. And he can't help you this time."

Adele accepted her advice. "I doubt that anyone will respect me until I'm out of these rags." She had no need to wear rags, not when her own trunks were at Fordham, but she had simply not had the time or inclination to change yet. Not with Rafe so sick.

Mistress Gallett went back to the lord's beside, and she watched him tossing and turning. Leaning over him, the old witch muttered some unintelligible rhyme while her hands hovered above his head and then his heart, gradually moving the length of his body and back, her voice growing stranger while she chanted in singsong.

Adele tensed as she listened to the strange, foreign-sounding words, torn between the church's teachings and her desire to save Rafe's life. It was all she could manage to keep from crossing herself in protection, just like the superstitious soldiers waiting outside. The low chant continued, and the room seemed to crackle with energy, further convincing her that Mistress Gallett was casting a spell.

Adele watched with some fear, and when she glanced at Sadie, the young beauty stared at her with a mocking smile. It was as if the girl were aware of Adele's inner battle between Christian belief and the old religion. Finally, Mistress Gallett turned from the bed and, glancing from one young woman to the other, sensed the growing tension between them.

"Get them fires going, Lady," she said to break their staredown. "And once the fever's broke, give 'im spoonfuls of this."

Gallett pressed a small pot containing a dark, sticky substance into Adele's hand, seemingly plucking it out of thin air. The healer must have had the substance hidden about her person, for Adele had seen nothing in her hands when she went to the bed, nor had she taken anything out of the basket.

The two women pulled on their cloaks and, carrying the basket, headed for the door. Val watched them unmoving from his post beside the settee, neither greeting them as friends nor treating them as enemies, silent as if he too had been bewitched.

"Will you come back tomorrow?"

"I'll know when it's time, Lady," said the old woman. She opened the door to admit a draft of cold air.

From all the shuffling and bumping taking place, Adele realized the guards had been listening at the door. Now they scrambled out of the women's way, desperate to avoid bodily contact with the witches.

After cackling in amusement at their fear, Mistress Gallett hissed at them and thrust out her arm. She pointed to each man in turn, chanting some gibberish. Eyes wide with terror, those nearest her crossed themselves, hugging the stone walls so as not to be touched by her, convinced the old woman was bewitching them. Her wild laughter still echoed down the corridor long after she had gone, the eerie sound sending a chill creeping along Adele's spine.

Now that the Gallett women were gone, Adele realized the soldiers were staring at her, hostility apparent in their scowls. She had sent for the witches, bringing the stink of brimstone into their castle. Because she had called on the devil's own, was she evil also? Adele could almost read their minds, and cold fear prickled down her back. If these men reacted out of superstition and cast her out, she was certain Rafe would die.

"Symme," she called, peering at these grizzled faces in the half-light, searching in vain for the smooth-cheeked squire. Symme did not appear, and no one offered to get him. Anger and fear mingled to harshen Adele's voice. "Are you deaf? Bring Symme to me. And get Adric, and Ivo and his brother," she added, divinely inspired as she recalled Rafe's men who had accompanied them on the journey.

The soldiers glanced at each other, surprised she knew their comrade's names. Was this a common slut who traveled with the troops, or could she really be who she claimed?

"If you want your lord to live to see another day, then do as I say," Adele snapped, deepening her voice, making it echo through the corridor. As she had hoped, her warning set them in motion. One of the younger soldiers took off running to fetch the men she named. Adele nodded in thanks and stepped back inside the room. She shut the door.

Here, in the safety of the firelit chamber, she leaned weakly against the door and tried to draw an even breath. She had come within a hair's breadth of being thrown out into the night with the two witches. Mumbling hasty prayers of thanks, Adele forced herself to action.

There was already a pile of extra logs heaped beside the hearth, and she struggled to stack as many on the fire as the grate would hold, poking the embers into flame. In the bedside chest were wool blankets and a wolf robe.

Going against all she had learned about cooling cloths and cold water to reduce a fever, she would increase his temperature to sweat the poison from his body. Not entirely sure if this would cure him or make matters worse, Adele followed Mistress Gallett's instructions. They were the last hope she had.

The sound of running feet outside the door told her the men were here. Having no time to waste, Adele did not wait for them to knock. She opened the door, bringing them inside the room before purposely shutting it to thwart curious eyes and ears.

"How is he now, my lady?" Adric asked hopefully, his face drawn with worry.

Symme's eyes filled with tears when she shook her head. He went to the bed to see for himself, and looked askance at Adele when he saw she had heaped more covers on his sweating master.

Quickly Adele explained what they had to do. Ivo nodded in agreement; he had heard of this being done successfully when he was in France. They all agreed it was worth trying, for nothing else they had done was working.

"We're going to sweat out his poison?" Symme asked a bit doubtfully. He alone knew that this novel treatment had been prescribed by Mistress Gallett. So far, the others did not know they had consulted the witch. They would not be left in ignorance for long; the other soldiers would soon spread the word. Until then, Symme intended to do what he could to aid Lady Adele's fight to save his lord.

The room grew hotter and hotter until they were all bathed in perspiration. Two charcoal braziers had been lit. Adric and the other men brought a constant supply of wood to feed the blazing hearth as well as heaps of dry bedcovers and a steaming jug of ale to mix the healing potion. Merrily following the humans, Val escorted the party out of the sickroom and down the stairs into the dark night.

Adele was so exhausted that she dozed against the side of Rafe's bed, holding his hand and sponging away sweat pouring down his face. Later, when she lay on the settee to sleep for an hour, Symme took his turn at the bedside.

They kept up this routine all night until everything became a blur of leaping flames and stifling air, so hot that it was difficult to breathe. The men stripped off their tunics, working bare-chested to stoke the fire and turn their master so the sodden draw sheets could be changed. Once during the night when Adele woke to see the room filled with lurid light from the fire and with gigantic black shadows moving across the wall and ceiling, she wondered if she had died and gone to hell.

Sometime close to morning, Symme gently shook her awake. "Lady, come here. Does he not seem easier?"

Bleary-eyed, Adele followed him to the bed. The candles had burned down to stubs, but the leaping orange flames from the hearth gave off enough light to see by. When she looked down at Rafe, her heart stopped. He looked dead! His handsome face had a damp, waxy pallor, and with his eyes closed and his hands folded on his chest, he looked as if he had been laid out for burial. She clapped her hand to her mouth to keep a wail from escaping, but Symme still smiled and pointed. Almost too weary to comprehend, Adele finally saw what he meant—Rafe's breathing was even! When she touched his brow, though it felt clammy, the fever had gone.

"Oh, dear God!" Adele cried, turning to Symme to embrace him. "We've done it. Adric, Ivo, come quick!"

The other men roused at her shout and ran to the bedside, with Val bounding along beside them. They looked at Rafe, shocked at first, their reaction to seeing him lying so still the same as hers. Then, while they watched, his eyelids flickered and Rafe opened his eyes.

Val wriggled the top half of his body across the mountain of bedcovers to gently nuzzle Rafe's hand and give him a tentative lick of affection.

They gasped in unison as Rafe smiled at the dog's greeting. The expression was faint, but it was unmistakably a smile! Wearily, Adele tried to think what it was she must do once the fever had broken. Then she recalled the black concoction Mistress Gallett had pressed into her hand.

The sticky substance smelled vilely of congealed blood and a bitter, pungent herb Adele could not identify. Still she sat beside Rafe and, using a small spoon, pushed the mixture into his mouth. His eyes opened again, and Rafe gasped in surprise. Adele felt his hand move against her side and she clasped his fingers, bringing them to her mouth to kiss.

"Here, sweet, eat this. 'Twill make you better," she coaxed. To her delight, Rafe obediently opened his mouth, though he grimaced like a child after taking each spoonful. A few minutes later he was asleep. Adele did not know if she should take off the extra covers now, or wait to be sure his fever was really gone. She had already told Adric to let the fire die back to normal. The shutters had also been flung open, allowing the sharp December air to blow refreshingly cold inside the room.

Knowing that Rafe had passed the critical stage was such a relief that Adele felt the muscles in her neck and shoulders gradually relaxing. She recalled that lurid scene of bare-chested men bathed in sweat stoking the great fire until the air inside the room was so close that she could hardly breathe. It had been a hellish night. But with God's grace, they were now on the other side of the horror, and Adele offered a prayer of thanks for Rafe's deliverance. Events had gone according to Mistress Gallett's prediction. Once the fever broke, Rafe had truly taken a turn for the better.

Outside, morning light already parted the gray clouds. It had been a moonless night with a cold wind. Adele was sure there must be some omen attached to such weather, but she was too weary to recall it. Everyone but Symme had returned to their quarters: Rafe's loyal squire dozed beside his lord's bed, with Val sleeping beside him.

Aware that after a night's activity in this overheated

room she must look even worse than she looked last night, Adele attempted to braid her untidy hair. Without a brush, it hardly seemed worth the effort.

There came a tap on the door. Going to answer, Adele was delighted to see Margery. The two women hugged each other and shed copious tears of joy. Margery had brought a clean shift, a wool gown, hose, and slippers; best of all, she had brought Adele's own hairbrush.

"Adric sent me, my lady."

While she washed her mistress's face, then began to brush her thick auburn hair, Margery confided in Adele how happy she was to be the animal healer's wife. She also mentioned that she still felt ill at ease because she had never asked her lady's permission to wed. Adele smilingly assured her maid that she could not have chosen a better man, and having them living happily together was a blessing Adele had not expected. Margery gave a heartfelt sigh of relief at the news and affectionately kissed the top of her mistress's head.

How wonderful it felt to be clean and to have her hair brushed. In wearing her own shift and gown, Adele already felt a head taller as she stood, allowing the dark green worsted to drop in folds about her legs. Margery had brought a plain circlet of plaited purple and lavender ribbon to hold her filmy sea-green veil in place. Then, with a flourish worthy of a carnival magician, Margery produced a hand mirror from her hanging pocket.

Adele stared at her own reflection, brightly illuminated in the light from the fire and the new candles Margery had brought. Though her features were as she remembered, Adele saw such a change in her own face that she might have been looking at a stranger. Her chin and cheekbones were more defined, and when she looked into those familiar green eyes, there was a steely glint she had never noticed before. Experience had wrought the change. Though only a year in actual time, these past twelve months had made Adele grow far older, completing her journey into womanhood.

They woke Symme, but it was with great reluctance he left his lord's bedside to break his fast, shooed out the door by Margery. The young man needed to eat.

Next came Willet, Rafe's body servant, to bathe and shave his master, unaware his lord was not alone. Arthur, the steward, had sent him to the chamber. Because he had a crippled leg, Willet did not travel around the country with Rafe, serving him only when he was in residence at the castle. Puzzled at finding a lady and her maid in his lord's bechamber, Willet bowed.

After introductions, Adele asked what the man had been told.

"Only that he'd been wounded," Willet answered, glancing toward the bed. "I never seen him look so pale afore."

"Likely he's never been like this before, you daft lad." Margery laughed, shooing Willet, with his bowl and razor, toward the bed. "Go on, shave him and whatnot, then get out of our way."

Meanwhile, the two women bundled up the used bed linens and prepared a new change of sheets and pillowcases for the invalid's bed. Rafe lay unprotesting while Willet shaved him and brushed his hair. The servant had just washed off the razor and declared his task finished when the tramp of men's boots halted outside the door.

Without fanfare, three men burst into the bedchamber. They were led by Arthur, who stared dumbfounded at Adele and her maid, barely recognizing her now that she was dressed in her own clothing. The other men stared also, frozen in place: they were a young priest in his vestments, come to shrive Rafe and give him Extreme Unction; and a leech, a physician identified by the slimy creatures of his trade, here to suck out the last of Rafe's blood.

"Out of the way, woman," Arthur ordered as he recovered his composure. "We're come to tend Lord Rafe."

"Lord Rafe's fever broke in the night. Can't you see how much better he is today?"

Arthur glanced from Adele to his master's bed where Willet stood, undecided whether to leave or stay. "Well, lad, for once you did as you were told. Give me the razor, 'twill do to open his vein."

"No! You mustn't bleed him!" Adele cried in horror. "Can't you see he's already lost too much blood? That's why he's so weak. Bleed him and you'll kill him!"

"Go on, go back where you belong. We'll handle this," Arthur commanded confidently as he hurried forward, motioning for the leech to follow with his basin and jar.

The leech looked unsure how to proceed, dithering halfway between the door and the bed. The priest was less unsure. He placed a violet silk stole round his neck and prepared to administer the church's last rites.

Adele stood guard over Rafe, convinced that if they bled him it would be fatal. Though she knew it was standard treatment, bloodletting had never made sense to her, especially when the patient was already weak from loss of blood.

"You, Father, may come forward," she said, smiling as she beckoned the priest. Last rites, at least, could do him no harm. Uneasily, Adele wondered if he knew she had sent for Mistress Gallett. When she looked at Arthur's hostile face, Adele recalled the old woman's warning that if Adele did not stand her ground, she would be thrown out of the castle.

Out of pious respect, Arthur and the leech moved to the other side of the room and Willet joined them, allowing the priest to continue undisturbed.

In the middle of the rite, Rafe apparently recognized the prayers being said over him. His lips moved as he followed the priest, the Latin words barely audible. Rafe even made his confession as the young priest bent low to hear his mumbled words.

Adele started to point out Rafe's new found strength to Arthur as further proof of her progress in treating His Lordship, but one glance at the steward's thin, set mouth told her it would be in vain.

When the sacrament had been given and the priest had blessed all present, he apologized for having to leave, explaining that he was urgently needed elsewhere. Adele thanked him and held open the door, instructing one of the waiting men-at-arms to escort the priest from the castle.

Clearly, Arthur was annoyed by the turn of events, for he had considered Adele to have no power and this was an indication to the contrary. He had intended to have her removed this morning, but when he'd come in, he'd found that the woman he'd felt sure was a commoner playing at importance appeared to be what she'd claimed—the Lady St. Clare. Worse, trunks and other possessions belonging to a lady of that name had arrived here months ago. The fine gelding in the castle stables and that black hound who watched him from the corner also reputedly belonged to this mysterious Lady Adele.

Rafe started to speak, and Adele leaned closer, eager to hear what he said—deliberately turning her back on the angry steward.

"Am I dying?" Rafe asked, aware he had just been given Extreme Unction. He had heard the last rites said often enough over dying comrades on battlefields from here to Anjou.

"No, sweetheart, you're so much better this morning," Adele reassured him as she took his hand.

"Ah, my lord," Arthur boomed, hurrying to the bed, where he virtually swept Adele aside. "I've brought Roger the leech to treat you."

Again the leech stepped forward, his jar of parasites and blood bowl at the ready. Arthur began to roll up Rafe's sleeve in preparation.

"No! Stop this instant! You'll not bleed him. I forbid it!" Adele cried, mustering every ounce of authority she possessed.

The leech immediately fell back, hearing her unmistakable tone of command. Arthur's face turned crimson, and he looked as if he might explode.

"Damn you, you interfering woman! If you don't step

aside, I'll have you thrown out of Fordham. If my lord dies, it will be your doing."

From the bed came a distinct chuckle, faint but unmistakable.

"Well, Arthur, my lad, you're a cheering bedside companion. Am I that close to meeting the grim reaper?"

Flustered, Arthur stammered an apology. In his anger, he had forgotten that his master could hear what was being said.

"And don't be so sharp with the maid," he said groggily. "Likely the poor woman's doing what she thinks is right."

"It's not a maid he's talking to." Adele glared at Arthur. "Your steward's taking great delight in insulting *me*."

"Adele?" Rafe questioned as he struggled to sit up. "Is it really you?"

"Yes, it's really me," she whispered, kneeling at his side and taking his hand in her own. "They want to bleed you, and I won't let them because you've already lost a lot of blood. It would be sheer stupidity. I have a healing potion—"

"Aye, got from the old witch. We'll have no truck with witchcraft here," Arthur roared, seizing his opportunity. He pushed forward again.

All eyes were upon her. Adele saw Symme standing in the doorway, and before he had a chance to admit to sending for Mistress Gallett, she spoke. "I sent for the wise woman because I'd no more medicine to treat you. She gave me good advice and a potion which worked this miracle."

"Is it true that you brought the old witch here?" Rafe asked, strength rushing back to his voice.

"Nay, I sent for a healer. Though, I admit, I'd have sent for anyone with potions to save your life."

"My lord, you forbade that old witch from ever setting foot in the castle again!"

Rafe nodded in agreement at Arthur's reminder. He moved so he could see the window where gray morning light crept inside the room. "That's true, I did forbid it," Rafe croaked, his throat so parched he could barely speak. "Yet if her potion truly made the difference, maybe this time we can overlook it. I just thank God for letting me live to see another day."

Taking advantage of the lull in activity, Margery stepped forward and grasped the leech's arm. "Come on, me lad, time for you to go. You smell none too pleasant to be in an invalid's room," she added with a disdainful sniff. "If my lady says you're not needed, you're not needed."

Both men protested, looking toward their lord for support.

"But, my lord, bloodletting's the correct treatment," Arthur reminded indignantly.

"If Lady Adele says you're not needed, I'm sure she's right," Rafe said, his voice almost back to normal.

Finally, and with exceedingly bad grace, Arthur strode from the room with Willett and the leech in tow. As he was leaving, the physician apologized profusely for annoying Her Ladyship. The man was ever hopeful for further business from the nobility, who paid for his services in coin—unlike the villagers, who settled their debts with bread loaves and tubs of lard.

When the men left, Adele and Margery felt so triumphant that they were tempted to dance around the room. Rafe, however, felt too much recovered to blindly accept his medicine. This time he questioned Adele about the foul concoction she was trying to spoon into his mouth. "What's that stinking stuff you're giving me?"

"I don't know, but it makes you better. Open your mouth."

"It smells like dung and tastes like—"

Into his open mouth the spoon went, and Rafe made a terrible face as the sticky black potion ran down his throat. So much good had come from the other doses, Adele decided this time to give him a second spoonful. As soon as he opened his mouth to protest, she pushed it in. After the second dose, Rafe put up his arm for her to stop, the sudden movement making him wince in pain, for his limbs had stiffened from disuse.

"No more! You're worse than the leech, only you're trying to poison me instead of bleed me. What day is it—nay, what month? I seem to have been in limbo for weeks."

"'Tis still December, but I don't know the day," Adele admitted. After Rafe's nightmare encounter with Lorkin Yates's dagger, the days all ran together. She did not know when one ended and the next begun.

"I can't believe you're here with me. Everything's beginning to come back. How did you get me to Fordham?"

"Gerard Montsorrel helped bring you home. We thought you would soon be better, especially at home. Then your wounds became infected and you were burning with fever."

"Oh, that always happens—I've always gotten over it," Rafe dismissed casually as he struggled to sit against the mound of feather pillows. Symme still waited by the door, and Rafe motioned him forward. "Come here, lad. Let me look at you."

The young man wept with joy to see His Lordship returned from the dead, but his being the one who'd sent for Mistress Gallett weighed on his conscience.

"My lord, you mustn't blame Lady Adele. I suggested she send for the witch."

"It doesn't matter whose suggestion it was, lad. Her fool spells don't work, but at least some of her potions do. I'm living proof of that," Rafe said, his jovial side uppermost.

Adele smiled.

Chapter Fourteen

A week had passed and Adele still could not believe the miraculous change in Rafe. At first it had been hard for him to stay on his feet for long, but that soon changed as his strength flowed back. His endurance lengthened with each passing day.

When he was able, Rafe took great pride in escorting Adele about his castle, which had been brought up to date, incorporating the most modern defenses. Indulgently she listened while he outlined the special design of the inner and outer portcullises and drawbridges, and the advanced method of constructing the castle sluice pits. Even the dungeons were a point of pride; though Rafe hoped he would have little use for them, they were relatively dry and rat free.

Adele did not interrupt him as, like a small child showing off his new toy, Rafe demonstrated the latest style of bow. Warming to the subject, he then introduced his bowmen to her, mentioning that many of them were Welsh, for everyone knew the best archers came from Wales.

Everyone but me, Adele thought, hiding a smile as she considered his statement. Though very much a nobleman as he showed her about his castle, Adele discovered yet another side of the man she loved, the excitable boy.

They stopped short of climbing the towers, for Rafe found steps tiring and he disdained the gnarled stick Ivo's brother Yves had carved for him, using it only when they were gathered in the great hall, and then only so as not to hurt Yves's feelings.

Though she had grown up in a castle, Adele was amazed by the sheer size of Fordham. Its great curtain walls towered as high as Esterwold's keep, and its rushing moat, fed by a mountain stream, looked more like a river.

Fordham's interior was somewhat spartan—as befitted a military installation—but the lord's quarters were the exception. The solar's fine molded ceiling incorporated the De Montford crest, which was also chiseled above the great stone hearth. On either side of the family crest hung old elongated shields belonging to Rafe's father and grandfather. As a young man in search of adventure, his grandfather had left Anjou to join the Norman Duke William's invasionary force, taking part in the conquest of England in 1066. Their backgrounds were surprisingly similar; Adele's forebears had also left their native land to take part in the conquest, and both families had been rewarded for their service by parcels of land in the newly claimed country.

For the first few days they supped together in the solar. Rafe ate sparingly, finding himself barely able to stay awake to finish his meal. Adele had used all the black potion and she'd sent Symme to Mistress Gallett for more, but he could not find her. Without the potion, Adele worried that Rafe's health would decline. But she'd worried unnecessarily, she discovered, for his healing progressed until he was finally able to resume his place at the lord's table in the great hall.

The first time Rafe came down to sup with his men, the

241

soldiers jumped to their feet, and their resounding cheers rang the rafters as they made their pleasure known at having him back amongst them again.

With the added promise of the festive Christmas season just around the corner, and just when Rafe seemed to be getting back to normal—even able to ride for short periods—there came an unpleasant intrusion from the outside world.

Though dry, it was a cold, gray day. Adele sat by the fire working on an altar cloth, embroidering the holy article as her secret penance for consulting a witch to save Rafe's life. She was doubtful that such penance had much value, though, because in her heart she knew that if the same situation arose again, she would again defy the church's teaching and seek out Mistress Gallett.

Each afternoon Rafe rested, and though he chafed at his invalid's regimen, he adhered to it. Adele knew he would not abide by her wishes for much longer. Once he considered himself healed, Rafe would do exactly as he pleased.

Outside, a party of riders were admitted to the bailey, and she heard the thud of their many hooves. When a servant finally came to the door, she was not surprised, for she had halfway been expecting to be disturbed. "There are men here to see Lord Rafe," the servant told her. "Their lord says it's very important."

Adele nodded. That meant she would have to wake him. She had intended to change his dressings, but there was no time for that. She roused him and helped him pull on a red wool tunic and his black hide boots. As no one had asked her to join the guests, Adele hung back.

Rafe, noticing, said impatiently, "Well, come on. All that haste and now *you're* dawdling."

She smiled and they descended the stairs to the great hall together.

"De Vesci!" Rafe cried in surprise, his voice so strong that no one would have guessed how close to death he had come a few short weeks ago.

The Lord of Alnwick came forward and they embraced. Adele curtsied to Eustace De Vesci, remembering this important man from their pilgrimage to St. Edmundsbury.

"Rafe! By God, you look fit. Maybe I was misinformed—I'd heard you were ailing," De Vesci said in surprise, glancing from Rafe to Adele.

"No, you weren't misinformed. Had it not been for my flame-haired angel, you'd likely be coming to my funeral." Rafe laughed, motioning for their guest to join him beside the hearth.

Now that he had become an avowed enemy of the king, De Vesci never traveled without protection. His troop of men sat at the trestles which had been hastily set up for them in the great hall. Platters of coarse bread and meat and cups of ale were brought to refresh them.

Gascon wine and tender spiced meats, accompanied by fine white bread and chunks of pungent white cheese, were brought to the lord's table. For the most part, the meat and aged cheese lay untouched while De Vesci explained what had lately been taking place across the land. Many more men had joined the rebel cause, coming from Wales and the west country to stand with the northern lords. King John was systematically attempting to flush out these traitors.

"You're virtually my neighbor and are still uncommitted," De Vesci remarked finally, when all had been discussed. "Why is that? Surely you're no lover of Softsword's policies."

"No. I favor the middle road proposed by Archbishop Langton. The archbishop's certainly no friend of John's, but neither does he support outright anarchy. What of this new charter drawn up by the barons? I've yet to read it. Have you presented it to him yet?"

"No, that will come later," De Vesci explained with a scowl. He'd apparently hoped for more fire from Rafe, and likely a vow of commitment. "Have you recruited your tenants and freeholders yet?"

"No, De Vesci. I'm barely off my deathbed," Rafe growled, beginning to see where this discussion led. Eustace De Vesci was seeking a man to join his cause, an ally to count on in his fight against the king.

"Time's wasting. If you present the charter in the spring, that doesn't give us much time to recruit an army to go up against him. He has men. Pembroke, Arundel, Warwick, Devon—they trot after him like little dogs."

"You know I'm with you or neutral," Rafe assured, rising as De Vesci picked up his gauntlets and signaled his captain to ready the men for departure.

"Lady Adele—always beautiful and sweet natured," De Vesci said in parting, kissing her hand. His dark eyes glowed in appreciation as he admired her soft curves encased in gold and black brocade.

"Good day, Lord Eustace. Will we see you again at Christmas?" Adele asked as he fastened his thick, sheepskin-lined jack.

"Possibly. That all depends on your good lord's conscience." His leave-taking after that was abrupt.

The visit marked a turning point in Rafe's recovery. It also caused an abrupt change in his outlook, for, instead of showing joy at being alive, Rafe grew dour and preoccupied. Most of his time was spent with his soldiers while he made a complete review of their armaments, discussed the castle's readiness to withstand a siege, and ordered extra practice at the archery butts. He also demanded a higher level of skill from them and doubled the time devoted to training for battle. Rafe was preparing for war.

Despite the storm on the horizon, the castle's inhabitants made preparations for the holiday season. Adele loved the smell of baking which wafted along the castle corridors, and she anticipated eating the fruit-filled puddings and breads wrapped in brandy-soaked cloths and stored in kegs in the pantry. Honeyed fruits were being prepared, thick with sweet yellow crystals. Game had been hung in the cellars to ripen for the feasts of the twelve days of Christmas.

Adele found it all very exciting, yet at the same time found it difficult to visualize overseeing such massive preparations when she became Lady of Fordham. Lady Adele of Fordham Castle! What a grand title it sounded. Yet nowadays, each time she thought about marriage, instead of joy she felt sadness. By now, she had expected Rafe to at least broach the subject of their marriage. He had not mentioned it.

At first, he'd been so weak that she was overjoyed just to have him alive, giving little thought to the subject. But things were far different now, and the change had been brought about by Eustace De Vesci's visit. Even Rafe's joy at being alive had vanished. These days he had only one all-consuming purpose: protect his castle.

Though Rafe was well enough to ride, they had not taken that promised tour of the countryside. Today he had ridden out alone to a neighboring manor, despite the biting wind and threat of snow, ignoring all her admonitions to take better care of his health.

Not to be planning for their future was bad enough, but Adele was forced to admit they no longer had a present. True, Rafe still kissed and embraced her, but those displays of affection were uncharacteristically chaste. And Rafe had not made love to her since St. Edmundsbury.

While he was ailing, she had not expected passionate embraces. But he was no longer an invalid—finding the energy to drill his troops, to ride about the countryside, energy for everything but her. She could no longer take comfort from the excuse she had used in the beginning. At times Adele felt so neglected that she wondered if Rafe had fallen out of love with her. Whenever that terrible thought entered her mind, her heart pounded with dread and her palms grew clammy. Their love had been so passionate, it was terrible to even think such a thing. Rafe had become the other half of her soul!

Adele clutched her cloak tighter about her neck to keep

out the wind. Winter at Fordham felt much colder than at Esterwold. Here they were further north and cold winds swept down from the Scottish Highlands, raking the open moor with its icy blast, stunting everything in its path.

Today Adele had chosen to go out alone, needing to walk and think. This was such a departure from the norm that Val had looked stunned when she told him to stay behind.

Whenever her dog was beside her and she was riding Moonlight, life always slid back into that old familiar, happy pattern, allowing her to pretend that all was well. But it most certainly was not! The pain of Rafe's neglect grew sharper with each passing day. Adele needed to rehearse what to say to him, for she could keep silent no longer.

She was almost ready to return when the thud of hooves blew to her on the wind. As Adele crested the next rise of ground, she saw a rider below. It was Rafe! She would recognize his big chestnut anywhere. But Adele did not want to see the man alone just yet, for she had still to decide what she would say. She held back, not rushing forward with a shouted greeting as she once would have done.

Rafe drew rein beside a stand of stunted trees bordering the road. Someone obviously had waited there to speak to him, for a cloaked figure stepped from the trees. Adele could see it was a woman, and she wondered who. Rafe sat motionless in the saddle, looking down at the woman. Adele could not hear their voices, or even if they spoke. Then she saw Rafe dismount and step toward the woman.

A burst of laughter pealed out, and in shock Adele recognized that tinkling sound. The woman tossed back her hood, and a mass of black curls tumbled around her shoulders. Sadie Gallett reached out her shapely arm and touched Rafe. A mingled wave of jealousy and betrayal swept over Adele.

Here was her answer to all her puzzling questions—

Sadie Gallett had come back into Rafe's life. That was the reason they no longer made love, or why he had not made plans for their future. The uneasiness she'd felt when first she had seen the lovely Sadie had been a warning she did not heed.

Adele retraced her steps, stumbling over the rough ground, blinded by tears. She could not stay to watch—yet her vivid imagination would well supply the picture.

How long had Rafe been seeing Sadie? All those days when he rode about the countryside—when she had foolishly rejoiced that he felt well enough to ride—had likely been trysts with the witch's daughter. A bitter smile curled her lip as she blinked back tears. Rafe's surprising stamina for the saddle had been fueled by a far different thing than she had imagined.

At the noon meal, Adele sat silently waiting for her opportunity to speak with him alone. Rafe had returned and was discussing the mobilization of men from the surrounding villages with a tenant named Bennet—a man who farmed the valley where Fordham's moat became a river. They spoke at length about the king's soldiers' confiscation of his neighbors' property, but all she could think about was his love for Sadie Gallett.

The men's talk droned on until she could endure it no longer. Bennet spoke down his nose and had an annoying habit of constantly clearing his throat, both of which irritated her beyond measure. Though Rafe looked askance when she got up, excusing herself from the table, he did not ask where she was going; to Adele it was further proof of his waning affection.

Her vision blurred by tears, Adele could hardly negotiate the stairs to her chamber. Supposedly for appearance's sake, Rafe had given her a chamber of her own. Though at the time she had not thought it would mean the end of their lovemaking, she had been wrong. This morning she had discovered the real reason for the change.

This comfortable firelit chamber which she had found so pleasant was now made ugly by the motive for its existence. Had Rafe loved her true, he would never have moved her this far from his chamber. These colorful tapestries, the green velvet bed hangings, and the thick sheepskins before the hearth became a mockery, symbolizing a security that did not exist.

Adele pulled on her boots and grabbed her cloak. She would go for a ride and hope the cold December wind would blow a little sense into her addled brain, for she seemed to have used very little where Rafe De Montford was concerned.

Once again Adele stopped Val from following, though he had bounded up to her hopefully when he saw her put on her cloak and had followed her to the stables. Poor dog. The large black beast's head hung down and his tail was tucked between his legs.

"Not this time, love," Adele said, patting the dog's smooth head as she led Moonlight from the stable. The lad who saddled her horse warned her it was going to snow, but she loftily assured him she was not afraid.

Across the two drawbridges she rode, her horse's hooves thudding hollow on the wooden boards as she picked up speed. Once she was clear of the bailey, she took the downhill track onto the moor. This countryside was certainly appropriate for solitude, for she saw no other living creature as she rode into the buffeting wind. Rugged, cold, cheerless were words she now ascribed to Fordham's rolling miles. If she headed northeast, Adele knew she would reach Eustace De Vesci's lands, so she changed direction. Not only did she want the wind at her back, the possibility of encountering that rugged Northumberland lord was not appealing. Somewhere to the south would be Montsorrel's lands. Beyond that, Summerhay and Hugh D'Avranche. Or maybe by now Summerhay was held by another of King John's lapdogs.

The wind whipped tears from her eyes, stinging them across her cheeks. Out here she was free as a bird, but Adele discovered that such freedom was an unwelcome state. She wanted to belong to Rafe. Even when she had exchanged verbal blows with him all those months ago, she had secretly wanted him. She could admit it now that it was too late. How ironic to think that after she had brought him home wounded—even risked her own immortal soul by consorting with a witch to save his life—everything had been snatched away by a woman whose heart was black as the arts she practiced. A very woman she herself had summoned. She simply could not compete with Sadie Gallett's spells and love potions which could ensnare a man without his knowledge.

Adele heard hooves thundering behind her as she raced across the open moor. When she looked back, she was shocked to see a rider astride a chestnut stallion. Rafe? He was following her!

Urging Moonlight to greater speed, Adele turned onto a narrow track which led sharply downhill, thinking to escape him, for his big chestnut could not maneuver as well as her dainty gray. She could not speak to him now, for she would blurt out all her pain and sense of betrayal; she wanted to be clever, to say all the right things instead of bursting into tears and revealing just how much he meant to her.

The chestnut gained ground. Damn! Did the animal have lightning in his hooves? Poor Moonlight galloped flat out as they flew along the bracken-fringed track, past boulders and stunted trees, over springy heather and gorse.

"Damn it, Adele, slow down before you break your neck!" she heard Rafe shout, the wind whipping his voice away and making it faint.

Adele . . . Her name echoed out of the gusting wind, but she was deaf to his warning. There had been much pain in the year since she met Rafe De Montford, some his doing, some not—she could endure no more. She had to get away from him, from all the emotional upheaval he caused. She wanted to ride forever across this bleak and lonely land.

Long before they came to the crossroads, Moonlight

was flagging. Adele chose a level path thinking it would be easier for her horse, though she had no idea what lay ahead. She didn't even know which direction she'd turned. It could not be north, she decided, for she now had the wind at her back. Before her lay a patch of woodland, boulders strewn randomly across the heather-clad land. The icy wind seared her face, seeming suddenly to have shifted direction for she rode into the teeth of the wind, its cold blast numbing her cheeks. The first drops of moisture stung her eyelids, which she slitted against the wind.

"Stop!"

Adele gulped in horror, for Rafe's voice sounded right behind her. A moment later he grasped her reins, and Moonlight snorted as he was pulled alongside the fierce chestnut. Slowly her horse came into line, losing speed, until he finally trotted, docile as an obedient dog. Furious at the unexpected turn of events, Adele shouted at the gelding and kicked her heels into his flanks, but the horse stubbornly refused to move.

"Let me go!" she screamed, when Rafe grabbed her arms.

"Tell me what in hell you're doing, woman," he yelled.

Adele struggled free of his grasp and swiftly slid from the saddle. It was to no avail. Rafe also came out of the saddle and pinned her arms against her sides.

"Answer me!"

"I'm out riding, you blockheaded dolt," she yelled above the wind. "Or I was, until you arrived."

"Where exactly are you going, my lady?"

"Does it matter?"

"In this country it matters. Look at the sky. We're in for a snowstorm."

"A little snow doesn't bother me."

"Around here we usually have more than a *little* snow," Rafe corrected, turning her about to shield her from the wind. "What's the matter with you? Have you lost your senses?"

"Quite likely."

Baffled, Rafe stared at her, genuinely at a loss. "For heaven's sake, Adele, tell me what I've done? Because I know it's going to be my fault."

"How astute of you."

A couple of snowflakes settled on his cap, and Rafe dragged his hood over his head. He did the same for Adele.

Eyes flashing, she shook back the hood, defiantly letting her bright hair stream loose in an untidy tangle. More snowflakes floated down to melt against her face.

"I know I've not been paying enough attention to you lately, but, sweetheart, you have to understand. There's months of neglect to put right at Fordham, and an impending war doesn't help—"

"Oh, stop apologizing for things that I understand," she cried. Her vivid imagination had already supplied a conclusion to that horrid scene she'd not been able to watch, the lewd picture uppermost in her mind when she said, "Think back to this morning. Surely you can guess." Though it was not her intention, Adele felt tears spring to her eyes. She did not know if they were tears of pain or anger.

"This morning?—I know I left you alone, but I've little choice right now. De Vesci wants an answer, and God knows, when the king's men finally come to the gate, they're going to demand one, too. I have to know where my neighbors' loyalties lie—"

"Lie? Oh, yes," Adele cried, seizing on the word. "You men are good at that. Do you think I care about your neighbors' war preparations? I want to know how you could be with *that woman* when all the time you said you loved *me*. You told me you'd petitioned the king for permission to marry me. Lies! Like a fool, I believed you . . . until this morning when I saw you with her. How many other times have there been? How many nights have you spent together since you moved me out of your chamber?"

Her shouted accusations, delivered with such anger, stunned him. Rafe blanched before his face grew hard as granite.

"You have your own chamber, Lady, because we're not yet wed."

"Nor will we ever be as long as Sadie Gallett shares your bed."

There, right or wrong, she'd said it. Adele tried to dash away her angry tears, but could not because he pinioned her arms. She sniffled and glared at him, finding his expression hard and unyielding, without a flicker of guilt. Oh, what had she expected? The wind seemed to have lessened and more snowflakes swirled about them in the fading gray light, settling on her nose and eyebrows, clinging to the bright, curling tendrils of her hair.

"You thought . . . Oh, Adele . . . have you so little faith in me?"

"Sadie Gallett told me that she, too, once thought she would be your wife."

"When did you meet—ah, she came with the old woman that night, didn't she?"

"Yes. Why didn't you tell me about her?"

"Because there was nothing to tell."

"Oh, don't play me for a fool! A beautiful woman like that in love with you and there's nothing to tell?"

Rafe shook her, dislodging a piece of snow from her hair which slipped onto her face. "Listen to me. I never loved her. Are you listening? I don't now, nor ever did, love Sadie Gallett. And despite what you think, I'm not sleeping with her."

"But you were lovers."

"She was a beautiful girl who offered herself to me— with no promises. Only a fool would have turned her down. There was never anything of love about it. It was years ago. In a roundabout way, it was the cause of her mother being thrown out of the castle."

"What do you mean?" Adele asked, licking melting snow from her lips.

"I rescued Mistress Gallett from a crowd of village lads who were going to duck her in the pond. I thought her knowledge would be valuable in treating my men. It worked for a while, until Sadie began to feed me love potions and take pieces of hair to make a poppet. She even persuaded her mother to cast a spell to make me marry her."

"That's why you sent her away?"

"Father Paul convinced the men they'd go to hell if the witch stayed. I'd no choice. This morning Sadie Gallett asked after my health. She also wanted to know if you were still here. There was no more to it. Had you spied on us a little longer, you'd have seen for yourself."

"I wasn't spying."

"What else do you call it?"

They glared at each other through the thin haze of snow sifting around them. In the background the horses tossed their heads, shaking snow off their ears, harnesses jingling in the eerie silence that had descended. It was as if nature itself awaited the outcome of their quarrel.

"So what did you tell her?" Adele whispered at last, licking moisture from her lips.

"That you'd be at Fordham as long as I draw breath."

As if from a great distance his words registered, the emotion behind them softening her anger. Adele swallowed, desperately wanting to believe him. Had she truly made too much of a chance encounter? She'd assumed the meeting had been arranged, yet it could have happened the way he said. Rafe had given her no reason to doubt his fidelity in the past.

Snow crusted the edge of his hood and collected softly on his broad shoulders; behind him the horses' breath wafted like smoke. Perhaps her jealousy was misplaced after all. Rafe had ridden out in the storm to search for her. He could have been neglecting her of late simply because he was using all of his energy in preparing his people for the coming hostilities. Less than two weeks ago she had prayed to God to spare his life, and her prayers had been granted. Now, simply because Sadie Gallett had spoken to him, she was jealously accusing him of infidelity.

Her anger, which had been fierce enough to boil her blood, had burned itself out. Adele gazed up at Rafe, barely able to make out his features in the gloom, seeing his eyes as black as his hair beneath a coating of snow. Once again Rafe pulled her hood over her hair, and this time Adele let it stay. His arms went round her back, imprisoning her arms, but lovingly. As Rafe drew her close, a surge of emotion rocked her body and she leaned into his warm strength, abandoning herself to his comforting embrace.

"Come on, sweet, let's go home. No more doubts, no more jealousy. Promise?" he whispered against her ear, his breath tantalizingly warm against her cold flesh.

Feeling ashamed of her outburst, Adele buried her face against his chest, and her voice was muffled as she said, "No more, I promise."

"I owe my life to you, and I love you more than ever."

His sincere words thrilled her and she nestled even closer. "You know I'd do it a thousand times over for you," she confided, pressing her cold cheek against his neck.

Rafe enfolded Adele inside his cloak to warm her icy limbs. Thus wrapped in his embrace, Adele felt so loved and secure that she could have stayed like that forever.

Rafe rested his face against the top of her head as he suggested, "What say we go home before we're buried?"

Adele smiled, so relieved to have his love reconfirmed that she had almost forgotten the accumulating snow. "What if we can't find our way back?" she asked in alarm when she finally roused herself to look around the whitening landscape.

"They will send a party to search for us if we are gone much longer. We'll meet them halfway."

Heads down against the sifting snow, they rode side by side along the desolate track. The afternoon's fierce wind had become a soft moan as it sent eddies of snow around the thickets of scraggly blackthorn and gorse bordering the trail.

They had ridden as far as the first rolling hill before they saw movement on the horizon, black against the snow. A little closer, and the shapes became six mounted men. Rafe hailed his soldiers, and they gave a resounding cheer in reply, relieved to have found both their lord and his lady.

When they finally reached the castle, they thudded over the drawbridge in the fading light. The snow was coming down heavily now obliterating paths and landmarks, turning all into a sea of white. Adele felt weak with happiness and relief. She had not realized how dangerous the storm would have been had she stayed out on the moor. When the wind rose, blowing the snow into drifts, she would have been hopelessly lost; she might have died from exposure had no one come to rescue her. Adele shuddered at the thought, realizing that her own willfulness could have sealed her fate. With that sobering reminder uppermost in her mind, the safety of Fordham's mighty walls made her doubly thankful.

They rode inside the bailey, and the great bridge was winched securely in place behind them, shutting out the inhospitable night. Gray light reflected off the snow cast wavering shadows across the keep as the party dismounted in the sheltered bailey.

"Thank you for joining the search," Adele said to the snow-frosted soldiers who, once they dismounted, shook themselves off like animals. "I won't ride out in weather like this again and risk being taken by surprise."

The men respectfully tipped their heads to her and bid their lord good night, then led the horses inside the lighted stables to be rubbed down and fed.

Rafe was grinning at Adele and she sheepishly smiled back, aware of his amusement as the lantern above the stable bathed them in yellow light.

"Very convincing, my lady," he commented in an undertone, "I almost believed you myself."

Adele was somewhat ashamed that because of her jealous suspicions the men had all come out in such foul weather to search for her. "I'm sorry I caused such a stir. I truly didn't expect the storm."

"Apologies accepted, Lady. Just promise not to do it again."

"If you promise not to meet beautiful women on the moor again," she countered, trying to sound lighthearted, though she was still uncomfortable with the knowledge of Rafe and Sadie being lovers, however long ago it may have been.

Rafe hugged Adele and kissed her brow, her cheek, and her soft mouth. "Then I cannot meet you, my love, because you're the most beautiful woman I know."

"Oh, Rafe," she whispered, seeking his warm lips and drinking in the reassurance of his kiss. "Don't ever leave me. I couldn't bear it."

"You have my word."

For a few minutes longer they stood clasped in each other's arms.

They walked inside the castle to be met by the appetizing aroma of baking bread and roasting meat drifting from the kitchens. Here inside these walls was instant warmth and light. Giggling maids were helping the soldiers loop evergreen garlands across the end of the great hall in preparation for the Christmas feasts. Everywhere they went, they encountered smiling faces as Rafe's men welcomed their lord back.

There were some questioning looks cast in her direction, though. With a prickle of unease, Adele suspected that not everyone accepted her story of being caught out in the snow. She knew she had to bear their doubt with good grace, proving to Rafe's people how truly she loved their lord. Luckily, the part she had played in his recovery was common knowledge.

The villagers had even begun to bring their ailing children to her in the hope she could cure them. Adele was humbled by their faith and prayed to the Blessed Mother to aid her in her attempts. She had already decided that when she became lady here at Fordham, she would have the infirmary cleaned and stocked. Her own knowledge of cures was limited, yet she knew she could learn much from others. For one, Mistress Gallett might teach her how to blend many salves and potions. It was a fine line she must walk, being careful not to appear to dabble in the black arts, or the local priest would condemn her as a witch also.

Whatever the future held, Adele had already made a vow never to let jealousy come between her and Rafe again.

Chapter Fifteen

While she dressed for the banquet Adele hummed a Christmas carol. This afternoon on the snowy moor she cast away all doubt about her place in Rafe's affections. She had been immature. She could not expect his undivided attention, for he had far too many responsibilities for that. She smiled at her own foolishness. She still had Margery, Val, and Moonlight—and best of all, she still had Rafe.

During their absence, unexpected guests had arrived at the castle; a number of stranded travelers had also sought shelter from the storm. These people would stay at Fordham until the roads cleared. When she rode inside the bailey, Adele had seen a number of strange horses there, but it had been too dark to identify any insignia on their saddle cloths. She had no idea who would join them at tonight's feast. The maid who brought up her washwater said there were minstrels and players amongst the travelers who would entertain them in exchange for shelter.

Margery made Adele sit still before the hearth while

she brushed and braided her hair, weaving gold ribbon and strands of pearls into the thick plait which hung down her back. Tonight Adele would wear a narrow gold circlet on her brow—a gift from Rafe to replace the one she had sacrificed to Lorkin Yates. For one foolish moment Adele caught herself wondering how Rafe had acquired a lady's accessory, but she thrust the thought away. It did not matter where the circlet came from, or at what point in Rafe's life it had come into his possession. He now gave it to her with love, and that was all that mattered. She was growing up.

Tonight Adele wore her splendid new tunic of ivory silk brocade over a marigold velvet gown. The fur-lined tunic felt soft and warm against her body, lightweight yet thick enough to ward off the fierce drafts wafting through the castle's arrow slits and cavernous chimneys. Adele also wore matching marigold velvet slippers, their fur lining plush and warm against her silk-clad feet.

When Margery was finished, Adele spun about the room, twisting and turning, imagining she was dancing with Rafe. There might be dancing tonight, now that they had minstrels. It didn't matter what the entertainment, this would be a night to remember. Eyes closed, she pictured Rafe's smile and recalled the touch of his hand, the image making her heart race. Tonight she could truly say—in contrast to her misery this afternoon—she was as lighthearted as a child.

Down to the great hall she hastened, followed by Margery in a forest green wool gown, also a yuletide gift from Rafe. Everyone in the castle had benefited from their lord's generosity, from Adric's russet wool tunic and Symme's sword with the jeweled hilt to the lowliest kitchen maids who had each received a hair ribbon and a crystallized sweetmeat. Not even the animals had been overlooked: Val now wore a gilded red leather collar, and Rafe's large hunting hounds, who lolled before the hearth, all wore matching brass-studded collars. Adele smiled when she considered Rafe's thoughtfulness.

259

Though the household gifts had been doled out by Arthur, even his dour expression could not dampen the proceedings.

Adele swept regally inside the lighted hall and stopped in the doorway with an exclamation of pleasure as she admired the colorful scene before her. The evergreen garlands were all finally in place. Pungent boughs of fir and holly with trailing lengths of ivy crowned both hearth and doorway. Atop each table were beribboned yew branches surrounding candles. Scarlet-berried holly boughs festooned the gray stone walls, and a decorated Christmas bush of holly, bright with colored ribbon and silver bells, was suspended from the rafters. It was a splendid transformation of this usually austere hall. Adele looked curiously around the trestles, seeing dozens of merry strangers, their faces illuminated by the flickering candles.

Each time the great door opened, the wall sconces flared in the draft, emitting trails of smoke and showers of soot. The cold winds bent the candleflames and stirred the Christmas holly bush, setting it swinging above their heads. Beyond the door, purple and blue shadows crept across new-fallen snow, the cold scene a sharp contrast to the warmth and gaiety within the hall.

From across the hall, Rafe watched Adele's wide-eyed reaction, saw her standing still, admiring the decorations. His heart lurched as he reminded himself how short-lived her delight would be.

He knew Esterwold was a poorer demesne and likely they did not decorate so lavishly for the Christmas season, so to please her, he had ordered even more display this year than usual, until even he hardly recognized his own cavernous hall. In her new gown, Adele looked like an angel come to earth, and Rafe's arms ached to hold her and protect her. He had designed everything to make this Christmas perfect for her—and now a bundle of parchment would ruin it all. He pressed his hand to his scarlet tunic, crackling the folded sheet he had thrust there to keep its contents secret until he decided what to do.

Rafe stepped from his dais and crossed the hall to meet his love. Freshly mindful of their guests, some of whom he knew to be the king's spies, Rafe lightly embraced Adele, giving her cheek a peck of friendship. So entranced was she by the festive surroundings, she never questioned his polite greeting. Offering his arm, Rafe led Adele to their table. Its red damask cloth had garlands of laurel and holly bound about with red ribbons.

"Everything's so lovely," Adele whispered against his ear. "I've never seen such lavish decorations. I know you took special care to please me, and you have, dear Rafe. I'll remember this Christmas for the rest of my life."

Never was a truer statement spoken, Rafe thought as he squeezed her hand. He found his mouth repeatedly settling itself in a grim line and forcing him to feign pleasure he no longer felt. He smiled.

"Yes, sweet, I wanted to please you," he said as, out of the corner of his eye, he watched the others seated nearby. *Be careful*, he reminded himself, flashing a squint-eyed nobleman named D'Isigny a brilliant smile.

"I'm surprised this is all off your own land as well," Adele said in wonder, discovering evergreens she had never seen before.

"Fordham's not all wild moorland," he explained, motioning to his server to fill their wine goblets. "Someday—and I know I've promised this before—we'll ride about the land so I can show you how much I have," he said, grinning at her.

Adele smiled and hugged his arm against her body, so filled with happiness it was as if the afternoon's quarrel had never taken place. She looked hopefully at the motley assortment of people crowding the lower tables, quickly identifying the minstrels by the small harps slung over their backs and their particolored tunics of red, green, and yellow.

Even a priest was there, his shabby vestments mud-stained, marking him as one of those travelers caught in the storm. As she scanned the tables, she saw men-at-arms

261

in unfamiliar colors, even a mendicant friar, several pages, and a corpulent merchant draining a large cup of ale.

Their more distinguished guests, two nobles, were seated with them at the lord's table, and Adele was formally introduced to them. Though dressed for travel and somewhat damp and bedraggled, these men of importance disdained the lower classes who cackled at the tables below the salt. When she later studied the younger man's tunic, Adele gasped in surprise to find the royal crest embroidered there. Quickly she tried to recall his name—was it Aubrey Ferrers from the county of Derby?

When she asked Rafe about the man's position in the royal household, he silenced her with a frown. Though puzzled by his reaction, Adele did not ask more.

Suddenly calls for silence echoed through the room. The priest had been prevailed upon to bless all under this roof, and he wished the gathering much joy at this sacred season. After the blessing had been given, the mood within the hall grew more lively. The three minstrels came forward, bowed before the lord and lady of the castle, then sang a sweet country carol, its simple words reminding all present that this season was about far more than holly boughs and full bellies.

The first platter of food was carried inside the hall and paraded before the gathering, succulent and steaming. Ahead of the cook, who bore the head platter, walked the steward. Arthur stopped before the lord's table and bowed before striking his staff three times in honor of the Trinity and also as a signal to the kitchen staff to bring in the remaining dishes. An endless stream of bowls and platters followed, paraded about the room, first offered to the lord and his guests. There were so many dishes the board virtually groaned. Finally came the glistening boar's head, the fat still popping and crackling. A cheer went up, for now it was truly a Christmas banquet. Everyone set to with a will.

Adele had never liked seeing the boar's head with its mouth stuffed with spiced crabapple and surrounded by a bed of greenery, though she knew it was a traditional part of the feast.

While they ate, the two nobles at their table inquired politely after Adele's health and her place of residence. For the most part, her answers were drowned by the noise filling the cavernous room.

Roast capons swimming in purple wine sauce, huge fish with gilded scales, spiced meat and fish spreads, crusty venison pasties all arrived in turn, providing a far more lavish selection than Adele had ever seen. She shared a trencher with Rafe, who gave her tastes of this and tastes of that, spooning spicy or sweet sauces, filling her wine goblet, yet as the meal progressed, Adele felt that something was very wrong.

At first it was difficult to place, for Rafe conversed pleasantly with his guests, was attentive to her needs, and took food from various platters for his own meal. Yet it seemed that his mind was elsewhere. When Rafe applauded the minstrels, or generously praised the cook, it seemed mechanical rather than heartfelt.

Tonight he looked handsome in his hollyberry-red tunic, a heavy gold chain and medallion about his neck. He was the perfect lord of the castle, his smile welcoming all to his feast—but he smiled only with his mouth while his eyes remained dark and troubled. Adele knew him well enough to recognize this counterfeit Rafe De Montford, even if their guests did not. How different he was tonight from the man who had rescued her on the snowy moor. Were these noblemen here to press him to commit to the king's cause? Or had they brought some other disturbing news?

There was no dancing, but she did not mind. Her pleasure had already been dampened by the strained undercurrent beneath Rafe's genial facade. Amongst the travelers sheltering at Fordham were some acrobats who tumbled about the middle of the room, entertaining the gathering in return for lodging. Unfortunately, the quality of their performance had shrunk in proportion to the quantity of ale they consumed. What should have been a skillful feat of balance deteriorated into a third-rate comedy as they fell down time and again, until the room rocked with laughter. Mercifully, the men were finally dragged off to the kitchens for a sobering dunk in the water butt.

Adele toyed with a crystallized apricot, vastly relieved when the two noblemen finally excused themselves. Their yawns had become embarrassingly loud and their heads had begun to nod. The men explained they had been on the road all day, intending to travel on to York until they'd been waylaid at Fordham by the snow.

"What's wrong?" Adele asked, taking Rafe's hand, waiting to speak until their guests had crossed the hall.

"Sweetheart, there's so much wrong, I hardly know where to begin."

Adele gasped and her heart plummeted as she tried to imagine what could have happened. "Because of those men?"

"Nay. Ferrers is only the king's lapdog. He delivered a royal letter to me on his way north. D'Isigny—the one with the squint—is also about royal business, but his is of a different nature. As soon as we can excuse ourselves, we'll go up to the solar to discuss it. Smile—act happy— I don't want spies carrying tales."

Adele did just that until her face ached. She even forced herself to laugh and clap for the minstrels. Then, waiting until enough time had passed, the host excused himself and bid his guests good night.

As she followed Rafe upstairs, Adele thought how handsome he had looked tonight in his red, gold-embroidered tunic. His dark hose and laced, knee-high black hide boots were also decorated with gold. When she first looked at him, he was so alluring that her legs felt like water; at his touch, shivers of anticipation sped along her arm. How she wished they were going upstairs for what she had anticipated would be the conclusion of tonight's festivities instead of to discuss some dire turn of events.

Inside the small solar, a fire burned invitingly and a tray of wine and cakes had been provided on a side table.

Rafe ushered Adele inside the solar and closed the door. Several of his most trustworthy men stood guard on the stair. Before Rafe withdrew the letters, he looked behind the curtains that separated the window alcove from the main room, making sure no spy was hiding there.

His unusual care made Adele even more nervous, aware that what he was about to reveal was of the utmost importance. He lit more candles from the hearth to give them light to read, then withdrew the folded parchment from his tunic where all night these letters had been a crackling reminder of unwelcome tidings.

Adele glanced at the first letter, seeing it was short and had the king's signature at the bottom beside the royal seal.

"First—from my lord and king—a demand for troops to put in the field and my sworn commitment. This was D'Isigny's contribution to my night of pleasure. When he leaves, my answer goes with him. That gives me until the snow melts."

"But you expected the king would press you to commit to his cause," Adele reminded, swallowing nervously, for she knew that this alone could not be his whole reason for gloom.

"True," he sighed, getting up and going to the hearth. "There's likely a dozen letters like this being carried from here to Scotland. I just didn't expect John's watchdog to be sitting at my table waiting for me to sign. But, no matter. You're right, it's no great surprise. The second letter is from Esterwold."

Adele's eyes widened in surprise at this unexpected news, and she sat straighter on the cushions. "From Bohun?"

"Yes. He gives me a few odd bits of news, namely that your old friend—the knight who helped you rule—has gone to his reward."

Adele gasped in surprise, her eyes instantly filling with

tears. "Oh, poor Sir George," she whispered, swallowing and blinking back grief. "But that's not all that letter's about, is it?"

"No. Unfortunately, that's only the opening," Rafe said, bracing himself. "The king's sending Bohun back to his own castle—" Rafe caught Adele's hand when she jumped to her feet with a cry of delight. "No, sweet, that's not good news. Apparently, your former neighbor, Cosantine, has ingratiated himself to such an extent that the king's given him charge of Esterwold."

"What!" Adele cried in shock, pulling free of Rafe's restraining hand. "He's castellan now?"

"No. Esterwold belongs to him. John gave him all the manors adjoining the property."

"He can't! That traitor! When he couldn't foist off an impostor as my brother—oh, I can't believe it! I thought he was our friend! The king's got no right to give away my land—does he?"

Rafe nodded, his face grim. "If he chooses, he can take any man's land, mine included. Theoretically it all belongs to the king. It is only on loan to his barons as long as they please him. He can confiscate property— and has, many times. Besides, you're still his ward . . . which brings me to the last letter."

Adele stared up at him, her heart thudding with shock. How could there be any more devastating news? Yet she had the terrible feeling there was, and somehow she could almost guess what it would be.

Rafe opened the sheet of crinkling parchment covered in small neat script and began to read. "Whereas it has come to our attention that you did not heed our bidding concerning our ward, Lady Adele St. Clare, I have relieved you of her care . . ."

Only the sound of the crackling hearth could be heard as they stared at each other. Rafe resumed his reading, each word dropping like lead. Adele ceased to hear as the missive droned on until Rafe reached the final paragraph.

"Lord Ferrers will have charge of our ward as far as

York where she will enter the household of our dearest friend, Thornton le Wylde, to whom she will then be wed."

The breath choked in her throat as Adele realized what Rafe had just read. The king had betrothed her to another man! "But, you . . . did you not ask him . . . for permission to marry me?" she stammered, tears spilling down her cheeks.

"Yes, I've petitioned him several times. In his usual evenhanded fashion, John has not only chosen to ignore me, he has betrothed you to another of his cronies. Oh— did you notice how he praised me for my judgment in withholding you from D'Avranche, a confessed traitor, keeping you safe in my castle until he could arrange your betrothal to his *dearest* friend—"

"Thornton le Wylde," Adele supplied. "Who is the man? Do you know him.

"Aye, he's a jumped-up pig farmer. Dear God, I must think what to do," Rafe said, rubbing his brow as he stared into the fire. "Short of imprisoning the bastard, I can't even prevent Ferrers from leaving. But I can keep him from taking you with him."

"How?"

"I'm not sure yet. Oh, sweetheart, I'm so sorry. I never expected this."

Adele came to him, needing his strength as she poured out her grief. This Christmas feast had held such promise. There was so much to be thankful for, especially Rafe's miraculous recovery. Everything was happily resolved between them, and tonight she had looked forward to making love to him, longing to rekindle the passion which had blazed between them.

For a long time Rafe held her safe, resting his face against her silky hair. Even their Christmas finery was a mockery. The lavish feast, the brightly decorated hall— all had been to make her happy. He could not have guessed how short-lived that state would be. Rafe's dislike of the king had grown until he could barely stand the thought of serving him, though he had sworn an oath of fealty to the crown. John's praise commending him on his wise judgment especially rankled, for surely the king didn't think him fool enough to be flattered by it. Rafe had no doubt that John knew he had disobeyed him. Why else would he send one of his spies to Fordham?

Rafe wanted to slit Ferrers's throat for bringing these letters which caused him and Adele such pain. He could not deny he'd seriously considered disposing of Ferrers and pretending the missive had never arrived. Doubtless that was what De Vesci would do, faced with the same dilemma. But he wasn't Eustace De Vesci. Rafe had always worked inside the law.

Adele's sobs finally lessened, her shoulders heaving silently until that too stopped. Spent, she leaned weakly against Rafe, hiding her face in his tunic. How she longed to shut out the world, to be able to stay with him in this room, safe forever from the king with his favorites and his foolish laws, easily made and swiftly broken. They could pull up the bridge to keep safe from their enemies and defend Fordham against a siege. Yet, in the end, she knew the king would have his way.

Finally, Adele raised her tear-stained face. "Couldn't you just pretend you never received the letter?"

"Don't think I haven't thought of that, but I'd have to kill Ferrers—or at least detain him. John knows I want to marry you, so his praise for my judgment in keeping you from Summerhay is only a ploy. He cleverly discovers men's weaknesses to use against them. He knows I disobeyed his orders. If D'Avranche hadn't fallen out of favor, the king would've made me pay through the eyes and nose for it. He's playing cat-and-mouse, seeing what I'm going to do next."

Horrified, Adele heard Rafe's explanation, for she had naively hoped the king did not know why he hadn't taken her to Summerhay. If Rafe disobeyed King John again, the monarch might strip him of his lands and title. She

would not let that happen—even if it meant marrying le
Wylde.

"You're sure he knows?"

"Positive. If I'd not petitioned for you, there might be
room for doubt. But he knew exactly where to find you.
Thank God you're sleeping in your own chamber, so at
least, for his spy's benefit, we've the appearance of
innocence."

"What good's that to me?" Adele demanded, pulling
away from him. In the past, Rafe had always found a
solution to bad situations, however difficult or dangerous
they were. Though the conclusion appalled her, she wondered if this was the one time there was nothing he could
do to change matters. She swallowed, before asking in a
small voice, "Am I going to York to marry le Wylde?"

"Never," Rafe growled, pitching the letter aside. "Let's
get this straight. Ferrers's orders are to take you to York.
He hasn't read this letter, because the royal seal was
intact. And it's not likely John confided in him. He may
not even know I want to marry you, agreed?"

"Yes, I suppose. But what good's that?"

"I'll delay my response to the king by asking silly
questions like how many knights does he want and where
are they to go? Anything to delay the inevitable. D'Isigny
will be none the wiser. He'll assume he has my sealed
commitment. As soon as the snow thaws, he'll be anxious
to leave, because he has many other lords to visit. Then
we'll have only Ferrers and his men to deal with."

Rafe scowled as he paced before the hearth, punching
his fist into his palm when he said, "I'd like to slit the bastard's throat, but I won't. We'll detain him and allow
D'Isigny to leave first. Maybe you could plead illness."

"He'd probably drag me off my deathbed to follow the
king's orders," Adele observed gloomily, finding her
mind devoid of useful suggestions.

"Not if he thought you had the plague."

She gasped. "The plague! You'll panic everyone."

"True. Then, the only thing which would make John's arrangement void is the prior marriage of either party."

"I was never married to D'Avranche," Adele reminded him gloomily. "I never even met him."

Rafe smiled, and for the first time tonight, his expression was genuine. "No, silly—not to D'Avranche—to me!"

"You!" she gasped in shock. "We aren't married."

"Not yet—but we soon can be."

"Without the king's permission?"

Rafe shrugged. "I'm willing to gamble. Things can't get much worse. In fact, I've been a prize idiot not to have done it before. Ever obedient to the crown, I went about things in the proper manner. This time I'll do as I please. Are you game?"

Her face aglow with delight, Adele laughed. "Need you ask? But how can we get married with them here? There's no way we could keep it secret."

Rafe grinned at her and he held out his arms.

"Who says? I'm no fool either. I suspect our noble friends will sleep soundly for some time."

Her eyes widened in surprise, and she smiled. Had he drugged their guests' wine? That would explain their sudden exhaustion. She smiled. "Who'll marry us against the King's will?"

He smiled.

"Oh, that's right," she gasped, her mood brightening. "The priest caught in the storm."

"Aye. It matters not from whence he came or where he's going, just so long as he's an ordained priest. I doubt he knows the political situation, either. Besides, I doubt he's incorruptible—a little gold can go a long way to buying silence. So, after D'Isigny leaves, you shall become too ill to travel. I'll start rumors that it might be the plague. That'll send Ferrers galloping north. By the time John finds out, it'll be too late. You'll already be married."

"It sounds wonderful, yet there's too much danger in it for you. The king's temper is legendary. He could strip you of all you own. Make war on you. Even take your life."

"Don't worry about that, sweet," Rafe said as he kissed her brow. "He could, but I have a feeling he won't. Once that charter's presented, all hell's going to break loose. Hopefully, he'll be far too preoccupied to think about us."

"And if the king won't recognize our marriage?"

"I'm a good friend of Archbishop Langton. Likely he can use the weight of Rome to support our claim. John won't want to infuriate them again. Now, don't worry, you wait here while I get the priest."

"Now?" she squeaked in surprise, patting her hair and smoothing her gown. "Can't I get ready first?"

"You look beautiful just the way you are," Rafe said and he held out his hand for his ring. "I'd better take that."

After he took the piece, to Adele's surprise, instead of leaving Rafe dropped to his knees before her. "I'm asking you to marry me, Lady. I love you with all my heart."

With trembling lips Adele whispered her answer as she leaned down to kiss him, thrilling at the pressure of his hot mouth.

When he gazed up at her, Rafe's blue eyes were soft and tender as he fixed forever in his mind this exact moment, how she looked, how her mouth tasted, how sweet was the sound of her whispered words.

Quickly they embraced and he hurried to the door. "I'll bring Margery and Symme to stand for us."

With that, he was gone. Adele tried to quiet her racing heart, hardly able to believe this was really happening. Her hands were shaking with excitement. Out of the pain of treachery and loss had come such delight. Once again she wondered if she was dreaming. Then she noticed the discarded letters and knew it was real. In his haste Rafe had left the condemning evidence scattered on the settie. Tempted to throw the parchments in the fire, she hid them instead in her embroidery basket.

The wedding party arrived one by one. First came Margery, a cloak over her Christmas gown, weeping with joy at the news. She clasped Adele against her ample bosom, wishing her happiness. Then Symme and Ivo slipped inside the solar, both men sworn to secrecy. Lastly came Adric, escorting the priest, with Val bringing up the rear, his tail wagging in pleasure at being part of this unexpected gathering in the wee hours of the morning.

The unshaven priest was still half asleep. He glanced bleary-eyed about the lighted solar, seeing first the lord and lady of the castle, then the others. He had been surprised to be asked to perform a wedding at this unearthly hour. At first he had hesitated, wondering what lay behind the need for stealth and haste, but the bag of gold Adric had pressed into his hand went a long way to persuade him.

It was highly irregular, of course, for no banns had been called, no confessions made—but this *was* the Christmas season. That was most important, for had it still been Advent, they would have needed a special dispensation—or more bags of gold.

There, in the early hours of the cold December morn, they gathered in the firelit solar, voices hushed, all but the priest aware that what they were about to do was treason.

If the sleepers below in the great hall noticed the unusual castle activity, they merely wondered at the strange habits of their betters before rolling over on the rushes and going back to sleep. Even the liveried men-at-arms who had accompanied Lord Ferrers and Lord D'Isigny slept on, blissfully unaware, as did their masters—the depth of their slumber induced by good food, ale, and a little something Rafe had gotten from the witch who'd cured him.

Adele stood beside him, her marigold velvet skirts brushing against his black boots, her shaking hand clasped firmly in his.

Behind them, Margery still wept quietly to see how beautiful they looked together: she pale and lovely with her bright crown of fiery hair, he dark and powerful standing protectively at her side. Their love for each other burned brightly in their tender smiles.

The priest produced a faded stole from inside his vestments, which by now had dried but were still mud-spattered. He unrolled the wrap and placed it around his neck, indicating he was ready to begin. With much throat-clearing, he began reciting the Latin sacrament of marriage.

The priest shortened the ceremony to the bare essentials, anxious to return to the warm place he had claimed beside the hearth, afraid if he was away too long that another would make the spot his own.

Adele and Rafe knelt before the priest, using the cushions from the settee as a kneeler. At last, the priest joined their hands to pronounce them man and wife. Rafe slid his ring on Adele's finger, then kissed her on the mouth.

"God bless you, wife. You're truly an angel come to earth," he whispered, recalling his thoughts when he had first seen Adele come inside the hall in her splendid new gown.

Overcome with joy and happiness, Adele rested her head on his shoulder. "Tonight you've made me the happiest woman alive."

Aware of the continued need for secrecy, the small wedding party quietly gave the happy couple their blessings with many hugs and kisses. Again Margery shed abundant tears of joy as Adele hugged her and thanked her for her years of faithful service. Even Val received a parting hug from the bride. Then the wedding guests slipped away in the shadows, leaving Rafe and Adele alone.

Chapter Sixteen

When all had gone, the room's silence was broken only by the crackling fire and the wind moaning through the battlements. Adele looked through an arrow slit at the white countryside beyond the castle walls, shivering with a mixture of cold and excitement as Rafe moved behind her. The welcome heat of his body enveloped her in a comforting wave.

"All done without incident," he reported after he had closed the door behind Symme, the last to leave. Rafe had also scanned the great hall, where all seemed peaceful.

"See how cold and lonely it looks," Adele said, leaning back against him as he looked over her shoulder at the white outside world. "We're like two travelers, just you and me adrift on a sea of white," she mused dreamily.

Rafe smiled at her statement. *You, me, and a few hundred other souls,* he mentally corrected, but what matter? Rafe hugged her close, resting his head against hers, intoxicated by the perfume of her body. Before them spread the vast, rolling landscape of his northern lands, covered in snow which reflected its own light so that it was never really dark outside. True, they were locked safe and sound in the light and warmth inside his castle. But he wondered gloomily how long this would remain his castle.

Though to Adele Rafe had professed nonchalance about his defiance of the king, he knew John well enough to have qualms about the wisdom of his action. This time next year he could be earning his bread by hiring himself out to fight for other nobles, while one of John's friends enjoyed Fordham's splendor.

Adele moved in his arms, startling him for an instant, so deep in thought had he been. She brought him back to the present with a jarring thud. Good God! This was his wedding night. He was holding the most desirable woman in England in his arms and he was wasting precious time worrying about the future wrath of his king. He was being crazy not to fully enjoy the treasure for which he'd risked so much.

"Let's go to our chamber, love," he suggested, her ear cool against his feverish lips.

Adele's pulse raced. She still half expected to waken to discover that none of this had really taken place, but she knew it was real by the warm strength of his arms around her, the heat of his kisses. Even now, they tantalized the exposed nape of her neck, and his husky invitation promised all manner of delight.

"What if someone sees us?" she asked, ever mindful of his safety, unable to be so cavalier about this move which could spell ruin for the man she loved.

"Ah, there's something I never told you—there's a secret way from the solar to my bedchamber. Just in case Ferrers looks in your chamber, Margery's put a mound of pillows under the covers."

Rafe led Adele to where a colorful tapestry depicting Adam and Eve's expulsion for the Garden of Eden covered the wall.

"Rather an appropriate subject, don't you think?" he

275

suggested with a wicked grin as he pulled aside the hanging. Revealed was a narrow door set in the stone.

In less than a heartbeat Adele was inside Rafe's bedchamber. There, the familiar great bed with the blue velvet hangings looked inviting and warm. The fire was already banked for the night, and a jug of wine and two glasses were on a tray beside the bed. She shivered with anticipation, almost afraid of the intensity of their passion for they had been so long apart. Uneasily she thought about Rafe's barely healed wounds, but when she turned to question him about his pain, he was already shaking his head.

"No—don't give it a thought," he said as he read her mind. "Come here to me, Lady De Montford. It's been a long, long time."

His words gave her a little thrill of surprise as she realized that, tonight, she had truly become Lady De Montford of Fordham Castle.

"Yes, it's been much too long, husband," she whispered, using that name for the first time and finding it thrilling.

Adele moved as if through water, her legs weak, her hands trembling. From all those months of loneliness, the days of longing, Rafe's passionate love promised solace.

He held her against him for a long time, not speaking. Adele understood his sudden quiet mood. There had been so much strife to overcome before they reached this point, he wanted to savor it.

Presently Rafe released her and turned to pour two glasses of wine. They stood before the hearth holding up goblets of red wine and solemnly toasted their blessed union. After he had drained his goblet, Rafe pulled off his tunic. Adele's heart bumped erratically, her excitement mounting as she gazed at his upper body. How magnificent he was, sinewed and strong, his chest broad and his shoulders square.

How she had longed for this moment, her wedding night being one of her most cherished fantasies. Tonight only Rafe's wounds marred his perfection, painful reminders of how close he had come to death. But they were also reminders that he'd survived for her.

Adele traced her fingers along his arm. "Now that you're a married man, must you keep risking your life?"

"You already know the answer to that," Rafe answered gravely, glancing down at his injuries. "I did learn one thing from FitzAlan's tourney, however."

"What's that?"

"Never to fight in borrowed mail. The sleeves were too short. Had I known we were taking part in a tourney, I'd have brought my own and this would never have happened."

"Have you forgotten we were supposedly on a pilgrimage, sweet? Mail shirts have no place there," she reminded. She drained the last of the heavy wine. "Though it was something your friends did not remember."

"And their carelessness gave them away to Softsword's spies. Doubtless some are paying dearly for their mistakes."

"I wish we'd never heard of King John."

Rafe chuckled as he took her empty goblet. "You've much company in that. From what I hear, fully half of England feels the same way."

She smiled at him and rested her head against his hard shoulder. "I won't let that man spoil my wedding night, even if he is the king. I forbid you to mention him again."

"Done. Because, love, I'd much rather talk about you," Rafe whispered, reaching for her gold circlet and lifting it from her brow. He pulled loose the ribboned coif that Margery had carefully created, spilling strands of pearls and golden ribbons on the rushes. Soon Adele's magnificent cloak of lustrous hairs spread in waves about her shoulders. Rafe took a handful of the perfumed locks and brought it to his mouth to kiss. He inhaled her unique scent which had haunted him both sleeping and awake since he'd first held her in his arms. He still could hardly believe that a woman could be this beautiful, this loyal, this passionate, and, hardest of all to credit—his!

Adele slid her hand gently across his chest and shoulders, avoiding the bandages. Just the touch of his hot, smooth flesh made an expectant shiver run down her spine. Under her fingertips his hard muscles seemed to have been sculpted by a master, yet they were not cold, unyielding marble, but made of living, pulsing flesh.

"Oh, Rafe, I love you. You've made this the happiest Christmas of my life," she whispered against his neck.

"I'm sorry I had to wait for such bad news to act. Sometimes I'm too law-abiding for my own good," he confessed wryly. He unlaced her tunic and drew it over her head. "Just think, if I'd done as I pleased, we could have wed months ago."

She smiled at him, moving, twisting as he pulled off her gown, the marigold velvet falling to the rushes. Her linen shift followed until Adele was covered only by her cape of shimmering hair, her flesh pale and translucent in the firelight, her soft, smooth body perfectly formed.

"You're truly my angel," Rafe whispered, his eyes dark with passion as he stroked her back and swept his hands across her silky skin, molding her curving hips.

With one swift movement Rafe swept Adele into his arms and carried her to the bed. There he laid her a top the blue velvet cover. Growing more impatient as his passion mounted, Rafe balanced on one foot to drag off his boots and held on to the bedpost while he pulled off his hose.

Adele giggled as he wobbled about until his clothes were finally scattered over the rushes. She welcomed him with open arms as he leapt inside the covers, pulling quilts and blankets up over them. With a deep sigh of pleasure she slid into his embrace, thrilling to the warmth of his body against her chill flesh.

Now that Rafe was holding her tight, her hips pressed against his pulsing flesh, she gave no further thought to his wound or whether the king would punish him for his defiance. She thought only of the delight of their lovemaking. Whether this was to be the last, or the first, night spent together as man and wife, she wanted to cherish every moment.

The fragrant heat of Rafe's body awakened delicious memories. Adele burrowed against him, her tongue making a tantalizing passage from his ear to his neck to his shoulder, deliberately arousing him until he finally grasped her head between his hands and welded his searing mouth to hers.

Here, in the dark-curtained island of his great bed, they would make love as never before. Adele's heart sang as Rafe kissed her brow, her cheek; his mouth moved slowly over her shoulders to her breasts which ached for his touch. Unconsciously Adele thrust forward, filling his hands with her sweet flesh. Rafe captured her pink nipple in his mouth, drawing on it until her flesh hardened in arousal. His hot, insistent touch sped heat to the very core of her being until her legs ached for him; her belly and the heated flesh between her legs throbbed with desire.

Instinctively Adele sought that long, burning flesh that seared her thighs, and she gently caressed it, aware that Rafe was close to the point of no return. He was still a few moments longer before rolling her onto her back, the weight of his body a blessed torment as he pressed her deep into the feather mattress. Adele's thighs strained against his.

For an instant Rafe fumbled, seeking her portal until she opened eagerly to receive him. So desirous of each other were they, as they came together, their hips ground against each other in desperate abandon.

All thought of slow, casual lovemaking fled. Only passion held sway as they embarked on that journey which would culminate in total surrender of both body and soul. Adele clung to him as if she were drowning, their mouths hot, open, seeking. Every nerve ending of her body responded to the rhythm of his thrusts, making her groan in intense pleasure as Rafe moved faster and faster.

His whispered endearments were muffled in her hair. Rafe's hands clamped tight about her shapely hips, raising her off the bed as he drove deep inside her, taking Adele on a dizzying journey which always seemed new yet achingly familiar.

Finally the dam burst in a flood of agonizingly sweet mutual fulfillment. Lost to reality, Adele drifted, floated, until she gradually grew aware of tears trickling into her ears, of her bruised lips and throbbing body—and of Rafe.

For three days the snow held. It was agony to have to act as if they were mere acquaintances, never to steal a kiss or a touch. Though he was only one man, Aubrey Ferrers seemed to be everywhere at once. After the first day, Adele no longer doubted Rafe's assessment of the King's reason for sending Ferrers here. Around corners, at table, walking the battlements, climbing the towers—no place was safe from his stealthy prowl.

Manor payments were usually made on quarter days. This winter's date had been December 25. Tenancies had ended then and rents came due. This year, however, because of the weather, Rafe had sent word through his bailiffs that payment was excused until further notice.

Once the winds shifted and the thaw began, the day for the collection of rents was chosen. A parade of tenants came across the lowered bridges and into the bailey, where trestles were set up to receive the lord's due. At mid-morning the sun came out, warming and brightening the proceedings. Unlike many other lords, Rafe gave each tenant a cup of ale and a hunk of bread while they waited.

As Rafe had spent much time away from the castle this past year, he had also decided to hold his lord's court simultaneously with the collection of the quarter-day dues.

Adele thought it very unusual to hold either event outside—she had always opened Esterwold's great hall to conduct her manor court—but she assumed that because Rafe had so many tenants, it was wiser to hold these events in the open. Arthur oversaw the collection of rents—some paid in cash, some in goods—keeping his steely gaze on the bailiffs to make sure they dealt honestly with his lord's revenue. Though cheerless, Fordham's steward was brutally fair, and it was rare for a peasant to exercise his right of appeal to his lord for any overcharging.

Adele was disappointed that she must watch the court as a bystander, for she would have liked to sit beside her husband as was her due. *Husband*! Each time she thought of Rafe that way she felt a little thrill of excitement. Had they been able to bring their marriage into the open, today she could have shared this important part of castle life with him.

But even here, Aubrey Ferrers snooped about. He examined the bailiff's charges, looking over Arthur's shoulder at the columns of figures. He had been charged with making sure the Lord of Fordham had not cheated his royal master by collecting more revenue than he reported. Though Arthur found this scrutiny most irritating, Rafe had warned him not to cross the nobleman, so he grimly endured the snooping without protest.

After a long, tiring day, the court adjourned. Two sentences for lashing had been carried out: one to satisfy an angry father whose daughter's virginity had been stolen, the second in punishment for the far more serious charge of pilfering from the church collection box. However, the accused was determined to have been starving and new to the area, so Rafe chose to be lenient. The rest of the charges carried various fines, the crimes ranging from eating a neighbor's turnips to brawling outside the parish church. Each offender's name and his crime and punishment were duly noted in the manor records.

Soon the short winter day was spent. The sun slid behind a silver-tipped bank of clouds before the last tenant trudged over the drawbridge heading home to his village. Once the bridges were cleared, each was winched closed. Rafe was taking no chances of a surprise attack in these unsettled times.

In the great hall, the festive decorations for the Christmas feast were still in place. Every day the wandering minstrels serenaded the lord of the castle at his noon meal and again at supper. Though the weather showed every sign of clearing, few of the stranded travelers had made any move to leave, reluctant to abandon Fordham's pleasant safety. The one exception was Lord D'Isigny.

"If it please you, Lord Rafe, I'll be leaving tomorrow," he announced through a mouthful of food that night as they sat at table.

"And you want my written commitment to take with you?"

D'Isigny smiled mirthlessly and nodded.

Probably due to his squint, D'Isigny never quite looked one in the eye, a habit Rafe found most unsettling. "Do you go straight to Northampton to the king?" he asked casually.

"Nay, I've more work to do. Likely I'll be waylaid by a few more snowstorms before I'm done."

Adele heard their exchange, and her heart thudded uncomfortably as she reviewed the plan which would be set in motion once D'Isigny left.

"And you, my lord Ferrers, I suppose you're anxious to be back on the road as well," Rafe remarked, turning to the sly Ferrers. The man watched all activity inside the hall with a hooded and calculating gaze.

"There's no great hurry. I'll wait for the lady to decide," Ferrers said, turning to Rafe and forcing a smile. "Do you know when that will be?"

"Oh, I think Lady Adele will be ready to leave whenever you choose. Most of her belongings were never unpacked. Shall I have her trunks loaded on your wagon?"

Ferrers barely concealed his surprise at De Montford's offer. He had been especially cautioned to look for signs of De Montford's maneuvering to keep the woman at Fordham in disobedience to his royal master's wishes. However, from what he had seen, all had been above-board. Not once had he caught either De Montford or the king's ward acting inappropriately.

"Why, yes. That would be splendid . . . if that's agreeable to you, Lady?"

Adele quickly swallowed the bread in her mouth, not expecting to be asked a question. Generally, visiting noblemen treated her as if she were either a half-wit or a piece of furniture.

"Yes, of course, my lord," she replied with a gulp as the bread stuck in her throat, "The sooner the better. Likely my lord Rafe will be glad to see the back of me, for I've inconvenienced him enough," she added with a smile.

Rafe glanced sharply in her direction, and Adele marked his silent warning to take care not to say too much. She had thought her latter remark to be a stroke of wit on her behalf, but she obeyed him and said no more.

"Nay, Lady, a beautiful guest like you is an asset to any household," D'Isigny interjected, overhearing the remark.

Surprised that he even knew what she looked like, Adele treated the squinty lord to a smile of thanks before returning to her meal. They continued to eat, making small chat, while the minstrels played and sang carols and rounds. Sadly Adele watched Rafe, longing to touch his sun-bronzed hand resting close to hers on the table, his strong fingers curved about a cup. When she looked at his lips, she remembered his kiss and how it felt when his fiery passion had kindled her own . . . Adele drained her cup and declined a refill from the server. She must be careful not to watch Rafe with such longing, lest it show in her face. She was sure Ferrers watched her like a hawk.

Presently the minstrels, showing no sign of fatigue, began a rousing country tune. The piece was popular with those seated at the lower tables, and they noisily tried to repeat the chorus, which grew longer with every verse. The level of noise in the hall increased greatly as tipsy men tried to outdo each other for sheer volume until Adele's head began to ache.

She politely excused herself, glad to get away from the uproar. Each time she thought about the part she must play in deceiving the king's spy, her heart jumped and her hands sweated. Much depended on the success or failure of her performance. If Lord Ferrers chose to wait out her ailment, as well he might, they would have to think of some other way to trick him into leaving for York without her.

By mid-morning of the following day, Lord D'Isigny, riding at the head of his liveried soldiers, clopped over the drawbridge. He waved farewell to Rafe, who stood watching from the battlements. Tucked safely inside D'Isigny's pouch was his sealed response to the king. If he was lucky, it would be spring before that letter found its way into the royal hands.

One down and one to go.

That afternoon as the pale sun washed the bailey, its rays transforming patches of snow into puddles of mud, Rafe's soldiers struggled to load Adele's trunks onto Lord Ferrer's supply wagon. She was alarmed to see her worldly possessions disappearing inside the canvas-topped wagon.

Even Val's wooden crate was hauled out to the bailey. The dog was not inside, for she intended to keep Val free as long as she was able. She could not help wondering what would happen if Ferrers left without her, yet took all her possessions with him to York—including her horse and her dog.

When Adele asked Rafe that same question, he grinned. "I'm one step ahead of you, sweet. That wagon has a bad axle. They'll be lucky to haul it to the bridge before they have a catastrophe."

"What if that just delays him? I don't know how long I can pretend to be dying."

"If you're dying of the plague, Ferrers will be halfway to York before he gives that wagon a second thought."

The following day dawned cold and gray. Lord Ferrers surveyed the sky after he had broken his fast, wondering if they would get far before the rain. "Is not the lady Adele up yet? I don't want to tarry, with that sky."

Rafe feigned surprise. "Perhaps too many late nights," he suggested, noticing that many of the stranded travelers still lounged about the hall. A couple had left yesterday, but most were still there, including the two clergymen and the fat merchant who played chess all day and devoured his food and ale. Well, the announcement that was about to be made would soon thin out the ranks. Rafe hid a smile as he anticipated the hysterical flight of these unwelcome guests.

As time passed and Adele did not appear, Ferrers asked impatiently, "Shall we send a maid to rouse her?" He cast an anxious glance at the gray sky.

"Yes, a good idea—ah, here's her woman now."

On cue, Margery emerged from the shadows, holding her skirts in her hand as she hurried across the hall. "Oh, my lord, my lord," she wailed, entering wholeheartedly into the play-acting. "My lady's unwell. She's hot and sneezing. Will you send her a posset from the kitchens?"

"Why, of course. I'm sorry to hear it," Rafe said solicitously. "I'll have them send food as well."

"Nay, she'll eat nothing. I've already tried milk sops."

"I trust it's nothing serious," Ferrers said, looking questioningly at Margery's agitated face. "Is it, woman?" he demanded as a wave of unease invaded his peace of mind.

"Likely she took a chill being outside on quarter day," Margery offered hopefully. "A hot posset will soothe her."

By afternoon Lord Ferrers had decided to wait another few days to start out for York, allowing Lady Adele to recover from her indisposition. A cold rain had begun in late morning, and the thought of crossing the moor where snow lay in vast white islands was not appealing. He had challenged Lord Rafe to a game of chess, and they sat companionably beside a charcoal brazier, engrossed in their game, cups of spiced mulled ale at their elbows.

Margery tentatively approached the two men.

"Lord Rafe," she whispered, coming to his side as she tried to speak privately to him.

"What is it, woman? Can't you see I'm playing chess?"

"It's important that I speak with you alone," Margery continued in a whisper, amazing even herself as she produced two large tears which plopped from her cheeks.

Lord Ferrers could not help but hear the exchange, and his attention was immediately captured. He looked more closely at the distraught woman.

"What is it?" he snapped, leaning forward.

"My lady's getting worse," Margery whispered, "She's coughing now and she . . . she . . ."

"She what? Out with it," Rafe demanded, half rising from his chair. "She what?"

"There's spots all over her arms, my lord," Margery wailed.

"What?" Ferrers asked, eyes narrowing. "A rash, you say?"

"Aye, my lord, and it's spread since morning. We must send for the wise woman to treat her. I don't know what else to do. Will you come see, Lord Rafe? I'm afraid."

Lord Ferrers had paled and he pushed back his chair.

"Is this a ploy to keep her from journeying to York?" he snarled suspiciously.

"Nay, my lord, I know when my lady's ill. I've been with Lady Adele since she was a babe," Margery added indignantly.

"We'll come with you to see," Rafe said, glancing around the hall to see if anyone else had heard Margery's tearful tale. There were a few curious glances cast in their direction, but Ferrer's soldiers continued to throw dice and the fat merchant still snored contentedly beside the hearth.

The three hurried along the castle's chill corridors, then up the stairs to Adele's snug tower room. A fire was burning in the hearth, and a young maid scuttled aside as the two noblemen marched into the room.

The bed curtains were half drawn, making it gloomy and hard to see the patient in the big bed. Rafe was thankful for that, since Ferrers would not be able to see much either. He wondered how they had feigned a rash. For a moment a terrible thought flashed across his mind. Margery had sounded so very convincing. What if she was not acting? What if Adele was really ill?

Rafe accompanied Ferrers to her bedside, gasping in shock as he noticed her pale arm outside the covers. An angry red rash crept along her arm. The rash was unmistakable. Rafe swallowed uneasily, and he felt his heart begin to pound.

"You say the rash is spreading?" he asked Margery who stood behind them wringing her hands.

"Over her body just since this morning," Margery revealed tearfully.

Ferrers stepped closer, suspicious. This illness had occurred so very conveniently, he considered cynically, almost as if it had been prearranged. When last he'd spoken to the lady, she was hale and hearty, clapping for the minstrels' songs, clearly enjoying her food. . . .

Ferrers looked down at the angry rash which even as he watched seemed to be spreading further, and a terrible thought crossed his mind. He *had* heard that people sometimes felt fit as a fiddle just hours before being struck down with plague. Just thinking about that made him sweat. Why, he'd sat close to the woman, even touched her hand. . . .

Rounding on Margery, Lord Ferrers took her arm and marched her to the hearth to interrogate her.

Rafe stood beside the bed looking down at Adele. She lay with her eyes closed. Her face looked very flushed, and sweat beaded on her brow before slowly trickling down her cheek. Why was she sweating? Surely that could not be feigned. Rafe's stomach lurched again as he wondered if fate had played the cruelest of tricks. Could Adele really be ill? Could she—oh, God, no, not that! Could she actually have the plague? So many strangers had crowded into the castle during the snowstorm, any one of them could have been carrying the deadly disease. As he stood there, Rafe could feel the blood draining from his face, and his hands grew cold and clammy. Oh, dear God, not his sweet Adele, not now when she was finally his. . . .

Then a strange thing happened. While Rafe stood looking at her with a stricken expression, Adele winked at him. He gasped and bent over her for a closer look. Had he imagined the movement of her eye? Rafe waited, peering through the gloom, tempted to get a candle for more light, yet not wanting to draw more attention to her. There—she winked again, and the corners of her mouth twitched slightly.

As if a great weight had been lifted from his shoulders, Rafe let out a sigh of relief. He closed his eyes in a silent prayer of thanks, gripping the bedpost as he suddenly felt faint.

Back came Margery with Ferrers, who was carrying a candle.

"Let's have a look at her in the light," declared Lord Ferrers, holding the flame higher to cast a yellow circle of light over Adele's face.

"See how she sweats?" Rafe pointed out quickly.

Ferrers saw the perspiration trickling down her flushed cheeks, saw the rash, and when she suddenly burst out coughing, he leapt back. Without warning, Ferrers thrust the lighted candle at the startled Margery and bolted from the room. Rafe stood there a moment longer wondering what he should do; then he too ran from the room to follow.

The young maid who had heard Lord Ferrers questioning Margery about her lady's illness raced ahead of them. When she heard Lord Ferrers mention that dread word, she panicked. Unable to keep any news to herself, she ran along the castle corridors screaming and wailing to all who would listen.

Within minutes, the great hall was in an uproar. Travelers and soldiers, anxious to know what all the commotion was about, crowded around to hear the terrible tale, which in the telling had grown by leaps and bounds.

Lady Adele was dying of plague!

The statement sent horror through all who heard it. Suddenly, anywhere but Fordham Castle seemed most desirable as the stranded travelers panicked. Scrambling for their possessions and disregarding the cold rain, the guests began a mass exodus—joined by some of Ferrer's men-at-arms as they streamed across the bailey. So sudden and pronounced was the leavetaking that Rafe had to order several of his soldiers aside to tell them it was not true. With effort, he managed to keep his own men from panicking. The kitchen staff, the sentries on the battlements, all jabbered and wailed as the tale was retold. Even the fat merchant who had been snoring beside the hearth was awakened by his fellow travelers and—though he hated to leave the warm fire and abundant food—he too disappeared into the driving rain.

From the battlements, Rafe watched in amazement, holding his aching stomach. He had laughed too much. They were so frightened they could barely wait until the bridge was down; some daring souls had leapt the last few feet before the bridge was completely lowered. They ran, tripping over each other, even exchanging blows when one forced his way in front of another. With cloaks pulled over their heads and held protectively before their faces, men walked, rode, and ran across the twin drawbridges to disappear into the gathering gloom. Rafe could not have asked for better fortune, for this rumor had effectively emptied the castle of its storm-driven flotsam.

Ah, yes, there was Ferrers now, galloping across the bridge at the head of his men. They had pulled the wagon as far as the outer bailey before it capsized in the mud and was abandoned. Ferrers had taken almost an hour to assemble his men and depart; Rafe had vastly underestimated his courage.

It took him almost two hours to convince all of his people that Lady Adele did not have the plague. Rafe told them that she had taken a chill, but was feeling much better now. No, he claimed, he had no idea how the addled wench could have mistaken Lady Adele's illness for plague and begun this mass panic. His dubious men heard him out, and Rafe realized that, until they saw Adele for themselves and could see that she was sound, they would not be convinced.

Rafe went to Adele's chamber to beg her to come down and show them she was well. He was concerned that his soldiers had been frightened unnecessarily. He had never intended to start a panic amongst his own people.

But there she was, whole, and sound, and beautiful. Rafe smiled at her in relief, and she gave him an answering smile.

"How?" was all Rafe asked as he came into the room and closed the door. "You had me worried out of my wits."

Adele smiled knowingly and led him to the bed, where a pan of hot coals and a half dozen hot water bottles were concealed beneath the covers.

"Ah, I think I'd have been sweating too, with all that," he laughed, breathing a sigh of relief. Adele had looked so convincingly ill, he was still not wholly recovered from his shock. "What about the rash?"

Pulling a face, Adele held out her arm, which still looked angry and red. "Not as easily cured. Margery used a salve to blister the skin, but the cream to repair the damage doesn't work as well."

"Wear a gown with sleeves long enough to hide the rash, and please, sweet, come down to show the men you're whole, then we can all calm down."

"What about Ferrers?"

"He's halfway across the county by now. It's safe to come down. Besides, the bridges are up and no one can slip in to surprise us. All the travelers have gone as well, and Ferrers's men-at-arms. There's only us left."

Adele gasped in delight. "Then we did it!" She moved inside the circle of his arms to press her still damp face against his.

"Yes, we did. Things went even better than I'd hoped."

They went down to the great hall together, entering the room where many of the soldiers and servants still gathered. Their chat, their worried talk, stopped as if by magic when they saw their lord with Lady Adele. She looked just as they had seen her yesterday, wearing a blue tunic, her auburn hair hanging down her back in a loose braid, looking as well and as beautiful as ever—definitely not dying from the plague.

After a stunned silence, the men greeted their liege. The captain of the guard, gathering his wits, gruffly ordered his soldiers to return to their posts. The men obeyed the order, though they were still baffled that such a foolish rumor had begun. They left, muttering amongst themselves.

"There's still a few days of Christmas left, my love," Rafe said as they exited. "What say we celebrate them together as they were meant to be celebrated?" Rafe gave her a relieved smile as he hugged Adele against his side. "Shall we sup alone at our table amidst the holly and the ivy?"

"Oh, Rafe, I'd like that. And I still can't believe Ferrer fell for it."

"You did it, sweet. You certainly missed your calling. It's a pity women can't be players; you would surely be famous."

"All I want to be famous for is being the best Lady Fordham this castle's ever had," she confided. They walked up the steps of the lord's dais.

Pages and maids bustled into place, and the servers nudged each other, ready to pick up dishes and decanters to wait upon their lord.

"That wish has already been granted. There'll never be another Lady of Fordham to match you," Rafe told her. He took her hand and pressed it to his lips.

Chapter Seventeen

Yorkshire's winter weather proved to be a strong deterrent to the king sending any other spies to Fordham. As the weeks passed without incident, Rafe began to relax. John Softsword's vengeance was usually swift; by now he had likely chosen a dozen other men's lives to destroy.

The weeks stretched into months which were blissfully uneventful. Rafe introduced Adele to his people as the Lady of Fordham, and she was wholeheartedly accepted; even Arthur made a shamefaced apology for his earlier lack of respect. Whether his remorse was genuine or was prompted by Rafe, Adele did not know. Taking the steward at his word, she accepted his apology and assured him there were no hard feelings between them. As a further show of goodwill, Arthur assisted her in reestablishing the castle infirmary.

It was well known that Adele had nursed their lord back to health; that act by itself would have made her place secure. She was gladly accepted. Though she was concerned about the soldiers' reaction to her bringing

Mistress Gallett inside the castle, Adele was relieved to find they did not hold it against her. Many of Rafe's people still had a touching faith in the woman's ability to cure their ills, and she retained a steady stream of patients from the surrounding villages.

In the castle, Adele was still mindful of the people's healthy fear of the witch. She carefully weeded out the legitimate cures from the more questionable ones offered to her by the old crone. And she publicly burned the grimoire discovered in the infirmary during its cleaning, just in case, to reassure the castle inhabitants she would not resort to using black magic in her treatments.

As spring approached and the roads dried, Rafe and Adele traveled south to visit Gerard Montsorrel and his wife. Much was afoot in England these days, and the momentous events were not taking place in the wild stretches of the north country. Rafe and his troops were needed to fight not only the king's hostile faction, but the more radical rebels who wanted to depose the king in favor of his young son and control England through a regency.

As Rafe had predicted, after King John was presented with the barons' charter, he had no time to waste in pursuing so small a matter as the betrothal of a lowly ward. Far greater concerns occupied his time: there were open rebellions to crush, avowed insurgents to strip of their possessions, and, more importantly, his own royal personage to protect.

As expected, King John had erupted in one of his royal rages when faced with the barons' charter, and had rudely dismissed the courier. However, too many of his nobles were dissatisfied and the growing tide of revolt could not be stemmed.

Spring burst forth with pink and white apple blossom, the surrounding woods starred with a white and yellow carpet of primroses and anemones beneath the sparse-leaved trees. Where they stayed at Montsorrel, the season was more gentle, devoid of icy winds searing the moors and spring squalls blown in from the sea.

Though Adele enjoyed Barbara's company, she fretted over Rafe's safety when he and Gerard were in the field. It seemed that they were constantly skirmishing with those barons who disliked their staunch support of Archbishop Langton.

Easter week saw the dissenting ranks swell with an influx of forces from Wales and the west country. Then, in May, John's castle at Northampton was attacked by rebels. However, the attackers lacked siege equipment and finally had to abandon their assault. John's enemies had not won, but their audacity greatly affected his defiant stand.

London fell. Partially through trickery, it was true, but the king could no longer overlook the dangerous situation. He was aware that if he did not at least appear to accept the barons' charter, he would be deposed and his young son put on the throne instead. He did so.

When Rafe and Gerard arrived home, riding triumphant at the head of their troops, Adele thought the fighting was over. She was vastly disappointed when Rafe warned her it might only just be beginning. He was soon to embark on another journey, and this time she could travel with him. King John had agreed in principle to sign the barons' charter; their representatives were to meet him at a location in southern England to finalize their agreement.

For Rafe not to have to fight and merely witness the king's signature seemed far preferable. Adele was thankful that Archbishop Langton's moderate approach had finally won out.

At present King John was firmly entrenched in Windsor Castle, which he considered to be the safest and most defensible castle in his realm.

The travelers jogged through the winding country lanes in fragrant early summer, headed for Staines. As they rode, Adele was reminded of that other journey made not very long ago—when they had gone on the pilgrimage to St. Edmundsbury. This time, however, their goals were clear and there was no undercurrent of intrigue. The countryside was at its best beneath sunny blue skies. In the fields, ears of corn and barley showed verdant, and all the birds in England seemed out to serenade them as they rode past.

Adele had brought Margery and a new maid called Tess to serve her on the journey. She had been disappointed when Barbara had begged off, but Adele quickly overcame her disappointment when a happy Barbara revealed her reason for staying behind at Montsorrel Castle. Her fervent prayers to Saint Edmund had finally been answered. Lady Montsorrel was with child!

At noon they stopped to take their meal in a green meadow sprinkled with buttercups and daisies. A sweet-voiced thrush perched on a nearby branch, his melodic voice serenading them while they ate. When their meal was finished, Adele stretched full-length on the grass, idly plucking daisies. Rafe leaned over her to kiss her mouth, his back to the sun, leaving his face in shadow.

"Do you still love me?" she whispered, reaching out to stroke his face. Rafe caught her hand and kissed her fingertips. Though she knew his answer before he spoke, she never tired of hearing it.

"Even more than yesterday," Rafe replied softly as he trailed a daisy across her brow. He gave her a false stern look. "If you keep asking me that question, someday I might surprise you and say no."

She laughed and playfully punched his shoulder. Rafe caught her to him and they rolled together down a gentle slope until they came to rest at the bottom. As he held her in his arms, Rafe's kisses grew more thorough and meaningful.

"When this is over, are we going home?" Adele asked, knowing how much he loved his land and wanting to learn to love it also.

"I hope so. I've had enough of fighting and bickering."

"With me?" She gave him a hurt look.

He laughed, "No, I meant with John's friends and foes. I find bickering with you quite delightful."

Rafe imprisoned her wrists while he spoke, and she was a willing prisoner.

"I've loved you for a year," Adele said, making no effort to break free.

Rafe lay beside her and raised her arms above her head. "I've loved you far longer than that," he confided. "Had we more privacy, I'd prove to you just how much."

Adele shivered with delight at the hidden promise in his words, aware that his suggestion was futile. Already the grooms were leading forth the horses, ready to resume their journey.

"I'll hold you to that promise," Adele said, gazing into his blue eyes, seeing an image of herself reflected in his pupils, a miniature Adele all flaming hair and bright blue gown.

"Come, sweet, we must be on our way," Rafe said as he trailed kisses across her sun-warmed cheek. "We have to reach Staines before nightfall."

With a reluctant sigh, Adele roused herself, seeing Margery and Tess already mounted and waiting for her. This stolen hour had been so pleasant she wished they could have stayed here all day. Once they reached Staines, she knew they would likely be crammed into a stuffy inn with scores of other travelers and no hope of privacy.

As they rode south in the warm afternoon, no one could have guessed there was strife in all of England. Peasants toiled in the fields here, blissfully unaware of the king's struggle with his barons, the notion alien to their minds, for they had no quarrel with the king. Some peasants did not even know his name, so little did royalty affect their existence. This great charter that promised so much had been drawn up by nobles for nobles; the peasants' lives would continue in the same uneventful drudgery as before.

On the morrow, the barons were to meet the king at a place named Runnymede—a point selected midway between Windsor and Staines.

Adele had not asked Rafe what he would ask from the king in return for a renewed oath of fealty. Many men demanded land and the return of their confiscated property, titles, and privileges. Beyond wanting to keep what he already had, Adele could think of nothing lacking in Rafe's life.

In the early morning hours they gladly departed the crowded Bear's Paw Inn, where they had spent a cramped and drafty night. No one was sorry to leave the sagging old relic behind. When today's ceremony was over, Rafe had made up his mind to head north and hope, for a while at least, the king would leave him in peace to rule his Yorkshire lands.

As their small party neared the appointed place, they met other knights and their retainers—some of the nobles accompanied by their ladies—all traveling in the same direction.

The passing hedgerows were strung with budding briar roses, and here the trees were already in full bloom. This southern climate was much warmer in contrast to Fordham; there, spring had only recently crept across the moors. Yet though the weather could sometimes be inhospitable, Fordham was Rafe's home and now hers as well. Adele could honestly say she missed its rugged, untamed landscape. It sprawled open and free, not narrowly defined and orderly as was this southern land.

At Runnymede in the flat green water meadows of the Thames, the two opposing parties met. The common spectators were kept well back. The appointed barons and King John and his ministers took part in the ceremony, but it owed much to display and little to sincerity.

Adele craned forward to see, for she stood in the forefront of the crowd, assured of a good view. She was surprised to see the king was so short and needed high-heeled boots to bring him up to most men's shoulders. He was splendidly dressed, taking great care about his personal appearance, having lavished extravagant amounts on his

297

adornments. King John's reddish brown hair was graying, and though Adele had heard he had been handsome in his youth, she did not find him so now. The monarch wore his shoulder-length hair curled under, and he affected a short, pointed beard and mustache, which accentuated his wide cheekbones and shifty eyes.

Here at Runnymede, in the water meadows of the Thames on June 19, 1215, King John officially signed the Magna Carta. The ceremony was for public display, as he had already signed the document's first draft the previous week. By the king's signing and acceptance of the great charter, a truce was called between John and his barons, a peaceful resolution brokered by Stephen Langton, Archbishop of Canterbury.

One by one, the richly dressed nobles came forward to publicly reaffirm their allegience to the crown. As a condition for the oath, many men had asked for the return of their confiscated lands and the release of family members held hostage by the king, favors John sourly granted, knowing he had little choice.

Finally it was Rafe's turn, and he stepped forward and went down on his knees before the seated king in his splendid, gold-trimmed robes.

"And you, De Montford, what favor do you want in payment for your loyalty?" John asked in a scornful voice.

"Just your blessing on my marriage to your ward, the Lady Adele St. Clare," Rafe said. The king's sudden intake of breath told him the king had not been aware of their marriage.

John laid his beringed hand heavily on Rafe's shoulder. To his surprise, Rafe saw a smile twitching the lips beneath the brown mustache. "So, at the last you outmaneuvered us. Should we not punish you for your disobedience?"

"Nay, Your Grace, you should reward me for helping keep your head on your shoulders," he said quietly. "I was ever a staunch supporter of Langton's policy of reconciliation."

Rafe's bold statement surprised the king but did not

raise his ire. "You've ever been an insolent bastard," he observed pleasantly. "Yet strong armed with a sword and a man of your word. Do you ask for nothing else? This is your chance while I'm effectively neutered."

"Nay, Your Grace, I doubt either of us will live to see that day."

The king liked the meaning he chose to read into De Montford's remark, for he considered himself most skillful with the ladies. "Hmm, you're probably right there."

"There is *something*, Your Grace. Not for me, but for my wife. Will you return her castle of Esterwold to her?"

John sighed wearily and waved at the clerk to write down the request. "It's yours, De Montford, poor hole that it is. I found that old knight who'd so coveted it was a poor excuse for a soldier." He laughed somewhat wryly. "Perhaps if he'd been as strong as you I might not be in this place—and he might not be dead. Esterwold is yours."

"Thank you, Your Grace."

With that, Rafe placed his hand in the king's and swore the binding oath. Then he got to his feet and backed away as Gerard Montsorrel moved forward to take his oath.

In the nearby trees birds sang a heavenly chorus, and the sky looked exceptionally blue. Rafe squared his shoulders and picked up his pace as he strode toward the waiting spectators, overwhelmingly thankful to be alive.

Adele stood waiting for him, looking especially lovely in her green mantle and silver veils. His heart quickened as he saw her smile of greeting. Today he would give her the two gifts which lay closest to her heart: the king's acceptance of their marriage, and the return of her birthright, the ancient keep of Esterwold.

What more could they have ever wanted?

Lair of the Wolf

Chapter Seven

Sharon Schulze

On January 1, 1997, *Romance Communications*, the Romance Magazine for the 21st century made its Internet debut. One year later, it was named a Lycos Top 5% site on the Web in terms of both content and graphics!

One of *Romance Communications*' most popular features is The Romantic Relay, an original romance novel divided into twelve monthly installments, with each chapter written by a different author. Our first offering was *Lair of the Wolf*, a tale of medieval Wales, created by, in alphabetical order, celebrated authors Emily Carmichael, Debra Dier, Madeline George, Martha Hix, Deana James, Elizabeth Mayne, Constance O'Banyon, Evelyn Rogers, Sharon Schulze, June Lund Shiplett, and Bobbi Smith.

We put no restrictions on the authors, letting each pick up the tale where the previous author had left off and going forward as she wished. The authors tell us they had a lot of fun, each trying to write her successor into a corner!

Now, preserving the fun and suspense of our month-by-month installments, Leisure Books presents, in print, one chapter a month of *Lair of the Wolf*. In addition to the entire online story the authors have added some brand-new material to their existing chapters. So if you think you've read *Lair of the Wolf* already, you may find a few surprises. Please enjoy this unique offering, watch for each new monthly installment in the back of your Leisure Books, and make sure you visit our Web site, where another romantic relay is already in progress.

Romance Communications

http://www.romcom.com

Pamela Monck, Editor-in-Chief

Mary D. Pinto, Senior Editor

S. Lee Meyer, Web Mistress

Chapter Seven
by Sharon Schulze

A chalice of mead in his hand, Garon settled back into the great carved chair on the dais and watched as the people of Glendire—his people now, he thought with satisfaction—finished the preparations for the feast.

Glendire was a fine keep, strong, despite the depredations of recent years. 'Twould be well-kept and prosperous once more, he vowed, and soon, if the king would allow him the time to make it so. After years of a soldier's harsh life, he found he now looked forward to this new challenge, a challenge that, as a younger son, he'd never expected to face.

Saving the king's life had changed his fortune, given him far more than his father and brothers had ever had. And unlike his father, what Garon had, he'd keep, seeing the fruit of his labors grow and flourish. The king's favor, a fine keep, good lands—it was a crown of blessings, with a beautiful, spirited wife its central jewel.

Likely he should be down on his knees even now, thanking God for His favor. But since 'twas not the time or place for that, instead he raised his chalice in honor of this bounty, casting his gaze over his hall once again.

Unlike at the tension-filled feast before the wedding yesterday, the servants now wore expressions of relief, some even pleasure, as they went about their tasks. It appeared they'd accepted him, English though he was, as their lord and protector.

Perhaps they'd tired of paying the toll of war. Of a certainty, they'd lost much in their conflict with Longshanks. Glendire wore the signs of its sacrifice. Few young men remained, and many of those bore the scars of battles hard fought. Fields were left untilled, major repairs were unattended to. And their lord and his children—aye, even his daughter, last of the Llewellyns—given over in payment for their family's loyalty to their homeland.

Yet despite the peace and the vows made today—oaths of honor, loyalty, fealty—Garon knew his battle for the soul of Glendire had just begun. In time the people, he hoped, would gratefully accept his stewardship of their home and of their lady. He would need their cooperation as he worked to restore Glendire to its former glory.

He raised the mead to his lips and drank deeply of the honeyed brew. Mayhap his life might soon taste as sweet as the mead, especially now that his lady-wife had sworn fealty to him. That vow mattered as much to him—nay, more—than the vows she'd made to him when they wed.

He drank again, savoring the subtle bite of the wine along with its sweetness. Aye, the Lady Meredyth—Merrie—was like the mead: a sweet taste upon his lips, yet she carried a kick he'd ignore at his peril. He'd forced her hand this day, for he knew well that she'd permit no harm to come to her people. Indeed, 'twas doubtful she'd have freely sworn her fealty to him so soon had he not threatened their safety. He'd yet to discover what price he would pay for her submission to his will.

His blood heated as he considered the possibilities. 'Twas ever thus when he prepared himself for battle.

Excitement thrummed through his veins, sharpening his senses and making him feel truly alive. Yet this sensation was different from what he felt before war. This conflict of arms—aye, 'twas that indeed, he thought as his lips quirked up in a smile—this contest of wills with his bride, served to raise his spirits . . . and more.

Garon shifted in the chair. His body hadn't forgotten for a moment the pleasure he'd shared with Meredyth. She'd felt it, too—from her response he could not doubt he'd given her satisfaction, an ecstasy as sharp and keen as a dagger's blade.

But that same blade had pierced his heart, he feared. He poured more mead into the chalice and stared down at the shimmer of candlelight reflecting off the wine. Longshanks' Wolf, vanquished by a slip of a woman? Had the conqueror become the conquered?

The truth could be a weapon he'd do well to keep hidden, lest she rend his heart in two.

Meredyth awoke to a thunderous pounding noise. She lay still for a time before she realized that the sound came from deep within her skull, which felt as though it had been broken apart. Her jaw throbbed in time with her head, and when she tried to move her mouth, she discovered that a coarse cloth was tied tightly over it. Panicked, she drew in a deep breath through her nose, then choked at the musty stench filling her lungs.

Dear God, what had happened to her?

Where was she?

A wave of nausea flowed over her, adding to the blanket of pain covering her from head to toe. She felt bruised everywhere, and her body shuddered with cold. How long had she lain there, her linen gown scant protection from the frigid air surrounding her?

Her mind still clouded and muddled, she couldn't remember what had happened. But whatever it was, she couldn't simply remain here, waiting for her attacker to return and finish his evil work. 'Twas time to move, to act, for she seemed to be alone now, and she might not have another such chance.

Meredyth closed her eyes, drew in several shallow breaths, and forced herself to a sense of calm. Then she opened her eyes to survey her environment.

Shadows surrounded her, flickering in the dim glow of some far-off light. She lay facedown on a rough, damp stone floor, her hands bound behind her. 'Twas no wonder she ached, for she was trussed up tighter than a Christmas goose. Keeping her eyes fixed upon the faint, distant light, Meredyth took silent stock of her aches and pains. Most of her hurt seemed to emanate from the back of her head, and the tightly knotted gag pressed hard against the worst spot.

It seemed someone had clubbed her in the head. But who? She could not remember anything. Forcibly emptying her mind of fear, of panic, she let her thoughts flow where they would, allowing random images to float before her mind's eye in an attempt to recall the recent past. With startlingly vivid clarity, she saw a man's face—strong, handsome, his dark eyes pinning her in place, staring straight into the depths of her soul. His lips settling upon her own, fostering such a yearning . . .

'Twas the Wolf.

Her lord and master.

Her husband.

Meredyth's heart tripped faster in her breast as the flood of memories filled her aching head. Sir Garon Saunders, his armor shining in the sun as he rode his mighty destrier toward the gates of Glendire, his blue banners unfurled behind him. The Wolf, standing naked beside the tub as he readied himself to bathe. Her husband, taunting her with his desire—a desire she'd matched full measure.

Holy Mary save her, had Garon done this to her? Had she given her home, her people, her life, into the hands of a murderous monster?

'Twould serve him well, no doubt, to be rid of her

now—now that she and her people had sworn their fealty to him and his dreaded overlord, Longshanks. He'd taken away her home . . . he'd taken her. Had she served her purpose already, and made her life forfeit because of it?

Nay, it could not be! For the passion between them alone, he'd be a fool to rid himself of her so quickly. A woman for his bed, a trophy of war to sit at his side, proof of his warrior's might, a symbol of his king's favor.

Her mind thus cleared, other recent memories rushed to the fore. Though she had not yet come to know her husband well, he'd not treat her thus, she knew it deep within her.

But Sir Olyver . . . Aye, she'd not put this past that slimy snake! He'd been watching her with that evil expression in his eyes, savoring her as though she was a tasty morsel for his delectation. Then escorting her to the Great Hall . . . the darkened stairwell, a sharp pain in her head . . .

But what did he hope to gain by this? she wondered as a glorious burst of anger sent strength into her body. She shifted on the floor and wriggled about until she could lean against the rough stone wall. Perhaps he'd hidden her away in one of the many caverns that riddled the limestone cliffs beneath the foundation of Glendire. If so, she ought to be able to find her way out.

Whatever Sir Olyver's reason for taking her, she refused to let him win!

'Twas careless of him, indeed, not to bind her feet; she'd use his oversight to her advantage, she vowed. By pushing against the wall with her shoulders, Meredyth worked her way up till she could stand. She swayed but remained on her feet despite the dizziness. She refused to give in to it, for she had to escape this place before Sir Olyver returned.

Though 'twas difficult to walk with her hands bound behind her, she headed toward the flickering light, staying close to the wall and pausing every few moments to listen. The area seemed familiar to her—possibly a part of the series of caverns beneath the cellars of the keep.

She'd played here with her brothers when they were children, hide-and-seek among the nooks and crannies.

She'd been very good at that game.

A metallic squeal, as of rusty hinges, sounded in the distance. The rhythmic crunch of boots on stone followed hard on the sound, moving ever closer.

Heart pounding wildly, Meredyth veered off into the darkness, moving as swiftly as she dared. She kept the wall to her left and concentrated on not making any noise. She stopped when the footsteps halted, and she listened.

A man cursed. Meredyth held her breath and prayed he'd not come her way.

The footsteps began again, heading away from her.

She slumped against the wall and closed her eyes. Praise God he hadn't set off into the caverns in search of her! Grateful for the reprieve, she prayed her memory would serve her well, then moved deeper into the caverns.

"My lord?"

Shaken from his reverie, Garon looked up. Dame Allison awaited his notice at the edge of the dais, hands clasped tightly before her as though to still their trembling. Was he such an ogre, to strike fear into this simple woman?

"What is it?" he asked more quietly than was his wont.

"The hall is ready, my lord, and the feast prepared. Why is my lady not here with you?"

Garon set down the chalice and stood, swiftly scanning the room. 'Twas crowded with people, both English and Welsh, but of his lady-wife, he saw no sign.

"Mayhap she's yet in our chamber," he suggested, "sulking, for she sought refuge there as soon as the ceremony in the bailey had come to an end."

" 'Tis unlike her to sulk, my lord," Dame Allison said, censure coloring her voice.

Garon smiled, for Merrie in any mood had the power to stir him. "Mayhap, then, she merely seeks a period of reflection to illuminate the value of our joining."

Dame Allison stepped up on the dais and came to stand at his side. "Of what value *is* your joining to my lady?" she asked in a low voice, her expression filled with accusation.

What nonsense was this? Garon swept his hand across the table, sending the chalice flying. "You forget yourself, woman."

"Nay, my lord, 'tis you who've forgotten—if you ever knew." Dame Allison trembled with rage. "Where is the advantage to my lady in your marriage? You English have taken everything she treasured from her—her family, her people, her home, her noble name, all lost to you. You left her with nothing but her pride, my lord, and even at that you forced her to humble herself before you this morn."

"Your words are far different from the cries of celebration after the people of Glendire swore fealty to me, madam." Garon met her gaze with his own, weighing the honest anger he saw in her eyes. "Why do you attack me thus?"

Before she could answer, Sir Olyver crossed the dais to join them. "Mayhap she thinks to distract you, Sir Garon. To give her mistress more time."

"More time?" Garon glared at the other man, mistrusting the smirk upon his face. Though Olyver's expression was ever thus, something about it now, spoke to Garon of plots and schemes well-savored.

"More time for what?"

"To make her escape, mayhap? When I went to your chamber just now, to escort Lady Meredyth to the hall for the festivities, she was nowhere to be found. It appears she's gone missing." Sir Olyver eyed the chalice, lying overturned in a puddle of mead on the table, then met Garon's gaze. "Could it be that your bride seeks to avoid the"—he cleared his throat delicately—"demands her husband might make of her?"

Garon grabbed Sir Olyver by the arm and dragged him close. "You forget yourself, sirrah," he growled. Of a sudden, he became aware of the silence surrounding them.

Thrusting the other man aside, Garon straightened and turned to face the fascinated crowd filling the room.

"Has any among you seen the Lady Meredyth?" he demanded.

A chorus of nays was his answer.

She could not have left the castle without someone's notice! He pushed past Dame Allison and Sir Olyver and stood poised at the edge of the dais. "Send for a guard from the gate."

Or mayhap she hadn't left at all, he thought as he considered the source of the news. Could this be a ploy, a simple ruse to stir him to anger with his bride?

"The rest of you, search this keep from top to bottom. Your mistress may have come to harm," he added, hoping it wasn't so.

"My lord, look!" someone shouted from the gallery.

"Lady Meredyth!" another called from the far end of the Great Hall.

The crowd parted to reveal Meredyth standing just within the room, a cloth tied over her mouth, her gown dirty, and her face pale as milk and smudged with dirt. She swayed on her feet, her hands held behind her.

"Merrie!" he cried, rushing toward her. She appeared about to topple over, but she somehow managed to straighten before he reached her. He grasped her shoulders, realizing as he did so that her hands were bound behind her. "By Christ, what happened?" He drew his dagger and cut her bonds, then swept her into his arms.

Meredyth rested her head upon Garon's shoulder and fought back tears. Her aches and pains were as nothing, now that he held her in his arms.

Then Meredyth looked up and saw Sir Olyver Martain moving away from the dais. Forgetting that she still wore the gag, she tried to shout. Then, fingers numb and clumsy, she struggled with the knot and pulled the cloth free. "Stop him!" she cried, but her voice was little stronger than a croak. She struggled within Garon's hold. "Stop Sir Olyver now!"

A scuffle broke out on the dais as two of Garon's men sought to subdue Sir Olyver. He broke away from their grasping hands and, drawing his sword, leapt back to stand with his back against the wall. "What is the meaning of this?" he demanded.

Garon eased Meredyth into a chair and freed his own sword from its scabbard. "Meredyth?" he asked as he stalked toward Sir Olyver, then stood before him, holding him at bay.

"He struck me in the head, then hid me away in the catacombs beneath the keep." Her throat dry and her voice still rusty, she accepted the goblet Dame Allison handed her and swallowed a mouthful of the rich wine.

Sir Olyver shook his head, his eyes wild as he stared at her. "She lies, my lord. Surely you'd believe your own man over a lying Welsh—"

Garon stepped forward and in a single move knocked aside the other man's sword, then brought the tip of his blade to bear upon Sir Olyver's throat.

"Not another word," he warned, "else I'll slice your throat here and now."

Meredyth slumped back into the chair in relief as two of Garon's men grabbed Sir Olyver's arms and bound them behind him.

"Take him to the dungeon," Garon ordered. He sheathed his sword and dropped to his knees beside her chair. "Merrie—"

He framed her face with his hands, hands that trembled slightly, she noted with disbelief.

"Dear God, if he'd harmed you . . ."

Meredyth gasped as Garon's lips covered hers in a kiss of such tenderness, she thought she'd swoon from the sensation. His taste filled her mouth, more heady than the wine she'd consumed and far more intoxicating to her senses.

His hands crept up into her hair to cradle her head, brushing against the lump there. The pain made her gasp.

And cleared her head of Garon's enchantment.

313

They both seemed to come to their senses at the same moment, for Garon snatched his hands away from her and stood, just as she would have pushed him aside.

'Twas all she could do to hold her head up and maintain her composure. What had she done? How could she remain true to herself, to her people, when she could leap so readily into his arms?

She must be strong.

For if he were to learn of her feelings for him, Lady Meredyth Llewellyn would be utterly vanquished.

The Wolf's conquest would be complete.

Watch for Chapter Eight by June Lund Shiplett, of Lair of the Wolf, *appearing in July 2000 in* Manon *by Melanie Jackson.*

SWEET FURY

CATHERINE HART

She is exasperating, infuriating, unbelievably tantalizing; a little hellcat with flashing eyes and red-gold tangles, and if anyone is to make a lady of the girl, it will have to be Marshal Travis Kincaid. She may fight him tooth and nail, but Travis swears he will coax her into his strong arms and unleash all her wild, sweet fury.

___4428-5 $5.99 US/$6.99 CAN

Dorchester Publishing Co., Inc.
P.O. Box 6640
Wayne, PA 19087-8640

Please add $1.75 for shipping and handling for the first book and $.50 for each book thereafter. NY, NYC, and PA residents, please add appropriate sales tax. No cash, stamps, or C.O.D.s. All orders shipped within 6 weeks via postal service book rate. Canadian orders require $2.00 extra postage and must be paid in U.S. dollars through a U.S. banking facility.

Name_____
Address_____
City_____State_____Zip_____
I have enclosed $_____ in payment for the checked book(s).
Payment <u>must</u> accompany all orders. ❏ Please send a free catalog.
        CHECK OUT OUR WEBSITE! www.dorchesterpub.com

Silken Savage

Catherine Hart

Captured by a party of Cheyenne while traveling through Colorado Territory, beautiful Tanya Martin refuses to let her proud spirit be broken or her voluptuous body abused. But she has not anticipated the reaction of her heart to A Panther Stalks, the brave who has claimed her as his prize. Tanya soon becomes her captor's willing slave, overcome by a passion she cannot resist.

___4462-5 $5.99 US/$6.99 CAN

Dorchester Publishing Co., Inc.
P.O. Box 6640
Wayne, PA 19087-8640

Please add $1.75 for shipping and handling for the first book and $.50 for each book thereafter. NY, NYC, and PA residents, please add appropriate sales tax. No cash, stamps, or C.O.D.s. All orders shipped within 6 weeks via postal service book rate. Canadian orders require $2.00 extra postage and must be paid in U.S. dollars through a U.S. banking facility.

Name_____
Address_____
City_____ State_____ Zip_____
I have enclosed $_____ in payment for the checked book(s).
Payment <u>must</u> accompany all orders. ☐ Please send a free catalog.

DESPERADO
SANDRA HILL

Major Helen Prescott has always played by the rules. That's why Rafe Santiago nicknamed her "Prissy" at the military academy years before. Rafe's teasing made her life miserable back then, and with his irresistible good looks, he is the man responsible for her one momentary lapse in self control. When a routine skydive goes awry, the two parachute straight into the 1850 California Gold Rush. Mistaken for a notorious bandit and his infamously sensuous mistress, they find themselves on the wrong side of the law. In a time and place where rules have no meaning, Helen finds Rafe's hard, bronzed body strangely comforting, and his piercing blue eyes leave her all too willing to share his bedroll. Suddenly, his teasing remarks make her feel all woman, and she is ready to throw caution to the wind if she can spend every night in the arms of her very own desperado.

_52182-2 $5.99 US/$6.99 CAN

FRANKLY, MY DEAR...

SANDRA HILL

Selene has three great passions: men, food, and *Gone With The Wind*. But the glamorous model always finds herself starving—for both nourishment and affection. Weary of the petty world of high fashion, she heads to New Orleans. Then a voodoo spell sends her back to the days of opulent balls and vixenish belles like Scarlett O'Hara. Charmed by the Old South, Selene can't get her fill of gumbo, crayfish, beignets—or an alarmingly handsome planter. Dark and brooding, James Baptiste does not share Rhett Butler's cavalier spirit, and his bayou plantation is no Tara. But fiddle-dee-dee, Selene doesn't need her mammy to tell her the virile Creole is the only lover she gives a damn about. And with God as her witness, she vows never to go hungry or without the man she desires again.

___4617-2 $5.50 US/$6.50 CAN